Talk

Dirty to Me

Look for Dakota Cassidy's next novel
Something to Talk About
available soon from Harlequin MIRA

Dakota Cassidy

Talk
Dirty to Me

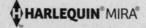

Recycling programs
for this product may
not exist in your area.

ISBN-13: 978-0-7783-1619-0

TALK DIRTY TO ME

Copyright © 2014 by Dakota Cassidy

This is a work of fiction. Names, characters, places and incidents are either the product of the author's imagination or are used fictitiously, and any resemblance to actual persons, living or dead, business establishments, events or locales is entirely coincidental.

® and TM are trademarks of Harlequin Enterprises Limited or its corporate affiliates. Trademarks indicated with ® are registered in the United States Patent and Trademark Office, the Canadian Trade Marks Office and in other countries.

For questions and comments about the quality of this book, please contact us at CustomerService@Harlequin.com.

Printed in U.S.A.

For my agent, whom I lovingly call Agent Fab, Elaine Spencer. You're a gladiator, my friend. There are no words in the English language to adequately describe how dear I hold the notion that you have always believed.

Also, to the many folks who've been involved in making this project a reality:

My editor, Leonore Waldrip—for seeing this one little crazy idea/book in its earliest stages and passing it on. Add to the mix your amazing sense of humor and genius brainstorming, makes you a keeper.

Emily Ohanjanians, your insight, attention to detail, and overall brilliance will forever influence the future words that flow from my fingertips.

An enormous nod to the show *Hart Of Dixie,* my inspiration for writing Southern fiction. I love every "bless your heart, Lemon Breeland, Lavon Hayes, Annabeth Nass, Zade" moment spent with you each week. If you're a fan of the show, you'll know what I mean when I cry, ZADE forever!

To all of my amazing readers—really who else can I count on to talk about anti-inflammatory cream and one's (ahem) nether regions (all in one whacky conversation that I swear didn't begin related at all) with me at three in the morning on Facebook but all of you? I treasure our conversations. I hold your thoughts and continued support in the highest regard. Thank you for always being so willing to laugh (and sometimes cry) with me!

One

"He looks really good, considering." Emmaline Amos sniffed, pushing her way past an enormous bouquet of white lilies standing by Landon Wells's casket at Tate and Son's Home Of Eternal Rest.

She pulled Dixie Davis with her, away from Landon's casket and into the privacy of a connecting mourning room where she set Dixie on a couch surrounded by pictures of Landon.

The scent of dark wood paneling, vanilla candles, and Old Spice invaded Dixie's nose, making her "ugly cry" hangover pulse in her temples with the force of a sledgehammer.

Dixie lifted her sunglasses, thwarting another ambush of tears, so grateful for the opportunity to have had a few moments alone with Landon without the intrusion of the long line of people who'd shown up to pay their last respects.

She muttered up at Em, "Why does everyone always say that, Em? Landon's *dead*. There's nothing good-looking about it. I always thought that was a crude thing to say."

Em huffed, brushing the brim of her black sun hat, and sat down beside her. She gave her a nudge to make some room. "It's not crude. I was complimentin' him. New adjective, please," she drawled, her Southern lilt like macaroni and cheese to Dixie's homesick ears. Comfort food for the soul.

"Crass?"

"Crass is harsh, Dixie."

Landon Wells, her best friend ever, was dead. That was harsh.

Harsher still, Landon's other best friend, Caine Donovan, was just outside that door.

Don't forget he's your ex-fiancé, too.

Right. Dixie started to regret her terse words with Emmaline. She couldn't afford to alienate the one and only, albeit totally reluctant, ally she had left in her small hometown of Plum Orchard, Georgia.

Maybe what was making her so snappish was exhaustion after the long drive from Chicago. Or the anxiety of returning to said small hometown where everyone knew her name and mostly wanted to throw darts at her picture.

Maybe it was the precariousness of her life in financial semiruin that made her voice what she'd been thinking for almost two hours as mourner after mourner repeated Em's words while she'd waited for her private viewing of Landon's body.

Or maybe it was the likelihood that a good portion of the female population of Plum Orchard High, class of 1996, were just outside this very funeral home with metaphoric stakes soaked in the town's specialty, homemade plum wine, just waiting for Reverend Watson to perform her public exorcism. Then they could seal the deal by driving their angry pieces of wood right through her despicable heart.

It would be nothing less than she deserved.

She'd been a horrible person in high school and beyond, and here in Plum Orchard where time seemed to stand still, no one forgot.

You were horrible long after high school, too, Dixie. To Caine...

Point. Most of her anxiety had to do with the fact that she had no choice but to see Caine Donovan again.

Bingo, Dixie. The thought of seeing him left her feeling fragile and raw.

To this damn day his memory still leaves you breathless.

Acknowledged. Dark, star-filled nights under a scratchy army blanket in the bed of Caine's pickup truck, the scent of magnolias clinging to their sticky skin. It was just one of many of the images—both good and bad—she'd warred with since her return to Plum Orchard became a reality.

She scrunched her eyes shut before reopening them.

"Sorry," Em said, dragging her from her internal war. Her blue eyes held sympathy beneath her wide-brimmed hat. "I'm glad they gave you some time alone with Landon before the latecomers swarm in to pay their last respects. I can't even imagine how much this hurts." Em squeezed her shoulder with reassuring fingers.

Dixie let out a shaky sigh, hooking her arm through Em's. "No, I'm the one who's sorry. I'm tired and on edge, and you've been so kind to me through this whole process when I totally don't deserve—"

"No, you surely do not, Dixie Davis!" Em's voice

rose, then just as quickly reduced to just above a whisper. She peered over her shoulder as though unseen eyes might bear witness to her bad manners. God forbid. "You were a mean girl back in the day. My high school years were torture because of you. And might I remind you, people don't forget, especially here in little ol' Plum Orchard. Why, you're lucky I even picked up the phone during Landon's last days, knowing it was you I had to talk to on the other end of the line," she finished on an offended harrumph.

But Dixie knew better than to take Em's outburst personally. Em was as kind as she was generous, and nothing, not even a faded-around-the-edges grudge, would keep her good heart from beating selflessly.

For all her leftover high school anger with Dixie, Em had called her religiously with updates on Landon's last days, because he'd asked her to. Em always did what was right. That was just who she was.

Still, Dixie gave her a sheepish glance, and bumped her shoulder playfully to ease the lines of Em's frown. "This is about the cheerleading squad, isn't it?"

Em's arm stiffened. She lifted her chin. "You told me my legs looked like sausages in that stupid cheerleading skirt, so I couldn't be on the squad. But my split jumps were better 'n Annabelle Pruitt's, and you knew it."

True. Every last word of it. She'd been cruel, twenty or so years ago. Yet, comments like that, among the many she'd hurled at Em, obviously crept into a person's soul and hung around. From the moment she'd seen Em after being gone so long, Dixie had known she'd be met with extreme caution. Maybe some angry outbursts and plenty of tests to see if she really had changed.

So Dixie's next admission was without hesitation. "I did."

Dixie let her hand slide down along Emmaline's arm to thread her fingers through hers, giving them a light squeeze. "I'm not that person anymore, Emmaline. I'm really not. You were right then and now. Your split jumps were at least a hundred feet higher than Annabelle's. I lied back then out of jealousy. Your legs are long and gorgeous." They were. Em was undeniably beautiful.

Em ran a self-conscious hand over her bare leg and said, "Don't you try and flatter me after all this time. Not after I spent four months' worth of babysitting money on the ThighMaster because of you."

Dixie winced. "Then, if nothing else, you know, for every mean thing I did to you back then, I hope you'll remember, the Lord says to forgive is divine."

"The Lord didn't go to high school with you."

"Fair." Dixie let her chin drop to her chest, noting under the lights of the funeral home, the long curls of her red dye job were fading dismally.

Em's nostrils flared at the pin Dixie'd effectively poked in her bubble of anger before her rigid posture deflated, and she let out a half chuckle. "Don't you be nice to me, Dixie Davis. I'm not one hundred percent buyin' this 'I've changed' act. You've done that bit once before, and we all fell for it ten years ago, remember? Not so fast this time. So just keep your compliments to yourself." It was obvious Em was trying to keep her resentments in check out of respect for Landon, for which today, Dixie was grateful.

If not for Em, she wouldn't have been able to speak to Landon the one last time he was still coherent—nor would she have known about a single funeral arrangement. So Dixie nodded in understanding. "No rights allowed."

The tension around Em's crimson-colored lips eased some, her expression growing playful. She fingered one of the lilies in a fluted vase on the table near the couch. "And as a by the by, Lesta-Sue and the Mags said they'll never allow you access to the Plum Orchard Founders Day parade committee, if you were hopin' to worm back into everyone's good graces, that is."

It was a "take that" comment meant to hurt her—to remind Dixie, when she'd been head Magnolia, the town's decades-old society of women, and a rite of rich Southern girl passage, she'd once used her popularity and status to shun others via the town's elitist club. Especially Em.

If Lesta-Sue was here already, that meant the rest of the Mags would be here, too. Terrific. Surely, Louella Palmer, Dixie's head Magnolia predecessor, wasn't far behind.

Louella hated her, too. In fact, there was a special kind of hate reserved by Louella just for Dixie. Because she'd broken the girlfriend code ten years ago.

Really broken it.

But Dixie nodded again, and this time, if there was such an act, she did it with even less hesitation than the time before. "Lesta-Sue shouldn't allow me access to a public gas station bathroom after what I did to her. Stealing her high school beau of three long years by offering to let him get to second base with me was a horrible thing to do. So it's a good thing I'll be long gone by the time they break out the hot glue gun and crepe paper. I'm not here to stay, Em. I'm just here to say goodbye to Landon."

The statement tugged at Dixie's heart. She'd missed home—even if it hadn't missed her.

Em's dark brows knitted together while her gloved fingertips fluttered to the pointed collar of her black-belted dress with the flared skirt. "You're upsetting me, Dixie."

"How so, Emmaline?"

"You're still bein' sweet."

Dixie flashed her a warm smile. "Aw, thank you."

"Stop that this instant!" Em insisted. "It's unsettling. I should hate you just like every woman still left in this town who attended Plum Orchard High does." She stiffened again, as if her years of piled-up high school hurts caused by Dixie were warring with her naturally forgiving nature.

Em had just wanted to fit in back then, and Dixie'd used it to her advantage at every outlet. She wouldn't forgive someone for treating her the way she'd treated Em, but if regret counted, she had plenty of that to give.

Dixie shot her another smile full of more gratitude. "Yes, you should hate me. You still can, if you'd like. But I appreciate you, and everythin' you've done. So see? We balance each other out."

"The only thing that keeps me from shunning you just like the others is I can't help but feel badly for you, Dixie. I, unlike you, have a conscience. You've had a horrible patch. I mean, first we all hear you lost your fancy restaurant—"

"That was almost two years ago, Em." Two long years, scraping together a pathetic living with the degree she never quite got, and working odd jobs with her limited—really limited work skills.

Em clucked her tongue. "Two years, two days. Does the amount of time since the descent into financial devastation truly matter?"

Dixie had to nod her agreement. It only mattered to her. Her and the investors she'd let down.

"Okay, but then, your best friend, Landon, asks me to keep you—of all people—up to date on his journey to the end, knowing darn well I'd never say no because one, I grew to love him, too, and two, for gracious sake, he was *dying*. Then that best friend in the whole world of yours, I'm guessin' your only friend left, dies."

"You're a fine human being, Em. I mean that." Dixie refused to take the bait and let Em get a rise out of her.

Em pushed some more. "Adding to all that misery, there's Caine Donovan. Your heart must be in an emotional tizzy about seeing him after, what is it now? Ten years…"

Dixie remained stoically silent. About all things failed restaurant and especially all things Caine Donovan.

"You remember him, right? One-time Plum Orchard High heartthrob and all-county track star, now one of Miami's biggest real-estate moguls… Oh, and the man you claimed to love but bet on like a Derby horse?" Em was dropping a line into Dixie's ocean with a juicy worm on the end of it to see if she'd rear up and bite.

The bet. God, that damn bet.

But the truth was the truth. Her restaurant had failed because she'd been too busy partying and running up her credit cards to bother with silly things like managing the restaurant she'd convinced herself, with absolutely no experience at all, was as good a place as any to escape her hometown and run away from the horrible thing she'd done to Caine.

Her engagement had failed because at the time, Dixie Davis didn't know how not to turn everything into a three-ring circus.

And yes, Caine was successful, and she wasn't.

All ugly truths.

Topping everything off, there'd been Mason—the beginning of her end.

Dixie lifted her sunglasses once more and forced a smile, letting her eyes purposely meet Em's. "Sorry to disappoint, but there's no emotional tizzy here. Seeing Caine is part of the process of saying goodbye to our mutual best friend. That's all. He has as much right as I do. He was Landon's best friend, too."

Liar.

She'd practiced those words in her bathroom mirror hundreds of times before she'd left Chicago so they'd come off cordial and, above all, gracious. She'd almost convinced herself this imposed meeting was just that— two people who hadn't worked out, simply running into each other again and chatting niceties until it was time to go back to their lives.

But seeing Caine meant remembering how madly in love they'd been for a time. It meant hearing his voice, a voice so warm it could probably still make her thighs clench.

If they ended up in a close setting, it meant possibly brushing against his granite wall of a chest or watching him confidently smile while he arrogantly tilted an eyebrow at her. It meant that swell of clawing longing for him rising upward and settling in her chest.

It meant reliving emotions that still ached almost as fresh as the day they'd happened.

No one since Caine had ever touched her quite the same way. Caine Donovan was like a drug, and she was his junkie in need of a Caine Anonymous meeting.

Dixie chose to avoid Em dangling the Caine carrot under her nose. Talking about Caine meant stirring up all the emotions that went with everything that had happened. Today all her turmoil was reserved for Landon and her gratitude toward Em.

That Em had walked this far out on the ledge, offering to come with Dixie to Landon's funeral in front of all of Plum Orchard's very prying, judgmental eyes, was more than was her due.

The ache of more tears tickled the back of Dixie's eyelids. "You know, even though I knew Landon's death was inevitable, it really is just like everyone says—you can never prepare for it."

Em waved a hand around the room, chockfull of life-size pictures of Landon doing everything from zip-lining in Alaska over an icy glacier to cooking in Bobby Flay's kitchen. "Well, if no one else was prepared, this sendoff is a sign Landon was prepared. He knew how he wanted to go out, and he left strict instructions about it. You don't think his mother arranged those drag queens on stilts outside, do you? The Plum Orchard Bible study ladies nearly fell faint to the ground when they arrived."

A glimmer of a smile outlined Dixie's lips, lips still chapped and peeling from her nervous habit of tugging them. "He wasn't shy, was he?"

"Landon was whatever the antithesis of shy is."

That Landon had been. Loud and proud. Just thinking about him always made Dixie smile.

Yet, each time she thought she might smile, a new wave of loss washed over her, and it reminded her she'd never smile with Landon again. "I hate that he's gone." God, she really hated it. She hated even more the fact that she hadn't made it back in time to be with him when he'd passed.

Everything had happened so fast, in a blur of urgent phone calls from Landon's hospice care nurse, Vella, and Em's updates, to the humiliating decline from American Airlines of her very last credit card.

Em pointed to one of the pictures of Dixie and Landon on a nearby table, her eyes fondly roving it. "He hates it, too. Who wouldn't hate being dead?" She chuckled, eliciting a laugh from Dixie, too.

Dixie's shoulders relaxed a little in her ill-fitting jacket. She leaned into Em and said, "Landon's probably pretty upset he's missing this."

Em's hand strayed to her hair with a bob of her head. "Oh, you know better 'n all of us what Landon Wells was like. He had to have his nose in everything, or it drove him positively crazy. I'm sure wherever he is, he hates missing out on the circus outside these doors. Did you see the gentleman who looks like he just left the set of that movie *Coming to America?* And bless his heart, all those grief-stricken comments from parts near and far on his Facebook page made me tear up."

Dixie let slip a fond grin of recollection. "The turn-out would have tickled Landon's 'come one, come all' bone," she agreed, referring to the mass of mourners she'd witnessed on their way inside.

Eclectic defined her best friend, or maybe, he'd de-fined it? Either way, it was what made Landon Landon. His joy in everything great and small—his wonder at the differences in people, cultures—his determination to experience anything he could get his hands on and celebrate it with gusto. His ability to collect people from all walks of life and turn them into lifelong friends.

Shortly after college, he'd invested his trust fund wisely in several startup internet companies and was a self-made multimillionaire by the time he was twenty-five. Those companies continued to provide steady incomes to this day. And along the way, he'd added new ones—via winning bets on everything from a game of pool with a castoff royal to a polo match with some foreign politician.

Because of his savvy business acumen, Landon was able to retire at twenty-six. Since that time, he'd been to exotic, sometimes isolated locales Dixie'd never heard of, had experienced the gamut of a world traveler, from a pilgrimage in an ashram in India to bobsledding with the Swiss Olympic team.

Landon had lived and loved openly and freely, sharing his wealth wherever he went.

Dixie gripped the edge of the couch, her heart overloaded with the empty beat of grief. She'd miss everything about him: his pushy late-night phone calls about her nonexistent love life, his questions about her financial security, his inquiries into her cholesterol levels, and anything and everything else Landon had pestered/mothered/nurtured her about in their lifelong friendship.

The small room had grown oppressive with her sorrow in the last vestiges of the late August day. She reached into her bag and used one of her many overdue credit card bills to fan herself. "Mercy, it's hot in here."

"Are your ears hot, too? Because I hear through the iPhone grapevine Louella Palmer's in the back row of this very establishment, sittin' next to Caine, and chewin' his ear off as we speak. You know, the man you're not in an emotional tailspin over?" Em showed her the text in yet another obvious bid to take her licks. It only made sense she'd think the subject of Louella Palmer would be the straw to break Dixie's back.

Everyone in town probably thought the subject of Louella was a sore spot for Dixie. The real sore spot belonged to Louella, though, and she had every right to it.

Louella had once been her right-hand, helping her lead the Mags as if they were the mob—Southern contingency. They'd been frenemies of sorts then, and in the end just before Dixie left town, bitter rivals. Not only was Louella currently the head of the Magnolias, she was almost as good at mob relations as Dixie had been.

On the outside the Mags were refined and decorous, and they considered themselves the epitome of Southern grace and charm, but upon Dixie's harsh inner reflections these past few years, they were all nothing more than elitist snobs with Southern accents—and she'd been the biggest one of all.

Of course Louella was sitting with Caine. It gave her plenty of time to remind him anew how Dixie was spawned from the loins of the devil.

Caine was already here, too. Dixie's heart sped up as though someone had revved its engine, but her next words belied the storm brewing in her stomach. "You know what, Em? I hope Louella reminds him just how silly he was to ever get mixed up with the likes of Dixie Davis."

Take that. She would not bite on the matter of Caine Donovan or Louella Palmer. The whole town had witnessed their messy breakup with Louella smack dab in the middle, and in a town as small as Plum Orchard, people were sure to speculate about their eventual meeting after all these years.

It was only natural—expected even. So why was she so jittery about it?

Because what you did was unforgiveable, Dixie. Then you ran away without so much as an apology.

Em's expression was astonished, her eyes full of some good ol' Southern shock. "I can't believe you're not biting, Dixie. How can you even be in the same room with him after everythin' that happened between you?"

"Technically, we're not in the same room. I'm in here, and he's out there in the foyer." Right out there. "And I no longer bite," she teased, snapping her teeth in jest.

"For two people who were gonna get married and had the biggest breakup Plum Orchard's ever seen, in the middle of the town's square to boot, you sure are calm and collected."

Her spine stiffened. Em just couldn't seem to choose to love or hate her, and while Dixie recognized it as her due, the reminder of her and Caine's breakup was still like a knife in the gut almost ten years later.

There'd been rain, and thunder, and shouting, and accusations, and even a small fire and finally, the death of their preordained relationship, left splattered all over the whitewashed wood-stained floor of the gazebo in the town square.

Dixie shivered. She would not revisit that horrific night today.

"I bet your mother's still crying over all that money

wasted on your fancy engagement party. Caine's mama, too."

Poke, poke, poke. Dixie knew for a fact her mother, Pearl, was still crying. She'd told her so from her sickbed in Palm Springs when she'd made Dixie promise to pass on her condolences to Landon's mother. Though, her tears always had crocodile properties to them.

Pearl Davis didn't cry genuine tears over human beings. She cried over investments lost, bank accounts in the red, and the merging of two prominent Plum Orchard families lost to her all because of Dixie.

And Caine's mother, Jo-Lynne? She still didn't speak to Pearl. Regret, sharp and just as vivid as if their breakup had happened only yesterday, left Dixie fighting an outward cringe.

Dixie, Landon and Caine's mothers were all best friends once—the belles of Plum Orchard's hierarchy aka the Senior Mags. So it was only natural their three children were virtually weaned from the same bottle. Just over two years older than Dixie, Landon and Caine had been her protectors since birth.

While their mothers had played canasta every Thursday, planned church events at Plum Orchard Baptist, and been a part of every social organization a small town finds imperative to good breeding and proper social connectivity, they'd also planned Dixie would one day marry one of the two boys.

Either one would do as far as Pearl, Jo-Lynne, or Landon's mother, Charlotte, were concerned. They were all as good as family, the women used to say. That hadn't quite worked out as planned after Landon confessed to their families he'd only marry Dixie if she had male parts. And Caine's male parts didn't interest him in the least.

Caine and Dixie had always known their mothers' plans were fruitless where Landon was concerned, but as it turned out, the plan wasn't so far-fetched when Dixie and Caine's relationship took a turn toward romantic upon their simultaneous returns to Plum Orchard.

"So has Miss Jo-Lynne spoken to Miss Pearl since the 'incident' or is there still bad blood after all this time?" Em prodded with a smile.

Dixie shot her eyes upward. "Look, Landon, who knew you weren't the only busybody in Plum Orchard? Emmaline's going to carry the torch in your stead," she teased, warmth in her voice.

Em swatted her with her plastic fan. "Oh, hush, and don't you worry. There's still plenty of busy to be had from Landon, Dixie Davis. Plenty." She shot Dixie a secretive look with her sparkling blue eyes.

The same look she'd given her when Dixie had mentioned the phone call she'd gotten from Landon's lawyer, insisting she be at the reading of his will.

That phone call still made no sense, and it would definitely hold her up. Her plan all along was to get herself in and out of Landon's funeral lickety-split because she desperately wanted to avoid running into Caine, and Louella and the Mags, junior or senior.

Avoid running into them like she'd avoid a venereal disease—or hitting a brick wall at full speed, driving a Maserati. A foolish hope, no doubt. She should've known Caine wouldn't miss Landon's funeral, even if he was living in Miami now. Of course, Caine deserved to pay his last respects to Landon as much as

Dixie did. He'd remained one of the best friends Landon had long after she and Caine had fallen out of one another's good graces.

I will not pretend like neither one of you exist, Dixie-Cup. You're both my friends. Y'all will always be my friends, and that's just how it's gonna be, whether you like it or not. Landon had said those words with a sweet-and-sour delivery after dropping a fond kiss on her forehead.

She'd loosely maintained her friendship with Landon around Caine, as well. After Landon's refusal to walk on eggshells, he relayed information on Caine's life and exploits. While Dixie would never admit it, she ate the scraps Landon fed her like a hungry stray dog.

Dixie turned, folding her arms across her chest to find Em with expectant hope in her eyes. "Okay, this is me biting. Care to explain exactly what that 'plenty of busy to be had' means? You are Landon's attorney's secretary, so you must know something. You've been giving me the side eye since I got here yesterday."

Em's eyes snapped back toward the doors, connecting the mourning room to Landon's viewing room. "I'm just a lowly secretary. I know nothing you don't know."

Suspicion pricked Dixie's internal antennae, making her narrow her grainy eyes. "You *do* know something, Em. My spidey senses are dull from the long drive from Chicago and fraught with grief, so just spit out whatever it is that's made you so full you're gonna burst."

"I assure you, there's nothing." Em crossed her heart with two properly gloved fingers, gazing stoically at Dixie. And she didn't even blink. "Now, I think we should get a move on before we're thrown outta here for loitering."

Outside the door buzzed with activity from impatient mourners still waiting to say goodbye.

On a deep breath, Dixie took one last glance at one of her favorite pictures of Landon. One with his sandy brown hair, wide gray eyes and a smile he'd handed out as if he was handing out Halloween candy, Landon epitomized handsome.

Goodbye. How would she ever say goodbye to him?

"If you want to keep avoiding the man who shall remain nameless and absolutely doesn't put you in an emotional tizzy, you know, *Caine*—you'd better step up your game. He's four mourners, one a stripper from Glasgow, away from us in the line just outside that door," Em whispered low in her ear, holding up her phone to show her the warning text message from Augusta White.

Dixie's stomach dived toward the floor, twisting and swirling as it went. The temptation to take just one quick glance at Caine when they walked through those doors made her twitch.

Don't you dare look, Dixie. Do not. Her curious eyes would not betray her by peeking to locate his face in the crowd. His delicious, handsome, chiseled face.

No. She wouldn't allow it. She soothed herself with the idea that it had been close to ten years since she'd last seen him. He was almost thirty-eight now. Maybe he had a paunch and a bald spot.

It could happen. Early senior onset or something.

"Dixie, c'mon now. Let's go," Em urged with a squeeze of her hand.

With one last glance of Landon's smiling face, she picked up the photo and whispered, "Please, please remember this—wherever you are." Dixie closed her eyes and recited the words they'd used before they hung up after every single phone call, before every good-bye they'd ever shared. "I love you like I love my own spleen."

That's a whole lotta love, Dixie Davis, he'd say on a hearty chuckle. Landon's all-too-familiar response to her decades-old declaration of love echoed in her head, leaving her fighting back another raw sob.

Landon Wells—protector of all things defenseless, smart, rich and the best friend any girl could ever have was dead after a short, but incredibly painful bout with pancreatic cancer.

Everything was bad right now. The world was dull and pointless. The future was cloudy with a chance of lonely. Tears fell from her eyes, making her shoulders shudder uncontrollably.

"Oh, Dixie," Em whispered into her hair, wrapping an arm around her waist in a show of undeserved sympathy. "He'd hate you crying like this almost as much as he hates bein' dead, and you know it."

Dixie's throat closed and her shoulders shuddered, making Em grip her waist harder. "Stop this right now, Dixie Davis. We have an afterlife party to attend. Landon planned it all out. Rumor has it, Bobby Flay's gonna be there. You don't want to miss bacon-wrapped sliders made personally by Bobby Flay, do you?"

Em's words made Dixie set the photo down and take a deep breath, preparing herself to face the crowd outside. She was right. Landon would hate her grief as much as he'd hated the pity showered upon him when he'd first been diagnosed. He'd told her to live, and while she did all that living, he wanted her to love again.

Someone, he'd said into the phone during their last

phone call, his husky voice deep and demanding in her ear even in the last throes of his illness. *Love someone until it hurts, Dixie-Cup. And for everyone's sake, don't cry over my lifeless body. You're an ugly crier, girlie.*

A deep, shuddering breath later and she turned her swollen eyes to Em's compassionate gaze. "You're right. He'd hate to see me cry."

When Em propped open the door to the viewing room, Dixie stumbled, forcing Em to tighten her grip around her shoulders. "You and your love of astronomically high heels. You'll break an ankle someday, Dixie."

But it wasn't her heels that made Dixie stumble. It wasn't the endless rows of heads that shot up as they stepped into the chapel to join the mourners, skeptically eyeing their first glimpse of the Horrible Dixie Davis after so many years gone by.

It was Caine Donovan and the momentary eye contact they made as Em pulled her away and down the seemingly endless candlelit aisle of the funeral home. The electric connection his deep blue eyes made with hers snapped and sizzled, sending blistering rushes of heat through her veins.

It was everything and nothing in one short glance, hot and sweet, dismissive and breathtaking. Her heartfelt prayer he'd developed a paunch and had lost all that luscious chocolate-brown hair had gone unnoticed by whoever was in charge of aging.

He stood beside a smug yet pretty, Louella Palmer, wearing a conservative black sundress and matching sun hat, her blond hair sweeping from beneath it. As Dixie and Em moved toward them, Louella's fingers slipped possessively into the crook of Caine's arm just as she turned her pert little nose up at them.

A reminder to Dixie she'd once broken the mean girl's girlfriend code.

Job well done.

"Ladies," Caine said with an arrogant nod and an impeccably unmistakable impression of Sean Connery. Em whisked Dixie past him so fast she had to run to keep up.

But she hadn't missed the subtext of his Sean Connery impersonation. Caine had once used that accent, and his uncanny ability to mimic almost anyone's voice, on more than one intimate occasion. His knowledge of just what a Scottish accent did to her naked flesh was extensive—and he was lobbing it in her face.

Perfect.

Em twittered in girlish delight, bright stains of red slashing her cheeks. "Oh, that man," she gushed, holding firm to Dixie so she wouldn't divert off their course to bacon-wrapped sliders. "He's so delicious. I can't believe he didn't take that gift and use it to make big money in Hollywood or somethin'."

Dixie flapped a hand at her to interrupt. "I know. He's so dreamy when he does his Sean Connery impression." And Frank Sinatra, and Jack Nicholson, and Brando, and even Mae West. Caine's ability to impersonate not only movie stars but almost any stranger's voice was something they'd once laughed over.

Dizziness swept over Dixie like a soggy blanket, clinging to her skin. But Em kept her moving to the end of the aisle and out the door. "Yes. That. All that dreamy handsome, well, it's dang hard to hate." Em's face was sheepish when they finally stepped outside into the hot August day.

The darkening sky hung as heavy as her heart. Spanish moss dripped from the oak tree above them, drifting to the ground.

Em crumpled some with her conservative black pumps. "Sorry. He's just such an honorable man. He makes despisin' him akin to killing cute puppies. Forgive me?"

Dixie gave her a small smile of encouragement, moving toward the parking lot on still-shaky knees. "I'll forgive you, but only if you call him a mean name in feminine-solidarity. It's the only way to atone."

Em pressed her key fob, popping open the locks on her Jeep. She looked over the top of the shiny red car at Dixie who stood on the passenger side and put her hands on either side of her mouth to whisper, "He's the shittiest-shit that ever lived. Shittier than Attila the Hun and Charlie Manson on a team cannibalistic virgin-killin' spree." She curtsied, spreading her black dress out behind her. "Forgiven?"

Dixie smiled and let loose a snort, adjusting the belt of her jacket to let it fall open in order to cool off, if that was possible in the last days of a Georgia August. "Done deal."

Em winked at her. "Good, right?"

With a deep breath, Dixie let go of the restrictive tension in her chest. "You're a good human being, Em. Right down to the cannibals and virgins." Dixie paused, letting their light banter feed her soul.

It was okay to laugh. Landon would have wanted her to laugh. She tapped the roof of the car with a determined flat palm. "All right, c'mon. Let's get to this shindig before I have to go to the reading of Landon's will. I really hope you weren't kidding earlier about the bacon."

Dixie slipped into the car, taking one last glance of the funeral home in the side-view mirror where her last true friend in the world was housed. Her mentor, her shoulder to cry on, her life raft when everything had gone so sideways.

And then Caine stepped off the curb and into view— his tall, hard frame in the forefront of gloomy clouds pushing their way across the blazing hot sun.

Whether she'd admit it or not, Dixie watched Caine get smaller and smaller in the distance against the purple-blue sky until he was gone completely from her grainy-eyed vision.

Déjà vu.

Two

"**P**hone sex. You mean like—" Dixie dropped her voice an octave "—'Hello, this is Mistress Leather' phone-sex?"

"Correct, Ms. Davis. Phone sex. The act of engaging in verbal fornication."

Dixie took a moment to process the entirety of the phrases "phone sex" and "verbal fornication" and what that entailed, but it was proving difficult. After so many sliders, she thought maybe not just her arteries were clogged, but her brain cells, too.

Yet, she tried to let the words of Landon's attorney sink in as casually as if he'd told her she was now the proud owner of one of Landon's classic cars.

So Landon Wells, the man Dixie was sure she knew everything about, right down to his preferred brand of underwear, owned, among various other assorted businesses, a phone-sex company he'd won on a bet in a high-stakes poker game in Uzbekistan back in 2002.

Dixie tore her eyes from Landon's lawyer, Hank Cotton, Sr., and cocked her head in Em's direction, her eyes full of accusation while purposely avoiding the invasive gaze of Caine Donovan.

He'd remained brooding and silent while Hank read the will, but Dixie knew Caine like she knew herself. He was just waiting for the right moment to pounce on her with his cutting words.

Dixie chose to ignore Caine, turning to Em who'd known the whole time what Landon was up to. This was what her code-speak had been about back at the funeral home, and she'd held her tongue.

Em, from her seat beside Landon's lawyer where she flipped papers for him to read, folded her hands primly in her lap and made a face at Dixie. "Oh, stop lookin' at me like I'm Freddy Krueger. Might I mention, I *am* a legal secretary for heaven's sake, Dixie. I couldn't tell you. So I'm callin' the cloak of—"

"Client confidentiality," Dixie finished for her, lacing her words with bold strokes of sarcasm. "I know you're the last person I deserve common decency from, but at the very least, I expected more originality, Emmaline Amos. Something like, all memory of Landon's recently revised will was snatched from you by aliens, and no way in the world would you have kept this kind of shocking news from me as yet another form of payback had those despicable aliens not sucked your brains out through your nose with a pixie stick."

Em shook her head, her silky dark hair semiflattened by the sun hat she'd discarded. Her ruby-red lips curved into a wince of an apologetic smile. "Mmm-hmm. You know, I almost went with that story, but then there were all the complications that come with the pixie sticks, and I just couldn't get it to…gel." She threaded her slim fingers together to articulate her effort to gel, then let them fall back to her lap.

Caine sat in the corner, still silently sexy, his gaze burning a hole in the side of Dixie's head. As if this was all her fault. If the world came to a screeching halt, just before it did, the last words she'd hear before it all ended would be Caine declaring it was all Dixie Davis's fault.

Gritting her teeth, Dixie clenched her hands together in her lap to cover the bloat from the Alaskan king crab and sliders they'd consumed and lifted her chin. "I call traitor. You were traitorous in your intent. It isn't like I don't deserve as much, but this?" Phone sex wasn't something you kept from someone—not even Satan.

Em pouted, her heart-shaped face scrunching comically. "That's mean, Dixie, especially coming from *you*. And just when I thought you'd taken a turn, too. See why I was so hesitant to believe? I was just doin' my job. I do have children to feed. And a very large dog."

"Did you just say Dixie's taken a turn, Em? A turn for what?" Caine finally inquired with that delicious drawl, his growly voice warranting an unbidden stab of heat in places along her body Dixie had to mentally beg to pipe down. His square jaw shifted, going hard as his lips turned upward into a smug smile. "Satanic worship?"

If there was one person who could make her reconsider sidekicking it with Satan, it was Caine Donovan, making her heart race like a Kentucky Derby horse all while she hated him for still being capable of wreaking havoc on her emotions after ten years apart.

Instead of reacting to him, Dixie turned the other cheek, narrowing her eyes at Em. While it was true Em should have no loyalty to her, she couldn't help being upset. "Is it your job to taunt me, too? Because that's exactly what you did back there at the funeral home. You hinted. You bandied, and you took pleasure in it to boot."

Em slapped her hands on her lap, sending up a cloud of black material from her dress. "Bandied? That's a fancy Chicago word there, Miss Dixie, and I did not taunt. I was just tryin' to prepare you in a very round-about, non-confidentiality-breaking way for—for this… And of course I was dying to tell not just you, but everyone in Plum Orchard. It's the most scandalous news ever. I can't wait to see what the senior Mags have to say about this. But in the end, I couldn't betray our client."

Hank's nod from behind his glossy desk was of staunch approval. "That's true, Ms. Davis. We take our clients' confidentiality very seriously."

Em's head bounced again. "We definitely do. That also means I couldn't tell you lots of things until the reading of the will. As a for-instance, a small village in some east African town I can't pronounce will now reap the benefits of books, teachers, and medical care because of Landon."

"Africa isn't phone sex, Em," Dixie reminded.

"Then guess what? Landon owned one of the most successful phone-sex companies in the world, and he left it all to you and Mr. Smexy. You know, with condi-tions. Surprise!" She smiled and winked at Caine aka Mr. Smexy, who was back to sitting stoically in his corner chair.

He'd surprised Dixie when he'd shown up—surprised her and made her blood pressure pulse in her ears. Em had explained Landon's request Caine be present for the reading of the will, too. Something she'd also failed to mention while she was bandying and taunting.

Dixie shifted in her chair, still absorbing what she'd just heard. Forcing her lips to form a question, her eyes sought Hank Cotton's again. "So just to be clear, when you say Landon had a phone-sex company, you don't really mean, 'Oh, Daddy, do it to me one more time' kind of phone sex, do you, Mr. Cotton?" Did he?

No. That couldn't be what he meant. Yet what other kind of phone sex was there but the kind with ball-gags and chains and furry costumes? The palms of her hands grew clammy.

"Say that again, Dixie—just like that." Caine antagonized, drawing out his words. "All that honey pouring from your throat, husky and full of rasp is *hot.* It's a voice made for sinning. The only thing missing is your accent. Where did that go, Miss Chicago?"

The words he spoke were designed to hurt. Dixie knew he was taking pleasure in seeing the red stain of embarrassment flush her cheeks.

Deeper and deeper Caine shoved the knife of their memories into her chest.

Landon's lawyer, someone who hadn't been a resident in Plum Orchard when she'd left, sharply dressed in a dark suit and red tie, winced then straightened in his chair as though he realized control was needed.

He cleared his throat, breaking the awkward silence in his overly warm office. "I'd like to get back to the business at hand. So yes, in fact, I do mean that, Miss Davis. And it's very successful, lucrative phone sex, I might add. After Landon won the company, he turned a sagging Call Girls into a multimillion-dollar corporation."

A thought dawned on her just then, making Dixie relax into her hard seat. She nodded her head in sudden understanding. A nervous snort slipped from her throat. "This was Landon's idea of a joke, right? He told me before he died—" she puffed out her chest in Landon fashion ""—Dixie-Cup, don't you weep and wail long now, ya hear?' If you knew Landon, you'd know he'd go to any extreme to cheer me up."

Even from the afterlife. Where she totally planned to, when time and hiring a psychic to locate him allowed, hunt him down and kill him all over again for mocking her this way.

Hank shook his head with a firm sideways motion, his perfectly groomed, salt-and-pepper hair never moving.

His vehement nod meant a resounding no. Not a joke.

Hank leaned back in his plush leather chair and folded his slender fingers. "This is no joke, Ms. Davis. Landon Wells was very specific and quite detailed in his last wishes. He was the sole owner of Call Girls, and he hoped to pass that on to either you or Mr. Donovan in order to keep it in the family, so to speak. Clearly, his mother, Charlotte, wasn't an option. That left the two of you, his closest friends. And I warn you there's more to this. The will states that if you and Mr. Donovan wish to benefit from the entirety of the proceeds of his very unusual venture, both of you will have to earn it."

Dixie looked away from Hank for a moment, focusing on an abstract painting on the far wall, full of slashes of color and streaked with gold edges. The tumble of emotions displayed in oil reflected her muddled thoughts. "Earn it? We have to earn a phone-sex company? Meaning?"

"Meaning you'll both have to work the phones at Call Girls as operators. In essence, you'll be Call Girls employees for a two-month period with a general manager to train you, and watch your progress. As another stipulation, if you should decide to take on this challenge, you must both reside in Landon's house while you do—together or the offer becomes null. Landon had phone lines set up for you both at the guesthouse next to the other women he's employed. They're to help both you and Mr. Donovan learn the ropes of the industry, so to speak."

Em's finger shot upward. Clearly, there was something in this madness Em hadn't been privy to. "Do you mean to tell me Landon's plan is to keep the business and those women in his guesthouse here in Plum Orchard *for good?*" She grabbed a stray file folder and began to furiously fan herself with it. "What will Reverend Watson say? Oh, the ladies of the Magnolias of the Orchard Society will not like this. Not one bit."

Dixie actually had to fight a giggle at the thought of the Mags, especially Nanette Pruitt's face, the busiest busybody of them all, when she heard the news that Landon Wells planned to harbor harlots in what everyone in town, as far back as she could remember, lovingly called the "Big House."

"I'm the only person who knew the complexities of Landon's will, and the people asked to help him execute it. No one in Plum Orchard knows the extent of it yet. Leastways, I haven't heard anything through the grapevine," Hank soothed. "But yes, that was his intent. After finding out he was terminally ill, Landon had his general manager, Catherine Butler, begin the move—they only left their old offices a couple of days ago. Landon wanted the ladies of Call Girls moved from a lush apartment in Atlanta into his guesthouse, where he had Catherine set up operations in order to keep what he called 'his girls' closer to home. As Emmaline may have told you, Catherine's now happily engaged to Emmaline's cousin, Flynn McGrady."

Em's eyes widened, her hand immediately drifting to her cheek. "Cat knew Landon planned to keep Call Girls here?" She turned her gaze to Dixie. "Why, the two of them were just over for Sunday dinner at Mama's and not a peep about it!"

"Catherine was bound by legalities to remain silent until the will was read," Hank reminded Em. "I hope you won't hold it against her."

Dixie nodded her understanding and gave a tired sigh. "I don't know about Em, but I don't blame her. How do you say, 'I manage a phone-sex company, pass the fried chicken, please?' Especially with your mama in the mix, Em."

Em's mother, Clora Mitchell, was a lot like her own mother. Controlling, and angry about something that had no label. Dixie handled her situation by running away from it, and Em handled it by taking exhaustive good-girl measures. In her later years, Clora had loosened her stranglehold on Em a bit, but she was still as proper as they came. Clora'd faint dead with the knowledge she was related, even loosely, to someone working for a phone-sex company.

Hank cleared his throat. "We were talking about the guesthouse. That's where Dixie and Caine, if they choose to accept this challenge, will work during the course of their training. All of the appropriate permits are in place, and there's a formal letter to Reverend

Watson and Mayor Hale available should there be any doubt this is all done within the confines of not just county regulations but state, too."

Caine, who'd gone back to quietly brooding, cleared his throat and steepled his tanned hands under his chin. Dixie knew that look. It was the one where all the processing of pertinent information was done, and he was ready to play.

In three, two, one…

Caine fought to keep his voice even while trying to ignore Dixie and her gravitational pull. He was still damn angry with her. As angry as he had been the day they'd broken up, and that made him angrier. After all this time, Dixie still had the power to make him feel something he didn't want to feel.

"So let me get this straight. Landon left everything to Ms. Davis and I, but only if we actually work at Call Girls and live in his mansion *together?*"

Em coughed to disguise her laugh before pressing her fist to her lips to suppress another outburst.

Hank locked eyes with Caine, steady and sharp. "Yes. That's correct, Mr. Donovan. You each have two months to create your personas as phone-sex operators, and your, um…*specialty,* so to speak. Whoever garners the most calls at the end of the two-month time period wins the company. Full ownership. I have a list of what exactly *specialty* means in the phone-sex industry, and some other details to be hashed out, but that's the laymen's gist of it. You'll have full access to the house and staff, but I warn you, Landon left strict instructions that a court-appointed mediator will monitor your actions, so in his words, there'll be no funny business. Your reputations for one-upmanship precede you *both*."

Son of a bitch. Landon had covered every base, hadn't he? Especially the base that kept him and Dixie from finding a way that led to the other's demise.

If there was a way to manipulate herself as the front-runner in anything, from a sack race to a hot-dog-eating contest, Dixie would do it, and like the ass he was, he'd take the bait.

You knew us well, friend.

But why had he done *this?* In this particular way? Putting them together in the big house? The house where there were a million memories of them as a couple. Why had he put them together for an extended period of time anywhere? Landon had known how dark those days after he and Dixie broke up had been for him. This contest was like rubbing salt in a bloody gash. Putting the two of them together after their shitty history was diabolical and possibly even homicidal.

No way he'd survive being around Dixie for an extended period of time. He wasn't proud of admitting that, but it was the damn truth.

But wait. Caine finally smiled. The bastard was messing with them even from the grave. Damn, he loved Landon and his balls-to-the-wall sense of humor—even in death, he was busting their chops.

Dixie might have fallen for this act Em and Hank were putting on, but he wasn't. He barked an open-mouthed laugh at the thought. "Hah! You son of a bitch, Landon," he said into the room. "Best prank ever, pal. This one even gives Dixie a run for her money. And great job, Hank. Really. You should consider Hollywood. So let's get to why we're really here. Did he just want someone to witness his last prank? Wait, did he have you videotape this?" Caine craned his neck to scan the room for a camera. "This will end up on YouTube, won't it?" He laughed again.

And then he pulled up short.

Hank gazed intently at Caine.

Shit. He wasn't blinking. They were screwed.

"Mr. Wells said you might say something like this. I'm not sure you really understand me, Mr. Donovan. I repeat, this is no prank. If you wish to review Landon's will with the attorney of your choosing, I'm happy to oblige."

In his mind, he'd been busy sending Dixie back to Chicago where she belonged. Shipping Dixie and all the memories that came with her far away. Taking with her the dark circles under her eyes and the worry in her voice. Leaving. So he could do what he'd intended to do when he came back for the funeral. Stay a while. Catch his breath. Reevaluate where his life in Miami was going, or rather, wasn't going.

There was something missing from it these days. Something big. Something important. He wanted to know what that something was.

But now, he was back in the room with them all, hearing words like *Landon figured he'd think this was all some joke.* Which meant it was no joke.

Damn, Landon.

Dixie leaned forward, her beautiful face masked in more apprehension, and it made his chest tight, despite his wish that he could ignore it. She was thinner, almost fragile, maybe. Something she'd never been, but it wasn't just physically. It was in her posture, once straight and confidently arrogant, now a little slumped.

Shit.

Don't get sucked in, buddy. Don't you damn well do it. You know what it's like when she wants something. She could out-act Meryl Streep on an Academy Award–winning day if it meant she'd get what she wanted. Or have you forgotten all those tears she cried when you broke off your engagement? They looked damn real, pal. She's good. Too good.

Caine shifted in his chair and forced himself to ignore any and all signs Dixie was suffering any more than he was over Landon's death—or suffering over anything at all.

But there it was again, her voice a little small, a little hoarse when she asked, "What if I don't have an attorney because they cost money, ridiculous money, no disrespect to you—" She gave Hank an apologetic wave of her hand "—and there's no possible way I can afford to have someone review this? What if, as utterly shocking as I'm sure this will be for *some,* I don't want to work at Call Girls?"

Dixie didn't have any money? Bullshit. He'd heard about her closing her restaurant, but she came from one of the richest families in the South. She'd just ask her mother for more. Wasn't that what all women like Dixie did? There was a game here. Caine just didn't know what it was.

Hank's expression didn't budge when he gazed at Dixie. "If you don't want to participate, then you forfeit your ownership to Mr. Donovan, and he owns Call Girls and the profits from such in its entirety."

Aha.

Those words, so calm, so beautifully articulated tripped all the triggers Caine suspected Landon had counted on. He and Dixie in a hand-to-hand combat situation where, if it killed one of them, they'd do almost anything to win.

As it once was, it always would be.

Now he got it.

Dixie slipped to the edge of her chair, drawing Caine's eyes to her legs. He snapped them shut and instead listened to her ask, "So *he* gets everything if I decide to bail because I'm not game to pretend I'm Mistress Leather?"

"Mercy," Em muttered, letting her head drop to her chest, kicking up the momentum of her makeshift fan a notch.

Hank rolled his tongue along the inside of his cheek. "That's correct. And Landon suggested you use the title Lady. I believe—" he shuffled through more papers on his desk, tapping one before putting his glasses on "—yes. There it is in my notes. Landon thought Lady Lana would suit you, Ms. Davis. My notes here say he thought it was the perfect name for someone with 'a voice meant for sinning'." Hank slid his thin index finger into the collar of his Brooks Brothers shirt, loosening it to clear his throat.

Caine smirked, looking directly at Dixie. Lady Lana. *Nice, Landon.*

Yet, his victory was short-lived. First, when he remembered, even after their ugly breakup, Landon had kept their friendships on equal footing for the near decade they'd refused to speak to one another. Second, when he saw Dixie's pretty eyes finally spark, he knew he was in for it, too.

In the name of fair, Landon wouldn't play favorites.

"Really," Dixie drawled, her Southern lilt reappear-

ing. She leaned forward toward Hank, her gaze capti-
vating his, her body language, a glowing halo of sexy.
Just like the old Dixie.

Caine relaxed a little. Nothing had changed. It was
just another ploy.

She let her eyelashes flutter to her cheeks in that coy
way that made his pulse thrash. "And did Landon have
a name all picked out for Mr. Donovan, too? It would
only be fair." She smiled at Hank—the smile that was
both flirtatious and subtle, one she'd used often to get
almost anything she wanted back in high school. One
she'd used on him.

One you fell for, dummy.

Caine eyed Hank's reaction, at first taken aback.
Really, who wasn't when Dixie poured on the charm?
But it was only a momentary lapse before he read her
playful tone. "How well you knew him. In fact, he *did,*
Ms. Davis."

Caine gritted his teeth, bracing himself. *Damn you,
Landon. I hope you're getting your pound of flesh up
there.*

Dixie cocked her eyebrow upward in smug anticipation. "You have Mistress Leather's full attention,"
she cooed, using her husky-honey voice to encourage
Hank to spill. She swung her crossed leg and waited,
smoothing her hand down along her calf to her ankle
before pointing her toes.

Jesus.

Hank looked to Caine. "Landon's suggestion was
Candy Cane, with a play on Caine, but he was also par-
tial to Boom-Boom LaRue."

How do ya like that for some boom, Boom-Boom?

Three

Caine gripped the arms of his uncomfortable chair. Damn her, after ten years, for not only still being so sexy it made his teeth grind together, but for possessing the ability to suck any man—even staid Hank Cotton, into her vortex of charm.

Boom-Boom. *The hell, Landon?*

Why wasn't he getting the hell up, forfeiting everything to Dixie, and going back home to Miami? He could reevaluate his life anywhere in the world. It didn't have to be here. He didn't need the money. He didn't want the money. He wanted Dixie to go home and Landon alive so he could take him back out.

Worse, why was she still stirring things up in him better left unstirred? Just the brief glimpse of her with Em today at the funeral home dragged him right back to their short but tumultuous engagement.

When they'd both come home ten years ago, and she no longer felt like his kid sister, their constant sibling antagonism turned to something much bigger than he'd ever thought possible. When he'd stupidly believed

Dixie wasn't the reckless, cruel, entitled kid he'd left behind.

He mentally dug in his heels while she sat in her chair, daring him with her flashing eyes to come play the game. Not a chance she was going to sucker him again. Which brought him back to the same thought as he watched Dixie watch him. Why wasn't he hauling ass outta here?

"What's the matter, Caine Donovan? Are you afraid I'll beat you just like I did when you bet I couldn't spit watermelon seeds farther than you?" Dixie pointed to her pink-lipsticked lips, full and pouty-smug. "That's right—this mouth beat you by almost eight inches."

Caine made a fist of his hand, flexing and unflexing the tense muscles to keep her from seeing she was getting under his skin. "Your mouth was as deceptive as the rest of you. And you stood on a chair, Dixie. Hardly fair."

Dixie tilted her chin toward her shoulder, letting it nestle in her long red hair, gifting him that smoldering eye thing she used to do, knowing damn well it made him crazy. "Why, where in the rules for watermelon seed spittin' did it say I couldn't use a chair, Caine?"

Caine's jaw tightened to a hard line, shifting and grinding. *Resist.* "I don't need Landon's phone-sex company, or the money it makes. No matter how much."

No amount of money was worth being around Dixie again. No amount of money was worth the constant reminder that he was an asshole who couldn't tell the difference between the real thing, and the fake Dixie thing.

Yet. Here you sit.

Dixie rose to her feet, hurling her large handbag over her shoulder. That settled that. "Good for you, Richie

Rich. Unfortunately, I do." Wow, did she. After her drive here to Plum Orchard, her checking account was nothing but the kind of change you find in the cushions of your couch.

She needed the money. But did she need it enough to become a phone-sex operator?

Weren't you the one organizing an ad for your kidneys on Craigslist just three short hours ago?

But what if she didn't want to play Mistress Leather to dirty old men and oversexed college boys as a way to get herself out of this mess?

What if? What if you want to live the rest of your life never making the things you've done wrong right? What if you just sweep it under the carpet like you've always done? What if you just skip this part, the hard part, and fix something else you've broken instead? Something smaller, less difficult, maybe?

No. She didn't have to do this. She could skulk back off to Chicago and continue to lick her wounds in her studio apartment with the peeling pink paint, a stove that had only one working burner, a shower that dripped exactly two drops of water per minute, and a punk neighbor who sold pharmaceuticals for someone named Dime.

She absolutely could go right back to living just barely above the poverty level while she tried desperately to pay back money she'd charmed out of her mother's connections. Money she'd promised to handle with care—promised in the way the old Dixie promised everything. Loosely—offhandedly—with little regard for anything but what she wanted.

No. This was a way to finally do something because it was right.

Still, the more she played with the idea in her mind, the easier it was becoming to convince herself she could do this.

If getting back on her feet meant spanking a chair with a fly swatter for effect while she whispered the words, "You must be punished for disobeying me," into a phone, she'd do it. It was either that or starve at this point. Food won. Food and a warm place for Mona and Lisa, her twin bulldogs to sleep. "So, it's settled? I win. You lose. Where do I sign, Hank?"

Hank gave Dixie another "Hank look" translating to "not so fast." "Let's not be hasty. You have twenty-four hours to think about it, Ms. Davis. Mr. Donovan, too. Landon insisted upon a waiting period of sorts. In the meantime, Landon has offered his house and staff at your full disposal—to the both of you—while you mull this opportunity over. He wanted you both to be comfortable while you considered his offer."

She'd already had two years of broke since her restaurant had gone bust. Why waste time? Dixie shot her hand upward to avoid more naysaying. "I don't even need twenty-four seconds. I'm in. Pass the pen."

But Hank shook his head. "I'm sorry. Landon insisted that you both take the time to thoroughly think this through and get your affairs in order. He knew the two of you well, Miss Davis. His notes, and there were many, many notes—" Hank held up a stack of paper "—claim, on occasion, you're quick to jump before you think. Especially if it comes to any sort of competition with—"

"With me," Caine interjected with confidence, quite obviously pleased with himself.

Hank's lips pursed at Caine's interruption. He held

up the ream of paper again and pointed to it with a short-clipped nail. "Yes. Landon did say that, but Ms. Davis wasn't the only one he left remarks about. He also mentioned you're quite easily baited by—" he looked down at the paper, shifting his glasses "—the lovely and irresistible Miss Davis. His words, right here." He tapped the mountain of white again.

Dixie shot Caine a triumphant gaze. If there were notes to be had, she was grateful she wasn't the only one worth noting.

Caine's fingers flexed and cracked, signaling his legendary simmer.

"Thus," Hank continued, "he asked that you both take a hard look at his proposition. Landon was quite aware you both have lives and jobs elsewhere."

Well, one of them did.

"So please, each of you use the maximum time given, and we'll meet back here tomorrow at six with your decisions. Now, Landon had all the locks changed on the big house just prior to his death. I'll go get the set of keys he had made for each of you so you can settle in after such an emotionally trying day." Hank rose, whisking out of the office on expensively clad feet, quite obviously relieved to get away from Landon's tawdry business dealings.

Em rushed to stand next to Dixie, peering down at her with an expression of guilt. "Before you rush to callin' me a traitor, yes, I was the one who had the keys made and called the locksmith to change the locks. But I maintain, I only knew Landon owned a phone-sex company and he was leaving it to you two to fight over. I thought Cat and the girls were going to show you the ropes temporarily. He left me a beautiful letter to thank me for facilitatin' his…his passin', but there was nothing about keeping Call Girls here permanently."

Dixie's smile was as ironic as her tired nod. She patted Em's hand. "You don't owe me an explanation, and either way, I'm not staying at the big house." Not with Caine. Not knowing he'd sleep in one of the eight or so bedrooms—naked. He always slept naked.

A fleeting visual of his wide chest with a sprinkling of dark hair and thickly muscled thighs spread wide to reveal his most intimate body part shuttled through her mind's eye unbidden. Dixie bit back an uncomfortable groan.

"But the big house is so nice with every luxury available. Butlers and maids and a full-time chef," Em said, as though all those things in a gloriously opulent setting would make it easier to answer to the name Mistress Leather. "And bidets. He has bidets. Who can resist a bidet?"

Dixie pulled her purse closer to her side, running her fingers over the surface. She knew everything Landon had. Scratch that. Almost everything. "Yes, I know Landon has a bidet, and a slide in the pool, and a screening room, and a camel named Toe he couldn't bear to part with when he left Turkey so he hired a zookeeper to care for him at the big house. He told everyone all the time what he had. I'm not interested in his possessions—just the predicament he's left me in."

Dixie breathed deeply, pushing air in and out of her lungs to assuage her anxiety. "I don't want to stay at Landon's, and I don't care about the chef."

"You just care about the money, right, Dixie?" Caine interrupted, rising from his chair to saunter with liquid grace toward them. As confident as ever, he'd added a dash more smug to his repertoire.

Nice. Veiled innuendo.

Fine. She deserved all of the mud he could sling.

As she turned to look him directly in the eye for the first time in almost a decade, Dixie mentally reminded herself to stand strong and fight the bone-deep lust that never failed to consume her whenever Caine was in close proximity.

The way he moved with the sensual grace of a panther, the light bronze of his skin beneath his white shirt and navy suit, the ripple of his thighs, pushing against his trousers, still affected her.

But resist she would. Not an easy hurdle to jump when he moved in even closer and gazed down at her, waiting.

No. He wasn't waiting. He was laying down a dare in much the way she had earlier, but his wasn't based on desperation. It was steeped in anger.

Automatically, Dixie's chin lifted, her pride raising both metaphoric fists to the sky even as a wave of shivers covered her arms and the back of her neck. "Don't be coy about it, Boom-Boom. If you want to insult me then do it, but do it well. I'm not ashamed to say I need a job. So what?"

"And you're willing to call men you don't know *'Daddy'* for employment?"

Her cheeks went hot, but her mouth flew open. "You're just shy of accusing me of hooking for cash, aren't you?"

Caine's dark eyebrow rose while he jingled coins in his pocket. "Oh, I'm not shy, sweetheart," he reminded her.

She swallowed hard, the room growing oppressive. No. Neither of them had been shy. Their chemistry was what legends were made of. Hot, sticky, soul-baring legends. Her legs wound around him while he drove into her with forceful thrusts until she screamed, was the hottest, rawest sex she'd ever had. Everything—everyone since was just lukewarm.

She forced that to the back of her mind. "Well, I'm not shy either," she gritted, "as you well know. So here's the truth of the matter. The economy stinks. My restaurant went bust. I lost hundreds of thousands of some fine people's investment dollars. My 401K has tumbleweeds cohabitating in it, and I haven't been able to find a decent paying job in two years. So shoot me, Caine Donovan, for having the audacity to entertain the thought that this might answer a couple of long overdue prayers."

There was nothing Caine would love more than to hear the opportunity she'd jumped on when she'd left Plum Orchard had failed. He deserved to roll around in her failure.

Em stepped between them, casting Caine a pleading eye before turning to Dixie. "Suggestion? It's been a long, chaotic day. How about we go to Landon's and relax before someone says somethin' rash?"

Dixie straightened, preparing to leave before she took the bait Caine dangled in front of her and things escalated between them. They were older—wiser—and their behavior should reflect that.

She tugged her purse back over her shoulder with resolve. "I'm ready now. That Landon wants us to wait twenty-four hours is just enough time to grab a shower, eat some of Martha's infamous peach pie and Sanjeev's lamb curry, get a decent night's rest, and skip back over here to sign those papers." Her choice was made.

"You do realize this is ridiculous, don't you, Dixie?" Caine's voice grumbled, still so sexy-rough. "Landon's really yanking our chains, pitting us against one another. You know, just like back in the old days when the two of us competed over everything, and Landon looked on fondly at his two foolish best friends making asses of themselves? He's having a good laugh, wherever he is. What I don't get is why he'd do something like this. It's not like Landon, especially knowing the way we feel about one another. I don't suppose he left the reasons he did this in all that paperwork, Em, did he?"

Em's hands folded and dropped in front of her. "No. I don't know any more than the two of you know."

It was clear Caine's anger with Dixie hadn't dulled after almost a decade, and he wanted her to know. Fair enough. "Then don't stick around for the five W's. Go back to Miami and sell some more million-dollar, oceanfront houses to leathery-skinned women who have pocketbook-size dogs. You don't need the money. I do. You probably couldn't handle the challenge anyway." Dixie was methodically inviting him to try and best her. It was silly and childish and unlike the person she strove so hard to be, but gravy. Ten years was a long time to still feel this much hate coming from Caine.

The ripple of power Caine exuded reflected in his narrowed eyes. "Are you suggesting I let you have *everything?*"

"I'm suggesting you go home and admit defeat. Because, as you've mentioned, you don't need the money."

"And how is it that you've come to the conclusion I'll end up the loser?"

"It's simple logic. Me—woman—with a hot voice, if all the compliments I've been getting all these years are any indication. You—*man,* probably not a key component when attempting to arouse a male who wants to be called *Daddy* by his little *girl.*" Dixie had to fight the shudder those words evoked. That was most definitely not going to be her persona's *specialty.*

"Ah, but you forget one little thing, Mistress Leather," Caine baited, gracing her with a smile full of white teeth.

"What's that, Candy Caine?" Her eyebrow rose with total confidence. She hadn't forgotten anything. She had him by a landslide just by virtue of her gender.

Caine leaned into her, the slightest hint of his cologne dousing her nostrils before she took an unsteady step back. "You're forgetting *'Bond. James Bond.'*"

The tip of Em's index finger went directly into her mouth. She nibbled the chipped end of her nail, her brow furrowing, her eyes flashing danger zone signals at Dixie.

Oh, damn him and his Sean Connery bombs. Caine could create any persona he desired and melt the insides of millions of women into sticky goo. Dixie wanted to stamp her feet in frustration until she remembered one thing. Women didn't call phone-sex lines, or if they did, they sure weren't in the majority. Men were.

Hah!

Dixie was right back in high school when she said, "I think you're forgetting one little thing, Boom-Boom, name one woman you know who calls a phone-sex operator. *One.*"

Caine's lips flat-lined.

Uh-huh. "I bet you don't have enough fingers and

toes to count the men you know who've dialed a Mistress Leather, or variation thereof, do you, Caine Donovan?"

More flat-lining and nostril flaring.

She curtsied and winked. "Your serve."

"Don't be so quick to call me dead in the water. The women of today are empowered, unafraid of their sexuality, bolder about their needs and about expressing those needs. Add in Sean Connery, Johnny Depp, maybe a little Sam Elliott or for that matter, almost anyone they'd like to, uh...verbally play with, and I'm your man." Then he grinned. Wide. Smug.

Her nostrils flared.

"So I'll tell you what, Dixie Davis, you go right ahead and rev up your sexy, because I *dare* you to top that."

He'd used the word dare. Such a bad, bad word. Resist, Dixie. Fight it. Fight hard.

Instead of reacting, Dixie gathered herself together, her body rigid enough to shoot an arrow and looked Caine Donovan square in the eye.

The second gauntlet of the day she threw down was again silent, metaphoric, but it was no less meaningful. "Then I guess this is Donovan versus Davis. See you here tomorrow at six. Don't forget your thong and your flogging thingy."

"Flogger," Em corrected. "It's just called a flogger."

Dixie cocked her head at Em. "You know this how?"

Her face flushed red as she backed away from them. "I'm gonna go check on Hank and see if he's found those keys," she said over her shoulder, her embarrassment painfully obvious.

Caine rolled his tongue along the inside of his cheek,

his expression once again arrogant. "You bet I'll be here, Dixie, and I'll see your flogger and raise you some latex and hot candle wax," he retorted, still so smug.

Okay, conscience, fair is fair. I'm trying to be the best person I know how to be. I'm trying to leave my baggage at the airport carousel. But c'mon. He's baiting me. It's plain as the nose on my face. You can't expect me to take it and just lie down and die.

Her blood pressure soared. "Funny you should mention the word *see,* Caine." Dixie paused, putting the tip of her nail between her lips, widening her eyes with mock exaggeration. "You know, I wonder if Landon's company provides live video chats? I bet he does in this age of technology. So, I'll *see* your ridiculous latex and raise you one hot Southern belle in a leather corset, fishnet stockings and some ruby-red stiletto heels. A *real live* Southern belle, not someone just *pretendin'* to be a celebrity," she sniped with a smirk.

Caine leaned down, pinning her with his gaze, as though he were transmitting every last hot, lust-filled second they'd spent together to her mind's eye.

He trailed a finger along her cheek, making Dixie fight a whimper for the weak-kneed hunger his touch left in its wake.

It was all she could do to remain defiant rather than curl her jaw into the digit and sigh with years of pent-up yearning. His hand snaked around her waist, hauling her to him so their bodies were flush, his taut, hers softer but no less aware of the fire brewing beneath all that sinew.

Her clit throbbed in reaction to the rigid line beneath his trousers, aching with familiar need. Her leg begged her to allow it to wrap around his trim waist.

His hard fingers dug into her flesh, but Dixie didn't flinch. Instead, she issued what she was sure, if Caine actually decided to take Landon's offer, would be just one more of her many challenges. "What do you have to say for yourself now, Caine?"

Leaning in farther still, his lips stopped a mere breath from hers, creating an all-over tremble of awareness. The scent of his cologne, sharp and musky, lingered in her nose. "I say you look hot in leather, Dixie. Your ass was the finest in all of Plum Orchard at one time. Maybe even in the entire state of Georgia." Caine emphasized that point by reaching around her and grabbing a handful of it, kneading it until she thought her lungs had stopped working altogether.

Sliding his free hand along her bare leg, he traced his silken-padded fingers upward until they were under her skirt and had reached the edge of her panties, allowing his knuckles to skim the tender flesh where her leg met the apex of her thighs.

Caine pulled away then, almost garnering a gasp of disappointment from her, only to run his index finger along her cleft, pressing the silk of her underwear against the heat of her achy clit.

Shivers of need, desperate and wanton, made everything else fall away. Though her arms remained at her side, the all-consuming desire to twine them around Caine was a war she fought with steely resolve. He let his silken tongue dab at her lips, before he added, "Know what else I say?"

Her breathing was choppy, there was no hiding it, but she was delighted to find, Caine's was, too. "What else do you say?"

The delicious movement between her legs stopped

as suddenly as it had started. He smirked down at her. "I say you don't have the guts. That's what I say."

Just as Dixie was considering wiping the smirk off Caine's face with a good right hook, Hank and Em's footsteps sounded. She pushed at Caine, taking two unsteady steps away from the astounding effect he had on her body, away from the memory.

Em held up the gleaming keys and shook them.

Dixie snatched her set from Em and dangled them in Caine's direction with quivering fingers, and melting kneecaps. "I'll see you here tomorrow, Caine Donovan, and we'll see who has guts. Bring your impersonations. Bring whatever you think will help you win this. Just be sure to *bring it, big boy.*"

Dixie rounded on her heel with such fluid grace she owed herself a pat on the back for not collapsing. "Good night, Hank. I'll see you tomorrow at six sharp." She sashayed out of the office with the invisible words *I dare you* written all over the back of her suit jacket.

When she reached the top of the stairwell, she had to grasp the banister to keep from pitching forward. The throb in her temple returned, matching the unmerciful throb between her thighs, beat for agonizing beat.

She'd just consented to sell sex over the phone so she could win a new way to make a living, and in order to do it, she'd have to beat Caine Donovan, the one and only man who'd ever made her so insane with primal, wanton need, she would have done anything he asked.

Crazy must have taken a global vacation, but not before making one pit stop in her small town in Georgia.

Em skidded out into the hall, hot on her heels. As she reached the top of the steep steps she panted, "Don't do it, Dixie! I can barely afford to feed our dog, Dora the

Explorer. I don't know if I can take Mona and Lisa in, too. And seeing as you have nothing left in your 401K, you won't be leavin' me anything to help."

Dixie finally giggled, releasing her nervous tension. "I wasn't thinking about ending it all. I was just thinking about getting out of that room."

"Where all that hot man sucks up every last ounce of air? I know. I get it. He's like a vacuum packer—or at least, when you're in the room he is."

"That's not it either." The lie fell from her tongue like honey dripping from a bottle. "I was leaving before we ended up thumb wrestling till someone cried 'uncle.' You know what we were like, Em—always trying to one-up each other—fight to the death. That was years ago. I've grown up. So the last thing I want to do is engage in a pointless 'he said, she said' argument. I want to go back to my hotel and mull—plan—plot how in the world I'm going to pull this off."

Em clucked her tongue. "First, we're going back to *Landon's* so you don't break the rules he's set forth and forfeit everything because you can't resist being difficult. My mama has the boys for the night, and I'm free. I can dine on cold, leftover crab and artichoke dip in Landon's hot tub, which runs at a warm ninety-eight degrees. And second, remember this—your voice is pretty sexy, Dixie. All raspy and Kathleen Turner-ish. No doubt, you've made a million foolish men fall at your feet without ever having seen you. All they needed to do was listen. Bet you could beat the pants off Caine Donovan in a phone-sex-off with a voice like that if you set your mind to it."

If only his pants were the issue. Anxiety churned in Dixie's stomach. "But he can create thousands of different personas with his impressions, Em. He can be whoever a woman wants him to be. How can I ever top Sean Connery?"

"I can't even believe I'm sayin' this. What do you think the ratio of male/female callers really is? Ignore the story Caine was sellin' you and focus. You could beat him with your mouth taped shut with those odds. Women might be empowered these days, but the truth is, they don't have to work as hard as men out in the real world."

Good point. But… There was still Sam. "Have you heard his Sam Elliott impression?"

Em waffled, probably because she had. And it was a thigh-clencher. Still, she shook a stern finger at her. "Then you'll just have to work harder." She paused then, her smile ironic. "Funny, isn't it? You actually workin' for what you want instead of everyone doing the work for you? And besides all of the obvious, we don't even know if Caine'll take Landon up on this crazy endeavor I'm hereby callin' 'Survivor, the Porn Edition.' So before you even consider feelin' sorry for yourself, just remember your new mantra—outwit, outlast, outplay."

Em's words of encouragement warmed her. True enough. You didn't become a successful real-estate mogul by taking two months off. "You think?"

Em nodded with a vehement dip of her head. "He has a successful real-estate business back in Miami, Dixie, employees and everything. He can't just up and leave for a long period of time. So I'd lay bets by tomorrow, he'll be on a plane back to the Sunshine State. Today was just him blusterin' like men do when a woman has the nerve to call them on their game."

Dixie stood rooted to the top of the stairs while the

phrase, "What can Mistress Lana do for you tonight, unworthy one?" ran like a stampede of elephants in her brain.

Em roped an arm through Dixie's. "You're thinkin' too much. I can see it. Let's go to the big house and we'll talk it over." She stopped on the step for a moment, turning to Dixie, her eyes clouded with suspicion. "Wait a minute. Did Landon know what was going on with you financially? Did he know you were pushin' your last dime just to get here to be with him?"

Tears began to flood her eyes again, but this time Dixie didn't stop them, she let them drip down her face and hit the steel steps. "No," she whispered. "I could never tell him…."

"Because the first thing he would have done was meddle, and the second would be to set about making the boo-boo all better, and naturally, you have your pride."

"So you know what happened?" That last bit of her pride floated upward toward the ceiling.

"The grapevine is thicker than ever here, Dixie. Some took great pleasure in it when they read the papers and saw Dixie-Cup had gone belly up. Though I will tell you, I wasn't one of them. Honest." Facing Dixie, she held her right palm up.

"I didn't want him to rescue me. I went in with my eyes wide open. I left Plum Orchard to open the restaurant with them wide open, too—definitely one of my more harebrained schemes. But I never told Landon a thing. I lied to him and told him everything was okay, because he was so sick and he had enough to worry about. I let him believe I walked away from all of my investors."

"You're doin' this to pay back all those investors, aren't you? Because most of those investors were Davis family connections."

Shame and humiliation tinged Dixie's gut, but she refused to let it dampen her determination. "If I have to sell an organ on Craigslist."

Em let go of a heavy sigh. "That's what I figured. But it isn't like your mama's friends couldn't afford the investment, Dixie. They'll just write it off as a loss. And isn't that what bankruptcy is for anyway? So you don't have to pay anyone back?"

Dixie shook her head sharply. No. That was the easy way out. No more easy. "It was the easiest way to keep the bank at bay, but I still owe a debt as far as I'm concerned. I'll repay it."

Em's pretty blue eyes searched hers, a hint of admiration in them until they clouded back over with skepticism. "I just don't know what to think of you anymore, Miss Dixie," she said, her tone clear with conflict.

"Then think about other things. Like how uproariously, ironically funny it'll be when everyone in town finds out Dixie Davis, reformed mean girl in deep financial debt, is selling sex."

"You should've told Landon, Dixie. He'd have wanted to know. He loved you. He said that often to me durin' his last month. He said if he'd been hitting for the other team, it would always be you."

He had said that on a million occasions. He'd said it when he admired the color of her hair or what he called the sexy half curve of her lip when she was thinking. He'd said it when she was singing along with the radio, and her sultry voice made every song sound dirty.

Dixie smiled at the memory, and it grew wider. He'd

said, *The only person I'd change who I am for is you,*
Dixie Davis. You make this gay man pause from time
to time. But then I remember I can't change, and you
love Caine Donovan. Nothing can change that, girlie.

Something had.

Dixie shuddered a breath from her lungs and began
to descend the steps one at a time, taking Em with her.

Maybe it was Landon's spirit. Maybe it was just
desperation, but an ember of hope sparked, and if she
fanned it just right… "But he didn't know, and he didn't
hit for my team, and now here we are. So let's go back
to the big house and research phone sex, because I plan
to be the best Lady Lana Call Girls has ever seen. Caine
Donovan will rue the day he talks dirty to some lonely
woman with Johnny Depp's voice."

The pound of footsteps from behind them startled the
women. Caine flew down the stairs past them, ruffling
Em's hair on the way. "Race ya to the big house, ladies!" he yelled as none other than Christopher Walken,
taking the steps two at a time as if he was twelve, and
they were still walking the halls of Plum Orchard Middle School.

"So we have some work cut out for us," Em squeaked.

Dixie's eyebrow rose. "*We?* Won't that cause trouble
for you with Louella and the gang?" Louella was going
to have a kitten if she found out Em was helping Dixie
Davis—once girlfriend-code breaker extraordinaire,
now sworn enemy.

Em flapped her hand, but her eyes wouldn't meet Dixie's. "Bah. They pay me little mind unless they need
somethin' legal, so I pay little mind back. It's the same
as it always was—just like high school. I wasn't born a
Mag, so I'll never be a Mag. And since Clifton left me

for that no-good woman in Atlanta, they only tolerate me because I can be of help from time to time in the legal area. I was always an outsider, Dixie. That's still just as true as it ever was."

Dixie grinned. Em was bucking the system even though Dixie knew the lack of acceptance from the reigning queens of popularity and prominence stung. "Then we can be outsiders together." She tugged at her arm.

But Em hesitated. "Wait. Before we go any further, there's one more thing."

Dixie stiffened. "Now what? Oh, wait, I know. Landon owned a brothel, too, right? Is this the part where you tell me I have to get rid of my flannel pajamas for crotchless underwear, but you couldn't tell me before because it was *confidential?*" She accented the word with a roll of her eyes.

Em's hand fluttered to her neck. "Why, Dixie, I almost think that would be easier."

Hackles rose on the back of Dixie's neck. "Than?"

"Telling you about the court-slash-Landon-appointed mediator. Remember Hank mentioned that?" Em's feet were suddenly moving down the steps at a rapid pace, the skirt of her dress flying behind her.

Dixie followed suit, pushing the exit door to hold it open. "Vaguely. I was a little caught up in the 'oh, baby, I like it like that' at that point."

Em stepped around her and held her hand out with a grimace. "Meet your court-appointed mediator."

Four

Dixie stood at the foot of the bed in her appointed room at Landon's house. The house he'd bought, expanded and renovated from top to bottom. He had instructed she stay in the aptly dubbed Princess room, the room he'd always given her whenever she'd come back home during and after college to visit the big house.

Buttery lemon and pastel green leaves whispered across the wallpaper on the walls, surrounding the centerpiece of the room—a king-size canopy bed handcrafted in Italy of chestnut and ash and lacquered in a soft cream.

This was the bed where she and Caine had spent the nights just before their engagement party, wrapped in each other's arms, contemplating their future.

Caine would spread her out on the cool sheets while the sky outside grew heavy with stars. He'd rise up above her, running his possessive hands along her skin, paying special detail to the dip where her waist met hip, leaning forward and nipping at it while his hair grazed her shivering, frantic flesh.

Her hands always rose to caress his thighs, loving

the response he gave when he'd fall over her, taking her legs up around his neck and moaning the words with a rasp, *You, Dixie. I need to lick you or I'll damned well lose my mind.*

Those decadent, raw sounds coming from his lips always made her press her hips upward, begging.

When his head finally dipped between her legs, it was almost a surprise how the wondrous lust filled her up.

Jesus, Dixie, you're all I can think about day and night, were always the last words he spoke before he parted her cleft with his thumbs and slipped his tongue inside her, drawing long passes around her clit, making her beg him to capture the bud between his lips and suck the hard nub until she was thrashing her way toward insanity.

Rising up on his elbows, his glittering eyes held victory in them when they found hers. His raw power never failed to wrench the breath from her lungs when he demanded, *Look at me, Dixie. Look at me when I—*

"Dixie?"

The voice from over her shoulder jolted her with a yank from her memories and the indelible mark of Caine. Taking a shaky breath, she turned to find Sanjeev, Landon's trusted assistant, at the door with Dixie's lone suitcase.

She quickly took the opportunity to hide her embarrassment by gazing around the room she'd helped to decorate.

Her eyes scanned her surroundings and almost nothing had changed, from the thick carpet beneath her feet to the whimsical tea set on a corner table between the floor-to-ceiling windows, draped in shimmering silk, and overlooking the main house's pool. Despite the big house's lavish opulence, it was meant to enthrall those who stayed in it—not impress.

Landon had never cared what people thought about his outrageous spending. He'd only cared that, should they grace his doorstep, they grace it with the utmost comfort at their disposal.

Sanjeev, dressed in a traditional maroon kurta, put down her luggage then smiled at her. His olive-black eyes, set in flawless mahogany skin, gazed at her with warmth. "Landon said this should be your room for the remainder of your stay." He held out his long, well-defined arms and embraced her. He tightened his grip, as if he knew a hug was in order.

She leaned back in his embrace so their eyes met, ruffling his thick thatch of midnight black hair with her fingers. "Yeah, about that, Sanjeev… Did Landon, that crazy prankster, say anything else about my stay?"

His smile beamed wide. "He said I was to cater to your every whim, keep you well-fed, well-rested, and make sure you didn't spend wasted time mourning him."

She gave him a look of admonishment, clucking her tongue. "Aw, come on, Sanjeev, you know what I mean, and it has nothing to do with your out-of-this-world lamb curry or your saffron rice or even your pillow fluffing skills. The phone-sex thing. You must've known."

Sanjeev didn't miss a beat, though an erratic pulse throbbed at the base of his neck. "Of course I knew. I was his assistant. I knew everything."

Dixie tapped him on the shoulder with a chastising

finger. "So you knew Caine would be here, too." She didn't ask.

His nod held no apology. "I did."

"And a sneaky, late-night phone call, something along the lines of, 'Hey, Dixie-Cup, that guy who stomped on your dreams of marital bliss like he was stomping out a campfire is going to stay in the big house with you while you call men naughty boys' was totally out of the question?"

Sanjeev's eyes twinkled. "First, I believe it was you who stomped first with that dreadful bet. And oh, no, it wasn't out of the question."

The bet. She never, ever wanted to talk about the bet. "But it was disloyal to Landon?" She sighed in understanding. "I can't fault you for that, even if it wasn't in my favor."

His smile gleamed playfully. "As per Landon's reminder, I was bound by the 'I saved your life' speech."

Landon had found Sanjeev in the streets on one of his treks to India, dirty, infested with lice, homeless and alone at seventeen after he'd run away from an orphanage three years earlier. After living with Sanjeev for a year in India, Landon had acquired, via his multitude of connections, a visa for Sanjeev and brought him back to the States to live with him and manage the big house. That was eleven years ago, and never was there a better assistant to someone as whimsical and impulsive as Landon than Sanjeev.

Dixie rolled her eyes, knowing Landon would have cut off his right arm before he'd have sent Sanjeev back to India. "Well then, I hope you gave him the 'If not for me, the big house would have collapsed by now, and Toe the Camel would have died of malnutrition' speech," she teased.

And it was true. Sanjeev ran the big house like a well-oiled machine. Nothing, not even the tiniest of details went unnoticed under Sanjeev's watchful eyes.

"I will always remain loyal to his memory, but above all else, his last wishes. Though," he said, cocking a raven eyebrow, "I did warn him, during the hatching of the conditions of this will, a war the likes of which no one in Plum Orchard had ever seen was bound to ensue."

So Sanjeev knew the thought process behind Landon's last wishes. Interesting. But it wasn't the time to press. "And he said?" Dixie prompted, shrugging off her jacket and laying it across the bed.

"He said, and I quote, 'I hope you videotape it and put it on YouTube because it'll probably get a lot of hits and become the YT's newest sensation,'" Sanjeev responded with his comical imitation of Landon's accent.

Her head fell back on her shoulders as laughter, rich and free, spilled from her throat. It was so good to be where Landon's presence was strong—where his memory still breathed life into every nook and cranny— even if, in his memory, he'd left her between a rock and a hard place.

"So he really has a phone-sex company?"

Sanjeev's eyes were amused. "Indeed."

"These women are in the guesthouse right now?"

"They are. It's where Landon insisted they work."

Dixie eyed him. "Did he give any thought to what will happen to these poor women when he decided to drop them in Plum Orchard? You know what they're like here, Sanjeev. How they all gossip. It can ruin your life if you let it." She knew. She'd stomped on a life or two in her time.

"He gave it great thought. Surely, you know Landon did nothing without care, Dixie. He consulted all of them, and they made the decision together to come here, knowing how judgmental this town can be. However, when you meet the ladies of Call Girls, you'll understand why Landon left this earth at peace with his choice."

"The Mags will find a way to make their lives miserable all while looking for a way to have this shut down, Sanjeev. Did Landon think about the fact they could lose their jobs?"

"Have you thought about the fact that Landon has greased many a wheel in his time here on earth and in Plum Orchard—or that he was as careful about picking his lawyers as he was his locations for phone-sex operations?"

Dixie gave a halfhearted laugh, rubbing her eyes. "Point in Landon's favor."

"You look tired, Dixie. And I don't mean the kind of tired grief brings, or the kind a good night's sleep will fix. I mean soul weary. This worries me."

Ah, leave it to Sanjeev to look beyond the concealer under her eyes. "It's been a long couple of years" was all she was willing to admit.

He tugged on a strand of her hair, his eyes concerned. "And in those long years, you forgot to freshen your roots? Who is this Dixie?"

This was the Dixie who was too focused on her goal to pay everyone back and didn't have time or money to go to the hairdresser. She shrugged, casting her eyes down at her feet. "This Dixie was just caught up in other things."

"Then this assistant will fetch you some henna before you become too much more caught up. Pronto," he added with a wink.

Dixie kicked off her heels, sinking her bare feet into the Persian carpet. She leaned her shoulder against the canopy post to fold her hands in front of her. "I just can't believe he's gone," she choked out. Those words would never sound right. "So what will you do next, Sanjeev? Will you go back to India? I imagine Landon left you plenty of money to return in style."

Though Sanjeev leaving the big house and going back to his homeland left her heart as empty as a good bottle of wine after a long night of girl-talk, Dixie had always wondered if he yearned for the sights and smells of his native country. Much the way she'd longed for the comfort of her small town even with its irrefutable throwback to a simpler way of life, and its antiquated views on a woman's place in the world.

Sanjeev's eyes flashed momentary confusion. "I will do as I've always done. Maintain the big house and handle the multitude of charities Landon was involved in."

She cocked her head, her ears burning hot with new information. "So Landon isn't selling the big house?" He'd left the big house to Sanjeev and the numerous staff?

His arms went around his back. "No, quite the opposite, in fact."

Uh-huh. Suspicion pricked her spine just as it had with Emmaline back at the funeral home. "You know something I don't know, don't you?"

Sanjeev's eyes shadowed. "I know only the things I know."

"As clear as mud as always, Sanjeev," she said even though his evident secrecy made her grin.

Sanjeev's chin lifted as it always did when he was disgruntled about the fact that he still didn't have a full understanding of the subtleties of the English language. "For as long as I've been in your country, I will never understand you. Mud isn't clear, Dixie."

Dixie tilted her head, squinting one eye. "Know what else isn't clear?"

He took a solemn stance, his expression serene as he waited.

Dixie began to pace, a revived, caged energy freshly unleashed. Surely Landon had confided his reasons to Sanjeev for putting her and Caine together. "Why Landon would do something like this to me—to *both* of us? He knew where we stood with each other. Caine and I are in the worst possible place two people who broke up the way we did can be."

Sanjeev's eyes shifted downward in subtle recognition before refocusing on Dixie. "A place entirely of your own making."

Dixie nodded at his more than fair statement. "That's the absolute truth. You're right. But he's pitted us against one another like two children fighting over the last piece of Martha's peach pie. Why would he want to hurt me like this? He knows—knew—how painful the subject of Caine is for me."

Sanjeev smiled as though he were recalling a fond memory. "He's also the man who stood by you even after enduring Louella Palmer's public accusation that you had a sexually transmitted disease, lest you forget."

Dixie's fists clenched at her sides. "The *clap* to be precise."

Sanjeev raised his hands and slapped them together, jarring her.

"Still not funny."

"Oh, Dixie. It was almost a lifetime ago. Surely you can see the humor in it by now?"

"I'm not sure I'll ever see the humor in Louella Palmer, standing in line behind me at Lucky Judson's hardware store, randomly clapping while everyone was in on the joke but me."

The memory of that still stung as freshly as if it had happened just moments ago. A mix-up in her premarital test results, tests both she and Caine had agreed to have administered before their marriage, had resulted in the "teetering-on-senility" Dr. Wade Johnson somehow allowing his onetime receptionist, Louella, get her hands on them. Of course, she'd told anyone who'd listen Dixie had the clap.

"What is it your countrymen say about payback?"

"While I see your point, that's not the point. This phone-sex business isn't about punishing me for being a mean girl, Sanjeev. Landon loved me when I was horrible, and he loved me after I wasn't so horrible. Anyway, we're off track here, friend."

He pursed his lips, giving his cheekbones a hollowed look. "I'm not off track. There is no track. Landon didn't always have a rhyme to his reason. As you well know, he did many things on a whim—or because it simply pleased him, but never without the utmost caution. I don't know what would please him about seeing you suffer when he did nothing but indulge you almost all of your life, even at your worst, but I have no answers, only my orders to keep you safe, well-fed, and comfortable."

"Nothing concerning Caine Donovan is safe," she muttered.

Sanjeev acknowledged her words with a nod. "Be that as it may, we're here in this moment. Now, I have Mona and Lisa to bathe. They're as unruly as your hair, and I won't have them laying all over the bed I expressly freshened for you until I'm sure we're cleared for fleas. You, lovely Dixie," he said, pointing toward the equally opulent adjoining bathroom, "have an appointment at the guesthouse to meet your fellow employees. Freshening up wouldn't hurt you either. You're funeral worn." He chuckled at his joke, padding out of the room with a wave over his shoulder.

The silence of the bedroom engulfed Dixie in its subtle hues of silk and throw pillows, leaving her a moment to hear the throb of her panicked heart.

Meet your fellow employees, rang in her ears with a hauntingly Vincent Price–like quality. Sanjeev said it as though her new job was something as ho-hum as retail sales or file clerking.

Which brought a thought to mind. What were the women of phone sex like? Did they have office parties or swingers' parties? Celebrate birthdays with a cake from the local grocery store and attend in pasties and a thong?

Gossip at the water cooler about what a limp dick Dale in Idaho was for calling them from his mother's basement, and running up her phone bill just so he could get off to the sound of some imagined sex-starved woman who was just waiting for his dulcet tones to lull them into a pretend orgasm? Did they send each other the BDSM joke-of-the-day emails?

Oh, Dixie, reckless and impulsive be thy name.

The jingle of dog collars and heavy breathing startled her from her panic. "You're overthinking this, Dixie!" Sanjeev called out with a pant as he flew past her bedroom with Mona and Lisa dragging him down the long hallway.

Sure. She, Dixie Davis, was overthinking. Not something often credited to her, but on this rare occasion, certainly applicable. Reaching for her purse, she made her sulky way to the bathroom, paying little attention to her lavish surroundings.

She didn't notice anything but her purse vibrating the sound of a text message when she threw it on the countertop just under the gorgeous Venetian mirror she didn't want to look into.

The only person who'd ever texted her was Landon....

Dixie took a hesitant step forward, the tile beneath her feet no longer soothing her with its cool surface. Instead, it magnified the apprehension sweeping along her nerves like an out-of-control firecracker left on the ground to spin haphazardly.

With a trembling hand, she opened her purse on the vanity and snatched her phone out, stifling a shaky breath in order to read the text—from none other than Landon.

My beautiful friend, your journey awaits. Today is the first day of the rest of your life, Dixie-Cup. Carpe phone sex!

After freshening her makeup, brushing her hair into a ponytail, throwing on a cotton skirt and a tank top, impossible text message still on her mind, Dixie strolled along the winding path of arborvitaes and rosebushes to the guesthouse.

Which wasn't really a guesthouse at all. It was a mini version of the big house with only five bedrooms instead of ten, a pool lined with white travertine along its sloping edges, and an island, complete with palm trees, chaise longues and a bartender in the middle of it all.

As she made her way past the pool area, she noted not a single string bikini or Insanity Workout body to be had. The pool didn't have a ripple of activity swirling in the crystal-blue waters, dotted with solar lights beneath the surface where she'd expected to see a bevy of beauties playing volleyball on the shoulders of beefy men.

Her images of sex goddesses scantily draped in bikinis, dangling their feet in the pool while they whispered, "I love it when you touch me there" fled and were replaced by the sound of a voice that couldn't belong to someone more than ten years old.

She followed it toward the wide glass doors leading inside, scooting through the doors, and making her way across the terra-cotta tiled floor to the rounded entryway where the voice grew stronger.

"Ohhhhhh, I'm so wet for you!" an enthusiastic voice cooed. "You're so big and hard, I just don't think I can stand it! Doooo me, Enzo," the little-girl voice—far too youthful for phone sex—purred. "Do me like that, you Italian stallion!"

Dixie stopped all forward movement as if she was playing a game of life-or-death freeze tag, gripping the overstuffed chair in the twilight-filled foyer to keep her legs from collapsing.

She couldn't do this. The woman's voice, coming from Landon's old office, belonged to, at best, a teen-ager. How could she possibly support anyone who wanted to talk to a child—even if she was a grown woman merely pretending to be a child? How could Landon have supported it? Disgust bloomed in the pit of her stomach, mushrooming until she couldn't breathe.

This had gone much further than she'd gone in her head. It was one thing for two adults to consensually have make-believe sex with a phone as their barrier. That she could almost handle. But when a man wanted a child he could pretend to have sex with—that was well off her morality chart.

Not to mention—Italians and stallions?

That was her cue. Exit stage left.

Five

A hand clamped on her shoulder, a cool hand with a gentle yet firm grip. "I know what you're thinking, Dixie. You are *the* Dixie, right?" a soft voice asked.

She stiffened, caught in the act of running away. "If I said no, would that mean I could escape from this madhouse, and you'd never be the wiser?"

"Well, no. I'd be the wiser. I'd know you just as easily as if I'd run into you buying milk at the Piggly Wiggly. Landon talked about you all the time, and he must have showed us a hundred pictures of you." She paused for a moment, putting both hands on Dixie's shaking shoulders, forcing her to turn around.

What met Dixie's eyes was a creamy-skinned, fresh-faced young woman of no more than maybe thirty, with long chestnut hair spilling over her shoulders and down her spine, and a pair of the widest, deepest green-blue eyes Dixie had ever encountered.

Her coloring was naturally peach-inspired, and the clothes she wore, a T-shirt that read Georgia Tech and black capris, were as simple as Dixie's. "I'm Catherine, Cat for short, Butler. I'm general manager of Call Girls."

"Gage's new fiancée, right?"

Cat flushed a pretty pink—the kind of pink you flushed when you were wildly in love. "That's me. Em asked me to tell you she'd see you tomorrow. Something about the hot tub at the big house and cold king crab."

Dixie suppressed a smile. As a single parent with a husband who'd just up and decided he deserved a midlife crisis a little early, Em deserved a good pampering. "She deserves it after today."

"And you are definitely Dixie Davis. Landon always said you were even prettier in person than you are in your pictures. He was right. And that voice!" Cat said with obvious delight. "It's fantastic—so raspy and smoky. You're gonna give the girls a real run for their money."

Dixie grimaced. "I think today I don't want to be Dixie Davis, and I don't want to give anyone a run for anything with my raspy or my smoky."

Cat grinned, revealing adorable dimples. "If only trading lives with someone else was as easy as the words simply spoken, hmm? Now, before you set off to givin' someone hell—and yes, I can see that look on your face, Landon described your ire well—hear me out. The voice you hear in there on that phone is Marybell Lyman's, and she's not role-playing. It's just the voice our creator gave her. And it works for her, but we have strict rules about that sort of thing at Call Girls. I promise."

Still shaken, though to a lesser degree, Dixie's tongue got the better of her. "Clearly, the rules for Italians and stallions escaped Landon."

Cat chuckled. "What's the harm in making a small mob fish feel like a big ol' shark? That's why men call us, Dixie. To interact with women they've fooled themselves into believing are incapable of living without their magically lust-inducing words."

Dixie exhaled a breath of regret, ashamed she'd jumped to the same conclusions people still jumped to about her. "I'm sorry. I heard…and I just assumed—"

"Never you fear, Dixie. Landon wouldn't allow calls generated from men who wanted to talk to underage girls. He was a kind soul. In fact, it remains a strict rule. We entertain lots of fantasies here at Call Girls, but there are absolute no-no's, and if anyone's caught indulging a client in something that's off the table, it's cause for permanent termination."

Another sigh of relief shuddered through her, leaving Dixie unsure how to respond to this woman who looked as if she'd just fallen off the pages of *Seventeen* magazine.

She'd expected women who popped their gum, half-dressed in spandex catsuits, wearing six-inch stilettos and more eyeliner than Brugsby's Drugstore cosmetics counter could supply. Instead, a pretty, fresh-faced, articulate woman greeted her with a lovely smile and a lilting Southern accent.

One of these things was not like the other, and two of these things weren't even kinda the same.

Dixie squared her shoulders and pushed her hand toward Cat. "My apologies for my inexcusable manners. Yes. I'm Dixie Davis. It's a pleasure to meet you."

Cat gripped Dixie's hand, curling her fingers around it to give it a firm shake before letting it go. "No, it's not. Not yet anyway. You look like you're ready to find the nearest pitcher of sweet tea laced with bourbon to drown yourself in."

"Booze wouldn't go denied," Dixie confessed, dropping the tips of her fingers to the pockets in her skirt.

Cat tilted her head, her eyes glittering and playful. "So you made it this far, right? That's a sure sign you're at least a little curious. Do you want to soldier on? Or do we end this conversation with a pleasant but cordial 'it was lovely to meet you?'"

Dixie swallowed hard, her throat full of sandpaper, but she squared her shoulders. She was in. "We soldier. We definitely soldier. Battlefields and hand grenades ahoy."

Cat's grin was infectious. "I confess, we all wondered what you'd do. I laid the biggest bet in the 'Dixie pool' by the way."

"Bet?" *Why, yes, Dixie. You're familiar with bets. Those crazy situations where you challenge some poor soul, not nearly as skilled as you, to race you for the win? Sometimes they involve money—other times? Hands in marriage.*

She shook off the voice of her past and repeated, "Bet?"

"Well, yes. The bet that said you'd at least come see what you could see. You know, investigate what this was all about? Everyone else thought someone with the kinda means you come from would run away to your palace in wherever it is rich folk build their palaces. Not me, though. I just knew, from all the talkin' Landon did about you, you wouldn't turn tail. Knew it. So thank you kindly for the two hundred dollars I just won. Pizza night's on me." She let loose a breathy whisper of a giggle.

Dixie managed to ignore the fact that this as yet unnamed group of women had bet against her and her palace and blurted something random. "You have a pizza night at Call Girls?" Phone-sex operators ate pizza? Next someone would tell her hookers had expense accounts.

Cat grinned that contagious grin again. "Well, of course we do. We're not heathens, Dixie. Just because we call all parts southern on your anatomy words your mama would've washed your mouth out with soap for sayin', doesn't mean we blow up edible condoms and decorate them with whipped cream all the time. We're just like most everyone else. We have all sorts of things here at the office. Christmas parties—baby showers, 'Wear Your Pajamas to Work Wednesday.' You name it, and Landon insisted upon it. You know how much he loved parties, and impromptu parties were his specialty. It boosts morale if you can have a little party on the boss's dime, don't you agree?" she said with a conspiratorial wink.

She'd like to have a little something on the boss, all right. She'd like to have a chokehold on him. "I…" Dixie held up a finger, putting it to her lips for a moment and shook her head. "I'm going to stop now so I don't come off sounding like an uneducated, high-handed ass. Something I'm sure happens to you a lot. With first impressions being everything, I'll just say this is unexpected." Her head swam from so much unexpected.

"Your surprise is understandable, but I promise you, we're mostly all just average women who needed to find a way to make ends meet. Well, with the exclusion of LaDawn. She really *was* a—" Cat leaned in, leaving the lingering scent of jasmine and roses in Dixie's nose, and whispered, "a lady of the evening in Atlanta. Landon talked her out of the life and gave her a job here at Call Girls where she's been ever since."

Everyone's knight in shining armor, weren't you, old buddy?

"Some of us even have children, and Sheree has a husband who's out of work."

Once again, judge not lest ye be judged, Dixie Davis. "I—I'm sorry… I just thought…"

Cat crossed her arms over her chest as if she'd heard it all before. Yet, it didn't come across as a defensive gesture at all. "We know what you thought—or think. It's what everyone in this narrow-minded dink of a town still stuck in the 1950s thinks, and we've only been here just a few days. Some who call themselves open-minded think that. But I promise you we're not so different than the rest of the workforce. We're just more…er, colorful."

"Ladies, I bid you good evening," a cheerful voice with a British accent called from the sliding glass doors.

Dixie's limbs instantly froze even as her stomach heated. Oh, good. Candy Caine was on the loose.

"Michael Caine, right?" Cat said on a tinkling laugh, her cheeks staining the color all women's cheeks stained when Caine did an impression.

No one was left untouched by Candy Caine's charm. Dixie had to fight not to roll her eyes and whisper a warning to Cat to beware the Donovan spell. Instead, she stiffened her spine, lifted her chin, and activated her Caine-Away force field.

He made his way across the tile with his panther-like prowl, full of grace and a sensual glide of his cow-boy boots. His legs, thick and muscular, worked under his tight-fitting jeans, flexing in time with his rhyth-mic walk.

A familiar and unwanted clench, deep within Dixie's core, tightened as he drew closer.

He stopped a couple of feet from the women and grinned, holding out his hand to Cat, showcasing his enticingly visible pecs beneath his fitted navy blue shirt. "I'm—"

"Caine," Cat twittered, her free hand making a nervous pass over a long strand of her hair to smooth it. "Caine Donovan. I'd know you anywhere, too. We've heard a lot about you from Landon."

"Sorry I'm a little late."

Cat smiled at Caine. "I figured you might be. LaDawn said she heard at the diner you were over doin' Ezrah Jones's laundry for him. Is that true?"

Caine shrugged his shoulders. "He's had a rough go of it since Louise died, hasn't been showing up for poker in the park with his buddies from the VA. Just thought I'd check on him, maybe offer some support. Louise used to make cookies for me whenever I won a meet. She was a great lady."

Cat sighed a dreamy sigh. "You're as nice as Landon said you were. He told us all about your high school exploits, and how you three were thicker 'n thieves back in the day."

"And now it looks like we'll be thicker than phone sex," Caine joked, eyeing Dixie with that penetrating gaze that asked as many questions as it had ever answered.

"Damn. Guess I lost this bet, which might make pizza night a totally different ball game," Cat said to Dixie with a snicker.

"Pizza night?" Caine queried, raising one eyebrow and wiggling it.

Dixie's chin lifted defiantly, her eyes pinning Caine's. "Yeah, funny thing about pizza night... The women all bet I wouldn't show up today, but Cat. Cat had my back."

Cat dipped her head. "But we definitely didn't think you'd show up, Caine. You know, as rich and successful as your real-estate business is back in Miami."

Caine made a comically sad face, and in Daryl from *The Walking Dead*'s voice, he said, "It cuts me deep you think I'd run away from the chance to talk dirty when I have the best Sean Connery impression ever. It speaks volumes about our future working relationship, ma'am. We're lackin' trust."

Cat howled her pleasure, her slender shoulders shaking with laughter beneath her T-shirt. She pointed up at him. "Daryl—*The Walking Dead,* right? Lawd in all his mercy! Landon told us all about your celebrity impersonations. You really are as good as he said," she gushed.

Hark! Who goes there? What was that she heard in the distance? Yet another woman fallen prey to Caine Donovan? Dixie fought another roll of her eyes.

Turning her back on Caine, Dixie forced a smile to her lips and put her hand on Cat's arm to draw her away from the sexual napalm. "So maybe you could explain all of this? How Call Girls is run. What's expected of us? The thing about our chosen personas?" That troubled her the most, choosing a persona.

"You mean our specialty kinks, right, Dixie?" Caine made a point of reminding her, stepping around both of the women so he could peer into the archway that led to the great room and the subsequent bedrooms.

Dixie fought a scowl at his deliciously fresh, clean

scent, but couldn't fight the pop of her lips. "Why yes, Candy Caine. That's exactly what I mean. I'm all about finding out what my kink is."

"Um, we, in the business, that is, actually call them fetishes. Just an FYI," Cat interjected with another of her easy smiles.

"Fetish." Dixie nodded, mentally making a note of it for future fetish exploration. "Got it."

"Studious as ever," Caine remarked dryly, clearing his throat.

The reference to her lack of interest in her studies back in her high school days didn't go unnoticed. "That's what got me that 4.3 GPA in college," she reminded him with a flash of her eyes. "If memory serves, you had a 4.2." So humph.

"*Studying* was what got you a 4.3, Dixie? And didn't you leave college to cruise the seven seas on some rich guy's yacht?"

It was only two seas, thank you. Her blood pressure soared.

Just as Dixie was about to sling an arrow dipped in contempt back, Cat threw a hand up between, staring them both down with a matronly glare. "Okay, to your corners." She swished a warning finger at them, shooing them apart. "So let's just get this all out in the open, because even though I'm office manager, Landon was kind enough to allow me to take college courses online while I oversee Call Girls. So quite often, in between calls, I'm studying. Which means not only do I have other employees to protect, but my future career, as well. I can't do that if I'm breaking up petty disagreements between the two of you."

Protect? As if they both had a penchant for serial killing?

"Now, Landon told us all about the two of you and your ongoing love affair with a good war of words. He told us everything about your childhoods, Dixie's legendary mean-girl reputation here in Plum Orchard, your love of a good bet, your eventual engagement—the ugly ending to your engagement—the subsequent years you both spent hating each other over the ugly end to said engagement, all while he continued to remain friends with you both. Big yawn. Old news, right?"

Both Caine and Dixie remained stubbornly silent.

"Right?" Cat prompted, her expression stern and schoolmarmish.

Their grating sighs were simultaneous. "Right," they responded in unison like two guilty children.

"Good. So here's how this is gonna play out. I know there are hard feelin's between the two of you, and that's too bad, but they're absolutely not for the workplace. I run Call Girls, and I run a tight ship. If you decide to join us, I won't have the two of you taking potshots at each other, and making everyone around you uncomfortable while you do it. If you want to beat each other up over your history together, do it somewhere else. Do we understand each other?"

Like two chastised children, they both let their eyes fall to the tiled floor.

"And do not roll your eyes at me, Dixie Davis," Cat warned, planting her hands on her hips.

Dixie stopped mid-eye roll and sighed, letting her shoulders sag and her chin hitch forward like the petulant child she turned into whenever Caine was around.

Their bickering was bound to affect those around them, and that was unfair. "I'm sorry. We can really suck."

Cat giggled. "Landon told us all about your brand of suck. We were locked and loaded."

Caine's eyes were contrite when he shot Cat a sheepish grin after scrubbing his knuckles over his jaw. "I'm sorry if we made you feel uncomfortable, too."

"Apologies accepted. Now let's let bygones be bygones and get to introductions and the business at hand, okay? The girls are dying to meet you both."

Caine nodded his dark head. "Perfect. So let's set about finding our *fetishes*. Whaddya say, Mistress Taboo?" He didn't wait for Dixie to answer. Instead he held out his arm to Cat and smiled. "Shall we?"

Cat giggled again, soft and as lovely as she was, but a quick glance at Dixie had her clamping her lips shut and frowning before she regained her composure. She roped her arm loosely through Caine's, keeping a visible distance between them. "C'mon. I'll introduce you to everyone and familiarize you with what goes on here."

Dixie stuck her tongue out at Caine behind his back, and hurried to shuffle up to the other side of Cat, grabbing onto her free arm and winking. Her chuckle was throaty, but her words held the ultimate dare. "Let the games begin."

Back in her room, freshly showered and comfortable in an old T-shirt, Dixie snatched her phone with Landon's text from the nightstand and raised her fist to the ceiling with a shake. "You suck, Landon," she muttered, making Mona and Lisa stir.

After an hour with Caine, Cat and the women of Call Girls, Dixie's head was still spinning. She'd thought she'd made her choice the moment she'd thrown down the challenge to Caine in Hank Cotton's office.

Now? She was regretting her impulsivity. Once Cat had explained the inner workings of the phone-sex business, and only after Dixie was done mentally rolling her eyes at Caine, who'd smiled, joked and blatantly flirted with the ladies while making it appear this challenge was going to be akin to some leisurely stroll in the park, she'd waffled.

As she processed bits of information such as, she was her own boss and her hours were flexible, but some of the best, most loyal U.S. clients called in at night between the hours of midnight and three. And it was up to her to create an interesting, yet alluring phone-sex operator pseudonym, a website for that pseudonym, and an area of sex she specialized in. Scripts on how to handle difficult client calls, calls that got out of hand, all kinds of calls, calls, calls were readily available to them.

Shortly after meeting the women who ran the phones, and introductions, and all the details of the running of a phone-sex company, Dixie began to wilt, exhausted from the day's events.

Cat, clearly intuitive, had handed her the Call Girls phone-sex operator package, and told her to go get some rest before she made her final decision.

That was where she was now. Making her final decision. Her eyes flew to her bedside clock. And she only had eighteen hours and counting to do it.

Tick, tick, tick.

The only thing she had decided on, if she didn't chicken out, was the pseudonym Mistress Taboo. Caine had used it to taunt her, but it stuck like an earworm.

Flopping on the bed, she absently flipped through

the ream of papers Cat had given her while she stroked Mona's ear. Her eye caught the list of "specialties" Call Girls allowed, stilling her movement. "What, in all of heaven, do you suppose infantilism is, Mona?"

"Oh, you know, the usual. Men in diapers, baby bottles," Caine said, strolling into her bedroom on bare feet, in a pair of cargo shorts and nothing else.

The defined lines of his face almost always took Dixie's breath away. Tonight was no exception as the shadows cupped his strong jaw and enhanced his sharp cheekbones.

Her heart thrummed with the inevitable longing it had since the day she'd set her sights on him in high school. Dixie forced herself to look directly into his eyes instead of at the chest she'd once brazenly sat atop as he... Dixie gulped. "How unexpected to find you're so in the fetish know," she drawled, digging for the old Dixie, the one who was cocky and capable of keeping her composure catty and aloof all in one sentence.

Caine's eyebrow rose in that condescending way while his chest glistened in all its lickability in the dim lamplight. Coming to stand at her feet, he reached around her to give Lisa's broad head a scruff of his knuckles.

As the skin of his arm brushed hers, she sucked in a breath of air at the tightening of her nipples.

"Wanna see who knows the definition of more fetishes?"

"Almost as much as I'd like to see my spleen advertised on eBay."

Caine's eyes narrowed, glittering with amusement while his lips formed a sexy, cocky challenge of a smile.

"That's because you know you'll lose. What's the matter, Dixie? All bet-out for the day?"

"I'm all Caine'd out for forever. So what do you want, and why are you in my room? I don't recall hearing a knock."

Rising to her feet, she brushed a strand of her wet ponytail from her face, stepping around his solid frame.

"Door was open. And pillows," he said, jamming his hands into the pockets of his shorts as if he wasn't standing in front of her with no shirt on. "I know Sanjeev always has extra in here. I need another pillow. *Please,*" he tacked on with syrupy emphasis.

Dixie's throat grew dry and gritty. "There aren't a hundred people on staff who could find you pillows?"

"Unlike you, I don't want to wake the staff for something as ridiculous as a pillow. I know you're used to having someone at your beck and call, Powder Puff. I, on the other hand, fend quite nicely for myself and wouldn't dream of waking them."

"Look at you here in *my* room, fending," she mocked. His insinuation that she was selfish enough to wake an entire household over something as trivial as a hangnail infuriated her. In fairness, it wasn't exactly an untruth from her past, but it was no less infuriating now in the present.

And that was exactly what Caine wanted. Rather than rise further to his bait, Dixie turned on her heel, hoping the sway of her backside made him salivate just like it used to.

She threw the linen closet door open and peered inside, reaching for the chain to unsuccessfully turn the light on. The bulb was out. For all the fancy, highfalutin' gadgets Landon had in this house, he'd overlooked the simple things when he'd renovated.

The heavy oak door snapped back at her, smashing into her hip with a hard thud, meaning the spring was broken. Dixie spread her legs to hold it open, using her foot to keep it in place while attempting to adjust her vision to see the interior. The space had a small entry, and was just large enough to house some shelving full of soft, fluffy towels and silken bedding.

The door creaked when Caine came up behind her. Pushing her foot aside, he used his large hands at her waist to move her deeper into the closet. "I asked for a pillow. Not directions to the Fountain of Youth. What's taking so long?" he questioned, craning his neck upward to glimpse the top shelves.

Distracted by the light press of his fingers and the sting of the fleeting memory when Caine's hand was never far from hers made her forget about the door. "Don't let the—"

The door slammed shut behind them with a heavy thud, enveloping them in the quiet, Tide-scented darkness. Caine knocked into her, jolting her forward so her nose just missed the edge of a shelf before righting her with his arms.

Which left his rocklike, warm body pressed tight against her back.

Certainly a dilemma of her libido's highest order.

Six

"Uh, let the door shut?" Caine finished into her ear, leaving Dixie to fight the shiver his warm breath left in its wake.

Dixie attempted to inch forward and out of his nerve-tingling grasp, but there was nowhere to go. "Impatience be thy name," she said between the clench of her teeth.

"It's better than shithead, I guess," he murmured back.

"Didn't I mention? Impatience is your *middle* name."

"That's downright mean, Dixie."

"It's downright true, Caine."

"Viper."

"Mistress Viper to you, thank you very much." Dixie twisted uncomfortably, bucking against Caine's hand in the process. "Now quit name-calling and open the door. You know how claustrophobic I am." Just the thought of how claustrophobic she was made the claustrophobia in her stabby and irritable.

His sigh was a wash of raspy honey in the dark. "Stop wiggling around, woman, and let me—" one hand moved from her waist followed by the sound of the jiggling door handle "—open the damn thing…"

Chalk it up to a long day, but locked in a closet with Caine was the final straw that broke her raw nerves' back. Though, the fight to keep from having any square inch of her body touching Caine's worked to distract her fear of the pitch-black closet swallowing her whole. "What is the problem, Caine?" she snapped.

"I can't—"

"If you use the words *can't* and *open* in the same sentence referring to that doorknob—"

"You'll what?" he huffed, his chest pushing against her back.

"I'll suffocate you with one of these fluffy towels." She heard him jiggle the door handle again.

"Ready your weapon. I. Can't."

Slapping his hand from her waist, Dixie managed to turn around in the tiny space, her nose brushing the springy hairs on his chest. "Let me try." She twisted the handle, her heart pounding out her body's awareness of Caine's. "It's locked, damn it."

"Oh, Sherlock, still such a cracker jack," Caine cooed in another of his flowing British accents.

"Oh, Holmes, still just a sidekick with a big mouth."

"Move over, Dixie, and let me give it another try."

Dixie snorted to the tune of the irritation in his tone. "You do that, Hulk. I'll wait over here in the two square inches of space, cowering weakly so the big, strong man can save me."

They attempted to switch positions only to find themselves so closely fused their bodies were forced to make contact—delicious, heated, full-bodied contact. Her slip of a T-shirt left little between them, the material so worn over time it was like having on nothing at all.

"So now what, Dixie-Cup?" he grumbled huskily, his chin brushing the top of her head.

Dixie had to close her eyes to keep from swaying as the comfort of the familiar assaulted her. She would not allow her head to move just a hair forward and rest on his chest.

She gritted her teeth. "Get us out of here before I claw my way past you to get to that door. And stop calling me Dixie-Cup!" Because pettily lashing out was going to make this situation better.

Caine's fingertips twitched against hers. Knowing him the way she did, she also knew he was smiling into the dark. "But I've always called you Dixie-Cup, Dixie-Cup."

"No. Landon called me Dixie-Cup. You called me a liar." Dixie's chest tightened with the familiar constriction of his taunts.

Caine's fingers wound into the length of her hair, tugging her head back. "You were a liar," he replied smoothly, yet the edge to his voice was hard…raw.

Rivulets of sweat began to form between her breasts, and she wasn't sure if it was panic because the closet was hot and suffocating—or because Caine was. Fear of both made her strike out again. "Move, Caine, or I swear I'll scream!"

His response was to drag her to him, her spine arching, driving her against him, a moan rising to her lips when an aching rush of wet heat grew in her cleft. Her body's reply to him, to the gruff tug of her hair, and the once familiar command it wrought, infuriated her.

"Go away, Caine. Better yet, go back to Miami."

Caine's silky lips skimmed the darkness. "Like hell, I will. I was here first," he said, reaching a hand down to grip her hip, drawing her closer to the rigid outline of his cock, sharply defined against his cargo shorts.

She gave him a shove only to have the sound of the thump of his back hitting the door cut into the darkness. "You don't want Call Girls. You want to best me so you can flip your middle finger up in the air in my direction while you tell everyone over a round on you at Cooters you whooped mean girl Dixie Davis."

"Actually, I was going to buy everyone dinner while I did that. I'm disappointed to find you think me so damn cheap."

Don't take the bait, Dixie. Be the adult. "The point is you want to win."

His chuckle was thick to her ears, tipping her off to the fact that she wasn't alone in her arousal. "Oh, you bet I do. And in the process, adding a multimillion-dollar company to my portfolio won't make me sad."

"A portfolio. Nice luxury if you can get it," she managed, stifling a breathy sigh when he let go of her hair and cupped the back of her head.

Caine's body curved into hers even as his mouth continued its agonizing path upward. "Are things really that bad off, Dixie?"

Were things really that bad off? Was the sinking of the *Titanic* just a little boating incident? But Dixie stiffened at his question—the question that sounded warm and sympathetic. Oh, no, sir.

She wasn't falling for that old trick. The "draw someone into your web by being a kind shoulder to cry on, then wait for the moment you could use their misfortune to up your own game" trick. She was once the master. "Things are none of your business."

"Pride is a sin, Dixie," Caine murmured into the darkness, his voice growing heavy, his body melting into hers.

Fight the Caine charisma, Dixie. Fight it like you own a Justice League cape. "Falling for the notion that you're even a little concerned about me is a sin." Summoning what was left of her shredding will, she returned her focus to her claustrophobia. It was the lesser of the two evils. The mere thought they'd be stuck together like this until Sanjeev came to tell her breakfast was ready fed her fear.

Her heart began a panicked staccato. The heat of their bodies coupled with the stifling lack of air served her focus on her claustrophobia mission well. "We have to get out of here, Caine!" She shoved at the solid wall of his chest again. Yet it only made him tighten his hold.

"Dixie?"

"What?" she yelped, her voice thin.

"I'm going to do something that's probably going to piss you the hell off, but I want you to remember one thing after we get out of here."

Her rising panic squeezed her throat, but she managed to sputter, "Like?"

"Like this is for your own damn good."

The moment the words escaped Caine's lips was the moment he forgot he was trying like hell to remember she'd trashed him. He hauled her to him, planting his lips firmly over hers. His tongue sliced through the soft flesh, quieting her anxieties with the movement of his mouth.

When he suckled her tongue, devouring it in slow sips, Caine forgot everything but his unquenchable thirst for Dixie. The way she angled her lips to fit his, stifling a needy groan. The whisper of a whimper that made him rock-hard, even now, ten years later.

She made him feel things he didn't want to feel. She reminded him, everything after her didn't measure up.

But that didn't stop him from tearing at her T-shirt, driving it upward until her breasts sprang free. The moan he emitted from his mouth, primal and raw, was predatory, possessive when he gathered her breasts in his hands, tweaking her nipples to sharp points.

Christ, she felt like everything he'd been lacking in all the failed relationships he'd had since her.

When she wound her arms upward around his neck, clinging to him in the way that had always sparked some primal instinct in him, he thrust a hand inside her wispy panties to touch her, sliding between the lips of her pussy.

And all he could think was, here he was, lost again. Lost in the ultrafeminine vortex of Dixie. Powerlessly, helplessly lost.

He wanted to punish her for opening this hellish box of feelings he'd kept shut tight by sheer will and the determination to never get caught up in her and her lies again.

His breathing was ragged when he tore his lips from hers, as though he'd lose something of himself if he didn't. He couldn't see it, but he knew her penetrating gaze was eating him alive in the velvety darkness. "Damn you, Dixie," he hissed after a harsh pant.

Damn her and this new fragility that left him wanting to fix the things that had left her looking so bro-

ken. Damn her for reopening the wound of his anger
and spilling it all over him. Damn her for making him
question himself, question whether this was all another
game, whether she was just crying wolf, or she really
needed help.

He didn't want that. He didn't want to get tangled
up in her again.

But fuck. He did want *her*.

The zipper of his cargo pants was a vague sound
compared to the rush of her pulse, sounding out the
rhythm of her throb between her thighs. In a move so
swift, even Dixie questioned the dexterity of it, Caine
swapped positions with her, leaving her exposed back
against the cool oak door.

He yanked her arms upward over her head, fisting
her wrists together in his hand. It made her chest crawl
with white-hot heat, with a need so deep Dixie knew
it would never be like this with anyone else. With his
free arm, he lifted her at the waist until her legs circled his body.

And Dixie went willingly, wantonly hooking her ankles behind his back, holding her breath when he let
the head of his hard shaft slide between the lips of her
wet sex. Her head fell back, exposing her breasts to his
mouth, breasts Caine ran his molten tongue over until
the head of his thick shaft sat at her entrance.

In that suspended moment, Dixie forgot his harsh
words the night they'd parted. She forgot how much
she'd hated to still love him even though breaking off
their engagement was what any real man worth his salt
should have done.

She forgot the sting of humiliation during their engagement party, when Louella Palmer, microphone in hand, had, instead of reading a lovely speech about their courtship, declared Dixie had a sexually transmitted disease, and she had the test results to prove it. All while the entire population of five hundred and fifty-six people in Plum Orchard, Georgia, were given a front row seat to her humiliation.

She forgot the words of harsh reality he'd flung at her when Louella let Caine hear the voice mail Dixie had left her, crowing her victory. *I'm not some damn race horse, Dixie!*

She forgot how desperately she'd wanted Caine to really believe she'd changed since her high school days, and how easily she'd slipped back into that mean-girl role because she could never resist the chance to win—at everything.

She forgot how much she'd hurt Louella by pursuing Caine in the first place. She forgot how in the end, even after her apology, she realized it would always be like this. She would always be Dixie Davis, untrustworthy mean girl to him, and he'd always be fine, upstanding, kind-to-small-children-and-puppies Caine Donovan.

She forgot that back on that dreadful day, he'd been right, and she'd been wrong.

Dixie forgot all of that when the crown of his heated cock rested at her entrance, and her hips lifted, inviting him in. She forgot everything but the all-consuming desire tearing at her—a need that had to be sated or she'd die from the want of him.

Nine years of memories resurfaced in a tidal wave of reality.

Dixie let her hips slide downward in slow increments, sucking him deeper into her body until Caine drove upward with such force she wobbled in the strength of his arms, wincing when the pleasure-pain of his powerful entry stretched her. Each ripple of his abs pressed into her. Her nipples grew agonizingly tight, scraping against his smooth chest.

He angled his hips and pushed upward again. The violent thrust of his cock, wide and thick, only heightened her need. The sweat accumulating between them allowed for a slippery glide of skin on skin.

Dixie's clit raked against the flat plane of his abdomen as he took another possessive thrust, growling what sounded like surprise. "Has it been a while, Dixie? You're so damn tight and hot, so fuckably hot..." Caine's lips curved into her ear then, nipping her lobe and preventing her from striking back with an answer.

Caine's response was a heavy chuckle. "Some things never change, do they, Dixie?" he asked, driving into her slick entrance again, filling the emptiness inside her until she melted fully into him.

Harsh air escaped their lungs, full of rasp, heaving and choppy. Caine jammed his hands under her, cupping her ass, trailing his finger between her cheeks, forcing her to use his body as leverage to rise up and crash downward again.

Their rhythmic thrusts were madness; stroke for stroke, Dixie grew wetter, hotter until there was no sound but that of their bodies connecting.

Dixie's fingers went to his lips, pressing them to the fullness of his mouth to suppress his words, the fear of them slipping from his throat sliced through her haze of need.

She couldn't hear the words he used to speak.
Wouldn't.

Caine reached for her nape, digging his fingers into the flesh of it. "So good, Dixie—so sweet," he said from a clenched jaw, tensing and flexing.

Dixie didn't know if her response was to Caine's words or the incessant throb of her wish to be pushed over the edge—hard. And at that moment, she didn't care. She contracted around him, welcoming the intense fire burning her from the inside out, allowing it to be the only feeling in existence.

She rocked hard against the tightly corded muscles of Caine, accepting his last plunge into her wet depths. Her orgasm exploded, ripping through her, eliciting a hoarse cry of completion.

They slumped together, their chests crashing, the sheen of their sweat mingling.

A scrape against the outside of the door and a low growl had them both scrambling. Caine pulled out of her with haste, but she didn't have time to mourn the loss before she heard Em's voice. "What is it, Mona? Or are you Lisa? Isn't it enough that you woke me? Stop scratching at the door, or you'll wake the entire house, young lady!"

Still shaken, Dixie slid down Caine's body, dragging her T-shirt with her. Her underwear. Where was her underwear? Panic seized her.

She heard Caine zip up just before he reached over her head and began banging on the door. "Em! We're in here!"

There was a scuffle of dog paws scraping on the floor, and Em's gasp before the familiar sound of the jiggling doorknob drowned out everything else.

Dixie didn't have time to regret. She didn't have time

to be grateful she'd never missed a day of her birth control pills. She didn't have time to clean up.

She didn't have time to despise her body's blatant betrayal just because Caine had whipped out one of his best assets and had driven her mad with it.

She didn't even have time to see the look on Em's face when the light from the bathroom spilled into the dark closet, so damn invasive and harshly bright when she and Caine stumbled out together in a tangle of limbs and rumpled nightwear.

Dixie shielded her watery eyes, gulping in the cool air as Mona pawed at her leg with a whimper, and Caine's hand went to her spine to right her.

She swatted him away, angry with herself—angry with him—damn angry.

The silence that greeted them when her eyes fully adjusted was a mixture of two things: surprise and shock.

Em, wrapped in a blue terry-cloth robe, finally mumbled, "Mercy."

Lord, please have.

Em's gaze was pensive. She twisted one of the pink curlers in her hair. "I want to ask. Should I ask?" She shook her head, her brow furrowed. "No. I won't ask. It's ill-mannered."

Caine, smooth and composed as always, patted Em on the back with a casual hand and a charming grin as though they hadn't just made torrid love inside a locked closet. "We just got locked in while we were looking for extra pillows." He turned his back to them and reached into the interior of the closet, pulling out a fluffy pillow and tucking it under his arm. "See? Thanks, Em, and g'night, ladies," he called in Paul Hogan's Australian lilt before jamming a hand into the pocket of his shorts and strolling out of the room.

Dixie sagged against the wall in relief like the dirty whore she was. That they didn't have to discuss the whys and wherefores of what had just gone on was a blessing.

Em plucked at her hair, her smile devilish. "Snookie bump?"

Dixie caught a glimpse of her hair in the mirror and cringed, running her hands over the ends that stuck up in every direction. Her ponytail was smashed upward in a crazy likeness to the ultra popular bump. *That's because you bumped—hard—against a linen closet door—with a man you tell yourself you despise more than you despise collard greens, Dixie Davis. It's the sex-bump. Wear it well, for it's your new tramp-stamp.*

Dixie cracked her knuckles while Em waited for an answer with a smug grin. "We got stuck in the stupid closet while we were looking for some pillows. The lock's clearly broken, and so is the spring on the door. So, long lost court-appointed mediator, maybe you could make a note to have Sanjeev fix that, huh? Now, I'm going to bed." She harrumphed, turning on her heel to make an indignant exit.

"Hey, Dixie?" Em yelled.

"I'm going to bed, Emmaliiiine," she bellowed back, yanking at the ridiculously lavish comforter and climbing in, hoping her cheeks weren't as red as they felt.

"That's lovely," Em said, sweeping through the bedroom. "I remember how you always told us your beauty rest was important. You know, like the time all of us cheerleaders, and me, a *lowly alternate,* stayed up late sewing the costume for the football team's mascot while you got your eight hours of much needed rest?"

Dixie dragged the covers over her head and huffed in exasperation. Yes. She'd done that. Yes. She'd been a dreadful excuse for a human being. Yes. Did no one ever let go? It had been twenty years. "Okay, Em. I get it. Mean girl in the house. How many more nails do you have left to hammer into my coffin anyway? Is there a daily quota you have to meet?"

Em giggled. "Before you snuggle into that fine linen, I'd take a look at what Mona's chewing on right this second. It looks suspiciously like somethin' you wouldn't find in a linen closet. Niiight, Dixie!"

She cocked her ears, noting the snarfing sounds her bulldogs made when they were eating something.

Dixie threw the covers off and hung off the side of the bed.

Mona stilled all motion. Her beautifully soulful brown eyes stared back up at Dixie's.

Guilt. There was guilt in those big brown eyes. There was probably guilt in hers, too. For she and Caine had been caught red-handed by Em, fornicating. So much fornication.

Dixie reached down and tapped Mona on the nose with narrowed eyes. "Give Mommy back her underwear right this second, young lady!"

Seven

Caine paced the length of Hank Cotton's short driveway, listening to the wooden sign announcing his law practice flap in the thick breeze. He glanced upward to the darkening sky. A purple cloud with fat black lines and puffy gray hues settled directly over the sharp peaks of the well-maintained mint-green-and-white Victorian, where Hank's office was housed.

A storm was brewing, bringing with it the perfect setting for what he was about to do.

Stay here in Plum Orchard instead of going back to Miami where he knew damned well he should go. He'd come here thinking this was a good time to reassess his career, grab a break from his hectic life in Miami. He was burnt out, bored, lacking—lacking something he just couldn't figure out.

Plum Orchard, *home,* was the perfect place to do it. Now, with the messed-up mix of emotions he was feeling after last night, he knew he should go.

Yet, here he was.

Jamming a hand into the pocket of his jeans, he fingered his phone with the text he'd found from Landon bright and early this morning, and narrowed his eyes. Bawk-bawk-bawk, Candy Caine! it read in Landon's typically comedic voice.

Translation—his best friend was razzing him from the great beyond, daring him to give in to the worst label one man could give another. Chicken-shit. He didn't even bother to wonder how Landon had set up timed-release texts before his death. He was too caught up in how the hell he'd survive being around Dixie for two months.

"Damn you, you son of a bitch," he muttered, still madder than a coon cornered in a barn. Landon knew the two of them well, and he'd sure as hell known that throwing down the chance to whoop Dixie's pretty backside was like last night in the linen closet. A temptation Caine couldn't resist.

To leave Plum Orchard now would be as good as admitting he couldn't beat Dixie. Admitting he couldn't beat Dixie was akin to he-man suicide in this off-the-wall imaginary competition they'd created through the years.

Ridiculous? Absolutely. Shouldn't he be long past their childhood rivalries? Wasn't he enough of a man to take the high road?

No. Because when he veered off to the high road, it wouldn't be long before Dixie'd come along on her pretty pink Schwinn with the matching woven basket, honk the horn with the stupid frilly purple streamers at him and kick dust up in his face to remind him who'd won this round of Donovan versus Davis.

The memory made Caine smile—a smile he didn't even bother to fight. There were plenty of good memories involved with their legendary rivalry.

Those were the memories that had shaped his childhood. They mingled with the familiar scent of magnolias in his mother's carefully tended yard, bag after bag of pork rinds and six-packs of Dr. Pepper.

And Dixie.

No matter where he went, whom he dated, Dixie had always been the one woman he couldn't exorcise. Last night, locked in that closet, her luscious body open and willing, had turned what Caine hoped was nothing more than an idealized memory of her into his worst nightmare come true.

Dixie Davis still had the ability to get to him, burrow under his skin until she was so deeply rooted, he didn't know where she left off and he began. Nothing about that had changed.

Not the long talks he'd had with himself about how he was romanticizing the ghost of their relationship, forgetting the bad and remembering only the good. Not even the bottle of Jack he'd indulged in when he'd learned Landon had passed and he knew he'd have to see Dixie again after all these years had been able to talk him out of the realization that her presence in his life wasn't ever going to let him have any peace.

From the moment he'd seen her at old man Tate's funeral home, her wide, blue eyes puffy and red from crying, her long hair sexily tousled and now a faded red, the soft curve of her full lips chapped from her familiar habit of tugging at them, that voice in his head told him to get the hell out of Georgia. Because she'd never looked sexier. The years they'd been apart had been kind to her—even in grief.

Knowing he was able to see past her weary exterior and still find the woman he'd have once given a major organ up for was a sure sign it was time to hightail it out of here.

"But you're not gonna let me, are you, you interfering pain in the ass?"

Caine, my friend, if I've said it once, I've said it a thousand times. This thing between you and Dixie, this imaginary fight to the death at all costs, is like the chance to travel back in time and watch a half-naked, Russell Crowe–ish prisoner do battle with skilled, equally as half-naked gladiators. Not gonna happen on this watch, pal. It's too delicious.

Caine barked a laugh right there in the middle of Hank's cobbled driveway when he thought back on that conversation they'd had after Dixie had pulled one of her stunts. He ignored the curious glances of Nanette Pruitt and her pack of nosy Plum Orchard seniors staring at him from across the street, out on their customary after-dinner stroll.

Damn. His eyes scanned the lay of the land with a desperate glance, spotting a sugar maple he could probably hide behind if he sprinted. The last thing he needed was a lecture from Nanette Pruitt, and no doubt, if word had leaked about Landon's will, lecture she would.

"Caine Donovan!" she called out with a flap of a stark white handkerchief she held, crossing the street in her signature militant strut.

He halted all action. *Caught, Donovan.* If he were to turn his back on one of his mother's oldest friends, she'd hear about it, and Jo-Lynne Donovan would make him pick his own switch for his whippin'.

Caine threw a smile on his face, the one he reserved for the old money of Miami real estate, and turned around.

Nanette stopped dead in front of him, the rolls of her neck lavish with her customary pearls. Her modest sundress decorated with swirly flowers in yellow and blue floated in the humid breeze just below knees that matched her neck.

Behind her trailed her faithful comrades in piety, Essie Guthrie, Kitty Palmer and Blanche Carter. He noted the absence of Bunny Taylor who, last he'd heard from his mother, was visiting her new granddaughter in Atlanta.

Nanette reached up with a hand that was beginning to show the signs of age and pinched his cheeks. Just like she used to when she taught him history in the second grade. "Why, it's our very own Caine Donovan. In the flesh, ladies, out in the middle of our brand-new lawyer's driveway, talkin' to himself. Have you come home to handle the riffraff that nuttier-than-a-pecan-pie Landon left out back in his guesthouse? May the good Lord rest and keep him." She paused, raising her eyes heavenward in good Christian honor before continuing. "If anyone can take care of that lot of giggling Jezebels, it's Plum Orchard High's answer to Paul Newman, don't you think, girls?" she called to the three women behind her as though their spoken approval actually made a lick of difference.

Everyone in town knew Nanette didn't need the endorsement of her cohorts. She'd long ago taken up residence on the throne of moral high ground and decency. "You were always a good boy. So what will you do to rid our charming town of those…those…"

"Ladies of the non-biblical persuasion was the title you decided on at last night's meetin' of the Senior Magnolias, Nanny," Essie Guthrie offered with a nod of her pin-curled, fading brunette head and a wrinkle of her bulbous nose, smack full of distaste.

Caine mentally flung arrows at Landon. He was probably sitting on some cloud upstairs, sipping what he lovingly referred to as "champs" with his personal hero, Liberace, having a hearty laugh over the uproar he'd left behind.

But Landon poured some serious money into the town, and while the town didn't necessarily love his lifestyle, they loved the money he dumped into improving it, hand over fist, and it kept them from openly making their displeasure known. But it had never stopped them from talking behind their hands about him or Dixie and Caine for accepting who Landon was.

Landon knew what they said, and he didn't care. When Caine found himself bent out of shape over a snide comment from one of the Senior Magnolias, Landon had laughed at his raging. *I don't do what I do for Plum Orchard because I need the acceptance of a bunch of hypocrites. I don't do it as a way to shut them up. I do it because this is my home, and I love my home. I love it more than I hate their ignorance.*

So the ladies must at least have an inkling about Call Girls by now. But his salvation, for the moment anyway, was the hope they didn't know everything.

He shaded his eyes when a stray band of sunlight shot through the thickening clouds. Gazing down at Nanette, he summoned something he could latch onto from his Sunday school days to keep their fake saintly wrath at bay. "Now, Miss Nanette, that's not very neighborly of you, is it? What would Reverend Watson say? Wouldn't he want you to welcome those who've strayed from the flock? Maybe make them some of your famous lemon meringue pie? Weren't we always taught not to judge?"

The group of women rippled with muffled laughter before almost simultaneously clamping their lips tight after Nanette cast them the eyeball of fire and brimstone.

No one preached the Word to Nanette Pruitt. "Well, I can't get to forgivin' if they're still sinnin', now can I? They're a disgrace, Caine Donovan. Delilahs, every last one of 'em! They make no apologies for speakin' the devil's words and collectin' money for it to boot. Why, just last night while I was enjoying a lovely cup of tea at Madge's Kitchen, that awful La-Someone—"

"LaDawn," Blanche Carter provided in a meek whisper, tilting the white umbrella she held back down over her fretful eyes.

Nanette's sigh expressed her impatience, but her cool smile never faltered. "Thank you, Blanche. *LaDawn* was swishin' her way through that diner like she's a local. Lookin' like that, they're bound to corrupt the fine young men of Plum Orchard. One of them has tattoos and piercings, and her makeup looks like somethin' straight out of a Halloween parade. What are they doin' here, Caine?"

"Now, Miss Nanette," Dixie's husky voice chided from behind the group of women.

She sauntered over the sidewalk in her cute cutoff shorts and red T-shirt, the heels of her wedge sandals striking against the pebbled driveway. "Do you really think anyone could corrupt the fine young men of Plum Orchard quite the way I did?"

Her eyes strayed to Caine for only a moment, a dark, sultry reminder, before she rounded on the group of women and smiled. That smile that was meant to take you off guard, make you forget whatever your beef was with her just before you were sucked into the charismatic vortex of her charm.

Dixie hooked an arm through Nanette's and didn't bother to wait for an answer. Instead, she smiled brighter, if that was possible, winking at the Senior Magnolias with a sweep of her long lashes. "Ladies, it's *so* good to be back home," she cooed, taking a deep, appreciative breath before tilting her coppery head in Essie's direction and patting Nanette's arm with affection. "Essie? It's always good to see you. How's Jackson? Still conquering the New York stock exchange?"

Caine took a step back and grudgingly reveled in the magic that was Dixie. Not twenty-four hours ago, these women had spent the better part of Landon's memorial gossiping about her return.

Yet, when face-to-face with her, they'd rather bite their own tongues off than be considered impolite. His mother chalked it up to some Southern good breeding, cliquish thing he neither understood nor cared to understand. It was plain old hypocrisy. Period.

But Dixie knew this game, and she knew exactly how to play to Essie. There was nothing Essie loved more than her boy Jackson and her daughter Shelby, except maybe her bloodhound Bowie.

Essie's round face flushed with instant pride, her return smile fond if a bit hesitant. She let a tentative hand stray to Dixie's, giving it a light squeeze before yanking it back and tucking it into the pocket of her skirt with a look of guilt. "Aren't you just the sweetest thing for askin'? Jackson's well, as handsome as ever. Shelby's good, too."

Dixie smiled and nodded her head in approval. Her blue eyes flitted to Blanche who'd remained quiet since revealing LaDawn's name. "And, Miss Blanche? How's Henry feelin'? Last I heard from Mama, he was nursing his shoulder and some bursitis? She suggested a liniment she's used when I talked to her this week. Why not give me a call, and I'll pass on the name of it? Mama swears it has miraculous properties."

Magic. Caine had to give it up to Dixie. She'd managed to cast a spell over the hierarchy of Plum Orchard, diverting their attention and turning it into a gabfest.

No doubt Dixie was good at making you feel as if you were the only person in the world, he mused. Maybe it was how she paid such close attention to the small details of another's life, or maybe her concern, completely fake, of course, was what made people believe she was genuine.

But Caine knew better, and as he watched her play her flute, leading all the women in a dance they didn't even realize they were dancing, his eyes narrowed.

Leave it to Dixie to launch herself right back into the fold with nary a reminder of how she'd once talked Essie's son Jackson into toilet papering Nanette's entire house by promising to make out with him.

Or how she'd locked Kitty Palmer's daughter Louella in a porta-potty to keep her from riding atop the Miss Cherokee Rose float after being disqualified from the town's biggest pageant for getting caught drinking plum wine in the bed of Gordy Hansen's truck.

Dixie took a quick glance at the watch on her slender wrist, her lips thinning before they curved into another pleasant smile. "Ladies, I hate to cut our catching up short, but I have an appointment with Mr. Cotton I absolutely can't miss." Her eyes strayed to Caine's once more, flashing him a fiery glance. Clearly, she understood why he was here, and she didn't like it.

He rolled his tongue along the inside of his cheek and grinned at her over the heads of the women. Yep. That's right. He was here, and he was here to win.

Boom.

"An appointment?" Nanette's question was sharp, maybe even sharper than her keen knack for even a hint of gossip. Each of the Senior Magnolias' ears virtually stood at attention. "Why ever would you have to see Hank, Dixie Davis? Didn't you sort out that mess of a bankruptcy back in Chicago?"

The Senior Magnolias stiffened one by one, twittering to the tune of their shuffling feet. Blanche cleared her throat while Essie leaned so far forward, fiddling to adjust her hearing aid, Caine was sure she'd tip over.

Dixie widened her eyes, mocking surprise at Nanette and the women. "You mean you haven't heard, Miss Nanette? I thought the entire population of Plum Orchard would know by now. Must be a slow day 'round here. Bless your hearts, but it has been an *entire day* since the reading of Landon's will." She paused for effect, the kind of effect that had each of the women waiting on the edge of their seats and left Caine fighting an exasperated sigh.

Aw, hell. She was going to do it. Right here. She really did have bigger balls than any man he knew. Which just went to show, Dixie was still the same old Dixie he'd known back in high school. Their short run as a couple, when he'd thought she'd changed but later found out it was all just a part of her endgame.

Everything was about the coup.

Kitty Palmer's hazel eyes jutted upward at the rumbling sky just as a plump raindrop splattered on the brim of her floppy, orange hat. She stomped an impatient foot. "Well, tell us, Dixie, before I can't stand it any longer. Besides," she remarked with a squirm, casting her eyes downward, "rain always makes me have to use the facilities."

Dixie leaned into the group real slow, gathering them together as though she were going to share a classified government secret. She turned her back to Caine, purposely, of course. Though when she did, he wished her supple back end wasn't so well encased in those shorts or her long legs weren't so shapely.

Caine fought the instantly sharp reminder Dixie was all woman, and waited for the land mine to explode, one he'd stepped right into.

Dixie shook her head in astonishment. "I just can't believe you Magnolias, the backbone of Plum Orchard, don't know."

Nanette's irritation exploded in the way only the most God-fearing of them all would—tight-lipped and narrow-eyed—yet still the picture of decorum. "Just spit it out, Dixie Davis, and stop beatin' around the plum tree, young lady!"

"It isn't just me who has to see Hank Cotton. It's Caine, too. We're in this together, right, Caine?" Dixie shot him a smirk, her pink lips curling upward as a light rain began to fall.

"In what together?" Blanche asked just above a whisper filled with drooling anticipation.

Dixie's round eyes went demure as if she wasn't enjoying every second of this game of cat and mouse. "You know all those ladies at the guesthouse? The ones you haven't even given a chance just by virtue of their clothing and makeup choices?"

Blanche and the rest of the ladies bristled.

"They're working," Dixie whispered from behind her hand.

"Workin'?" Nanette squawked.

Dixie nodded. "Uh-huh. The ladies in the guesthouse are just doing their jobs. As *phone-sex operators.*"

Nanette gasped, her hand at her throat. "That's not true, Dixie! You're playin' one of your horrible pranks again. Same old Dixie!"

Dixie put her fingers to her heart, making an *X*. "No! Swear it on Mama's Hermes bag collection. Landon owned a very successful phone-sex company. It's worth millions and *millions,*" she emphasized.

Nanette backed away from Dixie as though she'd seen the devil himself possess her. Her eyes went wide with outrage while the Senior Magnolias rushed to rally behind her.

Dixie's face went sympathetic. "But that's not all. Guess what else? I have the chance to inherit Landon's phone-sex company—all of those luscious millions, as long as I can talk dirty, that is."

"You have to speak fornicatin' words on the phone to strange men?" Out of nowhere, a fan appeared in Nanette's hand. She liberally batted at the air near her pudgy face before she spoke again, but when she did, it was as though it physically pained her. "It's unseemly, Dixie Davis! *How could you?*"

Dixie's heart-shaped face softened, yet her tone held light reproach. "Now, Miss Nanette, how could I not? The good Lord and Landon, in what I'm sure was full heavenly cooperation, have opened a door for me. One that will help me dig my way out of my financial ruin. Would a good woman turn her back on what's clearly the gift of opportunity from above?" Dixie frowned and shook her finger. "It'd be like turnin' my back on all those morals y'all tried so hard to teach me."

Caine shook his head. Oh, she was good. So very good.

Nanette harrumphed her displeasure while Kitty held her hand to the spot where her heart beat. Caine saw the wheels of her razor-sharp, fueled-by-the-morality-police mind try to combat their very own words. "I can almost understand *you* doin' unsavory work. You were always a wild one, young lady. But what does that have to do with one of Plum Orchard's finest?" She waved a hand in his direction.

And the final bomb...

"I can't believe, while y'all were over here shootin' the breeze, one of Plum Orchard's *finest* didn't tell you himself." She gave Caine a "shame on you" eye roll. "So here's the story. Now, you girls be sure and pass this on to everyone proper. We wouldn't want any mis-understandings. Deal?"

Four heads nodded their consent while four mouths struggled to pick their jaws up off the ground.

"Caine and I have to compete against each other if we want to win Landon's phone-sex company. That's why he's here at Mr. Cotton's, I assume. To accept Land-on's crazy challenge. Whoever has the most calls at the end of two months wins all of it. That means our town hero will be speakin' those unsavory words—to—" she leaned in conspiratorially—"are you ready for this?"

Every woman nodded her head, eyes round with hor-ror. *Great.*

"To *women!*" Dixie whispered on a giggle.

Caine closed his eyes and sighed. His mother would know about this in fewer than twenty minutes.

"It'll be just like old times, don't you think?" Dixie asked. "Me and Caine tryin' to best each other to the bitter end? So many good memories." She sighed and clapped her hands together with over-the-top glee. "Anyway, I have to run now, ladies, but I sure hope you'll remember to save me a seat at the next Magnolias tea, seein' as I'll be in town longer than I planned. I've missed those pretty sandwiches with the crusts cut off." With a wave of her hand, Dixie gifted them with one last innocent wink of her eye and pushed her way past Caine to strut up Hank Cotton's driveway.

Just as she escaped into the stark white door of Hank's office, the sky opened up and let loose its fury, pummeling them with fat splotches of water.

While he held umbrellas and helped the Magnolias back across the street to the dry confines of Madge's Kitchen, he did his best to avoid Nanette's glare and dodge the shocked stares of her crew.

Son of a bitch.

Dixie ran her fingers over the face of her phone before sticking her tongue out at it. At six o' clock on the dot, she'd received another text message from Landon that read, Are you ready to rumble, Dixie-Do?

She shoved the phone in her back pocket and strode past the pool toward the guesthouse with purpose, determined to hang on to the victory of her earlier coup and her conviction she would take no prisoners with this phone-sex thing and beat Caine.

She was convinced he'd shown up at Hank's extra

early just to rub her nose in his acceptance of this bizarre contest.

A smile flitted across her lips when she remembered Caine's handsome face changing from smug to furious as she'd told the Senior Magnolias the costarring role everyone's golden boy played in Landon's game. Which was as good as grabbing her old cheerleading bullhorn and shouting it from the gazebo in the middle of the square. By this time tomorrow, Caine would be as tarnished as she was....

Then she straightened and kicked herself for slipping back into the ways of her ugly past. Not only had she wanted the Mags to know she wasn't going away any time soon, she'd wanted to hurt Caine for making love to her. For hitting refresh on her closeted emotions.

But after signing a stack of papers at Hank's office, agreeing to the strict rules of the phone-sex game while Caine simmered in a puddle of rainwater, she'd promised herself she would not gloat.

It was ugly and childish, and while no one brought out the ten-year-old in Dixie like Caine did, she was going to do everything in her power to ignore him and her inner elementary-school demon.

That last bit of one-upmanship in front of the Magnolias was the absolute end, and while it was a fine way to go, it was also a promise she was sticking to. For real this time. She had to stop clinging to a pain she herself had created.

Her focus lay solely with clobbering her opponent, and in doing so, it wouldn't do to spend hours masterminding ways to best him. Caine was banking on two things—that she'd want payback for the end of their engagement, and on the fact that she'd lose her "eye of the tiger" while she plotted his doom.

That Dixie no longer existed.

It was going to take grit and determination and a lot of dirty, dirty words to win this without resorting to some sort of scheme.

The dirty words.

They made her flush hot from chest to forehead. Mercy. How was she ever going to say those words out loud?

She jammed her hand in the pocket of her shorts, remembering the second text she'd had from Landon today. *The kinkiest girl gets the worm, Dixie-Cup!*

Dixie let her chin fall to her chest, closing her eyes. She paused just outside the doors leading her into Landon's den of iniquity and repeated the mantra she'd been saying over and over in her head since she woke this morning, determined not only to forget every luscious moment in that closet with Caine, but to win.

Because as hurt as she still was about losing Caine— maybe always would be—he still made her burn whitehot from the inside out. Caine's scent, still fresh on the shirt she'd burrowed her nose in just before she'd drifted off into a fitful sleep, had left her aching and empty. Full of so many memories of their short-lived romance, she'd had to war with herself not to run straight back into poverty's arms simply to avoid reliving that moment when she'd known, no matter how many corners she turned, she'd always be the old Dixie to him—the girl who'd chased after him until she'd finally caught him, then ruined everything by doing something awful.

That one moment in time at their engagement party had shattered her soul, pulling the carefully woven fabric of the rug that had begun to make up the new Dixie, the Dixie who'd come to terms with what a deplorable human being she'd once been, right out from under her. It was, and always would be her own doing, but she didn't need constant, agonizing reminders.

If Caine, and Louella, and everyone else who hated her knew karma had taken a chunk of her back in Chicago on their behalf, maybe that would satisfy them. If they knew it wasn't just her restaurant that had blown up in her face, if they knew her life had blown up in her face, if they knew about Mason...

Tears bit the back of her eyelids. Not even Landon knew about Mason.

No time for tears. Rolling her head on her neck, she straightened her shoulders with resolve and ran directly into Caine's wall of a chest.

His hands reached out to steady her, but she brushed their strength off, attempting to step around him.

"Evenin', Dixie. You ready to get your sexy on?" Caine tumbled into the night, blocking her entry. At eye level, his thick chest covered in a soft, faded black T-shirt, made her mouth water. His abs rippled when he lifted his arms and spread them across the doorway, bracing himself by pressing those magical hands against the frame.

Her gaze moved past the hard-angled planes of his body with conviction, her weak legs stiffened in order to keep her stance menacing. *You are a cucumber, Dixie. Cool as such.* "Move. Please."

Caine dipped his dark head low, bending at the waist so he was almost eye-to-eye with her. "Aw, Dixie. Are you disappointed to find I'm cleaning my chain mail and greasing my arrows in preparation for our phone-sex battle?"

Her chin lifted with righteous indignation—their eyes meeting squarely. She didn't budge.

Instead, Dixie launched her words at him full throttle. Anger was the costume best suited to hide all other emotions. "Don't be silly. When have I ever backed down from a battle? But were I you, I'd add a little something you seem to have overlooked on your medieval shopping list."

Caine grinned, infuriatingly, cooing his question in the gravelly velvet whisper of Sam Elliott. "What's that, Dixie?"

Heavens. That low, slow drawl left her almost as girlishly giddy as Sean Connery's did. He knew how much she loved a rough cowboy who sold big, manly trucks.

Remain strong.

Dixie ran her hands along her arms to hide her goose bumps, keeping her tone even, she replied, "A chest plate. You'll need it to protect you when I shoot that final arrow right through your heart, the one that leaves Landon's Call Girls millions to me." She made a face and used her forefinger to jab him in the ribs.

Caine surprised her when he threw his head back and laughed. "Still just as headstrong as always, huh, Dixie-Cup? I know you, Dixie. You're a wild woman when I'm inside you, but as bold and as brash as you are, as manipulative and cruel as that pretty mouth with the flaming-hot voice slitherin' out of it can be, it won't ever be able to play the dirty games. We both know that was my thing." He growled down at her with a chuckle.

Caine's reference to being inside her made her jiggle with butterflies. "I'm more determined than I ever was.

Maybe even more so than that time we played those six rounds of strip poker at Dwayne Hicks's house, and I was losing by three hands. Just you remember who ended up naked, Donovan, and minus almost five hundred dollars in his wallet."

Caine's lips brushed the shell of her ear, and Dixie froze in order to ward off the inclination to lean into them. "You cheated then. Will you cheat now, too? Because if you play the game fair and square, I'd be happy to see you have to take your clothes off," he said so low and husky it made the tips of her ears burn and her nipples pucker against her flimsy bra.

Don't bite, don't bite, don't bite. Stop biting, Dixie! "Why didn't you just go home to Miami, Caine? Don't you have a successful real estate-empire to run? Don't empires crumble when their leaders go missing?"

Aw, Dixie-Cup. You bit...

His expression was the standard cocky. "I have a whole office full of staff for that, Dixie. Besides, I was due some time off. What better way to spend it than being back home again where everyone knows my name, catching up on old times with some of the guys from high school, visiting my mother and driving you right out of your mind?"

"Well, at least you're honest about your motivation."

His already hard face went harder, the deep shadows of the evening playing across his clenched jaw. "Someone has to be. Honest, I mean."

Caine's caustic remark, meant to dig up her lying, cheating past, would hurt more if she weren't already at peace with her past. Not even Caine could manage to jam that knife any deeper into her gut than it already was.

Dixie'd made a promise to herself when she'd finally turned the mean-girl corner. She would own her past misdeeds. All of them. Every ugly, manipulative, hurtful one of them. But there would be no dwelling or groveling.

She'd simply set out to right her wrongs with as much kindness as those scorned would allow. And those scorned who refused her kindness would end up in the pile of her "regret wreckage" while she let them continue to hate her.

She'd been well on her way to redeeming herself when she and Caine had become engaged. He'd gotten to know the Dixie she aspired to—the Dixie that struggled daily to be good enough for someone so honorable, so revered by everyone who crossed his path.

Yet, when the true test came, when she'd slipped up once, he'd chosen to believe she was always going to be the worst human being in heels, hell-bent on making Plum Orchard's hottest man hers at all costs. He hadn't given her the opportunity to apologize. He'd believed that she would never change. How could she marry a man who left no room for mistakes?

It was then that she'd known she'd never be good enough for Caine Donovan.

So she'd shown him, hadn't she? By leaving him and never looking back. And she was going to continue to show him. Right here. Right now.

As the humid air picked up, sending her hair flying in every direction, she gave Caine an intentionally haughty gaze. "So here's the deal, Donovan. You can poke, taunt, bring up, remind me over and over about how utterly dreadful I was back in the day. In fact, I welcome it because it's true. But let me make one thing clear. Your innuendo about what a scheming, dishonest, manipulative man-eater I was rolls off me like water off a duck's back. It's old and unoriginal at this point. I'm here for one thing and one thing only—to pay off my debts and hopefully, find a new career…somewhere in this mess. So you stay on your side of the playing field, and I'll stay on mine. Don't cross that line or I swear, I'll stomp all over your Italian leather shoes with my ten-dollar Payless pumps."

His nostrils flared at Dixie's order, but he remained silent. Seeing she had him and his sense of honor under her thumb, Dixie backed up and planted her hands on her hips. "Now move. I have a job to learn and a website to launch. Mistress Taboo is in the house!"

When he didn't budge, she planted a hand on his chest, trying to ignore the warm skin covering his well-structured muscles. *"Move, Caine."*

Caine faked her as though he were stepping out of the way, but instead, his arms snaked around her waist like bands of steel, hauling her to him with a grunt.

"So we're going to just pretend nothing happened in that closet last night?" He ran a firm hand over her backside to cup a cheek with a hot groan. "Like this didn't happen?" he asked, his strong, magical fingers reaching under her T-shirt to stroke the hot skin of her belly.

Dixie forced herself to go limp in his embrace. She hung there, staring up at him with a dead gaze. "That's exactly what we're going to do. For not just the good of you and me, Candy Caine, but everyone else who has to suffer our ridiculous Hunger Game–ish behavior. What happened last night happened. Now it's over, and in moving forward, it's going to stay over. Because really,

Caine, why would you want to sleep with a woman with so few morals as me? What does that say about *you?*"

Their eyes met, glaring, scanning, searching. Using every ounce of will, Dixie kept her stare blank but determined. She had to or her heart would never survive the next two months. "So let go of me. I have men to entertain. So many, it'll be like it's rainin' 'em."

Caine set her down, his eyes in the coming darkness perplexed when she brushed him off. "You're really going to do this. Huh."

Dixie's lips thinned. "I'm really going to do this, and I'm going to do it so well, my mean-girl legend will be virtually forgotten, and in its place, Mistress Taboo will reign supreme!" Shaking from his embrace, she managed to scoot around him, stomping into the lavish entryway. She gave a rebel yell to all the Call Girls ensconced in their bedroom offices. "I offer myself as tribute to the phone-sex games!"

There was a bark of Caine's amused laughter before his return shout echoed in her ears. "May the odds be ever in your favor, Mistress Taboo!"

As she left Caine outside, more handsome than he'd ever been—more sex on a stick than even her tortured dreams had accurately remembered, she left him knowing that no matter what Caine thought of her, no matter the awful things he thought her still capable of, it didn't matter.

Because Dixie Davis was still mad about Caine Donovan.

Eight

Marybell Lyman of the infamous little-girl voice sat across from Dixie at her appointed desk, her saucer-like eyes wide after scanning the website Dixie had managed to design with a template she'd found online.

Dixie winced, twisting a strand of her freshly dyed hair around her index finger in nervous anticipation. This had to be right, and soon.

Doubt seized her. Maybe all those sparkly, torch-size candles in the shape of a heart surrounding her make-believe online bed were overkill? Or maybe the words of the slogan itself, mimicking dripping ice cream cones filled with vanilla confections and sprays of confetti-colored sprinkles, were too over the top? Mistress Taboo—for those who like "All Things Missionary."

"Too much?"

Marybell shook her head, the spikes of her red-and-green Mohawk stabbing the air. "No. Not at all, it's—it's pretty daggone sexy. Maybe we should consider another name? Missionary and vanilla isn't exactly taboo."

Dixie rolled her eyes. "Some people think talking

about any kind of sex is taboo. Just ask the people in this town."

Marybell laughed, sweet and tinkling.

"I really thought I could pull off a fetish, but when push came to shove, I had to rethink. But I love the pseudonym. So maybe my specialty is not having a fetish at all? Do you think it'll scare potential customers off?" That was the last thing she could afford to do.

"I think you should be whoever you want to be, Dixie. Damn what other people say." She swiveled the screen toward Dixie and pointed to the cartoon caricature of a redhead, dressed in a white corset with satiny red ribbons cinching it together so tight, her enormous, animated breasts spilled over the top like a freshly popped can of crescent rolls. "Is that you?"

Dixie winced again, marveling at the fact that the cartoon hadn't tipped right over with only that tiny waist to hold up her bodacious hips. "If only I could get my hair to hold a curl like that," she said on a self-conscious chuckle.

Marybell pinged a stiff strand of her Mohawk with a black, glossy fingernail and smiled. "Yeah, me, too."

Dixie's nervous laughter filled up the bedroom turned office, annoying even her.

"You're nervous."

"Like the last weaponless soul alive after a zombie apocalypse."

"It's the dirty words, right?"

She blew out an anxious breath, twisting her hands together in a fist. "It's the everything."

Despite her contradictory appearance, despite her short-cropped leather jacket, leopard leggings, multiple piercings, three tattoos, and one partially shaved eyebrow, Marybell was as sweet as her voice. When Dixie was paired with Marybell as her official Call Girls liaison, she'd made every attempt to hide her reservations and her relief LaDawn wouldn't be her mentor.

LaDawn Jenkins was one tough cookie, and frankly, she scared the breath out of Dixie. She was surly, short with her words, and the dismissive glance of disdain she'd sent Dixie by way of the end of her nose was enough to make her want to pack up Mona and Lisa and long-distance run back to Chicago.

To say LaDawn was less than thrilled two new phone operators would be cutting into her profits was putting it lightly. She was the gold medalist of dirty, and the tiniest of threats to her burgeoning call list were grounds for some scathing remarks aimed at Dixie, who'd barely left their introduction with her skin intact.

So in phase one of this contest, she was glad Marybell was her leader. Not in a hundred years would she have put Marybell Lyman's youthful voice with the young woman who looked no more than twenty-five or so sitting before her. Though, according to Marybell, or MB, per her request, she was actually almost thirty, proving one should never judge a book by its cover.

Judge not lest ye be judged. Another lesson learned.

Marybell reached out a hand and patted Dixie's arm with a thump. "You're letting LaDawn get under your skin. In no time at all, you'll be sayin' the *P* word like it was hyphened on your name. So let's give this a practice run. You up for that, Dixie?"

Again, she silently wondered how Marybell had ended up here. She was incredibly bright and articulate and full of encouraging words. The world was her oyster. Unlike Dixie, whose world was more like stinky, week-old dead fish.

Dixie stared down at the cheat sheet—the one filled with all matter of festively colorful words. It wasn't like she didn't recognize most of them—on the contrary. Maybe one or two were dicey, but she knew what they meant. Saying them out loud was another story altogether.

"Dixie?"

"Sorry. Ready."

Marybell wrinkled her nose, the light of the desk lamp catching her gold nose ring. "Breathe."

"Can't."

"You'd better. It's a deciding factor when pretendin' you're having the big 'O.'"

Oh. Dixie snorted out a breath, easing some of her tension.

"We're just practicin' right now. Loosen up, Dixie. Relax."

"Says the pro…"

"I'm no pro. I've only been doing this for a couple of years. Now LaDawn? That's a pro. She has more callers than Facebook has users. She's my phone-sex idol."

"Wasn't she—?"

"A hooker."

"Companionator!" LaDawn's thick Southern accent called out from one of the adjoining bedrooms where the constant beep of phones ringing drifted about. "I gave my companionship to lonely men. You'd do best to get that right, Marybell. I won't have you ruinin' my unsoiled reputation!"

Marybell's eyes rolled. "Companionator. Got it, LaDawn," she shouted back. Her eyes caught Dixie's again, warm and easy. "Either way, she knows how to lure tons of men in and keep them on the hook for hours. And LaDawn can do it all. So don't go comparing yourself to her just yet. She's the Jedi master of phone sex. You're just a youngling."

Dixie's fingers drifted to the edge of her note pad, smoothing the corners. "Well, I guess I won't ever get my light saber if we don't get the show on the road." She shoved the squares of paper away and with one last deep breath, urged, "Go. Just do it."

"Ring-ring—horndog calling!" Marybell chimed, pointing to the earpiece Dixie was supposed to click to the On position when it buzzed.

On a gulp, she pretended to flip her earpiece on and read from her cheat sheet, "Hello, this is Mistress Taboo. Are…you…um, worthy?" Weak. Dixie's voice was weak and watery to her ears. Ugh.

Marybell flipped her an encouraging thumbs-up and fluttered an engaging grin. "Okay, that was good, but don't ask if your caller is worthy like you're unsure. He has to prove he's worthy enough to talk to you. Demand that. Be firm, Dixie. You're the one in control, no matter how out of control your client would like to be. Always remember you're the captain of the Good Ship Vanilla. Vanilla sex can be just as hot and nasty as a virtual BDSM session. Don't let anyone steer you off course." She waved a finger at Dixie to commence their practice call.

Vanilla. She'd decided on sticking with what she knew. If Dixie'd learned nothing from her tainted past, she'd learned if there was a will, she'd find the way, and her way was the good old-fashioned way.

"Let's go again before I have to start my shift, Dixie.

Ready?" When Dixie nodded, she called out, "Ring-ring!"

Pay back every penny, Dixie. Her chin lifted. "This is Mistress Taboo. *Are you worthy?*" she husked out in a growl, finding a focal point on her desk to concentrate on. To help put her in the mood, she let her eyes smolder seductively in the way she once had when she was on the boyfriend hunt.

Marybell's hazel eyes widened in surprise beneath her heavy black eye shadow. "Well, hell-to-the-lo, Mistress Taboo…."

Dixie closed her eyes, swallowing hard. If she could just transport herself back to high school Dixie—if she could just summon up all those wiles she'd flung about at the boys as if she was lobbing pennies to peasants. If… "Well, hello to you, too. Now that you know my name, I think it's only fair you share yours, don't you? So I know what to call ya when we're doin' the do." Her words were suggestive, breathy, swishing from her tongue like the Dixie from days of yore.

"I don't think I should tell you my real name." Marybell's impression of a male voice bordered comical, coming from the throat of a woman whose dulcet tones conjured up colorfully winged fairies and Disney princesses. Marybell rested her chin on her hand and smiled again with a nod of encouragement to continue.

Dixie nodded back as though she actually knew where Marybell was going next. "Then who would you like to be tonight? Tell Mistress Taboo." Her cheeks flushed. Had that really been her?

Marybell picked up a manila envelope from the desk and fanned herself with it to indicate she approved of Dixie's hot response. "Why don't you just call me Bob?"

"Bob? Ohhh, that's sort of hot—and anonymous. It's perfect. Mistress Taboo approves," she purred, twirling her hair around her finger. "So, *Bob*—what's on your mind tonight? What are you in the mood for?"

"Heaven be," a voice stuttered from the lavish white oak doorway.

Dixie's head popped up, breaking the sensual co-coon she'd somehow managed to immerse herself in.

Em stood frozen just beyond the wide door leading to Dixie's assigned workspace.

Dixie cocked her head in Em's direction and motioned her in. "Look who finally came up for air from all that leftover crab and hot-tubbing. Marybell, do you know Em?"

Marybell smiled and waved in Em's direction. "Nice to meet you."

Em's crimson lips attempted movement, yet no sound came out.

Dixie jumped up from her chair and crossed the small space to hold her hand out to Em who tucked her fists firmly behind her as though Dixie were offering to escort her into the bowels of Hell. "Give me your hand, Em. Come and sit with us. It's okay, I promise."

Em swatted at her, her voice suddenly found if not a bit rusty. "Oh, you hush your mouth, Dixie! You just caught me off guard is all."

"Off guard?"

"Stop behavin' like you don't know what I'm talking about. I mean, good gracious, I've never heard anything quite like it. It was like you were meant to do—to do—this." She made a sweeping gesture with her hand at the desk and every last sin it encompassed.

Dixie rocked back on her heels with a knowing nod.

"Ah, yes, the devil's work. I should think that wouldn't surprise you, Em. Wasn't your nickname for me back in high school Satan's Sidekick or S.S. for short? Don't think I didn't hear through the grapevine."

Marybell choked out a laugh while Em flushed a pretty pink. "You *were* mean."

"I was. Seeing me reduced to this should go a long way toward filling up my 'payback' account. Marybell was just givin' me a practice run. Do you want to see my cheat sheet? It has all sorts of interesting words—"

"I most certainly do not!" Yet, her eyes strayed to the stapled papers on the desk, curious and wide before snapping back to Dixie's. "I heard all I needed to hear. I was just checkin' in on you to reassure myself you're stickin' to all those rules Landon made before I left to go home for the night. It's my job."

So there. Dixie internally cheered Em's new backbone, fighting a grin. "Then job well done, Em. Landon couldn't have picked a better, more efficient mediator had he been the one mediating himself."

Em relaxed a little, finally inching across the room and perching on the end of a chaise longue positioned far enough away from command central for her comfort. "Don't you try and win brownie points with me, Ms. Sidekick. I know you and your low-down dirty tactics, all complimentin' me while you steal my number two pencils right out from under my nose because I was stupidly greedy for acceptance. You won't pull the wool over these eyes. No, ma'am." For emphasis, she pointed to her eyes.

Dixie grinned. "I'm going to buy you ten packs of pencils to make up for that incident, in any color your heart desires. No wool. All on the up-and-up. Cross my heart."

"You can't cross a heart you don't have," Em said, relaxing a little more.

Dixie placed her hand over her heart and slumped back in her chair. "Well, if I had one, you would have just pierced it, and rightly so. So where are you off to tonight? Home to the boys?"

"First I have to check on Mr. Smexy and be sure Catherine's got him under control, and then I have a personal mediation with my own snake to attend."

Dixie's eyes went sympathetic. The rumors she'd heard about Em's divorce were few and far between, but they weren't any less painful to hear knowing the breakup of her marriage left two boys without their father. "Clifton?"

Em's intake of breath was broken up and choppy. "You'd think after thirteen years of marriage to a woman who cooked and cleaned like she was born to do it, two fine young boys, and a pretty little ranch house, the old dog would at least be willin' to let me have my two favorite things in the world besides my boys."

"What are your two favorite things? If you don't mind me askin'," Marybell said, her coal-covered eyes genuine when she cast an interested glance in Em's direction.

"Our iguana Beauregard Jackson, the boys just love him to pieces, and—and…" She put a fist to her mouth, lines of worry crowding the sides of her sincere eyes.

Dixie slid her office chair toward her and patted her thigh, sensing Em's discomfort. "You don't have to tell us, Em, if it's too personal."

"My dresses!" she shouted with a burst of words rocketing into the room.

"Dresses? Why would Clifton want your dresses?" Dixie paused and caught herself, letting out a dramatic, Magnolia-worthy gasp. The cad. "He doesn't want to give them to his new harlot, does he?"

Em waffled, her eyes driving nails into the lush carpet at her feet. "Not exactly…"

Marybell's head shot up while Dixie was just plain confused. "Did your husband Clifton like to wear your clothes, Em? Was he a cross dresser?"

Emmaline's whimper confirmed Marybell's statement. "Yes. Clifton liked to dress up as a woman, and now that my shame is lying all over this house of debauchery's thickly carpeted floor, I'm going to sneak off to the woods out back at Coyne Wilkinson's and look for a cave to spend the rest of my life in. I hope my boys learned how to build a campfire after all that boy-scoutin' they do. We'll need warmth come winter."

"Clifton likes to wear women's clothes?" Dixie repeated, fighting a squeal of disbelief. Clifton Amos, descendant of one of the founding fathers of Plum Orchard, a flannel-wearing, coon-hunting, tobacco-chewing, six-pack guzzling, all 'round good ol' boy liked to wear women's clothes?

Em's face went instantly defensive, her eyes hot with more emotions than Dixie was able to count. "Yes, he likes to wear women's clothes, Dixie Davis. Shoes and nylons, nail polish and pretty underwear, too! I didn't know about it, and when I found out, I tried to understand it while I prayed no one in town would ever find out. It was a tryin' time, to say the least. But for all my prayin', Clifton just knew I couldn't find my way."

"Oh, Em," Dixie murmured.

"Now don't y'all misunderstand me. I don't hate the idea. In fact, it doesn't bother me almost at all. What I hated was that Clifton did it behind my back. I hated that he didn't think I was worthy enough to share his secret with. A secret he says is so deeply personal, it's only meant for someone who truly supports him. I hate that he thought I'd love him less."

"And where does the other woman in Atlanta figure into this?" Dixie asked.

Em's sigh was pained. "He'd go off to Atlanta on weekend trips to a secret world I didn't know about, and he didn't want me to be a part of. That's where he met the woman he left me for. He left me for her because she *understands* him," she said with gooey disgust. "Oh, that word! How could I have possibly understood him if he didn't ever tell me what I was supposed to be understandin'?"

Dixie's heart clenched for her frenemy. Left here in judgmental Plum Orchard to fend off unwanted inquiries about her husband's whereabouts had to be worse than anything she'd endure short of death.

Add in babysitting Caine and Dixie, and it made for a recipe with "stressful" as the number one ingredient. "Oh, Em. I'm so sorry, honey. How can I help?"

Em stood ramrod-straight, defiance marring her full lips. "You can help by not helping. Don't use it against me when it suits you. Because you have plenty o' times before. And I'm sure you will again… I think…"

"Wow." Marybell whistled, her eyes wide. "Wasn't this whole thing with you two twenty years ago? No disrespect, but that's a long time to hang on to a high school grudge, don't you think?"

"You have no idea what acceptance means to a soul as insecure as I was. It stays with you a long time, but mostly, I just like remindin' Dixie about it to get my licks. It's a self-preservation reflex. Sort of like the sign of the cross to ward off demons," Em teased.

"But it's also true," Dixie admitted. "I manipulated people to my advantage, I teased, I cheated and I lied. I might not have been stealin' people's lunch money and beatin' 'em up in the schoolyard, but there wasn't much I wouldn't do to come out on top."

Em's eyes honed in on Dixie. "Someday, we're gonna talk about what motivated you to be so mean, Dixie Davis. What made you tick."

"So what did make you turn over a new leaf, Dixie?" Marybell asked. "It's all people talk about. Dixie Davis the man-eater. Dixie Davis, Plum Orchard's answer to all things rebellious and wild. Bad Dixie. I've heard them talk about it all, when they're not talkin' about the rest of us anyway."

Dixie's stomach clenched. Mason. Mason brought this on. Instead, she said, "It just happened. I'm living a clean life free of man-eatin' manipulative deceit. You'll see."

"Did you have an intervention an' everything? Like, did they take your makeup and sexy push-up bras away so you couldn't woo unsuspecting men back to your lair?" Marybell choked out before resorting to stifling her squeals of laughter.

No. She'd taken them away from herself. But that enormous change in her life was deeply personal, and she wasn't willing to open up about Mason.

Dixie forced a straight face. "They didn't take my makeup, but I did have to give up my lace panties. That pained me like nothing else. And flirting? I went on a flirting fast. Probably the hardest part about a mean-girl intervention. You get lots of speeding tickets without the superpower of the flirt in your arsenal's purse. It was a dark, dark time…." She finished, finally cracking and joining Marybell in gales of laughter.

Marybell wiped a tear from her eye, smudging her eyeliner. "Someday, I want to hear all the stories. I'm countin' on it."

Em shook her head, pinching the bridge of her nose. "I don't know what's happened to me since you landed on Plum Orchard soil, Dixie, but I don't like it. Here I am, spillin' my guts all over Landon's house of ill repute. Sanjeev will never get it all out of the carpet at this rate."

"That's the least of what's been spilled here," Marybell snickered, winking at Em.

Dixie raised her right hand, palm forward, her eyes latching onto Em's. "No one, not a Plum Orchard soul, will ever hear a word of it from my lips, Em. Thank you for trusting me enough to tell me about it."

The turmoil on Emmaline's face instantly melted. Dixie noted Em's shoulders didn't quite sag the way they had when she'd entered the room. "C'mon, Em. I'll walk you out to your car before I have to start my shift."

This time when she held out her hand, Em took it with much less reluctance. But trust, total trust, was still far off.

As they strolled out of the guesthouse, entering the soft glow of the pool area, Em yanked her close and whispered in her ear, "I swear to you, Dixie, if one soul finds out, I'll know it was you or Marybell. No one, not even my mama knows. This would crush the boys at school, not to mention Clifton's parents. They have no idea. I don't care how progressive Plum Orchard claims it is. We both know this town's still stuck somewhere back in the 1950s. Why, if Landon hadn't been so important and had all that money and connections and done so much for this town, they'd have run him and his crazy ideas right out of here."

"I get it, Em. I—"

"I mean it! I won't have my children or my in-laws mocked like I was when I was a child. They know nothing about what their daddy's up to, and I still don't know how to explain it. Don't you hurt my boys or I'll borrow old Coon Rider's gun and shoot your kneecaps right out from under ya, you hear?"

The mother bear in Em stole Dixie's breath for a moment.

A well of admiration sprang from deep within Dixie's gut. She gripped Em's clammy hand hard. "As I stand before you, not even the jaws of life could tear this secret from my mouth. I'd rather be toe-up in Purgeeta's Cemetery."

Em's hard edge softened a bit, but her words were still cutting. She gave Dixie's shoulder a poke. "Just you keep that in mind. And remember, I'll be the sole attendee at your funeral 'cause Louella Palmer's gonna be too busy plannin' a party the likes of which Plum Orchard's never seen. A big gala that'll make Landon's off-to-the-afterlife bon voyage look like a kiddy party at Chuck E. Cheese's."

"Is that my name I hear being used in vain?"

Dixie's eyes swung past the string of colored lanterns lining the awning of the pool house to catch her first glimpse of none other than Louella Palmer, sashaying her way toward them through the huge silver palms along the cobbled path.

Her white sandals clacked against the stones. Each step she took marked Dixie's long-overdue dressing-down.

Dixie tucked Em behind her, but not before she tugged on a strand of Dixie's hair and muttered a fierce warning in her ear, "You remember what I said. Not a single word."

Dixie squared her shoulders as Louella approached. Incoming.

Em's stiff body fairly hummed with tension from behind her with maybe even a little fear. Dixie reached around and gave Em's hip a reassuring pat as if to say, "Not on my watch."

Still as ethereally pretty as ever, Louella was immaculate in a lime-green frock, one that hugged her figure just enough to show off the easy swell of her flowing curves, yet still met the confines of good Southern decorum. She strolled toward them, confident and lean, and her sure strides almost didn't betray her lingering anger.

But Dixie knew better.

A humid breeze lifted the soft tendrils of her blond hair, artfully arranged to fall loosely around her face. The barrette, partially holding her locks up, matched her dress, and her nails, a pretty pink, mirrored her toes.

Dixie flashed her a warm smile, opening her arms wide for a hug. "Louella Palmer! It's been too long."

Louella bent from the waist, ignoring her offer of a hug and instead offered up an air kiss somewhere in the vicinity of Dixie's cheek. She straightened, folding her arms across her chest. "So look who's back," she said, showcasing the kind of restraint that was the hallmark of etiquette and good breeding. It was in her tight smile and glittering, uptilted eyes. In the way she lifted her chin and stood so straight, her spine just might crack.

Dixie, in return, ignored Louella's cool reception and dragged her unwilling frame into a hug. She gave her a tight squeeze, then grabbed her hands, entwining her fingers with Louella's to spread her arms wide. Her sweeping glance was full of approval. "Look who's still as pretty as a picture. You positively glow, Louella."

Dixie was surprised to find it had taken almost two whole days before Louella came to pick her way through the remaining debris of the train wreck that was her life. Aside from seeing Caine for the first time, this was the meeting she'd dreaded the most.

Dixie decided to keep things light, whether Louella liked it or not. The best way to bury the hatchet was to steal the weapon from your opponent's hands before they could even lift an arm to swing it. "So what brings you to Landon's?" she asked on a smile.

"What kind of leader of the Magnolias would I be if I didn't come and pay you a visit, Dixie? We welcome everyone new and those returning. I didn't have the chance to give you my condolences personally. The Mags send their condolences, too, of course. I'm sure they'll be dropping by soon." There was a brief moment of genuine sympathy in her eyes, but they turned cool quick. "It's just that I was so caught up with Caine as my escort to the funeral, it darn well slipped my mind."

Dixie flapped a conciliatory hand at her, giving her another welcoming smile. "I know firsthand just how charismatic that man can be—even at something as somber as a funeral. Don't you concern yourself with something as silly as courtesies. Manners just fly out the window when it comes to the charms of Caine." She used the same hand to fan herself.

Em poked her in the ribs with a dig of her red fingernail, clearly to serve as a reminder that Dixie was egging Louella on by openly reminding her who the first of their once tight-knit group had been to experience Caine's charms.

Damn. Old habits died hard.

Louella folded her hands together, propping them under her chin, and tilted her head as though she was genuinely interested in Dixie's welfare. "So, how's the restaurant business treating you?"

Her first instinct was to shoot back. Louella knew as well as anyone else how life was treating her. She was here under the guise of her leadership of the Magnolias, but in reality, it was the first warning of an all-out attack.

The Mags stuck together, and when you were out, you were out with a vengeance. She should know.

If she were truly reformed, not even the woman who'd accused her of having a sexually transmitted disease would bear her wrath. So Dixie held up her palms in defeat, her gaze purposely humble. "Not nearly as well as I hope the phone-sex business will."

Em poked her head around Dixie's. "You should see how good she is at it, too, Louella. She took to it like a duck to water." Her voice had a certain amount of pride in it, and it might have been wonderful, even supportive. Em was just trying to ease the palpable tension—except Louella wasn't going to let an opening like that slide.

Dixie winced in preparation before Louella went straight for her jugular. "Now that doesn't surprise me at all, Emmaline. Not in the least. We all know Dixie's

good at ropin' men in like cattle. She's left her panties…
I mean *mark* from here to Atlanta."

That was only semitrue. "Well, to be fair, it wasn't
quite as far reaching as Atlanta. Maybe just Johnsonville, and I never left a good pair of panties behind."

Em jumped to Dixie's defense, startling her. She
waved an accusatory finger at Louella. "That's unkind,
Louella, and you know it! Dixie's in a bad spot right
now. Takin' such pleasure in someone else's pain makes
you ugly and cruel."

Louella feigned a look of wonder, her eyes hardening
as they zoomed in on Em. "Would you look at the two
of you? Bondin' over your bad spots. How cozy. Who
would have ever thought you and Dixie would end up
the best of friends in your despair. How quickly we forget," she added dryly, glaring at Em who was no doubt
now doomed to have the title traitor added to her list of
Magnolia betrayals.

By tomorrow, no one would speak to her for asso-
ciating with Dixie.

Dixie heard Em's sharp gulp and knew her fear of everyone finding out about Clifton was where it stemmed
from. She absolutely wouldn't risk exposing Em. Not
even if it meant begging and pleading. "Look, Louella.
Why don't we just call it even? Let bygones be bygones,
and leave Em out of this. She has nothing to do with
what's passed between us. She's only doing her job
working for Hank Cotton. Surely we can behave like
ladies after all this time? It's been almost ten years."
Her tone was pleading as she faced Louella, begging
her with her eyes to let Em alone.

Louella's ironic laughter met Dixie's ears. "Oh,
Dixie. It's funny, but I remember saying almost those

exact words to you several times in high school. I think
I might have cried once or twice while I did it, too. But
probably not near as much as you did at your engagement party, I'd bet."

Em stepped out from behind her and loomed her
extra two inches of height over Louella, her lips tight,
and her face full of outrage.

The swift rustle of Em's feet behind her caught Dixie
so off guard, she was unable to stop her from saying
what she said next. "You stop this right now! When will
enough payback be enough for you, Louella? As if telling everyone Dixie had a horrible disease and ruinin'
her future marriage to Caine didn't fill your revenge
cup to the very top, you went and crawled right between
his grievin' sheets and took advantage of a bereaved
man not hours after he dumped the love of his life, for
mercy's sake!"

Nine

Dixie's head tilted in time with Louella's surprised gasp. *What?*

Emmaline's face distorted with regret as she realized what she'd just done. "Oh, gravy."

Dixie imagined that revelation was just what this was to Louella. Gravy on her chicken-fried steak. To have slept with the man Dixie was supposed to marry was better than a cherry on top of one of Martha's ice cream sundaes.

Dixie gritted her teeth, trying to remember the rule about karma. Even as she imagined Caine's muscular, tanned limbs wound around Louella's leaner ones.

Her stomach lurched in response, threatening to let loose Sanjeev's carefully prepared dinner of curried chicken and jasmine rice.

She'd broken the girlfriend code ten years ago then she'd run away from the consequences. Whatever Louella dished out now had been fermenting for a long time.

Louella didn't remain silent for long. Her lips popped

in a smack of pleasure. "Well, now that that cat's out of the bag, I'm going to go collect my date for the evenin'."

Dixie's blurred vision caught sight of Landon's camel, grazing on a thorny twig at the far corner of the big house's vast acreage. "Toe's dating now?" she quipped before she was capable of stopping herself.

Louella's laughter tinkled, mocking and satisfied. "No, silly, but Caine is," she drawled, waving a hand at something over her shoulder.

Dixie and Em's heads swiveled to catch sight of Caine, stepping out of the doors of the guesthouse, his smile warmly aimed in Louella's direction.

She pushed her way past Em, giving her a searing look of contempt before gushing the words, "There you are, Caine. Ready when you are!" followed by the sound of Louella's girlish laughter and Caine's heavy footsteps leading them away from the guesthouse.

Touché.

Em's head fell back on her shoulders before she lifted it up and let her chin drop to her chest. Her blue eyes peeked up at Dixie, shame and sorrow rimming them. "I'm dreadfully unpredictable these days, aren't I?"

"Woefully so."

"Do you hate me?"

"How could anyone ever hate you?"

"Even I'd hate me after tellin' someone their intended, and the love of their life, slept with someone else but an hour after those two someones broke up."

It was only an hour? Talk about jumping in her grave. Dixie pressed her trembling fingers to Em's lips to prevent her from repeating the unspeakable. It cut too deep. "I don't hate you. You're unhateable."

A sigh of despair slipped from her lips. "I'm sorry,

Dixie. Truly. It was an awful way to make Louella hush her mouth, but I just couldn't stand her bein' so mean to you, and now look. I'm just as mean. I got on a roll, and it just slipped out in the way all my foolish attempts to defend do."

Dixie slapped her hands against her hips in her second gesture of defeat tonight. "I would have found out eventually, Em. If not from you, then one of the Magnolias would have let it slip when Louella sounded the warning bell to attack. There are no secrets in Plum Orchard. So what better way than to find out in front of the perpetrator herself?"

Em gnawed her bottom lip. "My moods are so unpredictable with my life in such a quandary that I forget myself. I'm edgy and angry one minute, fragile and weepy the next. I'm just a babbling mess."

"You're going through a devastating time with this divorce. You're allowed to have mood swings." Even if those mood swings would now result in visuals filling Dixie's head she'd never be able to purge. "Besides, if you'll recall, I broke the code first. Why shouldn't she?"

Em's eyes rolled. "Was it really girlfriend code, Dixie? Caine never asked her out again, and that thing she keeps calling a date doesn't really count as a date. If you pay for your own coffee—that's 'Dutch,' not 'date.' She has her 'D's mixed up is all."

"It's the rule, though. She saw him first and staked her claim. Out loud. He might've asked her out again if not for me."

Em flapped her hands dismissively. "He would not have. It lasted all of fifteen minutes if what Essie Guthrie said is true. Which says to me, he couldn't wait to get away from her."

"And yet, he slept with her…" God, that hurt.

Em's face flooded with sympathy. "You do know I don't actually believe a word of it, don't you? Louella never lost her penchant for embellishing the truth to suit her. So don't you worry, S.S. I'll pay dearly for my mouth workin' overtime. I'm bettin' she wanted to tell you that nasty piece of business herself so she could drive that knife deeper into your already painin' heart."

The idea they would launch a good ol' Mag attack on Em sharpened Dixie's protective instinct, a loyalty she hadn't felt toward anyone but Landon. She planted her hands firmly on Em's shoulders and looked her right in the eye. "Don't you even think about Louella and the other Magnolias. I won't let them cause you or the boys any trouble. Not even if the old Dixie has to pay them a visit." Her evil could just as easily be used for good.

Em's gaze narrowed. "I'm still not sure the old Dixie's really gone."

"Louella still has her hair, and she left the house with Caine, even after you told me she'd…they'd…well, you know." The hard lump in her throat prevented her from actually saying the words. "Surely, my restraint says it all."

She shook her head as if to say Dixie's declaration of restraint wasn't convincing. "But if we're bein' honest here, you have to admit, the old Dixie was supposed to be gone ten years ago, too. And you were real good for a little while. I was almost convinced you really had turned over that new leaf you kept talkin' about. Then boom!" Em's fresh, new spine had come out to play, and it wasn't ready to go home for supper yet.

Dixie's head dropped. She couldn't meet Em's eyes.

Em's pause of silence was a sure sign her mind just

wasn't able to process a kinder, gentler Dixie. Letting the handle of her purse slide to the crook of her arm, she crossed her arms over her chest. "Mercy be, I just don't know what to believe about you anymore. All I do know is if I wanna be right with myself, I have to do right. I wouldn't want my feelin's to be crushed so callously while someone stood by and let it happen."

Tears stung Dixie's eyes again. "Thank you," she whispered.

"I'll tell you this. The Mags have been gunnin' for you since they heard you were comin' back, and Louella's been the captain of that Hate Boat. It's like she picked right up where you left off."

"In more ways than one." Every fiber of her being was still in the process of rejecting Em's statement while every curious bone in her body wanted to know everything that had happened between Louella and Caine. *How* had it happened? Why had it happened?

Em glanced at the watch on her wrist and frowned. "I really have to go, Dixie. You gonna be okay? Or will you be plottin' Plum Orchard domination to keep you warm tonight?"

Dixie laughed, glancing back at the lights of the guesthouse where phone calls filled with untoward sexual hijinks awaited. "No plots. Promise. That's not who I am anymore. Bygones, right?"

Em rubbed her arm. "All right then, but you call me if you need me, hear?"

Dixie gave her a quick hug and wished her luck before shooing her off, escaping back inside the guesthouse on sluggish legs.

Making her way back to the bedroom where Marybell waited for her, she clenched her fists and bit the inside of her cheek.

But it wasn't in anger. It was in anguish. Anguish she'd rather be skinned alive than reveal. She might be reformed, but she still wasn't above pride, sin or not.

Louella had learned from the master, and her crush on Caine, while maybe not as lengthy as Dixie's, had been just as valid. Making Caine hers had been just as much her dream as it had become Dixie's.

If Louella wanted sloppy Caine seconds, she was welcome to them.

So much for making amends, Dixie. That attitude is exactly the kind of reaction one would expect from the former you.

That thought deflated her, making her steps swift and guilty when she had to pass Caine's office, conveniently lodged right next door to hers. She scooted inside, shutting her door on the memory of Em's revelation with a shaky hand.

Flopping down in her office chair, she closed her eyes, letting the release of tension flood her limbs.

Yet, she couldn't block out Em's words. Couldn't stop the endless loop of torturous visuals. She focused on the picture of her and Landon located on the right-hand corner of her desk, clinking their champagne glasses together at the opening of her restaurant.

His wide smile, one that always hinted a mischievous thought, soothed and rankled her at the same time. She traced the sterling silver frame with a fingertip. "How dare you not be here right now when I need you so much? Did you know Caine slept with Louella, too?"

But Landon's voice, full of the candidness he was known for, taunted her. *How dare you have an ounce*

*of anger left for Louella when you snatched Caine right
out from under your former friend's cute, upturned nose
to begin with, Dixie-Cup?*

Alone.

She was alone with a phone. She'd laugh at how
comical the rhyme was if it weren't for the fact that
her stomach had decided to take up residence under the
desk, and her tongue felt thicker than molasses.

Letting her head drop to her folded arms, Dixie
rested her cheek on the cool desk and forced deep
breaths in and out of her lungs to help subside her panic.
Waiting for the phone to ring was like knowing the
grim reaper would knock, but you had no time or date
for his arrival.

She peeked up at her computer screen, letting her
eyes roam the numbers indicating the visitors to her
website since it had gone live on the Call Girls' main
site.

Ten. No doubt a nice, round even number.

Ten visits in four agonizing hours? Not as nice.

With four more hours to go until her shift ended.
Ugh.

The constant jingle of Caine's phone through the
wall behind her set her tired, frazzled nerves on edge.
His Michael Douglas impression, wherein he'd asked a
caller if they'd like him to find her Jewel of the Nile, was
the last straw. She'd taken a lot of heat since she'd come
home, but listening to Caine speak to other women—
she just couldn't do it. So she'd thrown on her headset
and turned up the volume on 98 Degrees. If a call actually came in, it would interrupt the soundtrack.

What did he have that she didn't? Where were all the stats in her favor tonight?

All she had to do was look at his website to see. Her fingers toyed with the smooth surface of the mouse then pulled away.

She hesitated for only a moment before going to the Call Girls home page to click on Candy Caine's website. An image of a man with ripped abs, more hard definitions than a dictionary covering his body, and bronzed skin, popped up on her screen. His face was in the shadows but for his lean jaw covered in dark stubble.

Caine knew how much she loved stubble. He wore a low-slung pair of jeans, his right thumb hooked into the waist, and a lone candy cane dangling suggestively from the left right by that indentation in his hip that led to all things sweet.

The tagline read, Come and Get Your Candy from Caine.

Damn Candy Caine and his money. A live model was out of the question for her.

Caine's date with Louella hadn't lasted more than an hour, not that she was counting. When he'd reentered Call Girls, he'd strolled past the bedroom door she'd reopened with a wave and a wink before settling in to address his many admirers.

The bastard.

The light of her desk lamp, though dim, shone on her computer screen, giving more life to Caine's website than he deserved. With a grunt, Dixie flipped the button on the lamp's base, blanketing the room in darkness, leaving only the muted twinkle of the lights from the big house to shine through the lone bedroom window.

As she settled in for the next round of "How Many

Ugly Adjectives for Caine Can Dixie Come Up With while She Prepares to Board the Train Called Penniless," the gentle chimes of her earpiece rang, cutting off the music.

Her head popped up. She had a call. A real live call! She froze. Mercy, now what?

Her hand shook, so much so, she almost couldn't press the button on her Bluetooth. "This is Mistress Taboo…" Dixie cleared her throat, fighting the thin wobble of her unsteady words. Confidence. Marybell had said confidence was critical to keeping control. She squared her shoulders and lifted her chin. *"Are you worthy?"*

"Of?" the refined, definitely Southern voice asked.

If her caller didn't know, she surely couldn't supply the answer. "Of my attention, of course," she whispered with a semiconfident delivery.

There was a rustle of something that crinkled, and then he asked, "What does a man have to do to prove he's worthy enough for you?"

Not sleep with Louella Palmer moments after crushing her heart? *Dixie…* "Why don't you tell me how you go about provin' yourself when you want a woman." She drew the sentence out, pausing slightly between words, letting them roll off her tongue with suggestive inflection.

"First," he drawled, cultured and so honey-thick sexy, Dixie's nerve-endings fluttered. "I have a question."

"I have one, too."

"Ladies first," he offered, grumbly and smoky.

She let the dark interior of her office envelop her, allowing it to hide her embarrassment and forged ahead. "What's your name?"

"What's yours?"

"You already know mine."

"I know what your website says your name is."

Did this man want to talk dirty or not, for gravy's sake? He must be what Marybell had titled the "reluctant caller."

The kind of man who was angry that he'd resorted to phone sex to get his kicks, yet was still excited by the prospect. Kid gloves were in order here. He needed to feel comfortable. Though, how she'd make him more at ease when she was so uneasy was a puzzle.

"Then you have your answer, silly man," she shot back playfully, deciding it was time to divert. Most men, no matter how tough on the outside, were easily diverted by sweet, submissive words and praise. "Or would you rather I don't call you anything at all? Because I can do that, too, you know... You can be whoever you'd like to be, darlin'." Her eyes widened at how easily the endearment slipped from her throat.

"Walker."

"Like a zombie?" she teased, twirling a strand of her hair as though he actually could bear witness to her flirtatious gesture.

His laughter filled her ear, thick and sensual, oddly raising an unbidden goose bump or two at the back of her neck. "That's what you can call me—Walker."

She squirmed in her seat before catching herself. Whoever he was, he had a masterful command she couldn't, or rather, refused to define. He was calling her for sex, for goodness' sake. What other definition was needed?

Control, Dixie. And sex. They had to get to the heart of this phone call's matter. She had to, or she'd turn tail and hang up. "Very Texas Ranger. So, *Walker*...do you fancy yourself a big, strong lawman?" She rolled her eyes at how ridiculously porn movie she sounded.

But Walker didn't seem to mind. "Do lawmen call phone-sex operators? I'd find that questionable."

Dixie giggled openly before she remembered she was supposed to be sexy, not eight. Clearing her throat, she prodded, "Only naughty lawmen, I suppose. Are you a naughty lawman?"

"Not today."

The line between them crackled with a hiss and a spit while he paused, and she searched for a sexy response to his very unsexy answer. Now she wasn't sure if he fell into the reluctant caller category or the just plain ornery.

She was, however, in the "need your bread buttered" category. "Then who are you today? You can be whomever you want to be with Mistress Taboo." No fantasy was going left untapped on the Good Ship Vanilla.

"Taboo, huh? Vanilla sex isn't very taboo, you know. It's a definite contradiction to the meaning."

He had a point. "Ohhh, Walker," she cooed. "I disagree. Vanilla sex can be just as hot as any sex with floggers, and chains, and all of that control. If you do it right, that is."

"Define right," he ordered, yet it wasn't a harsh demand. The underlying tone to his voice was gentle.

That meant they were getting somewhere, and it frightened her. Yet, she fought the impulse to put the brakes on like she would have back in the day when a suitor thought she was genuinely going to allow him to get somewhere she'd never intended to go. She would do this.

Once more, Dixie let the darkness of her office envelop her, imagining it was an intimate atmosphere rather than threatening. She hunkered down in her chair, cupping her chin in her hand. "Well, everyone has their own definition, I suppose. For me it has to do with giving yourself up completely to your partner. Sexually, I mean. It's getting lost in the sounds of your lovemaking. It's reveling in the taste of your partner's skin, knowing their hot buttons and exactly when to push them."

"And have you done that, Mistress Taboo? Have you given yourself up to someone that completely?"

Dixie didn't know what made her answer truthfully. Maybe it was her heart, raw and still bleeding after tonight. Maybe it was the anonymity of pretending to be someone she wasn't. Maybe it was desperation, but she sensed if she didn't at least reveal a little of herself to her callers, if she allowed her fear to seep into her words, she'd come across as a fake.

And "Walker" was the only call she had right now. Dixie swallowed hard before answering. "I have, Walker." She stopped short for a moment when her voice hitched and more tears threatened to fall. "Utterly and completely." The admission came out breathless and unexpected before she remembered this phone call was about him. "Have you?"

"Oh, I definitely have," he rumbled into her ear, soft, sincere. "Only once, but it's something I'll never forget. Not ever."

She sighed into the mouthpiece, forgetting he was a client, forgetting that she was supposed to be the one in control of their phone call.

There was the wet muffled sound of something or someone snorting before Walker cut her thoughts off. "I have to go for now, Mistress Taboo. But I'll call again. Count on it."

"Wait—" her protest was cut off by the sound of him hanging up.

The strangest mixture of giddy and disappointed settled in her chest. Dixie laid her head on her arm to bury her strong reaction to this stranger with no face. Walker's words, so intense and soulful, gripped her heart with their seemingly genuine honesty.

Ludicrous, of course. Who was honest in phone sex?

Walker was probably married with three children and had a wife who didn't understand him much in the way Clifton claimed Em didn't understand.

And his real name was decidedly not something straight from a romance novel.

It was with that thought her silly, romantic bubble burst. Dixie yawned, fiddling with the mouse to bring her computer screen back to life in order to check the time. She hadn't been up past midnight in ages, and it was already pushing one o'clock and the end of her shift.

As silly as it was to consider Walker was anything other than a middle-aged husband, bored with his lot in life, the amount of time she'd logged in with him on the phone wasn't so silly.

Forty minutes times four ninety-nine a minute wasn't anything to sneeze at. It wasn't like a LaDawn payday, but it was better than the nothing she'd collected the first half of the night.

Removing her earpiece, Dixie put her hand to her forehead and saluted her minutes logged. "Thank you kindly, Walker of the sexy voice and romance novel name. You've brought me a small step closer to digging myself out of debt."

Ten

Dixie woke with flushed cheeks and a groan of frustration. She'd been dreaming about Caine. His hands on her, his words in her ear, his hard length pressing her into the bed. Scrunching her eyes shut, she gave them a good rub to rid herself of Caine Donovan.

Whether Em believed it or not, the idea that he'd slept with Louella Palmer had been planted, and her self-esteem was taking an enormous hit dreaming about him even after such an ugly revelation.

Her cell blared, startling her from the bed. She reached blindly, skimming the surface of the nightstand for her phone. She sighed when she saw the caller.

Her mother. Yay.

She swallowed the dread from her dry throat. "Hi, Mama. How are you feeling? How's Palm Springs?"

"Dixie Davis, am I hearin' things right through the grapevine? Haven't you disgraced our good name enough?"

There was always room for improvement.

Dixie pushed the covers off and slid to the edge of the bed, pulling Mona to her side. It didn't shock her that her mother didn't ask how she was, or that she wasn't concerned about how Dixie was feeling. She'd learned long ago that her mother was concerned with two things—the Davis name and her money.

"So you heard what Landon's done?"

"Of course I heard what that crazier 'n a bedbug fool's done. What I don't understand is why you're playing his crazy game. How could you, Dixie?"

"Do you mean how could I even consider talking dirty on the phone so I can pay back all those friends of yours who invested in me so you can still attend their social events without the embarrassment of your daughter's mistakes hangin' over your head?"

The moment she spoke the words, she regretted them. This wasn't the Dixie she wanted to be. Accept what you can't change. Love without strings attached. No more grudges. Over and over she'd repeated those words in her head. Words spoken by someone whose memory she cherished.

Her mother was never going to love her without conditions attached. It wasn't in her DNA. Pearl didn't nurture, she demanded. She connived. She orchestrated everyone and everything. Acting out wouldn't change that—ever. "I'm sorry, Mama. That was wrong of me to say. Yes. I'm talking dirty on the phone in the hope I'll win Landon's company. I'm sorry if it embarrasses you with the other Mags."

Pearl's outraged sigh crackled over the connection. "You'll make a fool of yourself and the good Davis name!"

"Better a fool than a pauper, right?" she joked, knowing it was futile.

"You don't have to be a pauper, Dixie. The Donovan money is still good."

No. Never again would she let her mother encourage her to find the easiest way out. In Pearl's superficial world, all Dixie had to do was find another way to lure Caine back in and everything would be right as rain. "No, Mama. I'll do this on my own or not at all. I think you'd better get used to the idea that the Donovan-Davis merger is off."

So off it hurt.

"It didn't have to be, Dixie. You were careless."

Disapproval—Pearl's specialty. Even though she was always prepared for it, it never stung any less.

Dixie kneaded Mona's soft fur. If only her mother meant she'd been careless with someone's feelings rather than just carelessly getting caught. "It was a long time ago, and it's over now. It's always going to be over. Now, I have to go because I have a date with Emmaline and her boys."

"Emmaline Amos? Why, in all of heaven, would you have a date with her?"

Because she's the only person who'll associate with me? But something in her mother's tone struck her as odd. Why would her mother care if her date was with Emmaline?

"She's not in the same class of people as you, Dixie. You'll do well to remember where you come from."

Long live the ultimate snob. "If you mean the class of people who are honest, genuine, and kind, you're right. I'm not in the same class. Now, I have to go. I hope you feel better every day and that Palm Springs is treatin' you good. Bye, Mama."

Dixie clicked her phone off before her mother could

protest. She wouldn't hear a single bad word about Em or another word about how she'd messed up the marriage merger of the millennium.

Dixie's blurry eyes reread the newest cryptic text message from Landon and clenched her hands into fists of sheer frustration. Don't believe everything you hear, Dixie-Doodle...

Whatever that meant.

She wondered for the hundredth time since this had all begun, what Landon had set out to accomplish by sending her text messages.

It was as if he'd known how their battle for his company would play out, and he was enjoying the role of incorporeal commentator. Despite wanting to kill him all over again for poking her at her lowest, mostly, it soothed her to see his name pop up on her phone.

The ringing of the bell over the door at Madge's brought with it Em and her two boys, instantly quelling her lust for Landon's blood. Em and her sons, Clifton Junior, and Gareth strolled in with Em's mother.

Clifton Junior, his lips a thin line, the slump of his shoulders screaming disinterested, stood beside Gareth, who beamed a smile at her, his front tooth missing. He poked his head out from behind Em's hip. "Hi, Miss Dixie."

Dixie grinned at him and crooked her finger. Em's children warmed her all over—even sullen Clifton Junior, struggling so with his father's absence. "Well, if it isn't Gareth Amos. Your mama's shown me all your pictures. It's nice to finally meet you in the flesh. What brings you to Madge's on this fine day? Shouldn't you be off at your big, important job so you can pay for your big, important apartment? How will you keep the lights on if you're here eatin' donuts?"

Gareth giggled, scratching his dark head. "I don't haf a job. I'm only five," he lisped a protest that turned to a squeal of joy when she handed him a jelly-filled donut.

Dixie looked at Clifton Junior. "Boy, five years old, and your brother still doesn't have a job? How will I ever collect social security if you don't have a job? I suppose next you'll tell me, at eight years old, you don't have one either, mister?"

When Clifton stoically refused to join in on her joke, Em nudged him, passing him a stern look. "Miss Dixie spoke to you. Surely, you have an answer?"

But Dixie held up a hand with another chocolate donut—Clifton's favorite. "No answer necessary. I like my unemployed men strong and silent. Both of which Clifton Junior is."

Like the tiniest bit of hope still existed, Clifton smirked, taking the donut.

Dixie smiled at Clora. "Clora, good to see you again."

Clora's chin, square and tight, lifted along with her eyebrow. "So you've come back."

Dixie bit the inside of her cheek. Clora had never liked her. She probably liked her less now that she was so closely tied to Em. Her disapproval was evident. "Like the dead risin'," she joked.

"Or trouble stirrin.'"

"Mama! I warned you." Em hissed over Gareth's shoulder. "Please be gracious."

Dixie flapped a hand. "It's all right, Em. You go right on and disapprove, Clora. I'd disapprove if my daughter was mixed up with Dixie Davis, too."

Em clapped her hands together, effectively quieting

a response from Clora. "Say thank you to Miss Dixie, then off you go with Grandma. Mama's got work to tend to." She gathered each boy up in a warm hug, one Clifton remained stiff in, and thanked her mother for taking them for the afternoon before ushering them off.

"I'm sorry, Dixie. You know what my mother's like."

Dixie smiled. She did know what Em's mother was like. She'd grown up under the same kind of control and endless unattainable perfection Em had. "Just like mine. You know, I was thinkin' about that last night after what you said to Marybell."

"You mean about how pathetically insecure I was."

"And I was out of control. Isn't it funny that our mothers raised us with the same iron hand of disapproval, but we each reacted so differently? I just could never win with my mother." And clearly, after today's phone call, still couldn't.

Em scoffed. "Right, except you had a daddy and piles o' money. I had no father and I wore clothes my mother hand sewed. But I think I can almost understand why you were so mean. I tried harder to please everyone, you spit pleasin' everyone in the eye."

Dixie nodded. "It's funny what shapes us—motivates us." Made you act out at every possible turn.

"How about we forget our controlling mothers and talk about you and Caine?" Em teased, sliding into the booth and latching onto the coffee Dixie had waiting for her. She peeked over the top of her oversize coffee cup and grinned.

"There is no me and Caine, Emmaline." She buried her nose in the vinyl red-checkered menu—one whose items hadn't changed much for as far back as she could remember.

"Oh, Dixie, who do you think you're kiddin' here, petunia? You still love Caine Donovan."

She flicked Em's menu, the delicious fried scents of home mingling with strong coffee called to her. "Focus. I invited you to breakfast—not a therapy session."

All she'd thought of since waking from that dream was how much she wanted to run right back to Caine, burrow her face in the hollow of his neck, beg him to let her back into his life. To recapture those perfect moments before she'd ruined everything or even before she'd found out he'd slept with Louella.

Being in Chicago had dulled those emotions—muted the sharp edges of them. Being back in Plum Orchard had continually plucked them.

Em tapped the table. "Have I apologized enough for what I blurted out last night, Dixie?"

"You have."

Dixie grimaced, the pain still as sharp as it had been the night before.

Em reached across the table and squeezed her hand, remorse still lining her creamy skin. "I was just sick over it last night. I'm sorry again and again, S.S. And I still don't think I even believe a word that comes out of that woman's mouth."

Dixie smiled at her nickname and blew a strand of messy hair out of her eyes. "Forget it. Let's forget everything but a big plate of greasy bacon while you tell me how things went with you and Clifton last night. How did the meeting go?"

Em plunked her coffee mug on the white Formica table and sat back in the red cushioned booth, fading and cracked. "You want to talk about me?"

Dixie's frown portrayed her confusion. "Of course

I do," she said gently. "I was worried about you in the
state you were in last night. Seeing Clifton couldn't
have been easy."

Em's surprise filled her gaze. "I can't remember the
last time anyone wanted to talk about me or even to me
unless it was my mama and the boys. But to have you
want to talk about me? It's like baby Jesus just dropped
by for a playdate."

"Then tell me all about it, or I'll be forced to make
you break out the lighted manger you put in your yard
every Christmas."

Her joke fell flat. Rather than laughing, Em's blue
eyes skirted hers. Shame cast them downward to her
lap. Dixie's heart clenched into a tight ball seeing her
struggle with her emotions.

As people scuttled around them, Madge's finest and
oldest waitress, Tammy, moving furtively from table to
table across the yellowing floor on orthopedic shoes,
Dixie sat silent.

When Em lifted her head, her eyes were swollen with
unshed tears. "Can you believe he brought that woman
with him to mediation, Dixie? Worse still? She's absolutely gorgeous. Forgive my horrible thoughts, but I
wanted to pull her hair and knock her long legs right
out from underneath her."

"But why? You're gorgeous, too."

Reaching into her mint-green purse to pull out a
tissue, she shook her head. "I'm not. I'm a used-up ol'
housewife who's been tossed out like week-old biscuits."

It struck Dixie like thunder right then and there—
she knew that look. She'd seen it a hundred times on
Em's face in high school. She'd had a hand in Em's low
self-esteem—her and the Mags. A big one.

Twenty years later, and the damage was part of who Em had become. And she had to make it right. Change it, fix it, *own* it.

Dixie shook her head in denial. "Please don't say things like that about yourself, Em. None of them are true. I don't care what anyone's said—what *I* said, you're beautiful, and funny, and smart. And you're a housewife who still has plenty of life left for livin'! The next night I have off—or any loose change I find in Landon's couch—whichever comes first—I'm going to treat you to a girls' night out just to prove as much to you. You'll see. The men'll line up."

Em was about to protest again when the tarnished copper bell on Madge's door rang out a new entry.

Or several of them. Louella and the rest of the Mags wandered in on a cloud of sweetly scented perfume and a colorful array of modestly heeled pumps.

As they swished past her and Em's booth, Dixie was dismayed to see Em sink deeper into the seat, obviously hoping to fly low under their radar.

Dixie knew better. There was no flying low or otherwise. If the Mags had their sights set on you, secret-government-agency-issued invisibility packs couldn't keep you hidden.

Unlike Em, she sat straighter, setting her menu aside and waiting until the group of her former henchwomen made eye contact. "Sit up, Emmaline Amos," she scolded. "Always look your enemy in the eye. It's one of the first mean-girl rules ever written."

"If you'll recall, I wasn't privy to the rule book."

"I wrote it."

"Then to thine own self be true. As for me, I'm just

gonna make myself as small as possible and hope they find a moth to pull the wings off of in my stead."

"Dixie Davis—look who's come home to roost!"

Em groaned out her misery from across the table, reopening her menu and setting it in front of her to hide behind.

Dixie plucked it up and away from Em's face, whispering, "Watch and learn, grasshopper."

Sliding out of the booth, she pivoted on her chunky wedges, likely considered much too high for this time of day by the Mags, and smiled at Annabelle Pruitt and Lesta-Sue Arnold as they weaved through the assorted white tables. "Annabelle, Lesta-Sue! So good to see you both. I see life's been treating the two of you well. You both look fresh and vibrant."

Annabelle, petite in her knee-length white skirt and blue-and-white polka-dotted silk shirt, let a polite smile tease her frosted lips. Her rounded chin grazed the large bow of her blouse. "I see your Southern charm's all but escaped you, and your appearance, too, Dixie. Where'd your good fashion sense and accent get to? Too much Chicago in you to ever come back to your roots?"

Dixie's denim miniskirt, clingy red top, and denim shrug vest was as close to her native land of Plum Orchard as she'd come in a long time. She gave them both air kisses before inviting them to slide into the booth beside her and Em. They naturally declined with polite protests. They weren't here to sit. They were here to stir the pot.

So Dixie decided to give them the spoon. "So what have you girls been up to since I left? Lesta-Sue, you married now?"

Dixie knew she was married. Married to the man

she'd once stolen right out from under Lesta-Sue's nose, a shameful act she'd be willing to redeem herself for, if only they were willing to let her. But that wasn't what this visit was about.

Lesta-Sue's pinched face and thin upper lip wrinkled. "You know I married Grover. I sent you an invitation to our wedding. I know it was after the 'incident,'" she whispered, hazel eyes wide and full of innocence, "but we hoped you'd come back sooner than this."

"Ten years is a long time to stay away." Annabelle, no longer blond but chestnut-haired, twisted her thick, side-swept braid between her fingers.

And it was game on. This was called the bait and bait. Wherein, they baited Dixie then baited her some more until she became so frustrated she exposed herself and did the Mags' dirty work for them without them ever having to lift a dainty finger.

Her cool reply said the ball was in their court. "There were other pressing matters keeping me in Chi-Town."

Annabelle's smile grew glib. "And we heard there are newer, more pressing matters keepin' you here."

A quick glance around Madge's told Dixie no small children were present. She tapped Annabelle on the arm playfully. "Oh, stop implyin', Annabelle. Let's all just be adults here and say it. In fact, why don't we all say it together? Just to get it out of the way. Ready?" She smiled at them as though they were two toddlers she was teaching a new word. *"Phone sex."* She let her voice rise an octave, enough to catch everyone's attention. "I'm engagin', in Miss Nanette's words, 'in the devil's acts,' over the phone, no less. I bet you're not surprised at this unexpected turn in my life, are you, girls?"

Heads turned in the group's direction as Annabelle's

cheeks went pink and Lesta-Sue took an uncomfortable step backward, righting the wobble of her sensible turquoise pumps.

"So, let's discuss, shall we? Then we can get all the awkward moments right out of the way. You know the moment I mean, too. It's the moment where you set out to humiliate me publicly for being such a sad sack of a human being all those years ago. How would y'all like to do that? Maybe over some pie? My treat," she cajoled.

Lesta-Sue cracked first, her manicured hands balling into fists at her side. Her sidelong gaze in Louella's direction bellowed *help*.

Louella must have flashed her the go sign. Her words were meant to push Dixie's buttons. "I can't believe your lack of shame, Dixie! Your daddy'd do a back flip in his grave if he knew what you were up to."

Dixie fought the urge to lunge at her by brightening her smile. The Mags knew any mention of her deceased father was a sore subject. She'd been a daddy's girl through and through, and she'd missed him terribly since he'd died unexpectedly of a heart attack during her first year of college. "I'd like to think Landon met Daddy at the Pearly Gates and told him in person. About the *phone sex,* I mean."

And as if on cue, Annabelle cracked next, embarrassed by the rise in Dixie's voice. Her stiff words came out in a stream under her breath. "You're just as disgraceful as you always were, Dixie. You should have never come back to Plum Orchard. No one wants you here."

"As well they shouldn't," she agreed, totally compliant, completely cool—on the outside. "I'm a bad person, Annabelle, and even as I apologize to you both for the million and one things I did to you in high school, like stealin' Lesta-Sue's boyfriend, Grover, and treating you like my lackey, I'm still not going to let that stop me from doing what needs to be done. When has someone's disapproval ever stopped me?"

With yet another attempt to cast public stones at her out of the way, Dixie waited. Come hell or high water, it was surely coming.

As Dixie suspected, the women turned their venomous attention to Em, still hunched in the booth, her face a mask of despair.

Lesta-Sue launched the first grenade. "And you, *Emmaline?* How could you consort with the likes of Dixie and her phone-sexin' when you have two young boys to think of? It would serve you right if those poor children were taken from you and given to Clifton to raise. It's repulsive!"

There was an unsettling stir in the crowd, heads turned with a rustle of discomfort, and all eyes fell on Em. Silence prevailed but for the jukebox playing an old Hank Williams tune in the background.

Dixie felt Em die a little. Felt it like she'd feel her own heart stop dead.

And that was all Dixie could stand. She'd fought her sharp tongue and scheming long and hard over these past couple of years.

She'd made as many amends along the way as she could, but dragging the only victim the Mags could find into this, one who'd never dream of hurting a soul just to make a public spectacle out of her, wouldn't stand.

Like the lighting of a sparkler, Dixie's infamous temper flared, dipping and rising to a new height before zeroing in on her targets in homing pigeon fashion.

The red haze of her anger sizzled, almost blurring her vision. "Speaking of the word *consort,* Lesta-Sue, a word you're very familiar with, before you cast disparaging, not to mention judgmental, stones at Emmaline—" Dixie addressed the crowd trying their best not to gawk with open mouths "—would you like to share with everyone in this fine establishment what you did the summer just before our senior year?"

Lesta-Sue sucked in a hitched gasp of air, her eyes sending warning signals at Dixie. "You wouldn't dare...."

Dixie's smile was cunning when she crossed her arms over her chest. She leaned into Lesta-Sue, her eyes full of mischief and menace. "Aw, you know better than that, Lesta-Sue. I would dare. Em's just doing her job, and y'all know it. So if, in fact, you so much as whisper a hurtful word about Em or her boys in the same breath as something so wicked ever again, I'll make it my mission to share the consorting. *The video* of it."

Em's hand snapped out, reaching for Dixie's arm, her fingers bit into her flesh with a trembling grip. Her face was paler than normal, her voice shaky. *"Please."*

With Em's plea, the angry haze filming her vision cleared almost as swiftly as it had arrived. "Pass that along at the next Mag meeting, would you, Annabelle? Just in case Louella missed it from all the way over there." Dixie pointed directly at Louella, then gave Em a quick tug upward, grabbing her purse and hooking it over her shoulder. She ushered her out, head held high until they stood just beyond the front window of Madge's.

The sweltering heat of early September clung to Dixie's already hot face in a wave of cloying slashes. On fast legs, Dixie moved down the sidewalk, ignoring the questioning gazes of Plum Orchard. Familiar faces all wondering, *What has she done now?*

Em ran behind her and thrust a hand to her shoulder, curling her fingers into it. "Dixie, hold your horses!" Flinging her around, Em's eyes searched hers.

Dixie threw her hands up in disbelief, furious with herself. "I just blew my stack as sure as Johnson Ridley blows up at least one box of fireworks by mistake every Fourth of July. It's wrong, Em."

That manner of retaliation should have been below her. For many years, her impulse to strike had been quelled by what she'd learned from one of the most painful experiences of her life.

But it had just all gone to hell, and Dixie didn't like the way it made her feel. Low-down dirty and out of control.

"I'm sorry I embarrassed you. I know you hate when the attention turns to you, but I just couldn't stand it."

"Girl, I realized you were just practicin' what you preach. It was pure genius the way you turned the tables on them. Hide out in the open, right? Expose yourself before they can expose you?"

Yes. That had been the exact strategy—to expose herself, not Lesta-Sue. Tears of frustration began to well in her eyes.

"I learn something new and useful from you every day, S.S."

She stiffened, swiping a thumb under her eye. "It's not something I want to teach."

Em gave her a shake. "You said you'd only use your evil for good, right? And you did."

"How is threatening to expose Lesta-Sue using

my evil for good, Emmaline? It's what the old Dixie would've done, and it was wrong and selfish. What I wanted to do was win and win *big*." She spat the word as though it were covered in filth. "I wanted to grind her into the ground in just the same way they wanted to humiliate and knock you down a peg."

That particular competitive gene was the bane of her existence. Her hot temper was a close second; it made her reckless and foolish.

Em smoothed her hands over Dixie's bare arms in a soothing fashion. "No, Dixie, don't you see? You said those things to protect the boys and me so the Mags wouldn't dig around about my troubles in front of a whole restaurant full of busybodies. Only good people do that, and I won't hear nothin' to the contrary. Good people speak up for people who're too afraid, or in my case, too pathetic to speak out for themselves. You saved me from those perfectly dressed, pink-and-blonde bullies. I, fair maiden Dixie, dub thee a hero."

Dixie gave her head a shake, her lips a hard line. "I'm no hero, Em! Don't you confuse the two. I feel like I stepped right back into my pink stiletto shit-kickers like I never took them off. The real problem with that is they felt sooo, so good."

"Well, you did wear them for a long time," Em conceded.

Dixie shook Emmaline off with brisk impatience, moving away from her to sit on the bench in front of Brugsby's Drugstore under the shade of the dark green and gold overhang.

The cheerful topiary beside her, one that had been there since she was a teen, was a painful reminder of all the times she'd sat on this very bench and plotted.

She let her head fall back on the peeling bench, huffing a tired sigh. "Plum Orchard was no place to come back to test my mean-girl overhaul, Em. It was easier in Chicago. I had less history to battle. Too many things have passed in ten years, and that's not including what's passed in just the last two days. I don't want to be that person anymore. I *won't* be that person anymore."

Em shoved her over, sitting alongside her. Crossing her feet at her ankles, she said, "Sure nuff, Chicago was easier. It's a big place full of more strangers than folk you know personally. You can't get by with that here. A test isn't really a test if it isn't hard, Dixie."

Yet another reason she never should have agreed to this phone-sex-off.

"And here's somethin' else to chew on, Dixie. I'm beginning to think you're not that person anymore already. Color me as shocked as anyone, but I'm this far from callin' you a new leaf. Really, Dixie, when was the last time you took up for someone weaker 'n you? There was no advantage to you in lookin' out for me and the boys."

Dixie gave her a weak, heat-deflated smile and coyly batted her eyes. "Does this mean you trust me now, Em?"

Her snort ripped through the humid air, full of laughing sarcasm. "Oh, no it does not, miss. One kind act does not eradicate all your sins. But it's a foot in the right direction, Dixie. Yes, ma'am, it is." Em gave her a playful nudge to her shoulder before patting hers and inviting Dixie to rest her head on it.

Dixie did so with a mournful sigh and a million emotions warring with her heart. Surprisingly, the least of which was malicious joy at besting the Mags. What troubled her was how little time it had taken before she'd exhibited signs of her former path of destruction.

Em plucked at Dixie's denim shrug. "So, want to tell me about this mysterious video of Lesta-Sue?"

"No, I do not."

"You don't play fair. How could you bring up something so delicious and not share?"

"Because the former me would do exactly that. I forgot myself there for a minute, and every resolution I've made, every truly good thing I've tried to do since I made all those promises to myself went right out the window. I will not allow the Mags to try and convict the people who've chosen to give me another chance just to get to me."

"Is that what this is with me, Dixie? Another chance?"

She hadn't thought of it like that when she'd come home. She'd only given thought to getting in and out with the stealth of an F-16. But she liked Em. She enjoyed her company, and the more Dixie liked her, the more she wanted Em to forgive her and accept her friendship.

"I suppose it is. You have something to say about it?"

Em leaned her head against Dixie's. "Not a word, Dixie. Not a word."

They sat like that for a time, Dixie pondering how she was going to keep Em from the Mags' angry wrath and anticipate their next move. She thought about how she was going to keep herself afloat and pay her debts off if she lost this phone-sex challenge.

She thought about Caine and all the painful longing he dredged up.

Mostly, she thought about how nice it was to simply

sit with Emmaline on a bench across from the white-washed gazebo nestled in the neatly manicured square, smelling the scents of summer nearing its end, and watching Plum Orchard go about its day.

Eleven

"This is Mistress Taboo. Are you worthy?" Dixie's voice bled through the walls to Caine's office, so husky and sultry it was ruffling his already ruffled feathers.

He threw his pen down, leaning back in his chair. His desk was cluttered with a collage of sticky notes he'd made an array of designs with in order to keep his mind off Dixie.

Erasing Dixie's memory was more difficult than he'd anticipated. Especially when he thought back to her trapped in that closet, clinging to him as though he were the last life raft on a sinking ship. Hearing her heartbeat against his ear, feeling her slinky thighs wrapped around his hips—all things distinctly Dixie.

When it came to Dixie, he was helpless—hopeless. All she had to do was give him that wide-eyed look of anguish when he taunted her unmercifully for all her scheming and lying, and he was lost. It seemed the only way to curb his insatiable need to make her pay with his cruel words was to haul her body to his and make insane love to her.

Losing her once had hurt like hell. Losing her twice

wasn't going to happen. He'd dug in his heels this time. There'd be no convincing him she was changed. There'd be no convincing him she'd dug her conscience up somewhere in the landfill of her devastation.

Huh, pal. I don't remember Dixie trying to convince you of anything. She just showed up, somehow very different than the Dixie you once knew.

Landon in his head. Again.

What made this doubly hard was the encounter he'd witnessed between her and the Mags today. He'd never, in the entire time he'd known her, seen her take up for anyone unless it meant the means to her endgame.

Yet today at Madge's, she'd gone at Annabelle and Lesta-Sue as if Em was hers to protect. That side of Dixie, fierce and so primal, had chipped away at the ice forming around the part of his heart that had once belonged to her.

He'd watched that go down from behind a potted plant and a plate of eggs, shocked as hell. Stealing glances at her defiant eyes and defensive gestures almost made him like her.

Like her?

Where the hell had that come from? He didn't want to like her. Loving her was hard enough. To like who Dixie wanted everyone to believe she'd become would be to forget it hadn't just been her life, her future that was smashed to a million pieces by the end of their engagement.

He'd fallen hard for her back then, heedless to the warnings of everyone around him, heedless to his own internal warnings. He'd just fallen. Leaving Plum Orchard without Dixie as his wife had been like a knife to the gut.

To forgive her? He'd never given it much thought. Leaving her unforgiven was what fueled his macho fire. It was all he had, and he'd be tarred and feathered before he wasn't on the ground blowin' on the flames that kept that fire burning.

Emmaline poked her head around the corner of his office space and waved at him, halting his dark thoughts. "It's my job as mediator to pay you drive-by surprise inspections of your work. So, you stickin' to the rules, Mr. Smexy?"

Caine grinned at her, stretching his cramped arms. "You bet. Did you expect anything less?"

She grinned, smoothing her dark hair with a pale hand. "From Plum Orchard's golden boy?"

There was that damn moniker again. How had he missed that catch phrase in reference to him all these years? "The one and only."

Her glance was one of reproach. "Well, if I was mediatin' anything else, I'd expect nothing but good form from you. But, we are talking about you and Dixie. That'd give Jesus himself pause."

The mention of Dixie's name made Caine tentatively inquire, "You okay?"

For a fleeting moment, concern crossed her face, marring her creamy ivory beauty. The wary look in her eyes shifted, and she let her face relax into one with no expression. "Of course I am. Why would you ask such a thing?"

He shrugged indifferently, as though the gossip around town after Dixie and the Mags' little confrontation wasn't the talk of every dinner table. Em was hiding something, something she was desperately afraid of.

Which made Dixie's defense of her even more significant. Whatever Em was afraid of was hers alone. He wouldn't add to her anxiety by saying anything more, but the Mags' anger just because Em had chosen to dine with Dixie, couldn't be the crux of what troubled her.

Still, Caine kept his reply light, his fingers busy making a colorful Christmas tree from the sticky-note pad. "Just checking."

Emmaline's posture deflated. "You heard."

Caught. "Who hasn't?" he replied honestly.

"Then did you hear about Dixie, too?"

The intensity in her question rang like a church bell, making him look back up. Em's loyalty to Dixie stunned him. Of all the people she'd dragged through the mud, Em had been her most utilized target.

"Well, did you?" she pressed, her grip on the door handle white-knuckled.

He was a crappy at playing innocent, but he gave it a go anyway. "Hear about Dixie?"

"Yes, about our Dixie! She took on the Mags on my behalf like some kind of avenger."

Emmaline's inquisitive eyes waited for his reaction to such a strong statement.

"And what did it get her? Bragging rights? See Dixie take out a Mag at a hundred paces? As if she hasn't done that a hundred times before, Em? It's just the first step toward regaining her rightful place on her tarnished throne."

Em slipped inside the room, closing the door as she did, coming to stand at the edge of his desk. She lowered her voice, tapping a painted fingernail on the wood to demand his attention. "Don't you be so callous, Caine Donovan. I won't hear you talk about her that way. She was like some kind of warrior today—for me—*and* the boys. Just you remember that when you go judgin' her by using her past as your weapon."

Caine threw up his hands and slid the chair away from his desk. "Not another word, because I'm afraid of you," he teased in his best Geico Gecko impersonation.

Left unmoved by his attempt at humor, Em warned, "Just a reminder that some things can change. Dixie being one of those things."

"If you say so, Em." Not happening. He wasn't ready to concede out loud he, too, had been impressed by Dixie today, because there had to be a catch. Somewhere. There'd be no more making him look like an ass if he had anything to say about it.

Finally she smiled, her limbs relaxing. "I do say so. Now get to work, Mr. Smexy. You have sex to make."

"Hey, Em? Before you go… First, did I ever thank you for keeping such close tabs on me during Landon's last…" Damn, it was still hard to say.

"His last shining moments here on earth?" she finished for him, her smile a mixture of fond and sad.

He'd only just left Johnsonville, where Landon's hospice care was located, when Em had called to let him know the doctors said Landon had taken a turn for the worse.

Caine nodded, his chest tight. "Yeah. That was hell. Everything just kept falling apart. My plane was delayed, damn rental broke down."

"You know something? If I didn't know better, I'd almost think Landon planned that, too. He often said he didn't want anyone seein' him in his last moments. But if it makes any difference, he knew right up until the end how much y'all loved him."

Caine blew out a breath of more regret. "From the

other end of a damn cell phone." The phone Em herself had held to Landon's ear.

"But you were still with him until the last second he was with us, Caine. He smiled when he heard your voice. He might not have been able to answer you because of all the pain medication, but he knew. I *know* he knew." She said it with enough conviction that he had to believe or let the guilt eat him alive.

"In all this, I never asked. Tell me he got to talk to Dixie, too." No matter what was between him and Dixie, she loved Landon.

Em smiled again, but this time it was beaming. "She absolutely did. She was havin' her own troubles gettin' to him, too. Which is why I'm convinced Landon somehow orchestrated his own death just like everythin' else."

That made Caine laugh. Yeah. That was Landon. He nodded his head. "Good, and listen, I know things have been rough for you and the boys lately, but if you need help with anything, around the house—maybe take the boys for a burger on my day off to get them out of your hair, whatever it is, you let me know." His mother had raised him alone after his father died when he was thirteen. No one knew better than he did how hard that could be.

Em's big blue eyes grew watery. She crossed the room and hugged him hard around his neck. "Thank you," she whispered, patting his cheek before heading out the door. "Now back to work, Donovan!"

"Aye-aye, Captain!" he repeated Scotty's infamous *Star Trek* line to the sight of her whisking out the door in a flurry of blue material and the scent of gladiolas.

Caine cracked his knuckles and rolled his shoulders,

uncomfortable with this new Dixie emotion that was neither lust nor love.

Like.

Hah.

For just a minute, you liked Dixie, buddy. Don't deny—testify!

More Landon.

"The hell," he muttered back under his breath, flipping on his earpiece.

The hell.

"This is Mistress Taboo—are you worthy?" Dixie injected as much sexy into her greeting as was possible at midnight. Curling her legs under her, she settled in to answer her third call of the night with a mixture of nerves and the almost debilitating fear of the unknown.

Her first call had been a complete bust, and the second caller hadn't made it past the first couple of minutes. Day two's numbers so far weren't going down in the phone-sex history books.

"Hi," the distinctly male voice forced the word out.

There was the sound of a loud buzzer in the background, resembling one you'd hear at a sporting event, the tinny drone of some sports announcer's voice, then nothing but the inhalation of air.

A breather. Dixie instantly recognized the profile described in the Call Girls manual. Shy, unsure, embarrassed.

They'd make a perfect couple.

"I'm new to this," he finally said.

Honesty seemed the best policy. They could be cohorts in newness together. She flexed her icy fingers and rolled her shoulders, willing herself to relax. "You know what? Me, too. So we'll be new at this together. Deal?" She kept her voice light, easing off the sex-kitten tone to it. She couldn't afford to scare off a possible long-term relationship with someone simply because she came on too strong. Slow and subtle won the race.

"You're new, too?"

"I am."

A sharp scrape against the phone was followed by an exasperated huff of more words. "Jesus. I can't believe I'm doing this. This was a stupid idea."

Stupid idea meet stupid idea, Dixie mused, clearing her throat. "Calling me, you mean?"

"Calling anyone for sex. I don't know what the hell I was thinking. I just don't do this sort of thing. I've never done this sort of thing. I'm sure you'll hear that a lot, newbie."

Dixie smiled at the teasing quality to his tone while she drew imaginary circles on her desktop with her finger. "Well, I don't know what I was thinking when I thought I could sell sex over the phone either. But here we are. Wanna try and make the best of it? The first two minutes *are* only two bucks."

He laughed with a notable release of tension. It was a pleasant laugh, too, deep and full. "I'm…" he faltered then righted himself, "Dan. In case you were wondering what to call me."

Dixie smiled to herself. Ice broken. "A pleasure. So what do you do for a living, Dan?"

"I'm an accountant."

"Ah, so you're good with numbers. I'm not very good with numbers." Unless they had to do with racking up a mountain of haters. Then she was a superstar.

Dan cleared his throat and coughed. "Good with

numbers, not so much with the ladies, if you know what I mean."

She shook her head in disagreement as if he were in the room with her. "I don't believe that, Dan. You have a good, strong voice. It's clear and downright pleasing to the ear. At least, it is to my ear. You're articulate and pleasant. So tell me, how can any truly smart woman resist that?"

He made a noise faintly resembling a snort. "Because I'm a complete idiot face-to-face. I stumble over my words. I never know what to say. I'm much better at formulas and fractions and summing up expense accounts than I'll ever be at pretending I'm some kind of Prince Charming."

How ironic to find Dan was better on the phone than he was in person, and she was better in person, where her body language and coquettish smiles did all the work for her.

"Who says all women want a Prince Charming anyway? He's overrated, if you ask this girl. Wasn't he the one who didn't even recognize Cinderella when she wasn't wearing her ball gown? I want real. I want genuine. I want someone who'll hold my hair out of my face when I'm throwing up." Throwing up? Dixie cringed, cupping her hand under her chin to keep from bringing her head to the desk.

Vomit. Ugh.

"Well, that was very real. I think I like you, Mistress Taboo."

Dixie's cheeks flushed hot. "Really unsexy was what that was."

Dan chuckled. "Maybe so, but it kind of brought things into perspective."

"The kind of perspective that has you hanging up and never calling Mistress Taboo again?" She put as much pout into her voice as she could, but it rang false even to her ears.

"No," he blustered then cleared his throat. "Not at all. But I figure if someone like you can get a job selling sex over the phone, you know, with the vomit talk, maybe there's hope for me."

Dixie didn't even bother to hide her laughter. "Exactly my point. How hard is it to inquire about the well-being of a woman who's caught your eye instead of wowing her with your high-falutin' prose?"

Dan's next words told her he had his doubts. "You make it sound so easy, but we both know it's not that easy."

"It can be, if you let it."

"Every time I see her, I just clam up."

Her. "Freudian slip?" she teased gently, hoping to find insight into the real reason he'd called. Dan was lonely and needed a friend who wouldn't lend him the sort of ear a man was likely to get over a six-pack in a Neanderthal's man cave.

His gruff sigh confirmed her suspicions. "Okay. There's this woman...."

"You don't have to give me her name, of course," Dixie rushed to assure him.

"Her name's JoAnne. She works in HR. I've been watching her for a long time, and I don't mean in the creepy stalker sense, so don't freak out. I don't want to hack her up and put her in a wood chipper."

"My relief, can you hear it?" Dixie joked.

"I just mean I've appreciated the view for what seems like forever."

Dixie's smile was full of dreamy envy for JoAnne, having someone so smitten with her. "And she's got you all kinds of tongue-tied, huh?"

Dan's laugh was sharp. "In ways you can't begin to imagine. She's pretty, and smart, and outgoing. She's everything I'm not."

"Oh, don't be silly, Dan. I bet you're very pretty."

His laughter filled her ear, and now it was warm and full. "I meant outgoing, though I'm sure no one would call me pretty. I'm not good with a lot of people in one room, but JoAnne always has people around her. People are drawn to her like a moth to a flame. She's amazing, and I'm dull and boring. We're...we're just very different."

His genuine admiration for JoAnne rang in Dan's voice, almost making her sigh wistfully. To have someone feel that much pride in someone they hadn't even had one date with was the epitome of romantic. It was the Cyrano de Bergerac of romances.

Dan didn't want to talk dirty with Mistress Taboo. He wanted someone to listen to him. Someone to offer him a sympathetic ear.

Leading her to wonder out loud, "But sometimes, don't you think it's those differences that make a whole package in a couple? As long as you can learn to appreciate those qualities you lack rather than resent them, of course."

"Don't get your meaning."

"I mean, maybe JoAnne can teach you to navigate a roomful of people, and you can teach her to listen in the silence? You can sit back and revel in her people skills, and she can learn that communication doesn't always have to involve the spoken word. Sometimes communicating a feeling is just in the way you hold a woman, or offer to rub that sore spot between her shoulders to ease the ache of her workday. You don't have to be Cyrano and look like Brad Pitt, who's highly overrated, if you ask me, to convey your feelings."

"Hah!" he barked. "There's no fear of that. Promise." His reply, rife with insecurity, made her wince.

The wheels of Dixie's sentimental heart began to turn. "Oh, hold that thought! I have an idea, Dan. Have you paid attention to where she eats lunch? Maybe what she likes to drink?"

"Coffee. She's always in the coffee shop at lunchtime in our office building. I see her there a couple of times a week grabbing a salad. I don't get out of my office much, but when I do, I always go to the coffee shop because it's close."

"So why not bring her a cup of her favorite coffee and open with telling her just how amazing you think she is in the very words you used with me? Tell her you need a little sparkle to shine up your dull, Dan. The worst she can say is no as long as you're respectful and polite. And if she does, then you'll know whether she's waiting for Prince Charming with his fancy lines or just some nice, reliable guy who drives a sensible Honda."

"Hey! How'd you know I drive a Honda?"

Dixie visualized his eyes, wide with suspicion. "It must've been the fact that you're not pretty. Only men who aren't pretty drive Hondas," she finished with a chuckle. "Oh, and also, you said you were a numbers guy. Most of the numbers guys I know drive Hondas and Toyotas because the numbers for longevity of the life of the car are pretty good."

The pause on the other end of the line was significant. Dixie relaxed into it, hoping Dan was processing her words, not preparing to hang up because she'd gone too far.

When he spoke again, it was with quiet reserve. "This is probably going to go in the books as a prime example of epic failures in phone sex. I'm going to be honest with you when I say, you stink at it, Mistress Taboo."

A snort escaped her lips at his very accurate assessment. "That I do, Dan. You're only my third or fourth phone call ever, and I haven't spoken a single dirty word yet. You're not helping."

"But you're very good at something else."

"What's that?"

"Listening. You're one helluva listener, Mistress Taboo. I guess sometimes that's all a guy needs, someone to listen who isn't another guy. Er, wait. You aren't a guy, are you? Because I don't know if I could live with myself if the voice that's been making me a little hot under the collar belonged to a man, but maybe that's a totally different conversation?"

Her laughter echoed in her office. "I'm not a man. I'm all woman. Swear it on my mother's homemade banana bread. So I guess my work here is done?" Dixie left it up to Dan.

"Can I call you again, Mistress Taboo? Maybe just an update on how it works out with JoAnne?"

"I'd love that, Dan." Oddly, strangely, she found, she'd be delighted.

"Until then," his warm, hearty voice assured.

Dixie nodded her head, almost sad to lose the connection. "Until then," she whispered, clicking her earpiece off and marveling at how oddly pleased she was.

Was it wrong to take pride in the most unsuccessful phone-sex call ever? One that had lasted, according to her time log, almost an hour.

Maybe.

Or maybe she was onto something.

Twelve

"I knew it, Dixie. I damn well knew it!" Caine roared from the bottom of the marble staircase of the big house. "Get your pretty backside down here right now!"

Sanjeev approached him, hands behind his back in typical respectful fashion, his black kurta immaculately wrinkle-free. "Ah, Caine. I know this face, this tone of voice. This is the face of a man who's been, yet again, cuckolded by Dixie Davis. Surely you know this path. You've traveled it often. Your return trip shouldn't come as a surprise." His lips lifted at the corners to obstruct a full grin.

Almost two weeks had passed since their closet incident. A torturous two weeks where he'd suffered the giggles and small, breathy moans Dixie made from beyond the office walls as she sucked more unsuspecting men into her web of flirty. There was some guy named Heath, and another one named Dan. And two who went by the name Mike, or was it three?—all calling—all the time—all fooled by her load of crap.

Fourteen days since he'd begun avoiding her, refusing to buy into the idea that she was a changed woman.

Three hundred and sixty-eight hours since she'd blown his mind with her soft mouth and sexy groans of pleasure.

Their silent standoff was about to end—big.

Caine tucked his laptop under his arm with a grunt and eyed Landon's most trusted assistant with his "don't push me" look. "Where is she, Sanjeev? And don't hide her from me, or I'll tear this place apart, slab of marble by insufferably pretentious sculpture until I find her."

Sanjeev's lips warred with another smirk, making Caine respond by clenching his jaw. He cleared his throat and stood straighter. "Now, Caine. I'd be so disappointed in you if you brought discord to my housekeeping. You don't want me to have to stay up for two days straight, cleaning marble chunks and sculptures with broken limbs, do you? Is the life of a man who chooses to serve so cruelly dismissive to you?"

Caine shook his head, his lips thinning. "Oh, no. Don't you pull that self-sacrifice bit with me, buddy. There's going to be no keeping me from my mission."

"And what is your mission today, Agent Caine?"

His mission, should he choose to accept it, was to throttle a hot babe. "Where is she, Sanjeev?"

He followed Sanjeev's serene eyes toward the back of the house, lined with ceiling-high windows and heavy hunter-green and ivory drapes made of silk.

Just beyond lay the second pool Landon owned. A sprawling Olympic-size square of sapphire-blue water surrounded by various shades of blue, clay and green mosaic tiles.

In the middle of it, down in the shallow end, right near the stone fountain of a naked man spouting water from his genitals, sat Dixie on the luxury liner of floats with a fruity drink in the cupholder. Lolling the day away, while she sunned and dreamed up new endearments to label her many phone-sex callers.

Her red hair was wrapped into a loose ball on the top of her head, exposing the nape of her long neck. The sunlight danced on the soft swell of her breasts, clad in a surprisingly modest, yet incredibly hot, chocolate-brown bathing suit.

Sanjeev placed a cool hand on Caine's arm. "A warning. I will not have wet feet in this house. I've just spit-shined the floor with my own saliva. Keep your battle of the sexes out of doors, please."

Caine barked a sarcastic laugh. "No worries there, friend. I'm going to drown her all nice and neat right there in the pool. No fuss, no muss."

"There will be no unsightly yellow police tape marring my view of the freshly vacuumed pool, Caine Donovan. Understood?"

"You suck the fun out of everything, Sanjeev. Buzz-kill!" he called over his shoulder, jogging down the steps leading to the sunken living room and past Landon's collection of Buddha statues. He pushed open the wide French doors and exploded out into the pool area.

"Dixie! Get out of the damn pool. *Now!*" His roar of a demand echoed off the white pillars surrounding the cabana area, but still she didn't budge.

The water sparkled with the heat of the late afternoon sun while Dixie floated on it as though she didn't have a care in the world, twisting a stray strand of her hair around her finger like she'd always done when she was deep in Plum Orchard domination thought.

And she was blatantly ignoring him.

Caine narrowed his eyes until her temptingly curvy

body became a blur of smudged lines. The hell she was going to get away with this—not as long as he was in the game.

He set his laptop at the end of the pool farthest from Dixie, scanning the area through the thick imported palm trees and assorted fringe of grassy plants. The incessant heat of the sun beat down on his head, pissing him off.

Shit, it was hot. Gritting his teeth, Caine stomped over to the tented blue-and-green cabana where, under Sanjeev's instruction, Landon kept an array of toys for the assorted children who attended free swimming lessons in the pool each week.

Mona and Lisa lay in the shade of a lounge chair, lifting their heads at his entry. He pressed a finger to his mouth and dug in his pocket for the treats he always kept with him in case he came across the chance to indulge them when Dixie wasn't looking.

Mona settled back instantly while Lisa's soft eyes shone with gratitude when he held out the Snausages. He gave them each a quick pat on the head as they licked his palm clean and whispered, "Be very quiet, girls. I'm hunting a cheater…er, your mommy."

He scanned the area under the tent, locating the enormous red tub that would hold his weapon. Popping the top open, his eyes landed on the first colorful gun he could find, still full of water. *Nice.* He scooped it up, kicking his shoes off and shrugging out of his shirt and pants.

Lining up the mark of his prey with the red tip and a vindictive smile of satisfaction, he broke into a run, and howled, "Cannonball!" just as his finger pulled the trigger.

Caine doused the top of Dixie's head with the super soaker. The stream of water made an arc of perfection as the waves his body created hitting the water shook the float. It wobbled until she toppled over with a scream of surprise.

He smiled with deeper satisfaction when the remnants of her frosty drink spread out in globs of orange bubbles along the surface of the pool.

So did her casualty-of-war iPod with the earbuds still attached.

Well, damn. She hadn't been ignoring him at all. But Caine consoled himself with the notion that it wasn't as if she didn't deserve it anyway. She was right back to doing what she did best. Manipulating the rules of the game and cheating.

Cheaters deserved to go down. In big, brilliantly blue pools, with cannonball-like splashes and squirt guns.

Dixie's arms flapped wildly as she struggled to rise to the surface, giving Caine enough time to ditch the evidence and swim back to grab his laptop.

Hair plastered to her face, she pushed it out of her eyes—eyes that shone bright like angry chips in ice blue.

He loomed at the edge of the pool by the steps, arms crossed at his chest, waiting.

And three, two, one… "Caine Donovan!" she bellowed at him when her vision was free of hair and dripping water. Adorably wet, her bathing suit clung to every enticing spot on her body. He grinned.

As a response, she lobbed her soaked iPod at him, hitting his shoulder with the pink square. "You've ruined it! What the hell was that about?"

She dragged her body through the water to the shallow end where he sat on a step. As her rounded hips sliced the rippling waves, Caine had to force himself to avert his eyes and focus on the pool's intricately woven deck.

He flipped his laptop open and pointed to her new tagline for Mistress Taboo. "What the hell is *that?* Care to explain, Mistress Taboo?"

Dixie's eyes focused on the screen for a moment, then she snickered, squeezing the bun of hair on top of her head free of excess water. "Oh, that."

"Yeah, that. *That* got you three hundred hits today alone." He emphasized again by tapping his finger against the screen where it now read: "The Mistress of Taboo Subjects—No Woman Trouble Too Small—No Problem Too Big. Let me help you solve all of your female mysteries."

Mistress of Taboo Subjects, his damn eyeballs. This wasn't therapy. It was phone sex. This woman and her way of bending a set of rules should be bottled and sold.

"Catchy, right?" she curtsied and shot him her infamously flirtatious, over the shoulder smile.

"Cheating, right?" he ground out even as his tongue ached to lick the beads of water between her rounded breasts. *Look away, Caine.*

Dixie waggled a pink-tipped finger at him in admonishment and teased, "Oh, no, no, no, Candy Caine. I didn't cheat at all. Nowhere in Landon's rules did it say I had to actually do the talkin' dirty to the clients. I made it my duty to check with Hank first. And he says, Landon's rules only claim I had to *acquire* the most new clients to win. And look," she purred, pointing to the screen as the counter dinged another hit. "More acquirin'. Hmmm."

Caine fastened his eyes on her face in order to keep his focus off her luscious legs. Not that it made much of a difference. It was either ogle her legs or witness the smug look of satisfaction in her eyes, both of which left him hotter than hell. "So, you plan to win by being some sort of sex/dating guru to lonely men who need a guide on how to properly get a woman into bed?"

She grinned, the cute dimples on either side of her face making an appearance. "Guilty."

Dixie reached up to tug the ribbon holding her matted hair, yanking it free and shaking it out with a scrub of her fingers so it fell around her shoulders in wet waves. She shrugged her shoulders in the way she used to when she was using indifference as her weapon of choice. The more indifferent she was, the harder the poor soul Dixie was indifferent to tried to get her attention.

It made his hands itch to haul her from the pool and show her all about indifference.

Caine slammed the laptop shut and shook his head. "I should have known you'd find a way around it. You couldn't dirty talk your way out of a paper bag."

"Well," she said, "I guess I don't have to worry about that, now do I, master impressionist?"

"At least we were on a level playing field then."

"Level, how? You can be a hundred different men. I'm but one woman."

Yeah. One. Hah! "So what you're saying is, you're not enough?"

Her eyes, full of fight one minute, shuttered, and he didn't like what he saw in them. "No truer words," she muttered before squaring her shoulders. "What I'm saying is, I don't offer the variety you do. Who wouldn't want to talk to the famous Denzel Washington instead of some nobody like Dixie Davis? I had to find something that would catch a man's attention."

And that was fair.

And he didn't like that it was fair. Screw fair.

Moving off the step, Caine moved in closer until they were chest to chest, planting his hands on his hips. "I'm going to beat you, Dixie, no matter what kind of con you pull. Only I plan to do it fair and square."

Dixie clamped her fingers together, making the shape of a duck's bill. With a snapping gesture, she opened and closed them under his nose. "Blah, blah, blah, Golden Boy. I don't know why you're surprised. This is what you expected of me, isn't it? To find that one, teeny-tiny loophole that would make you want to tear your hair out because I thought of it first? *Again.*"

He snatched her wrist, bringing it to his chest, forcing her body to lurch forward until they were hip to hip. The taut pull of his boxer-briefs told him he was playing with fire, but his anger with her and her silly games he just couldn't resist playing, would damn well trump his hard-on. "What happened to the new and improved Dixie? I thought she was all sunshine and lollipops these days. Miss Honesty and Light."

Dixie's eyes clouded over, but only for mere seconds before they were full of fire again. "She's fighting for her life, and to make a living. You don't need to make a living. You have one. In *Miami.*"

"But it's so good to be home."

Her lightly tanned throat worked a visible gulp. "I'm glad it's good for somebody. For others, it's an effort just to watch out for pointy objects."

Show no mercy, Donovan. "Nobody to blame but yourself for that."

She rolled her eyes. "Well, thank heaven if I happen to forget, you're never far away for the remindin'. If I need someone to pass judgment on me or call me a liar, worry not, I have you on speed dial. You know what this is, Donovan? You're just jealous that my Mistress Taboo numbers are beating Candy Caine's, even with your stupid Patrick Stewart impressions."

Captain Jean-Luc was popular, damn it. And judgmental? Hold the phone. How was the truth a judgment? Whatever. He wasn't falling for her reformed act again or the recent nagging feeling he was riding his grudge too hard.

Caine hardened his expression, not only to remind Dixie he wasn't falling for it, but as a reminder to himself. "And you're just reaching here. How can you possibly give advice to anyone about anything when it comes to relationships, sexual or otherwise?"

"Maybe I've learned a thing or two about them since we broke up."

Her voice was smaller than he found spiteful comfort in, forcing him to pause. Dixie played coy and sultry as if she'd been tutored by a skilled madam, but weak and vulnerable? Never.

Stand your ground, Caine. Do not believe. The hot babe with the mind-numbing body and breasts that fit with ease and precision in your hands is good at this game. You must be better. "And what have you learned, Dixie Davis?"

Instead of fighting the clasp Caine had on her wrist, Dixie moved in closer to him, letting their bodies almost touch. The smell of her perfume, something soft and peachy, made his nostrils flare.

The fruity scent of the drink she'd been sipping was still on her lips. She traced a circle around his nipple, making it pucker. "I've learned that you, for all your goody-two-shoes, holier-than-thou, impossibly high expectations, are not the only fish in the sea. There are some men in the world who'll cut a girl a break when she makes one stupid mistake on her road to salvation."

"Really? How many of those have you been through before you got it right on the way to salvation?"

Dixie's chin lifted defensively. "Oh, I've got it right now. And just in time, too, so don't you worry."

"Does this 'just in time' have a name?"

A flash of her smug smile almost made him forget her breasts pressed against his chest. "Jealous?"

"Actually, I was hoping to get the poor guy's number so I can do him a solid and warn him off you. Maybe save him from the fall."

"Walker loves me just the way that I am. Faults and all."

Caine's ears perked. "Walker?"

"Yes, Walker. His name's Walker."

"Where does saint *Walker* hail from, and why isn't the entire town of Plum Orchard talking about Dixie's new beau?"

Her eyes strayed to a point just beyond his shoulder before returning to his, full of conviction. "He lives in Chicago, and he's wonderful and kind, and no one knows about him yet. I'd like to keep it that way for now. At least until I have the opportunity to throw it in Louella's face when she's throwing you in mine."

Now that was the Dixie he knew—but wait. "Louella's throwing me in your face?" That statement puzzled him.

Her lips clamped shut before she said, "Forget I mentioned it. All you need to know, Candy Caine, is that Walker and I are an item now. As in, I'm all his and he's all mine."

How interesting. "And how does this Walker feel about you hooking up with me?"

Dixie's tongue darted out over her lips. "We hadn't committed as of that point. But all this…tension…with you was what made me decide to make the final leap."

Caine's eyebrow rose with amusement. "I made you decide to commit to Walker? Does he know that?"

"Yep… Well, not yet, but he will know everything as soon as I tell him. And I mean I'm committing fully—unequivocally—*forever*. Maybe even marriage committed."

Caine wrapped an arm around the curve of her waist, lifting her from the water until Dixie had no choice but to look him directly in the eye. He smiled at her before capturing her lips, kissing her until she relaxed against him, pliant and soft. Until her fingers dug into the skin of his flesh and her soft moan, one he recognized as a sign of her will breaking, slipped from her throat.

He pulled back with a sudden jolt, taking pleasure in her pink cheeks, noting she still had a small trail of freckles across the bridge of her nose.

The surprise on her face was only matched by the defiance in her eyes. He smiled again. "Dixie?"

"What?" Her voice, hoarse and thick, was one of many things that turned him on about Dixie—especially when it was as a result of his lips on hers.

"Send me an invitation."

"For?"

"Your nuptials to *Walker*," he said with a chuckle, before dropping her into the pool with a resounding splash and the sounds of her screeching protests at his back.

Dixie stomped out of the pool, grabbing her towel, and chucking her ruined iPod on a lounge chair. She'd done such a great job of avoiding Caine for an entire two-week stretch. Hiding in the shadows of the various potted plants Landon had scattered about the house. Ducking into doors when she heard his footsteps or his voice.

Eating her dinner microwaved so they wouldn't be tempted to use the sharp dinner knives as tools for killing.

Walking Mona and Lisa on the south side of the house instead of the north where Toe spent his days and Caine often spent time with Landon's very friendly camel, had all been in the effort to stay as far away from temptation as possible.

All of her covert operations had proven successful until today. In the meantime, she'd hatched this new plan to become her callers' advisor rather than their playmate. Her ridiculous attempts to talk them into having phone sex with her had become a joke—especially to LaDawn, who lorded her numbers at their first weekly meeting over everyone as if she'd invented phone sex.

But when Dan had called back two days after their first encounter to tell her he'd finally gotten up the nerve to ask JoAnne out on a date, the seed his call had planted sprouted wings. Even if it wasn't conventional phone sex, it worked.

Dan had left her a glowing review on the Call Girls main site, and since then, her numbers had jumped from dismal to decidedly less pathetic.

Dixie'd double-checked the rules with Hank to be one hundred percent sure she wasn't breaking any part of her contract. Despite what Caine thought, she wanted to win this fair and square. After adding a disclaimer on her website about her lack of training or certification in the hallowed halls of therapy, she'd begun to average four calls a night.

Since her meeting with Hank and Dan's recommendation, word had begun to spread about Mistress Taboo, and she'd gone a little bit viral. Something she was extremely proud of.

But now she'd dragged Walker into it. She hadn't heard from him since that first phone call. Though whether he liked it or not—or knew it or not—he was officially her fictional boyfriend.

His voice had made an impact on her, one she couldn't quite define—or was maybe a little afraid to define. Yet Walker had clearly lingered in her subconscious if the way she'd thrown his name at Caine was any indication. The upside to Walker? Being so full of all that integrity, maybe now that Caine thought Dixie was spoken for, he'd keep his inconceivably delicious body to himself.

Being back here where she'd created so much damage was easier to navigate when Caine wasn't in the mix. It was easier to focus on keeping her promises to herself when he wasn't around to pass judgment on her every move with his angry eyes.

Though, each time they came in contact physically was another time she died a little more inside. Her body's reaction to him meant plainly she was weak. Worse, in a desperate moment or two, she almost didn't care that Caine didn't like her. She just wanted him to make love to her with his signature relentlessly forceful passion.

Thankfully, her self-esteem had kept her desires in check. But today, the image of him in the pool, his skin lightly bronzed and glistening wet, his arms a tangle of corded muscle, the dark line of hair that wound under his belly button and into his boxer-briefs always stole her breath, made her wet with wanting him.

Even in the ungodly heat, Dixie shivered and peeked around the pool area, embarrassed by her wicked thoughts. Mona and Lisa slept contentedly under the lounge chair while the floor fan Sanjeev had set up for them misted their chunky bodies, keeping them cool and comfortable.

Annoyed, she yanked her towel from the blue-and-green chaise, wrapping it around her lower body. Now she had a new lie to contend with. The Walker lie. Idiot. "Walker? *Really, Dixie?* What kind of fool declares she's on the verge of marrying a man who calls to engage in phone sex?"

"The kind that wishes to make Caine the Neanderthal jealous," Sanjeev provided, handing her a frosty glass of sweet tea with a pink umbrella in it.

Her sigh was exasperated, but she accepted the glass with gratitude. "You heard?"

"I believe Wylan Landry three miles down the road by the county line heard."

Dixie offered him a sheepish look. "I'm sorry, Sanjeev. I was angry. No one gets my goat like Caine."

Sanjeev cocked his head. "I don't understand how

Caine can get your goat. You have two dogs, no goats. You don't have a goat somewhere, do you, Dixie? Isn't it enough that I clean up after Toe, Mona and Lisa? I don't have enough misting fans for a goat, too."

Dixie chuckled and shook her head, scrubbing her hair with the towel. "No goats. It just means he pushes my buttons."

"You don't have buttons either."

"They're internal. It's a metaphor. Never mind. The point is Caine makes me say things out of spite that should never be said in public."

"Someone can make you perform a task you don't want to perform? I assume there's money to be made in this," he teased with an easy grin.

Sipping her tea, Dixie wondered out loud, "What is it about him that makes me behave like a vengeful teenager? I've managed to keep my temper and my scheming in check for a long time now. I come back home, and in a matter of seconds, it's like I never stopped being a blight on humanity."

Sanjeev nodded his sympathy. "Love is indeed a puzzle, isn't it?"

"I don't—"

He held up a hand to prevent her protests. "Oh, but you do, Dixie. To deny you love Caine would be to deny the entirety of your youth. It would be to deny some of the most monumental pieces of your past, and the incidents that have shaped this new, improved you."

These days, it felt as if her heart was in a vise grip for all the pangs it suffered. Yes—there was truth in that statement. Back then, when she'd vowed Caine would rue the day he'd broken up with her, most of her supposed changing had all been empty, internal promises based on revenge.

Once she'd gotten past the initial hurt over the end of their engagement, everything she'd done had been based on showing Caine what he'd missed out on rather than the real work she'd needed to do on herself.

And then, one day, one ugly, agonizing day, the tables were turned on her, and everything changed…. "It doesn't matter anyway, Sanjeev. Caine's never going to see me as anything other than a manipulative liar. It's not without reason. But for heaven's mercy, I get it already. Every single thing I do is an excuse for him to remind me that I'll never be good enough for someone so filthy rich in integrity."

"Why not prove him wrong then?"

Hah! "Because even if Jesus himself dubbed me new and improved right in front of Caine's very eyes, he still wouldn't believe it. I'm not here to prove anything to anyone. That's not how it works."

"How what works?"

"Redemption. It's not about how many apologies you make. It isn't about begging for forgiveness. It's about being actively involved in turning your life around. Actively owning the things you've done to hurt people and stopping the hurt. For good."

She bit back the next piece of her journey. It was still too personal to share with anyone yet. To speak of it was to diminish the impact it had on her life so long ago. For now, that would stay where it belonged—in her heart and mind.

"Besides, you know what I discovered while I cried my eyes out and ate enough fried food to feed a small country, Sanjeev?"

"I'm all ears, as you say."

And here it was, the entire crux of the matter. The eternal weight of loving someone as moral and forthright as Caine, and what had kept her from begging him for a second chance, boiled down to one thing. "There's no room for error with Caine. I was always afraid I'd mess up back then, and when I did, I realized mistakes just weren't allowed where he's concerned. It's damn hard to impress perfection."

Sanjeev wrinkled his nose. "Ah, but, Dixie, Caine is as far from perfect as you are imperfect."

"He's a lot closer to perfection than I am, buddy."

"He fights his own demons where you're concerned."

Dixie grinned, pulling off her towel and laying it over the lounge chair to dry. "Demons and me in the same sentence. How unexpected."

"Caine has his faults, too, Dixie," Sanjeev insisted.

"They're not as big as mine. He wins."

"This isn't about winning," Sanjeev said stubbornly. "It's about what should be."

"What should be? Who's talking in riddles now, Sanjeev?"

Sanjeev threw up a hand at her and waved her off. "We have no time for this discussion. You have to nap before your shift, and I have to restock the pantry and somehow manage to squeeze in laundering your delicates before the *Waltons Mountain* marathon."

Dixie grabbed his arm. Sanjeev wasn't known for his comfort with displays of affection. Still, she latched onto his hand anyway and squeezed. "Don't be silly. You don't have to do my laundry, Sanjeev. I can do it. You don't have to cook for me either. Even though I owned a restaurant, lately, I've become an expert at microwaved meals. Please don't go to any trouble for me. Though, I appreciate it—and you."

Sanjeev's eyes assessed her for a moment. His head tilted at an angle as though he'd never seen her before, and then he grinned—a rare and wondrous thing. "That you won't make me suffer the indignities of my continued confusion when identifying a thong and French cut panties makes me appreciate you back."

Her throat tightened at Sanjeev's silent understanding before she teased, "Then John-Boy awaits."

Sanjeev squeezed her hand back before shrugging out of her grasp and calling to Mona and Lisa with a sharp whistle. "Come here, you bottomless pits! Dinner and a movie are at hand!"

Mona and Lisa snorted their way out from under the lounge chairs, stopping to nuzzle Dixie's hand before they followed behind Sanjeev, their wide hips wiggling in anticipation.

She stood, watching Sanjeev and the dogs retreat into the shadows of the house until they disappeared.

The sting of tears, born of Sanjeev's forgiveness, a small sign her efforts were genuine and from the heart, threatened to overwhelm her.

Smiling to herself, she gathered her things, warmed from the inside out.

"This is Mistress Taboo—"

"Yes. I'm worthy."

Her breath caught in her throat as her heart raced. *Walker.* "Well, hello, Walker."

"Howdy to you, too, Mistress Taboo. How are you this fine evenin'?"

Dixie fought to keep her words calm when her insides were all kinds of tangled. "I'm very well, thank you."

"So I see you're counselin' men now."

Walker had seen the change on her site, meaning, he'd thought of her since the last time they'd spoken.

Whoa. Dixie pinched her arm hard enough to make her bite the inside of her lip. A dose of reality was in order. Wasn't it bad enough that she'd used him as her make-believe boyfriend to hurt Caine, but now she was hoping he'd been daydreaming about her, too?

She repositioned herself in her chair in an effort to get hold of her spiraling emotions and began arranging the sticky notes she'd accumulated since her phone line had begun to pick up. She kept track of the callers she advised by writing down their identifying traits. "I don't know if counseling would be the correct word. It's more like just offering helpful advice from a woman's perspective."

"Who calls a phone-sex operator for a woman's perspective on love and dating?"

Dixie tilted her head. He sounded just like Caine. Damn him. Her heart rate slowed down appropriately. "You sound just like everyone else."

"Who's everyone else?"

"No one specific. Just everyone else." LaDawn, the Naysayer. She'd mocked Dixie's change of strategy, even after seeing the jump in her numbers.

"You have someone specific in mind. I can tell by the sound of your voice, Mistress Taboo. You don't have to tell me his name. Give him a fake name just like yours, if you want. We do need a point of reference," he coaxed sweetly.

She stuck Mike number three's note in the "Mike

pile" where four more "Mikes" just like him who'd called in the last week sat, and asked, "How do you know it's a him?"

"Isn't it always about a man?"

At least one man, yes. "How's Golden Boy?" she blurted out.

His laughter, so inviting and gravelly, made Dixie laugh, too. "And what's Golden Boy got against you counselin' men on their sex lives?"

Walker had begun to tread into personal territory, making her drop her notes on Heath, who used a fictionally tragic character's name as his phone-sex caller pseudonym. "It's kind of a long story," she said carefully. "Suffice it to say, I'm not very good at phone sex, so I found a way around it in order to put food on my plate."

His voice held approval. "So you're scrappy. I like that in a woman."

That Walker liked the part of her personality everyone else detested made her stomach tingle. Right or wrong, his words of approval left her with a forbidden glow. Maybe it was the hunger for support, or maybe… maybe it just was. "Or something like that, yes. I'm doing what I have to do to become fiscally stable again."

"That's pretty scrappy, in my opinion."

"You say scrappy, others say greedy," she let slip.

"Well, now who'd call Mistress Taboo greedy?" he asked, incredulous.

"Do you have an extra ten sets of hands to count with? I'm sure you'll need at least that many."

"Why's it greedy to do what you have to do to get work? In this day and age, it should be considered an asset."

Walker sounded genuinely interested, and at this point, there was nothing she'd like more than to have someone on her side. Though she reminded herself, this was about getting herself out of debt, not collecting minions to cheer her name in Dixie vs. Caine.

"Another long story, but we're not supposed to talk about me. We're supposed to talk about you. So let's do that. Do you have a problem with a woman?" Was it crazy to hope Walker's problems didn't involve another woman? Like his wife? Or, heaven forbid, his mother? She squelched that thought.

"I'd rather talk about you." His answer was definitive in all its silkiness.

Dixie let out the breath she didn't realize she was holding. "You don't want to pay four ninety-nine a minute to talk about me, do you? I'm supposed to be helping you solve your female problems."

"I don't have any female problems. We broke up a long time ago. Female problems solved."

Her ears perked to the tune of Walker's apparently womanless life. *Bad ears*. "Anyone you've been interested in since then?"

"No one quite like her."

Something in Walker's voice made Dixie push the envelope a little further. "Was that a no one like her as in 'she was the love of my life and all things incredible,' or was that a 'no one like her, she was the worst thing to happen to me since crabs?'"

Walker's pause was painfully pensive, his answer, carefully constructed. "It was maybe a little of both. Wait, that's not fair. She was more good than bad, now that I reflect. Frustrating as hell, kept me on my toes, but I loved the hell out of her anyway."

"Was she the love of your life type or just the fondest memory you have of love and it's now become bigger than it really was?" She asked the question only because she'd asked herself that question over and over about Caine.

Walker coughed, but his eventual reply was throaty. "She was, and remains to this day, the love of my life. She was the best and the worst thing to ever happen to me."

Dixie held in a wistful sigh. "I understand that completely." Caine had been the best and worst thing that had ever happened to her. And she still loved him anyway.

"So you had someone like that in your past, too, Mistress Taboo?"

"I did." *I still do.*

"What happened?"

"We broke up, of course."

"Why?"

"It was my fault," she was quick to reply.

"How could anyone as cute as you are…uh, as cute as you sound be at fault?"

Ugh. The constant explanations of her dirty deeds was like living *Groundhog Day.* "I just did something that made him change his idea of who I was—or who he thought I'd become."

"You didn't cheat, did you? I'd have to take back my scrappy compliment, if you did," he chastised, though his tone was still light and teasing.

She resumed organizing her sticky notes for her callers. "No. It was nothing like that. Though, I'm not proud to say, I once cheated, too… He was a high school boyfriend, and I was young, not that that should excuse it.

Anyway, I didn't cheat on him. I would never…" Dixie sighed into the phone. Trying to inject her personal experiences into her brand of "therapy" without exposing herself was proving more and more difficult.

For all she knew, Walker was a serial killer who got his kicks off of getting to know his victims in unusual ways before hunting them down, throwing them in a pit of dirt and flaying them alive while he screamed the word *infidel*.

"And then what happened?"

"I did something really stupid and petty, and then I behaved abominably, which led him to believe I'd always behave abominably."

Walker scoffed. "He sounds like a judgmental ass."

Dixie's feathers instantly became ruffled on Caine's behalf. "It wasn't without reason," she defended. Wait. Why was she defending Caine? For all the flak he gave her, she should be willing to throw him to the wolves. Yet, ultimately, no matter how he'd handled their breakup, he'd been right.

"Which begs the question, had you behaved badly before?"

Her eyes went wide. "Why would you ask that?"

"Well, you defended him like you were defendin' your mother, and you were quick to do it, too. I figure, with my superior detecting skills, if he wasn't a bad guy, or a judgmental jackass, you must've given him reason to believe you might slip up again."

Score one for Walker. "Fair enough. Yes. I'd behaved badly before."

"How bad is bad?"

"Hah! I was probably a nominee for the worst human being on the planet. In fact, I'd wager I could have given some of those villains on soap operas a run for their money."

"Like Victor Kiriakis, *Days of our Lives* bad?"

Dixie grinned, leaning back in her chair and throwing her feet up on the desk to stretch her cramped calves. "I'd like to think more along the lines of Joan Collins from *Dynasty* bad. She was definitely more glam than Victor."

Walker whistled. "Wow. That's bad."

Dixie nodded her head, forgetting once more that Walker was the client. "Yeah. Superbad, in fact. But I learned the most valuable lesson of my life. Since then, I've been trying to mend the error of my ways."

"What was the lesson? What turned Mistress Taboo into a fence mender?"

Her fingers, flicking the tip of a ballpoint, froze. She gulped back her discomfort, massaging her chest, suddenly so tight she couldn't breathe.

This was too deep. She'd never told a soul about Mason. Not even her Landon. So, she sidestepped his very personal question by brushing it off. "It was very *A Christmas Carol*. You know, bad girl reflects on her life and realizes she's all alone in the big bad world with no friends and a family who's all but given up on her ever being anything but a lying, manipulative, self-entitled brat? But without ghosts," she added with a chuckle.

"I'm familiar with the story."

"Then you know how it goes."

"So you don't want to tell me what really happened?"

What she really wanted was this introspection to end. "It's a little personal."

"And here we hardly know each other, right?"

She smiled her relief at his lighter tone, sinking back

in her chair. "It takes at least four phone calls deep before I reveal all my secrets. But I warn you, you'll need a shower and clean underwear when I'm done."

"There she is, the Mistress Taboo I know." His voice showered her with warm approval. "It's been real nice chattin' with you tonight."

"Is our conversation over already?" Again, she found herself wanting to ask when or if he'd call again.

Walker sighed, the phone close to his lips. "I think it is for tonight, Mistress Taboo. A man's gotta work to pay those phone-sex operator bills."

Her giggle echoed in the dark bedroom. "Well, all right then, Walker. I hope we can talk again soon."

"Me, too, Mistress Taboo. Me, too."

Walker hung up then, leaving Dixie to sink lower in her chair, resting her head against the back of it. In the deep velvet of 3:00 a.m., she gazed out the window into the inky early morning in the direction of Caine's window at the big house and wondered what he'd say if he knew what had happened to her in Chicago—what she couldn't bring herself to tell Walker.

Or anyone.

With a yawn, she prepared to leave, stretching before gathering her purse, and that's when she saw the shiny gleam of an object at the end of her desk, buried under her sticky notes.

Dixie scooped them up, dumping them in a completely incorrect pile in an effort to clear the mounting debris.

Her heart skipped a beat when she identified the shiny object.

A brand-new iPod touch.

As she was marveling over Caine's decency for replacing the iPod he'd drowned when he'd been so angry with her, her phone vibrated.

She dug in her purse, pulling it out and sliding her finger over the screen.

Darling Dixie—I'm sorry I haven't told you I love you lately. This being dead thing is a real bitch when it comes to communication. But who loves you more than his spleen even from all the way up here? Me. J

Dixie couldn't help but laugh, even as the yearning to talk with Landon one last time, to hear him say those words rather than just read them, stole her breath.

She held the phone close to her chest and smiled at his picture on her desk. "I miss you, you intrusive pain in my derriere," she whispered.

So, so much.

Thirteen

"You do know I'd rather be dipped in batter and fried than be here right now, don't you, Em?" She spread her arms wide to indicate the square in the middle of town where so many familiar faces milled about, exchanging handshakes and idle chitchat.

"You do know that there are people just linin' up at the mere thought, don't you, Dixie?"

Dixie rolled her eyes at her. "Of course, I do. That's why I don't want to be here. Fried isn't a color I wear well."

Em burst out laughing, her mood lighter than Dixie had seen it in almost two weeks, and she was working hard to keep from spoiling it with her own sour disposition. "Wasn't it you who said to face your enemies?"

"Whoever said anyone should take advice from me?"

"Apparently the men who call Mistress Taboo seem to think they should. Did you see the end of the week report for your numbers? They were incredible, Ms. Davis! Your calls are up by thirty-eight percent. Of course, I say that with absolutely no bias on your behalf—being the impartial mediator that I am. But the way this is going, I think that ornery LaDawn's gonna have to take lessons from you soon."

"Or kill me in my sleep." Yes, sir. Her numbers for calls logged were way up. So far up, she was working sometimes an extra two hours on her six-hour shifts, and her mountain of sticky notes was going to need a desk of its own soon. It was exhausting and exhilarating. More importantly, it was working, and in only two weeks' time since she'd instituted her new plan.

"Stop that now. Don't be so melodramatic. She was just teasing you."

Dixie muffled a snort with her hand. "Have you ever known LaDawn to just joke? Wasn't it her who said she'd run off all the other 'companionators' on her old block in Atlanta by threatening to pick them off one by one with a sawed-off shotgun her granddaddy left her in his will?"

Em's eyes twinkled sapphire blue under the strands of lights hung to perfection from tree to tree in the square. "You know, she's a little like you minus the violent tendencies, don't you think? All manipulatin' a situation to her advantage."

"She's a little like a serial killer."

Em licked her finger and swiped at the corner of Dixie's mouth. "You have lipstick on your face. Oh! Speaking of, look who's over in the corner, chatting up Ray Johnson."

Dixie kept her fear on the inside, and stared straight ahead. "LaDawn?"

Em clapped her hands excitedly as if it was Christmas morning. "Yep! And Marybell, too. I'm so glad they agreed to come."

"Please say you reminded them this wasn't a place

to drum up new business? I'm all for advertising, but I think if some of the women in town got wind of LaDawn's magic flogger, they'd hog-tie her and leave her on the train tracks."

"Of course I did, Dixie. You don't think I'd let them go into something like this without tactfully suggesting they leave their sexy apparatus at home, do you?"

Dixie shook off the bad feeling she'd had all night since, at Em's insistence, agreeing to attend the annual Plum Orchard Autumn gathering and potluck. Em didn't know the Mags the way she did. She didn't know what they were truly capable of when they wanted to hurt someone. Her giving nature, the generosity she granted everyone, would be her downfall.

Inviting the Call Girls was a kind, Em-like gesture. Her hope to integrate the operators she'd come to refer to as close acquaintances into Plum Orchard was naive at best, disastrous at worst.

Em's blind eyes and deaf ears clearly only heard the gossip everyone spread about Dixie. The Call Girls operators had been the subject of more than one overheard conversation, and the conversations were never about welcoming them into the fold with open arms and a basket of freshly picked peaches.

They were more along the lines of scripture, damnation, and "how-to" videos on performing exorcisms.

"Are you having those misgivings again?" Em asked.

"I'm having many things."

"Don't be so cynical, Dixie. Louella said it was a wonderful idea to invite the girls. And this is a perfect opportunity for them to get to know everyone. It has to be hard to get out and meet folk when you work the graveyard shift."

"Harder still to get out and meet people when you sell *sex* over the phone in the graveyard," Dixie quipped.

"I know the town isn't in love with the idea of Call Girls being here, Dixie, especially the Senior Mags. But Landon did everything right. Trust that. He got all the permits he needed from the county and the state. He knew his stuff, and he made sure Hank Cotton did, too. So they all might as well get used to it and make nice, because there isn't much anyone can do about it."

Except make the women of Call Girls feel so uncomfortable and out of place, they'd give a Mag their personal gas money to run them out of town.

Em's hopeful face, brighter than it had been since Dixie returned, was fading, pulling her up short. She rubbed Em's arm. "You're right. I'm sorry. Ignore my sour mood. I'm just tired and cranky from all those calls I've been takin.' I'm sure everything will be fine."

Em nodded her agreement with a happy smile. "I know it will. You'll see."

Dixie didn't want to blast Em's Mr. Rogers moment on the off chance Louella and the Mags would mind their manners. Yet the possibility existed they were merely laying the groundwork to humiliate the Call Girls for having the nerve to think a phone-sex operation was acceptable in Plum Orchard.

Dixie tugged on the bow at Em's waist. "But hold that thought, and just walk to the other side of this equation with me, okay? Wasn't Louella also the one who thought it was a wonderful idea to jump into bed with Caine two point two seconds after we broke up?"

Em wrinkled her nose. "Still don't believe it, and two very different things, Dixie. Now, before you ruin a perfectly good reason to wear that beautiful black dress, let's go have some punch and enjoy a nice night out."

"Punch. That sounds good. Let's have lots of punch with lots of alcohol." Dixie followed behind Em, pushing their way through the crowded grass of the square. She admired the Kelly-green dress Emmaline chose for tonight; soft and flirty, it covered only one of her shoulders, and brought out every good feature she possessed.

Judging by the appreciative glances of some of Plum Orchard's most decidedly un-bachelors, they admired Em's dress, and what was filling it, too. If only Em knew how beautiful she really was, inside and out, she wouldn't be single long, Dixie mused.

Pulling her up the stairs of the whitewashed gazebo, Dixie momentarily flashed back to the night of her engagement party. The air had smelled the same then—the end-of-summer heat easing to welcome in the crisp scent of falling leaves and fireplaces burning fat pine logs.

Then she sucked in a breath of air to fend off the horrible images that always followed that happy memory. The fire she'd started by knocking over the candles that matched her wedding colors while she'd raged.

The screaming.

Essie Guthrie's updo singed to a crispy frizz.

The rain that had made a tsunami look like a mere shower.

The buffet table, lined with assorted dishes brought by everyone in town was the same, too. The only difference was all the food was on the table, not splattered all over the floor after being trampled by three hundred people all vying to get out of the rain and under the safety of the gazebo.

Glasses of plum wine, Herbert Fox's specialty, sat on a far table in the corner, glistening with the deep purple liquid. Dixie grabbed a much-needed glass for both her and Em while scanning the familiar faces of the crowd and the people she'd grown up with.

Some were older; some were in the next stages of their lives. All of them, whether they felt the same way about her, were welcome sights to Dixie's homesick eyes. She stood in the back of the gazebo against the rail, absorbing her surroundings, inhaling the smell of Essie's homemade corn bread and Jeter Orwell's mother's fruit salad surprise.

Dixie sipped her wine, wistfully watching couples gather in the center of the square where a dance floor had been laid.

The first notes of one of her favorite songs, "We Danced," by Brad Paisley, filled the air, a slow intimate song about finding everlasting love on a barroom floor. She swayed with it, closing her eyes with a smile. A hundred years ago, she and Caine had danced to this tune at an old bar they'd frequented during their engagement.

The memory transported her right back to the dusty hardwood floor littered with peanut shells and hay and the odor of stale beer and sweat. Caine's hard chest beneath his old college T-shirt, pressed to her cheek, his chin resting on the top of her head.

The smell of his aftershave tingled her nose, his cowboy boots occasionally scraping her ballet slippers. The heat of their bodies flush with one another's, their hands clasped together at their sides, oblivious to everyone else as they swayed.

"I see you decided to venture out into the pack of

hungry she-wolves tonight? What gives, Dixie-Cup. You lonely for a public lickin'?" Caine asked from behind her. And while his tone was light, she wasn't up for his kind of lickin', one he'd surely lavish happily.

Her eyes popped open when he positioned himself behind her, placing his hands on her shoulders. She stiffened, then shrugged him off. It took every ounce of her will not to fall back against his hard chest in search of shelter.

No more touching. No more kisses that set her soul on fire. "I'm just enjoyin' a nice evening in a hometown I've missed more than I thought I did. You do the same, Caine. Oh, and thank you for replacing my iPod," she replied, attempting to skedaddle away from him without looking him in the eye.

Caine caught her arm, pulling her back to his side. "Wait, Dixie. *Please*."

The harsh grit in his tone left her helpless to deny him. That and his muscled goodness dressed in an ice-blue fitted shirt, blue jeans, and the very same cowboy boots he'd worn when they'd danced at Junior's—all so acutely male, it physically hurt.

Her legs trembled while she silently damned him. She'd never been so aware of any other man as she was Caine, and it infuriated her.

Lashing out at him was the only thing keeping her from begging him to take her back. "Is there something you'd like to point out to me that you haven't yet? Have we moved on from my character flaws list already? That was fast."

He took the glasses of wine from her hand and set them on the table. Cupping her chin, he ran his thumb over her lower lip, one that trembled in response. "Stop, and just listen to me, okay?"

Caine's eyes reflected something she'd never seen, rooting her to the spot. Sure, she was used to anger, amusement at her expense, lust even, but this—this softer, almost gentle gaze? That she didn't understand— or maybe it was just that she hadn't seen it in a long time.

He hitched his jaw to the big maple where a park bench sat beneath its sprawling limbs and thick leaves. "C'mon. Let's go sit."

Sit? To ensure she was an easy hit? Uh-uh. This was just another trick to get her back for finagling her way out of phone sex.

Since the Call Girls' weekly meeting, he'd had plenty of time to plot her payback—or at the very least, work up a good simmer. "What's this about, Caine? Are you angry that my numbers beat your numbers this week?" She looked at her wristwatch, tapping the face of it with a fingernail. "Or is it time to call me a cheat again? Can't you just tell me what horrible offence I've per- petrated right here? You know, in front of everyone? You're so good at that. You want a microphone, too? Let's ask Louella if we can borrow hers."

When Caine smiled, it wasn't with malice or arro- gance, it was easy and kind. And it was freaking her out by the second.

"No tricks. Swear it on my old stack of *Playboys*."

The corner of her lips almost lifted. "You had *Play- boys?*"

"Stacks of 'em."

"And everyone calls you the golden boy? Why is it that if Dixie Davis is making the nasty on the phone she's the town pariah, but if Caine Donovan does the same, he's excused from the fire-and-brimstone speech because he wears a cape and saves drowning puppies?"

Caine lifted his wide shoulders and grinned. "Stop exaggerating. I only saved *a* puppy. No plurals in there."

Yes, yes, yes. He really had saved Aida-Lynne Gorman's puppy that'd wandered off from her backyard by jumping into the overflowing creek and swimming after it.

Dixie rolled her eyes at him. "And on the day that you were born the angels got together, and decided to create a dream come true. I've heard it all—in a song, I think. Maybe I ought to let Kitty Palmer hear you invite a woman to discover how you *Pirate her Caribbean* in Johnny Depp's voice? I hear you lay it on thick almost every night from my thin office walls. You get zero points for originality, mister, after you've used it three hundred times. And what is it with the Johnny Depp fixation? Does every woman want to talk to Depp?"

"Depp's pretty popular," he said in Depp's voice, following that with a crooked, endearing grin… Damn him.

"That's neither here nor there. The point is…" She frowned. "I forget what the point was."

Caine's laughter, so genuine she was tempted to laugh with him, made her heart skip. "So come with me?"

Caution being the better part of valor, Dixie cast suspicious eyes on him. "Okay, but one cross word and I'll find a can of gasoline in Landon's barn and set your pile of dirty women with big boobs in Technicolor on fire. It'll be a blaze like Plum Orchard's never seen. Trust that."

Pulling her behind him, Caine took her down the steps, crisscrossing their way through the crowd and across the square.

For a moment, her hand in his, Caine leading them off somewhere, brought back a time when she would have followed him into the bowels of Hell if he'd just promise to be hers forever.

"Sit." He motioned to the bench directly across the street from Madge's.

Dixie looked around with suspicious eyes then swiped the bench with her hand and held it up under the lamppost's light. "If you ruin this black dress, Caine, I'll steal your credit card and order a hundred more. It's the only one I have left from my old wardrobe in Chicago, and even if it's a little tight after all the food Sanjeev lavishes on me, it's still designer."

"I dunno, it doesn't look too tight to me. You look really pretty tonight, Dixie."

Heat rose in her cheeks. "Take that back."

"I won't because you do look pretty. *Very* pretty."

Her hands went to her hips. "Okay. I know you've got something up your sleeve, what is it?"

He shoved the sleeves of his shirt upward over his arms. "No tricks up my sleeve."

Stubbornly, Dixie refused to sit. "I don't trust you. I'll stand."

"And that's the root of our problem."

"We don't have problems, Caine. We have catastrophes—tsunami-like issues of devastation."

"And we can't have a relationship like that."

A relationship? Her throat went dry, making her wish she'd brought her wine with her. Did he want to… No. He wouldn't be so cruel as to make her believe he

wanted her back so he could… No. "What relationship
are we talking about? We don't have one unless antagonism is the basis for a relationship," she croaked.

"But we do, Dixie-Cup. We have a working one."

Hopes dashed appropriately, she hid her disappointment and gave him a questioning glance. "We never
see each other during our shifts. You're in one room,
and I'm in another. Strategically planned, I'm sure, by
Landon, in an effort to keep us from lopping each other's heads off with industrial staple guns."

"We don't have a relationship because we do just
that—avoid the hell out of each other. Every time you
hear me leave to grab a water or some coffee, if you're
in the hall, you run the other way."

"I do not run." To imply she was a coward was un-
gentlemanly.

"Okay, you walk swiftly."

"I prefer to call it speed walking. It's good for your
heart."

"Call it whatever you like, it's still avoidance."

"And that's been working, hasn't it?"

"No. Yes." His lips thinned. "No. I don't want to
avoid you, Dixie. I don't want LaDawn and Cat and
the others to cordon off portions of the break room
by groups so they don't have to worry they'll witness
a murder on pizza night. Everyone avoids us if we're
even within two feet of each other. Sure, we're civil,
just as Cat threatened we'd better be, but the tension is
still there. I don't want everyone to act like one wrong
thing said could set us off, do you?"

Caine was right. Last week on pizza night, Sheree
had seen the two of them each grabbing a slice of pizza
from the same box just as she'd reached for one herself,

but she'd jumped back when Dixie had tried to pull it from his grasp and teased Caine he was taking the slice with the most cheese on it. She'd only been joking, but it had stilled all movement.

She saw his point. The last thing she wanted to do was alienate the only people who willingly spoke to her, even if it was through clenched teeth à la LaDawn. "We're dividing them. Making them choose between us."

"You bet we are. We're killing their comfort with just our bad vibes. We've got some time left to this competition, Dixie, but eventually, one of us will go home. For the girls, this is their home now. I don't want to shit all over that just because we acted like asses. Or more importantly, *I* acted like an ass."

Perplexed, she murmured, "Okay. Will the real Caine Donovan please stand up?"

"Why doesn't the real Dixie Davis come sit down?" He patted the place beside him with a convincing, heartbreakingly adorable smile.

It made her want to bracket his jaw with her hands, press her lips to his until he swept her up in his arms like he used to.

Instead, Dixie fought the impulse and took a cautious seat, finding the very edge of the park bench and sitting on it as if it was nothing more than a sliver of wood. "So what are you proposing here? Do you want to have more group hugs? Maybe prayer circles? What will make the girls feel less like they have to choose between us?"

"All we have to do is be friends again, Dixie. And that means I have to lay off razzing you every chance I get."

Dixie's lips pursed and her eyes narrowed until Caine was nothing but a delicious hunk of a blurry image. "But it's how you're able to breathe. It's your life force. You can't do that any more than I can stop buying lip gloss and conditioner."

Brushing her hair from her face with a tender finger, Caine said, "But I can, and I will if you will. I've been pretty hard on you, Dixie. I'm not saying it isn't without cause, but that reason's grown older and apparently outdated. Almost ten years older. It's time to let go of it and behave like adults for the sake of those around us. It's time. I keep hearing about how you've changed from Emmaline, and it occurred to me, I haven't even bothered to attempt to respect those changes by giving them a chance, let alone paid attention to them. We're always too caught up in knocking each other's knees out from under one another."

Dixie's jaw dropped open. "Something's very wrong here. We've always done this, Caine. It's just what we do."

Or it's what I do so I don't have to really face what I've done. Caine was the person she'd hurt the most, yet he was the one person she was most afraid to make amends with.

"No, Dixie," he said, his voice that odd gruff again. "We didn't always do this, but maybe it's time we change what we do. I will if you will."

She went for one last poke at him, to test his commitment to this cease-fire. "And if I don't?"

"I'm guessin' my stack of classic *Playboys* are set for a bonfire, and your makeup's going to find the trash compactor."

The inability to breathe kept her silent for a few moments while the music drifted to her ears and the conversations of the surrounding people floated over her head. *Now, Dixie. Now would be the perfect time to tell Caine you're sorry....* "O...kay. It's a deal."

"Besides, with you marrying Walker—"

Dixie blanched. Damn her and her need to win everything. "*Committing* to him."

He flashed her another genuine smile. "Right. Committing. I'd think you'd want to let what's happened go and head into your marriage with an open heart, free of old hurts."

Right. That's what she'd want if Walker were real, and she wasn't still madly in love with Caine who clearly was managing just fine without her. *Oh, Dixie, what have you done?*

She plastered a fake smile on her face. "Right. Free of old hurts is cleansing. So let's try it. But I promise you—one crappy word, one prank, trick, whatever you want to call it—you go down, Donovan."

He nudged her with his elbow and winked. "Same goes for you, Davis. So, friends? Maybe we'll grab dinner together, or whatever you call what we eat in the break room at three in the morning."

Sure. Dinner.

How did you go about being just friends with the one man you'd loved all your life? Yet the idea of a kinder Caine, one who wasn't calling her a liar and a cheat, spread a healing balm over her bruised heart. "Okay. Deal."

He stuck his hand out, and Dixie took it without hesitation, letting the warmth of it envelop hers, wishing she could cling to it, pull it to her cheek so he'd draw it back and kiss each of her knuckles the way he'd once done.

Caine surprised her when he pulled her to his side, pressing a gentle kiss to her cheek with warm lips.

Her eyes closed of their own accord as she savored this moment—a moment that felt like goodbye.

Caine let her go and slapped his hands against his delectable thighs, rising with a tilt of his head in the crowd's direction. "Good. I'm glad. I'm gonna go call up Jo-Lynne, and tease her about missing Kitty's potato salad."

Dixie's head bobbed its agreement with a slow nod even as her throat clogged. "Checkin' on your mama is important. Say hello to her for me, would you, and give her my best?" *Oh, and also tell her I'm sorry. So I can avoid chickening out with her just like I did with you.*

"You bet," he murmured, looking fifty pounds lighter now after agreeing to their truce.

As Dixie watched him push his way through the throng of people, his tall frame navigating it with ease, hot tears stung her eyes.

She had to lean forward and brace her elbows on her knees to keep a constant flow of air to her lungs. Suddenly her dress was even tighter, her push-up bra constricting.

Who were they as friends? What would it be like when Caine no longer sneered at her, but instead, greeted her like just another fellow employee?

Who was she if she wasn't cultivating some sarcastically flirty response to his taunts? It was as though a piece of her had just died. She didn't know how to breathe if Caine wasn't pushing one of her buttons. At least when they were at each other's throats it was an excuse to interact.

Now she was relegated to the friend pile, and somehow, that didn't seem nearly as intimate as being his nemesis.

So this was closure. Myriad emotions, now all tied up into one neat package with a pretty bow. Closure well and truly sucked. And hurt. Really, really hurt.

The tap of someone's hand on a microphone startled Dixie from her pity party. She sat up just as Louella's voice touched her ears.

"Fine people of Plum Orchard, I'd like to thank y'all for joinin' us tonight. Lots of announcements to be made here, folks, so if you'll just bear with me, we'll get right back to dancing in just a few minutes...."

Dixie tuned her out, kicking off her heels and scooping them up to let them dangle from her fingers. She scrunched her toes up in the cool grass, unsure where to go next.

She had two hours until her shift began. Yet the last thing she wanted to do was rejoin the festivities. Watching Caine give a test run to their new friendship was not on her list of most desirable things to do.

With a grunt, she rose, and with a lump in her chest, began to pick her way through the crowd to head back to the big house.

"And let's all put our hands together for some new additions to Plum Orchard!" Louella breathed into the mic. "First up, Miss LaDawn Jenkins. A former prostitute turned phone-sex operator, currently running amok with our young children, y'all, helping to shape their minds one foul word at a time."

Dixie's head shot up to the sound of all of Plum Orchard sputtering and gasping in horror.

Her shoes fell to the ground. She knew it. Knew it as sure as she'd known Em was a fool to believe the

Mags were anything but heartless bitches. Her stomach turned, sour bile flooded her throat.

Breaking into a run, she sprinted across the square, pushing people out of the way like some designer-clad linebacker. The freshly trimmed clippings of the box-wood bushes surrounding the gazebo cut into her bare feet with stinging slashes.

She crashed into Howard Fordham's back, yelping an apology when she knocked his baseball cap off, making a break for the stairs leading up to the gazebo where, from a distance, she saw Annabelle and Lesta-Sue waiting, modern-day Southern sentries, guarding their posts.

"Heads up, ladies!" she yelled in warning, familiar faces whizzing by her bobbing head in a blur, her pulse throbbing in her ears. She had one task—get that micro-phone away from Louella Palmer and wrap the cord of it around her neck until she strangled her to death with it.

She no longer heard Louella's voice. Instead, it had become like the voices of the adults in a Charlie Brown cartoon.

She didn't hear the outrage of the disgruntled crowd or the angry outbursts of protests as she knocked people out of her way, tripping and stumbling.

When Dixie became aware Annabelle and Lesta-Sue were in it for the long haul, staunchly standing their ground, she decided it was all or nothing.

If the Mags were looking for a good rumble, they'd chosen the worthiest opponent.

With a warrior cry, Dixie barreled toward them full speed, knocking them onto the steps with a grunt at the force of their bodies slamming against the wood. Dixie fell on top of Annabelle and wiggled her way up, using Annabelle's long torso for leverage.

She didn't think about the fact that her damnably tight dress had risen almost to her hips by the time she reached the final step. She didn't hear the scream Annabelle let go of when she discovered her nose was bleeding.

She heard nothing but the roar of her anger, screeching through her veins and throbbing in her ears, the huff of her lungs trying to produce enough air to keep them inflated long enough to get her hands on Louella.

Scrambling to the floor of the gazebo, Dixie stumbled to her feet and directed her wild gaze at Louella who still had the microphone in her hand—whose mouth was still moving—whose venom was still pouring from her lips.

That was when everything inside of her, every tightly wound ounce of restraint, uncoiled like the head of an uncontained garden hose. Dixie reared up, her eye of the tiger the microphone Louella held so smugly in her hand.

Dixie lunged at her with a rebel cry, knocking Louella and her pretty gold and chocolate-brown fall ensemble to the ground, making the crowd below them gasp again.

Louella, dazed on the floor of the gazebo, gave Dixie the opening to straddle her and snatch at the microphone.

The screech of feedback ripped through the air, the muffled sounds of Dixie's hands clawing at Louella's to wrest it from her mingled with their grunts and eventually, Louella's piercing scream when Dixie latched onto her hair and yanked hard.

She tore the microphone from Louella, pushing off her opponent's body and struggling to her feet. With a howl of rage, she threw it out into the dark, using every last ounce of energy she had left. A magnified thunk signaled it had landed on something hard and unyielding.

Dixie mentally brushed her hands together while gasping for the air wheezing from her lungs in harsh puffs. She bent at the waist, resting the heels of her hands on her knees, heedless to the fact that her underwear was the subject of much chatter.

Heedless to the fact that this also left her weak and vulnerable.

In hindsight, as her feet flew out from under her, Dixie realized, she'd forgotten the golden rule of a girl-fight.

Never leave your opponent conscious.

Fourteen

"Ow!" Dixie moaned with a flinch.

"This from a woman who took out not one, but three Mags in the space of two minutes?" Caine quipped. "Hike up your warrior panties and hold still. I can't see if you need stitches if you keep pulling away, honey."

He tried to stay calm while looking at Dixie's battered face, running his fingers over it to reassure himself nothing was broken. He tried to remember his mother's words about always being a gentleman, even as he considered driving over to Louella's and beating down her door so they could end this all now.

If Louella was doing this because of the rumor his mother divulged tonight on the phone when he'd told her about the argument Dixie had with the Mags at Madge's—that Louella had once been in love with him and he'd chosen Dixie without knowing Louella was even interested, he had a record to set straight. He'd never even been a little interested in Louella, and he never had a single clue she'd been interested in him.

It had always been Dixie.

Shit.

Dixie flapped her hands at him, pushing him away as if he was making something out of nothing. "I don't need stitches. I need aspirin and maybe a bag of peas. A steak, too, if you could manage it, and I don't mean some cheap steak for my eye. The bloodier the better."

Caine pushed her hands out of the way, running his fingers over the planes of her face to check for breaks, wincing when he got a close look at her swollen eye, bruised to a deep purple. "You need boxing gloves and a cage."

He winced. Jesus, she had some shiner. But what was that tingle in his chest? Pride. It damn well was. It was probably wrong, but seeing her tonight, flying up those steps to shut Louella up in defense of the Call Girls, had been a thing of beauty. This side of Dixie, the side he was seeing more and more of lately wasn't so different than the old Dixie.

Her goal tonight was the difference.

"Well, if this phone-sex thing doesn't work out, maybe I'll see if Craigslist has cages."

LaDawn and Marybell rushed into her room then, skidding to a halt in front of the bed he had insisted she lie down on.

"Are you okay, Dixie?" Marybell reached for her, shoving Caine out of the picture and tilting her chin up to pop one of her eyes open with two fingers. She gazed down into Dixie's blackened eye until she began to squirm.

Dixie jerked her head away, swiping at her eye with her thumb. "I'm fine. Stop fussing, Marybell. It's just a black eye."

"Just a black eye? Look at you, talkin' like the boxing ring is your home base," LaDawn crooned, her lips forming a smile. "And on behalf of lil ol' me, too. I do declare, I'm all kinds of flattered," she drawled, playfully punching Dixie's arm.

"Hah!" Dixie snorted. "Don't kid yourself. I was doing it to keep you in the game, LaDawn. If your numbers don't make me aspire to do better, then whose will?"

"Good thing you got there before I did," LaDawn assured her, arms crossed at her chest. "I was gonna show that stuck-up, frilly, tight-ass what a whoopin' feels like. I put on the nicest dress I have for this party, too. One that keeps my best companionator assets from fallin' all over the men of this backwoods town." She hiked up the front of her overflowing maxi dress to rearrange her assets.

Dixie rubbed her temple, trying to sit up, but Caine settled her back in. "Next time, you do the whoopin'. I'll just eat and watch the chaos from the safety zone, okay?"

"No. No, sir. There's not gonna be a next time for me." LaDawn shook her mane of platinum-blond hair, still tangled up in her big hoop earrings, as she dipped a washcloth in more water, wiping at the scratches on Dixie's legs with gentle swipes. "No way I'm goin' somewhere where nobody'll just let my past be. To think, they were all laughin' and pointin' at me behind my back, but smilin' right in my face and offerin' me home-cooked food on top of it."

Dixie grabbed LaDawn's hand, wincing when she looked up at her. "You will so go back. I'll take you back, tied and gagged if I have to—and you'll like it. You live in Plum Orchard now, LaDawn. Marybell, too. This is *our* town, not just Louella Palmer's. As long as I'm here, no one's going to treat you like anything else but the taxpayers you are. I'll make sure of it." She groaned, leaning back on the bed when Caine swung her feet upward, repositioning her.

LaDawn shook her head. "It's not your fault, Dixie. Landon told me it might be like this, but I took the chance anyway because I wanted off the streets for good—and he sure can talk good game with all the fancy stuff he offered. I think Landon coulda talked Jesus into the second coming if he could have gotten face time with him."

"Tell me about it," Dixie muttered.

"But I'll tell you this—I didn't think there was anything I couldn't take on. I was a companionator, for Jesus sake. Those of us who companionate, we have our share of haters, mind you, but they ain't like the people in this town. This small-town bullshit is fierce. At least the haters back home hate ya right up front. These people fed me baked beans before they attacked, Dixie. That's just not right."

"I'm so sorry, LaDawn," Dixie said, while Caine pretended not to listen to the real sincerity in her voice. It wasn't like the gooey crap she'd laid on with a trowel years ago. It was raw.

And real.

LaDawn's round face fell. She was one tough cookie, if all the stories Caine had heard from the other girls were true, but she appeared genuinely hurt that she'd been tricked into believing the Mags would allow the women to blend in with everyone else.

LaDawn shrugged her shoulders. "Just seems like they don't want anybody to have a chance to make good without bringing up your misdeeds every chance they get. I might not be sellin' dictionaries on the phone, but I ain't spreadin' diseases and stealin' women's husbands anymore either. That should count for something, right?"

Marybell shook her head, her Mohawk flopping forward and back. "You were amazing, Dixie. A-maz-ing. All ragin' and yankin' that microphone from Louella's hand like you were some kind of thug. I know I was next on her hit list, so thanks, Dixie. I'm not as tough as LaDawn. I don't think I could have listened to her say those things about me."

"Looks like you won't have to worry about it, for a little while, at least," Em chimed in, crossing the floor in bare feet, her stained dress brushing her bloodied knees. "Seems Annabelle's on bed rest—she has a concussion. And Louella needs to pay a visit to Johnsonville to see a specialist to get her broken nose set."

But Dixie didn't look as though she was taking pleasure in any of it. She looked worried. "Is Lesta-Sue okay? I landed on her pretty hard, Em."

Caine cocked his head. Now she was inquiring about the opponent's health?

Em nodded. "I saw, and why should you care? Those women were out to turn somethin' perfectly lovely into a circus. They don't deserve your pity, Dixie!"

"Everyone deserves a second chance, Em," Dixie said groggily, making Caine worry she might have a concussion, too. Dixie preaching about second chances was like LaDawn preaching abstinence.

Em's lips thinned to a fine line of red. "I should have listened to you. After all, you were once head of the Mags. Butter wouldn't melt in their mouths while they assured me it was a wonderful idea to invite the ladies.

Oh! I could just march right over to Louella's and give her a piece of what-for."

Dixie shook her head. "We need to let everyone simmer down now, Em. Don't go pokin' the beehive."

"I want to poke her eyes out!"

That Dixie wasn't plotting Louella's ugly revenge right now was blowing his damn mind. Maybe she was plotting on the inside.

But something about that notion just didn't sit right with him.

Dixie's face scrunched up. "Hush. Take that back. It won't solve anything," she scolded, accepting a cold pack Sanjeev handed her before he escaped on silent feet.

But Em wouldn't be pacified. She paced, rubbing her bruised arm. "I say we strike back, Dixie—strike now while the iron is hot!"

"Listen to me, Darth Vader, no striking. That's what feeds this childish behavior. We're behaving no better than I did back in the day. I'll handle the Mags. You'll stay out of it—for the sake of your boys," Dixie reminded Em pointedly.

What did Em's boys have to do with the Mags?

Appropriately chided, Em crumbled, her eyes full of tears when she turned to LaDawn and Marybell. "I'm so sorry, girls. I truly believed that piranha Louella when she said it was a wonderful idea to invite you. If I'd known you were virtually walking into the lion's den, I'd never have insisted y'all come."

Marybell gave Em a hug, squeezing her tight. "You were just trying to be a good person and make us feel welcome in a place where it feels like I don't even speak the language. Besides, the fried chicken was almost

worth it. And those biscuits Ben Johnson's wife made—
wow." She held two thumbs up.

LaDawn clapped Em on the back. "I'm not much of
a hugger, but it was nice you thought of us. Next time,
though? Don't think of us. I'd rather just live out my
days in Landon's backyard with Toe and the pool."

Marybell pinched one of Dixie's toes. "We gotta go,
Dixie. Our shift's comin' up. Cat said she'd drop by to
see you tomorrow and check on you. She was off doin'
her online classes and making goo-goo eyes at Flynn."

Dixie reached for the nightstand, trying to lift her
legs up and off the bed. "Wait for me. I'm coming with
you. I have a shift tonight, too."

Caine straightened and pressed a hand to the flat of
her chest, trying hard not to think about how good it felt
just to touch her skin again. He'd drawn the friend line
between them tonight and here he was already thinking about how good it'd be to cross it. "No. No work
tonight, Dixie. You need to rest, and I'm seriously thinking of calling in Dr. Johnson just to have him give you
a once-over."

"Why, so he can mess all the tests he's so fond of
up and tell everyone I have the clap? Not on your life,
Candy Caine," she teased him with a half grin.

"Ray took over his father's practice several years
ago. I think you're safe," Caine assured her, keeping
his hand on her chest, his concern heavy.

"You mean the Ray I was talkin' to while enjoyin'
some baked beans was a *doctor?*" LaDawn mused in
disbelief. "Shoot. Just figures. I think Ray liked me."

"And on that note, we're off to work," Marybell said
with a snicker, blowing Dixie a kiss before ushering

LaDawn out of Dixie's room, their chatter drifting along the hall until he couldn't hear them anymore.

Em motioned for Caine to move over. With gentle fingers, she traced the outline of the bruise surrounding Dixie's eye, her eyes welling with more tears. "I'm sorry, Dixie. I'm so sorry this happened. I should have listened to your misgivings."

"Or ten," Dixie reminded. "I remember I said approximately ten."

So Dixie had been suspicious the Mags would mess with the ladies. Damn pious lot. It was time he did some intervention. Landon never would've stood for this kind of harassment. He wasn't going to sit back and let those women shit all over Dixie and the girls.

Em shook her head, her eyes on fire. "You're all banged up, Dixie. We can't just let this slide. Next thing Louella'll think it's okay to launch anthrax attacks. She's going to do whatever it takes to get you outta Plum Orchard. We can't let this stand. Besides, wasn't it you who always said the one with the most toys wins?"

Dixie's voice sounded thin and so sad, it hurt his ears to hear it. "That was before I lost my toys. All of them. No, Em. No more return attacks. I didn't take up for you at Madge's because I enjoy the fight. Hard as that is for everyone to believe." Dixie gave Caine a pointed look. "I did it because I was afraid they'd try to attack your personal life. This isn't a war, Em. This is a petty, spiteful woman who hates the very ground I walk on."

Em flapped her hands as she rose from the bed. "No matter now. For now you need rest. I'll do enough fumin' for the both of us."

Dixie grabbed at Em's hand, her eyes soft. "Hey, before you go—thanks for having my back, Em. The bits of it I can recall as I lay on the gazebo floor, looked like you were scattering bodies and taking names."

Em's smile was full of the devil. "I couldn't let Louella take advantage of your semiconscious state, could I? Especially after I created this fiasco."

"You really slugged Louella. That's some right hook you have," Caine interjected with a wink of admiration, wrong or not, manners be damned.

Em turned and gave Caine a prim smile over her shoulder. "I did not slug. I merely thwarted. Louella was gonna dump potato salad on a defenseless woman. I'd thwart again if the need arose. Now, I have boys who need a bedtime story." She leaned in to hug Dixie and whispered, "Rest, my friend."

Em's hasty retreat left them alone on the bed with Mona and Lisa, and his questions. Staring at her bruised face, swollen and red, Caine couldn't stop looking at her. He couldn't stop looking for her ulterior motive. He couldn't stop thinking about how crazy it was that Em was the one who wanted to strike back and Dixie didn't.

Dixie slid off the bed, her hands reaching out as she swayed.

Caine caught her, tucking her to his side, his worry she was seriously hurt far outweighing the things swirling around in his head. "Honey—you need to let me take you to the hospital, for Christ's sake."

"I have no insurance. No hospitals. I'm fine. Now you go do Candy Caine things. There must be a hundred calls backed up for Sam Elliott."

"I'll pay for it, Dixie."

His offer of money made her stand up straighter. "Friends don't let friends pay their medical bills. I'm going to take a shower. No more talking. It hurts my head."

Caine stopped her, putting his hands at her waist. "No way I'm letting you take a shower in this condition all alone."

Dixie shook her head with a grunt. "Friends don't let friends see them naked in the shower."

"What do friends let friends do?" he asked in exasperation.

Dixie gazed up at him, her eye puffier by the second, her cheek purple and yellow. She'd never looked more beautiful. "I'm unclear on our particular kind of friendship and its classifications. For now, I know for sure we're not the kind of friends who see each other naked. We're just friendly friends."

"Well, this *friend* isn't letting you take a shower alone. Not after that crack to the head. Do you want to slip and fall? And friends do let friends see them naked. Girls do it all the time." He scooped her up in his arms, carrying her toward the bathroom.

She wanted to summon the will to make him put her down the entire trip into the bathroom. She really, really did. Mostly. The half of her that was determined to let him go wasn't nearly as strong as the half of her whose limbs felt as if they'd been softened like butter in a microwave.

He set her on the vanity, sliding her backward until her spine was against the wall.

"But you're not a girl, and we can always ask Sanjeev to help me." Dixie leaned against the mirror, afraid to look at her battered reflection while Caine filled a glass with water and dug around in the medicine cabinet.

He handed her two aspirin with a grin. "Nope. I'm not a girl. I'm Golden Boy, remember? And Golden Boy isn't leaving this bathroom until you do. Sanjeev, at this hour, is probably knee deep in his nightly prayers. So you got me, babe," he joked in Sonny Bono's singing voice. "Now, lift your arms up," he ordered.

Dixie did as he commanded, too tired to refuse. He slipped her dress over her head, and popped the clasp on her bra between her breasts. The cool rush of air against her hot skin made her hiss.

Or was that Caine's touch making her hiss?

"Dixie?"

Her eyes popped open at the sound of his voice to find their noses a mere half inch apart. She smiled at his handsome face, his clear eyes fringed with dark lashes, the stubble on his jawline—him. Her hand went to his jaw in a familiar gesture, forgetting their friendship truce—forgetting her pact with herself to keep her hands off him. "What?"

Caine ran a finger down her nose and smiled back before dropping his boots and socks on the vanity next to her. "Keep your eyes open. If you have a concussion, you can't sleep."

Dixie frowned. She knew there was a reason for that rule—she just couldn't remember what it was. "Or?"

"Or you might not wake up in time to try out for defensive tackle. You don't want to miss an opportunity to hone your skills with the big boys of Plum Orchard High, do you?" he teased, fingers sinking into her waist to lift her to her feet.

Dixie's arms went around his neck to steady herself again, her nipples scraping the fabric of his shirt.

The promise she'd made to herself to have no physical contact with Caine was well on its way to crumbling.

She gave a halfhearted shove at his chest, longing to rest her head on it instead of push it away. "Let me take a shower. Go handle your shift. All the Connery groupies need you. Plus, you don't want to lose the opportunity to find some new clients, do you? If I take a personal day, your chances of beating me just improved. I'll be fine. Really."

His arms tightened about her waist, the slide of his hands against the skin of her back making her shiver. "That's not going to happen. So if you're desperate for that shower—it's while I watch, or it isn't going to happen."

She chuckled at the irony of his words. "Kinky."

Caine hooked his thumbs inside her panties, sliding them down along her legs to her feet. She used her hands to brace herself on his shoulders, loving the feel of his fingers brushing her thighs then her calves, completely comfortable with shedding her clothing. He nudged her with the top of his head to lift her foot then pulled her panties off.

Maybe it was only her imagination, but his breathing sounded hitched when he rose to his feet and slipped another arm around her waist to lift her off the vanity and walk her toward Landon's custom-made shower. She'd once jokingly referred to the extravagance of it as a shower fit for an orgy—party of ten, please—it was so spacious and decked out.

Caine flipped the faucets on, adjusting the temperature before picking her back up and setting her in the water under the first set of showerheads, stepping in behind her, clothes and all.

Dixie's shock was bigger than her protest. "You'll ruin your clothes," was all she could manage.

"I'll send you the bill," he grumbled, leading her deeper into the enormous tiled space. He placed his hands under her forearms, guiding her to the long bench where he sat her down and set about adjusting the remaining showerheads. The water sprayed both sides of her body, soothing and warm.

Dixie closed her eyes, not caring that she was naked, and Caine was still fully clothed. It felt too good to have Caine take care of her, to see the way his jaw rippled while he concentrated on the task.

She continued to ignore those promises she'd made to herself regarding Caine and touching when he settled between her knees, shower gel in hand.

The sting of water on her scrapes made her wince, but Caine's hands, smoothing the gel over her skin, massaging her aching muscles as he went, distracted her enough to forget everything but the soothing motion.

"Tip your head back, honey, so I can wash your hair."

Dixie did as directed, letting the pulse of the water and the scent of her pear shampoo wash away the grime and sweat of her kill. Nothing mattered but Caine's fingers in her scalp, easing the tight tension, rinsing the thick ropes of her hair by squeezing out the excess water. She bit back a soft moan at the gentle pleasure his hands wrought, one that was sure to echo in the cavernous space.

Caine finished rinsing her hair, and then his fingers came to rest on the area surrounding her black eye. "You were really something tonight," he murmured, so soft and low, she almost didn't catch what he'd said with the rush of the water.

Her eyes were still closed but her grimace was ironic. "Yeah. Something."

Tipping her head back up, he thumbed away drops of water from her face with tenderness before cupping her chin. "What I meant to say was, you were awesome tonight."

Dixie didn't understand his concerned gaze. She didn't recognize this Caine—one who had sympathy in his voice and touch. And still her promises to herself continued to slip away. "Thank you," she replied, her voice gruff, her throat tight.

"I mean that, Dixie."

She began to shy away from what Caine meant as a compliment. "I was angry."

"You were incredible."

She shook her head, casting her eyes to the buttons on his soaking wet shirt as remorse began to weigh heavy and ugly in her gut. "I was a spectacle. Seems I suddenly forgot to use my words. I was wrong to approach the situation like that."

His fingers went to her chin so her eyes were forced to meet his. "*No*. No, Dixie. Louella created the spectacle. You did the honorable thing and tried to stop it before it went too far."

Seeing Louella now, so much like she'd once been, left her overwhelmed with such sadness. That she'd been responsible for hurting Louella so much, she'd turned cruelty into a defense mechanism, made her bones ache with regret. "I used to be Louella, Caine. Or Louella's turned into me. I'm not sure anymore," she whispered.

Caine's eyes pierced hers. "No one is you, Dixie. *No one.*"

Tears stung her blurry eyes, warm water cocooned her and exhaustion left her limbs shaky and her heart vulnerable. This Caine—the one who was looking at her with understanding, the one who was calling her something other than the dregs of society—was breaking her resolve. She didn't know what that meant. She didn't want to know if it meant the exact opposite of what it usually meant.

Dixie shrugged her chin from his hand, her shoulders caving inward as a small sob escaped her lips. She could take almost anything. She could take his stinging words. She could take his indifference. She couldn't take friendly understanding.

And then Caine was reaching up, pulling her close, and capturing her lips tenderly, delving between them with his silky tongue.

Her fingers automatically sank into his wet shirt, relishing the hard strength beneath the soaked material, pressing her palms against the bulges in his shoulders until she wrapped her arms around his neck, bringing him as close as humanly possible.

Her mouth opened beneath the weight of his, accepting his kiss, twisting her neck to get closer, and ignoring the sharp stab of protest in her sore tendons.

She moaned when he pulled away, moving along her cheek with care, gliding his mouth to the hollow of her neck, nibbling, tasting. Her nipples grew tight, hardening with need.

Caine sensed that, and cupping the underside of her breasts, he kneaded them, dragging the tips of his thumbs over the points until she was slippery with desire.

Her head fell back, exposing the column of her neck.

Her fingers drove into his scalp, clutching handfuls of his wet hair, her hips lifted, and her legs went around his waist, drawing him flush to her.

Caine licked at her neck, letting his teeth lightly graze the skin, dipping lower and lower until his hot breath teased her nipples. When his lips wrapped around one tight bud, Dixie thought she'd explode, the sensation so intense, heightened by this new connection between them.

Water rained down on them, pelting the hard tile, creating a steamy shelter that soon blocked everything out but Caine's mouth on her, devouring every exposed inch of her slick flesh.

Her back arched as his free arm went around her waist, and his hand splayed across her ass, forcing her hips upward.

Caine's hand slipped between her thighs, spreading her swollen lips open, dragging his fingers up and down until he made a wet path of heat. "So good," she whispered.

Dixie placed her hand over Caine's, guiding his finger to her entrance, lifting her hips upward until his finger slid inside her. She hissed her pleasure, rocking against his thumb now rasping against her clit in delicious circles. The wet slide of his tongue licking at her nipple, along with his finger driving into her greedy body brought her orgasm, fierce and sharply sweet.

Her chest tightened and her thighs clenched together, trapping his hand between them. Caine found her mouth again, drowning out her whimpers as she came.

Dixie gasped for breath when another dizzy spell left her clutching at his arms.

"I've got you. Just hold on to me, honey," he murmured, placing her hands at his waist.

She gripped his clothes, soaked through and through, hearing the crunch of his wet jeans as he brought her with him to turn off the faucets. Dixie sighed when he lifted her back up and hiked her legs around his waist to exit the shower, leaving puddles of water on the floor.

"Sanjeev'll have your head."

Caine chuckled, the deep vibration of it from his chest making her sigh with contentment. "You don't think this is the first time there's been water all over the princess bathroom, do you? Remind me to tell you about the three-way we had in here two summers ago."

Dixie giggled. "Two summers ago you were in the Baltic with Landon."

"You keeping tabs on me?" he teased, his eyes crinkling at the corners.

"Like some creepy stalker," she joked back.

Through weary eyes, she watched as Caine somehow found a fluffy towel and dried her from head to toe, slipping her nightgown over her head then stripping off his own clothes and managing to struggle into her old flannel bathrobe.

The brief glimpse of Caine naked, still hard from their encounter, made her mouth water and her heart speed up, but her body wasn't cooperating with her libido.

Caine took her by the hand and led her back into the bedroom. "Bed. Now."

Dixie climbed under the covers, grateful for the cool luxury. Mona and Lisa burrowed next to her, knocking the assorted pillows to the floor as her eyes began to droop.

Caine brought her fingers to his lips. "Hey, tiger, no sleeping until I talk to Ray and make sure you're cleared."

He settled behind her, spooning her, sliding her nightgown upward until the heat of his cock pressed into her back. Caine's hands roamed over the planes of her body, teasing. Lifting her leg, he spread her wide, flattening his palm against her swollen heat, smoothing his hands over the lips of her cleft until she bucked against him, writhing and needy.

Her arms went up around his neck from behind her, thrusting her breasts forward so Caine could slide his hand under her and cup one. "I want to bury my face between your thighs, Dixie. Taste you on my tongue when you come. Lick you until you scream."

Dixie shivered at his words, arching up and inward against his hot length in response. She reached behind her, finding the solid length of his cock, and pumped it, moving her ass up higher until Caine had no choice but to answer her body's question.

Right now, in her dazed state, the only thing that was clear was she needed his cock in her, driving away her fears, putting out the fire of revenge and replacing it with his hands, his mouth and his glorious tongue. "Please, Caine," she begged. "Please make love to me. I need this so much more than you'll ever know."

He stiffened behind her, his thick thighs pressing into hers, the crisp hair of them brushing against her smoother skin. "I want to touch every part of you, lick every inch of you, drown myself in you. But you belong to someone else. Walker," he grated the name against her ear. "I don't make love to someone else's woman, but Christ if it isn't killing me to keep from doing it."

She twisted her neck, pulling his head in for a wet, deep kiss. "I made Walker up. Make love to me. *Now,*" she begged with a whisper.

He growled a chuckle, gripping her tighter, stroking her tender clit. "Say it, Dixie. Tell me what you want me to do."

She was so turned on, so fragile, so vulnerable the words flew from her mouth with ease. "I want your cock in me. Hard. I don't want you to ever stop. I want you to make me come like you're the only person who can do it. Do it, Caine, please, please do it."

"I want to watch, baby. I want to see you touch yourself," Caine ordered, cupping her ass, rolling his hands over her skin, dipping between her wet thighs, dragging that wetness to his lips and licking his finger. "No one tastes like you, Dixie. *No one,*" he said before positioning himself between her thighs and driving upward.

Dixie buckled then, stifling a scream of raw, uncensored pleasure, coming almost instantly—her need was so deep—with Caine not far behind.

And then he was moving away, running a warm cloth over her, toweling her dry with hands that nurtured as she burrowed beneath the warmth of the comforter.

Some of the last things she vaguely remembered were Caine signing off with Ray, a brief kiss to her temple, and his secure arms around her with her cheek resting on his chest.

But the very last thing she remembered was she and Caine lying next to each other just the way she'd always meant for things to be.

Fifteen

Caine's feet pounded against the pavement, sweat pouring in familiar rivulets down his chest and along his belly. Fall was coming, but summer wasn't leaving without a fight. Thick humid air rushed at his soaking wet skin, his thighs and calves straining to meet his goal even though they burned.

His iPod blaring Nine Inch Nails in his ears, he ran the track at Plum Orchard High. It was too early for the kids to be there for practice, leaving him with the track and his thoughts to himself.

Running helped him think. And he had a shitload of thinking to do.

Dixie was going to kill him—no question about that, and rightfully so.

Caine didn't know what made him do it the first time, or the second time, or even now as he was contemplating the third. He just knew he was eating Dixie up under the cloak of anonymity.

He'd gone along with this damn contest with the idea he'd nail her with his anger at every underhanded, low-down dirty opportunity afforded him. Not very golden boy of him, he mused, but the lingering effects of the end of their relationship left seeing her again a bitter pill to swallow. One he did his best to remind her of like some kind of damn tyrant. It was his fail-safe against falling for more of her bullshit.

It was his wall.

Because of the bet.

She'd called him her judge and jury, and the arrogant ass he'd been kept him from seeing that until just the other night when he'd finally apologized.

Dixie had once shredded his idea of what his life with her as his wife could have been. She'd taken the woman he'd created in his mind and blown her to shit.

That was when he realized some things never changed. Dixie was always in it for the win, and in the process, fulfilling a long overdue wish from their two families.

She didn't love him—she loved to brag about winning him. She always got what she wanted, but back then, he'd decided, he'd be damned if she'd get him. Not a chance he was marrying a woman who wanted to hang his head on her wall like some trophy. No matter how much he'd loved her.

He'd kicked himself over and over after he left Georgia and moved to Miami. He'd watched Landon indulge Dixie all through her teenage years—through all of her heartless shenanigans. They'd argued about it more than once. But Landon had seen something in Dixie no one but him saw, and he'd done what he'd always done, remained friends with both of them.

When they'd both come back ten years ago, and the older, allegedly changed Dixie caught his eye and every other aspect of him, he'd finally become a believer.

He, like everyone else, began to worship at the altar of Dixie.

He'd called himself all sorts of asshole for not seeing through her bullshit in the same way he had when they were kids.

She'd been the same old Dixie—cruel and manipulative, hiding behind the word *changed*. His pride and lack of good judgment had taken an ass-whooping, and there was nothing he liked less than feeling as if he'd been had. So he'd licked his wounds far enough away to stay sane and suffered through any mention Landon made of her when he had to.

But since they'd met up again, the cat had grown tired of toying with the mouse. Dixie wasn't the same damn mouse anymore anyway.

She was a gentler mouse, a mouse with a conscience. One who protected her friends and stuck up for the underdog.

He didn't know what had brought about the change, but change she had. Though he'd sure like to know what made someone as vindictive and calculating as Dixie turn into Gandhi.

He'd watched her take on the Mags, defend Emmaline, make dinner for the women of Call Girls without asking—or rather, expecting—a single thing in return. She'd put up with the jokes and constant reminders of some of her more widely known hijinks with a smile and a good-natured nod of her head.

Sometimes he wondered if she did it because she felt as if she deserved some sort of continual punishment. As though Dixie thought it was everyone's rite of passage to take a bite out of her as payment for her cruelty.

Yet she suffered the wrath of her past everywhere she

went like a trooper. She strolled into Madge's every day, head held high, back straight and sat on a stool where she ordered Danish for the girls coming off the night shift with a smile on her face and a kind word for anyone who bothered to ask how she was.

If Dixie heard what everyone was saying about her, and most didn't even bother to say it behind her back, she ignored it. It took guts to come back and face that kind of ridicule. Desperation and her sad financial state aside, Caine had to give it up to her for lasting as long as she had.

And then there was last night. Hell if he understood that Dixie. Not a sign of retribution. No defense in place for attacking Louella and the other Mags. Just her firm resolve that she'd been wrong to solve the problem with her fists instead of her words.

And tears, tears that ripped his guts out. Bruises that made him want to make everything better with his hands—his mouth. Scratches he wanted to make disappear.

The vulnerability in her eyes and in her body language said she needed someone to lean on—even if it was only for the moment. That Landon's death, this crazy phone-sex challenge, the worry her debt had brought had all begun to crush her, and she was fighting to keep her pretty head above water, said something about who she'd become.

That was the Dixie he was crazy about. The Dixie he couldn't keep his hands off.

He slowed to a more manageable pace, dragging a hand over his jaw and kicking up dirt.

Shit. He'd just admitted he was still crazy about her.

That brought him to a slow walk toward the bleach-

ers. He dropped down on the hard metal, wiping his
forehead with a towel before draining his bottle of
water.

Leaning back on his elbows, he gazed out at the
track, one he'd spent hundreds of hours at with Landon
and Dixie. In the stands, just hanging out, drinking their
first beers, watching Dixie cheer.

They'd been an odd dynamic—the three of them,
both of them sharing separate friendships with Landon.
But Dixie had always been a part of his memories.

Now a piece of that dynamic was gone, and today,
when he needed someone to throw his thoughts at, he
missed that dynamic more than ever.

His phone chirped, signaling a text. Digging it out of
his duffel bag, he hoped like hell it wasn't his secretary
back at the office in Miami. It was getting harder and
harder to keep everything on track being so far away.

Caine shaded the phone with his hand, scrolling to
the latest message.

Buck up, buttercup! Decisions, decisions to be made,
my friend. Choose wisely. Choose for keeps.

Caine smiled at the phone, his chest tight with missing his best friend. "You son of a bitch, Landon."

Catherine rushed to her the moment Dixie stepped
foot into Call Girls. "Dixie! Mercy, girl, you should be
at home resting." She made a face and groaned when
Cat cupped her cheek to assess Dixie's black eye and
swollen cheek.

Dixie attempted a smile, though the muscles in her
face didn't much like it. "Hey, stranger. How've you

been? Studying hard so we can all call you Miss Bachelor's Degree?"

"Forget about me. What are you doing here?"

"Working."

Catherine made a face at her, distorting her pretty features. "Oh, Dixie, nothing's more important than your health. Two days off won't break you."

"Nay, I say. Two days off could be the deciding factor between survival and poverty. You don't want to see me out there livin' under the old bridge by the creek, do you? Besides, I don't need my eye to talk." Though, it would certainly help if her tailbone wasn't on fire.

Catherine grabbed her hand and led her into her office, motioning her to sit on one of the chairs next to her. Her eyes were full of sympathy and concern. "So the girls told me everything about last night. I was worried something just like this would happen. I told Landon as much, but I'll never forget what he said when I expressed my concern."

Dixie knew what Landon would say. No one knew the kind of discrimination and disapproval that PO could throw at you like Landon did.

Cat puffed out her chest, raising one eyebrow and smiling a cocky half smile in Landon fashion. "He said, 'Kit-Cat, never you worry. If those buncha nosy old biddies with sticks up their hemorrhoid-filled asses give you or the girls any trouble, Dixie'll look out for you. She'll have your back. Nobody knows how to handle those women like my Dixie-Cup.'"

Dixie's chest grew tight again for the umpteenth time. Landon had had faith, more faith than she deserved. She gulped, looking away from Catherine's intense gaze and focusing on the pictures on her desk of a beautiful, chubby little baby boy with sandy brown hair. "He said that?"

"You bet he did. Landon would be so proud of you, Dixie."

Dixie deflected another rush of tears by snorting a laugh, dropping the bag of Tupperware filled with homemade split pea soup for the girls on her lap. "You think he'd be proud I wrestled Louella to the ground like some kind of caged animal in front of Plum Orchard all over a silly microphone? Oh, and let's not forget my panties. Most of the town saw those, too. I think Landon would call me unladylike, not heroic."

Catherine shook her dark head, her eyes glittering. "Don't diminish what you did, Dixie. Why do you do that? You did something good, something right, and it makes me mighty glad you're on our team."

Good Dixie. Brave Dixie. Caine's words last night, coupled with LaDawn's and Marybell's, and now Catherine's, were too much. All this praise made her uncomfortable. She'd done two whole things right in her life to this date. That didn't deserve praise—it deserved an about time.

She needed to escape before she couldn't breathe. "Is that all you needed? My shift starts in five minutes and I'd like to catch up on what I missed yesterday."

Cat leaned forward and grabbed both of Dixie's hands, her eyes deep and serious. "Look at me. You're a good person, Dixie Davis, and I don't give a coon's ass if you don't want to hear me say it out loud." Letting go of her hands, she smiled and leaned back. "Now, before you go, first, holy smokes. Did your line ever ring off the hook last night. Yay for you—lots of lonely men lookin' for advice. Second, you have a visitor. If you're not up to visitors, say the word, and I'll send her on her way."

Dixie's stomach reacted with a jolt. "A visitor? Friend or foe?" she asked weakly. She'd need to take kickboxing classes before she could go another round with a foe.

"I'm callin' friend, because she was lovely and sweet, but then after last night and that mean old Louella, you never can tell with the people in this town, can you?"

"Who is it?"

Cat hesitated for only a moment. "Jo-Lynne Donovan. She's waitin' on Caine, but she asked to see you while she did."

Perfect. Ding-dong, Caine's mother calling. Yet, her own mother would never forgive her bad manners if she didn't speak to Jo-Lynne, even if they weren't actually speaking to one another because of her. She blew out a rush of air and gathered her things. "Where is she?"

"Waiting in your office."

Even more perfect. Her ex-almost-mother-in-law was sitting in the office where, as a joke, LaDawn had turned Dixie's screensaver into a floating penis shaped like a rocket ship. She closed her eyes for a second to get a second wind, then popped them open with determination. "Then to the lion's den."

Cat's gaze was filled with concern again. "You gonna be okay?"

"Could be I'll have matching black eyes," she joked on her way out the door. She hadn't seen Jo-Lynne since the night of her engagement party. Another one of the many regrets she had. Not only had she ruined the friendship between her and Caine's mother, but she'd screwed up having one of the best mothers-in-law a girl could hope for.

Jo-Lynne represented some of the very best things about her childhood. She was kisses and Estée Lauder-scented hugs, gooey slices of pecan pie, tater-tot hot dish, and a million Band-Aids on knees torn and scraped from trying to keep up with two boys for your closest friends.

She'd loved Jo-Lynne like a second mother, and she'd spit in her face as surely as she had Caine's by not even apologizing for her part in their engagement fiasco.

One deep breath, two silent prayers later, and Dixie was face-to-face with the woman who'd given birth to the man she couldn't manage to stop loving.

Jo-Lynne rose at the sound of the office door opening. Her features, a softer version of Caine's, were serene as always. She wore her hair in a silky, sandy-brown bob that hugged the shape of her face to perfection. A smile flitted across her red lips before it tipped upside down, and she was putting her navy purse on Dixie's desk and rushing to her side. "Dixie! Oh, sugarplum, what happened?"

More tears? *Really, Dixie? Who are you?* The concern in Jo-Lynne's voice, the way she dropped everything to examine her scrapes and bruises, unlike her own mother, had Dixie in the grips of another display of her out-of-control emotions. She'd called Dixie that all her life. Sugarplum.

In fact, she could only remember two or three times when Jo-Lynne had actually used her given name—and one of those times was at her engagement party. Just after everything had gone sideways.

Dixie held up a hand to keep her at bay. A hug filled with warmth and sympathy was far more than she deserved. "I'm okay. Really. Just some scrapes."

Jo-Lynne pointed to the garish chaise longue. "You sit down this instant, young lady, and let me look at you. You're an absolute mess!"

Dixie did as she was instructed because you just didn't cross Jo-Lynne. Her perfume, classic and as elegant as she herself was, drifted to Dixie's nose while her gentle hands, aged only slightly, smoothed Dixie's hair back. "So you gonna tell me what happened?"

"You don't know?"

"I certainly do not. I just got in tonight from Atlanta and came straight here to meet Caine."

Dixie shrugged in embarrassment, putting her hands in her lap. "I got into a fight."

Jo-Lynne nudged her over and sat beside her, holding Dixie's hand under the ceiling lamp to inspect the deep scratch Louella's heel had left. "With?"

"A gang of wandering thugs?"

"Try that again, miss."

"Some people?"

"One more time."

"Flash mob brawl?"

Jo-Lynne's lips thinned. "Dixie Cordelia Davis…"

That was the warning. All three given names spoken at once. "Louella and some of the Mags. Two, to be precise."

Jo-Lynne's eyes flashed, angry and outraged. "*They* did this to you?"

"I sort of did it first. Then they did this back."

Jo-Lynne gave her back her hand, folding her own hands in her lap. Here came the disapproval. "I'm guessing that spoiled Louella deserved it?"

Had the entire world gone mad? Had Plum Orchard

moved to some sort of alternate dimension where Dixie
was always right and everyone else was at fault?

She shook her head. "She didn't deserve to be mowed
over like I was driving a John Deere and she was an
acre of unkempt land. I shouldn't have resorted to physical violence."

Jo-Lynne pursed her lips. "I want to hear every detail."

Dixie explained only that she was defending a friend
then waited for her lecture on violence with quiet apprehension.

Instead of giving her hell, Jo-Lynne nodded her head
in agreement. "Well, it doesn't surprise me that Louella
was a part of pickin' on someone. I'm here to tell you, I
never liked Louella. I know I should because she's the
daughter of a Mag, and we're all supposed to be like
family, but sometimes you're forced to tolerate family
you don't like."

Dixie's astonishment bled into her words. "Wait. You
believe me without anyone backing up my story?"

"Of course I do, sugarplum." She patted Dixie's
hand.

She'd been far worse than Louella once. It was only
fair to point that out. "But I picked on people, too—
all my life, Miss Jo-Lynne. I coerced, connived and in
general mowed down anyone or anything in my path,
especially Louella." In fact, had Landon brought the
Call Girls into town just ten years ago, she probably
would have behaved just as reprehensibly.

Jo-Lynne's eyebrows rose. "So Louella gets a free
pass because you did it, too? I'd like to own a yacht, so
I should steal one just like all the other criminals? You
were a child. A rebellious, out-of-control one, but still

a child. Louella's no child, Dixie Davis. She's a grown woman who should be long past this kind of judgmental behavior."

Dixie stubbornly refused to agree. "I wasn't a child when I—"

Jo-Lynne's finger flew upward, cutting her off. She pressed it to Dixie's lips, giving them a pat. "No. You were still a child back when you were engaged to Caine, sugarplum, whether you knew it or not. Life hadn't taught you your lessons just yet, so you'd appreciate what you'd been given instead of taking it just because you wanted it. You had to learn those things in Chicago where no one cared that you were Dixie Davis, didn't you?"

After all the humiliation and heartache she'd caused both she and Caine, Jo-Lynne was defending her as though Dixie had never left her watchful eyes. As though she still thought of Dixie as the daughter she never had.

The revelation cut her to the quick. "Yes…ma'am…" was the best she could manage.

"So tell me, this fight with Louella, was it over this phone-sex business you and Caine are wrapped up in because of my dearly departed Landon?"

Dixie couldn't hear the words phone and sex come out of Jo-Lynne's mouth. It was like hearing her tell you about her private bedroom matters.

Rather than clap her hands over her ears, she kept her reply simple. "Yes. Louella called one of the other operators out in front of everyone at the annual autumn dance, and it was cruel and humiliating. I was determined to make her stop. I just didn't stop her in the way reasonable adults do."

Jo-Lynne was pensive for a moment as though she was tempering her words. "You know, the Mags don't like what Landon's done here, Dixie, and I'm not saying that I'd suggest the youth of Plum Orchard consider it a step toward a solid future in telecommunications. I realize some of the women involved haven't been afforded the kind of lifestyle the girls here in town have. They're makin' their way, is all. But I say who's it hurtin'? If it wasn't for some good old-fashioned makin' love, not a one of us would be here to begin with. It isn't for us to judge if it's right or wrong."

If one could call flogging and foot fetishes old-fashioned.

Jo-Lynne's justifications for the Call Girls were just shy of blowing Dixie's mind. "I'm not sure what to say. I didn't expect you to be so understanding. Mama certainly isn't."

"Your mama and I didn't always see eye to eye on everythin', especially about raisin' you. I think you know what I mean by that."

"Mama's a hard woman to please. We don't talk much anymore. Not since the restaurant fell apart…"

"There's somethin' I've always wanted to say, and because I don't give a hoot about what anyone, especially a Mag thinks, I'm just gonna say it. Your mama's a mean woman, Dixie. Cold and controlling and as superficial as the day is long. But you're a strong woman. You were a strong child with an even stronger will. Your way was to rebel against that iron fist of hers. She demanded you wear your skirts below the knee, you ripped the hem out and cut them to midthigh."

"I wanted her to love me." She cringed as her voice cracked. God. She'd really wanted that. Just once, she'd wanted her mother to love her instead of always reminding her she owned her.

Jo-Lynne smiled a watery smile. "I know that, Dixie. You're not the reason I'm angry with Pearl Davis. It has nothing to do with connections or money or any of the things your mama's so angry about. Those are all superficial things. It has to do with how she pushed and pushed you until you exploded."

Trapped. That's how she'd felt when she'd stupidly left college out of boredom and came back to Plum Orchard with no degree and no purpose. Her mother reminded her every day how time was wasting.

If she were deeply truthful with herself, at first, Caine had been an answer to all her problems. Marrying him would get her mother off her back and her approval—approval Dixie was hungry for, all in one fell swoop. But he'd become so much more. Suddenly, he wasn't just to-die-for gorgeous, or kind and honorable— he was everything she'd never had.

In the process of finding the answer to her mother's constant badgering, she'd found love without conditions and judgment, and she'd fallen head over heels for him.

But it had been too late to put the brakes on the bet.

A sharp rap brought their eyes to the door. Caine popped it open and smiled when his gaze connected with Jo-Lynne's—that warm, loving smile he'd always reserved for his mother. "There you are." He scooped her up in a hug, kissing her cheek, while Dixie hoped to blend with the chaise. "We still on for dinner?"

Jo-Lynne squeezed his arm affectionately. "Give me two more minutes with Dixie, and I'll be right there."

Caine's hesitance was reflected in his reluctance to leave. He put a hand under her elbow, his expression playful when he used a teasing Darth Vader impression to persuade her. "Mother, if we do not hurry, Madge will be all out of fried pork chops and gravy. How can we have enough energy for total universal domination?"

Jo-Lynne almost cracked a smile then waved him out with a determined motion. "Shoo, Caine. I'll be right there."

Caine sighed, running a hand through his hair. "Mom, Dixie's had a rough couple of days. Give her a break and let her be."

Caine's attempt to prevent what he clearly feared would be a confrontation was sweet, but falling on deaf ears.

"I can see that, Caine. Now out, young man!"

Poor Caine. He didn't stand a chance. Dixie put a hand on his arm, almost incapable of looking him in the eyes after their lovemaking last night. "It's okay, Caine. You go."

His fingers threaded through hers for a moment, dangling there for seconds, the connection making her heart pump harder, before he gave his mother a pointed look. "I'll be right outside this door." He hitched his unshaven jaw in the direction of the door. "Play nice."

The moment Caine left, Jo-Lynne pulled Dixie up by her hands and looked her square in the eyes. "There's something else we need to discuss."

Dixie swallowed hard. *Atone, Dixie.* If Jo-Lynne wanted to purge, scream, yell, call her names after what she'd done, she'd roll out the red carpet for her. She stared straight ahead, bracing herself for her due. "Yes, ma'am."

But Jo-Lynne's eyes were soft. "You were a horror, Dixie. From the day you were born you were cranky and colicky and difficult to please. I know, because I rocked you at many a Mag meeting when your mama needed a break. And I loved you like you were my own. Not much changed with you for many years. You were ugly to people. I knew it. Everyone knew it, but I still loved you. And then you did somethin' so awful to my son—"

"I'm sorry," Dixie rushed out the words she'd waited forever to speak, steeped in more remorse than she'd ever be able to properly express. "I should have said that the night it happened, but I'm so sorry I ruined everything. I'm sorry I embarrassed your good family name. Most of all, I'm sorry I hurt Caine."

Jo-Lynne cupped her cheek. "Never you mind about family names and all the other silly ideals they feed you here in the Orchard. My name doesn't matter nearly as much as my son's heart does—his happiness. So I'm here to tell you true, Dixie Davis—you hurt him back then, bad. I don't want that to happen again. But mostly what I want you to know is I love you, I always knew you'd work past it one day—and I can see you have. But if you do it again, if you hurt my boy like you did last time, I'm comin' for you. Understand, sugarplum?"

She managed a smile, keeping her sigh of relief to herself. "Understood."

"Now, give Miss Jo-Lynne a big ol' hug. Don't know if I'll still be standin' after I eat one of those greasy pork chops Madge makes with my cholesterol bein' so high. So let's hug it out just in case."

Dixie let Jo-Lynne pull her into an embrace, savoring the familiar hug scented with remnants of her childhood. She rested her head on her shoulder, fighting another slew of tears.

When Jo-Lynne pulled away, she held her at arms'

length and granted her a smile straight from her child-hood. "Look at you, even all beat up, you're still just as pretty as you ever were."

She didn't feel pretty, but she did feel less dark on the inside than she had in a long time.

"Now, you make sure you come over in the next few weeks for some of my chili and corn bread. I won't take no for an answer. I'll make sweet tea just like always, and—" Jo-Lynne pulled her in close "—I've forgiven you, Dixie Davis. All was forgiven, a long time ago, sugarplum. Now forgive yourself." She dropped a warm kiss on Dixie's cheek, gathered her purse, and she was gone, leaving Dixie to war with more acceptance, more generosity of spirit.

Forgiven. Used in reference to Dixie Davis? Yes. The world had become an episode of *Fringe*. This had to be the "other" Plum Orchard.

She paused for a long moment, looking at the clut-ter of messages on her desk and the unopened emails in her inbox from clients without really seeing them.

Her muscles ached, as did her mind, full of Jo-Lynne's words of forgiveness, and more—words of acceptance. As she sat in her chair, ready to attack her inbox, it was with a lighter load on her shoulders to-night.

Lighter than she'd been in almost ten years.

Sixteen

An hour later, her phone chimed in her ear, reminding Dixie she was supposed to be working. After Jo-Lynne left, she was finding it hard to concentrate. Her face was on fire, her eye throbbed, and her mind was a vacuum of mixed emotions that left her all tangled up and simultaneously warmed to the core.

Stuffy of nose, she grabbed a tissue and answered, "This is Mistress Taboo. Are you worthy?"

"It's Walker."

Her heart skipped that ridiculous beat it had the last time she'd heard his voice, so smooth and silky against her ear. Over the past few days, she'd toyed with what part of the country he came from. His accent said Louisiana; it was very like Harry Connick—cultured and sigh-worthy on the ears.

"You sound like you've been crying. Are you okay?" When he asked personal questions about her, she found she had to remind herself, it really wasn't personal. Those questions were more about the client becoming familiar with her and building a rapport. They were questions that were typical, a way to strike up a conversation much the way one would in a real life circumstance.

Except Walker's questions didn't quite feel as if they had anything to do with striking up conversation. They left her feeling a million things. Sometimes probed, sometimes cornered and exposed, but most times they left her hungry for more contact with him. Could be, her emotional state had her reading a whole lot more into this than was realistic. Maybe she was just overly sensitive these days, and talking with Walker hit her hot buttons.

"Mistress Taboo? *Were you crying?*" His question sounded almost possessive. As though he'd take out whoever had made her cry.

Another ridiculous notion. It had to be or she'd have to question her mental state. Callers easily became attached to the operators, but the operator probably shouldn't take girlish pride in the idea or worse, cultivate it.

Still her cheeks warmed, betraying her better judgment. "Nope. Just my allergies."

"You never mentioned allergies."

Why would she mention them to some man hiding in his mother's basement, making phone calls to a cartoon figure on a computer screen? And why couldn't she keep her perspective with this man?

She'd talked to plenty of men lately. Why did this one man make her question his every motive? "I don't think we ever touched on the subject of medical afflictions," Dixie offered, attempting to lighten the mood. "So how have you been?"

"How have *you* been?"

Again, Walker probably didn't intend for it to sound

as if it held meaning, but there it was, that intensity, that gravelly lilt in his deep voice that made her feel as if he had a stake in her well-being. "Oh, I'm real good."

"You know, I've noticed something strange about you."

What about this bizarre attachment to him she'd acquired wasn't strange? Had he noticed it, too? "What's that?" She tried cooing the words to come off flirty, yet it sounded contrived and forced.

"Your accent."

She sat up straight, forgetting her spine felt as if someone had run a train over it. "What about it?"

"It sort of comes and goes. Sometimes you're all Southern, and then all of a sudden, it goes away. What's that about, Mistress Taboo?"

Dixie laughed, almost relieved to hear Walker wasn't going to try and pinpoint the dialect of her accent. "That comes from the time I spent in Chicago. I lived there for almost ten years. It sounds silly, but I was trying to fit in so they wouldn't think I was some country bumpkin who didn't know her backside from a cornfield."

"Who are they?"

"Some business partners." Aka, the men she'd tried so desperately to convince she was serious about her failing business long after it was already too late.

"What did you do in Chicago?"

"I owned a restaurant."

"Shut the front door," he said on a whistle. "A real, live restaurant?"

"It was very real."

"So were you some kind of fancy chef?"

Dixie fought a derisive snort. "Hardly. It was nothing like that. In fact, I hate to cook. I just invested in it, talked a bunch of other people into investing it, and put my name on it with the promise I'd take good care of it." *Then I skipped off to shop like the spoiled brat I was while everyone else did the work. And while I was off partying and running up my credit cards, I lost everything because it was too late to save it.* Yep. That summed it up rather nicely.

"So there was a Mistress Taboo's Fine Dining somewhere? That musta been somethin' to see."

Dixie barked a harsh laugh. "No. No Mistress Taboo's anything."

"So, the million-dollar question. What made you leave the glamorous life of restaurant owning to become a phone-sex operator?"

"Yet another of my long, sad stories." Bad-ump-bump.

"You seem to have a lot of those," he remarked, though she didn't detect that it was offhand or cruel.

Dixie slumped in her chair, reaching a hand into the drawer of her desk to look for some aspirin, wishing she had an ice pack for her eye. "If you only knew." Ugh. No more conversation about her. "Hey, I know. Let's try something new. Why don't we talk about you for a change? What does Walker of the sexy accent do for a living?"

"Hey, I have another question."

"Your quota for questions about me is up. This is all about you," she reminded him playfully, popping two aspirin into her mouth and sipping at her bottled water.

His low chuckle relieved her. "Walker of the sexy accent does a lot of things for a living. But more recently, he's not so much making a living as he is behaving badly."

Dixie cocked her head. That seemed to be viral in the male species as of late. "We've established that I'm the queen of behaving badly. Nothing you could do short of murder would allow you to take my title, mister. But so funny you should mention that, I just had someone say almost those exact words to me."

"What a coincidence. Who would behave badly with someone like Mistress Taboo?"

She smiled into the phone at his teasing tone. "You show me yours, and maybe, just maybe, I'll show you mine."

"Okay, me first. I behaved badly with a woman."

She rolled her eyes at how little information he gave her. "Aw, c'mon now. I need details, Walker! I can't offer advice if I don't have the details. Unless they're gory details. I don't want to have to testify against you in court. You know how that goes. I end up all over *Inside Edition* as the woman who caught the Phone-Sex Strangler serial killer. I can't leave my house without the paparazzi hounding me. People tweet about me. We can't have that, can we?" she teased.

He laughed into the phone, which in turn made her insides a little like Jell-O. It caught her off guard. She'd never had a reaction like this to anyone except Caine. "Uh-uh. No details until you show me yours."

Would it hurt to share just a little so they had a common bond that might allow him to open up? *Would it hurt to recognize that you enjoy talking to this voice on the other end of the line? You're probably not the first phone-sex operator guilty of it....* "Someone apologized to me for behaving badly recently, too, but he wasn't doing anything I didn't deserve."

"How did you deserve to have someone treat you badly?"

His seemingly genuine interest in her softened her resolve to keep their phone call about him. Maybe just a little evasive confession wouldn't hurt. "I did an awful thing to this person a long time ago. Something I regret to this day. He was sort of taking out his anger about that incident on me. You know, poking me, reminding me of just how ugly I'd been over and over at every possible turn. So he apologized the other night." *Then he made mad, incredible love to me, making me love him even more.*

"So whadja do to him that was so bad he had to keep rubbing it in?"

She rose from her desk and headed for the chaise, hoping it would be kinder to her sore body than her office chair. Clicking off the light as she went, Dixie skirted the desk and tried to piece together an answer.

How did you explain the bet she'd made for a man's heart? Dixie blew out a breath of air before she began. "I guess the easiest way to explain it is this—I bet someone I could win his heart, and when he found out, he thought I didn't really love him, and that all I really wanted to do was win the bet."

The pause Walker made was deafening. Dixie held her breath until he asked, "Was there a reason he thought that? Seems kinda silly to marry a man just because of a bet."

Relief washed over her when she didn't hear judgment in his voice. "At least a million. We had a combative… Wait, maybe *competitive* is the better word. We had a competitive relationship throughout our childhoods. Ca…" She bit her tongue. "*He* always played fair, though. No matter what we were competing for, because he's honest and decent. I, on the other hand, cheated more often than not. Like I said, I wasn't a very nice person for a very long time, and my reputation for getting what I wanted at all costs came back to haunt me because of it."

"So who'd you make the bet with and why'd you do it?"

"I made a bet with a frenemy, I guess. I used her. She used me. We were always trying to best one another."

"Sounds like you did that a lot. Reputations, huh?"

"I'm the champ. Anyway, at first it was just a joke— a way to poke at this frenemy. I didn't mean it mean it. Though, I did know she was nuts about this guy. I just wanted to get her goat. She said there was no way someone as honorable and decent as him would ever fall in love with me. Because I was the person I was, I bet her I could not only make him fall in love with me, but get him to ask me to marry him before she batted her falsies."

"Falsies?"

"An eyelash."

"And then?"

Dixie sighed. "Well, then because I can't resist bragging about a coup, I called her up and left her a victory voice mail, announcing that I was engaged. To the man she claimed to love. She played that voice mail at our engagement party—in front of an entire town."

Walker whistled into the phone. "Ouch."

She closed her eyes. "Pass the morphine and sutures ouch."

"So, *did* you really love him, Mistress Taboo, or was he just a bet won?" Walker's question made her chest burn and her skull throb. "You can tell me. Swear on my Willie Nelson albums, I'll never tell a soul."

But she nodded her head in response, grateful for the dark cocoon of night hiding her undying shame. "When we first started dating, he was a way out from under my mother's thumb, but it turned much deeper the more I got to know him. The more time we spent together, the crazier I was about him. So yes..." She stumbled on the hitch in her voice.

"I didn't meant to upset you—"

"Yes!" she blurted out, cutting him off before realizing she'd lost her composure. "Yes," she offered more calmly. "I loved him. I just didn't have enough self-respect to tell him about the bet before he was humiliated in front of his family and friends. Every single day, I wish I could take it back. I'd do *anything* to take it all back."

When she'd finally realized just how much she'd wanted to be Caine's wife, she'd thought about telling him. She'd even tried once or twice, but back then, she'd been selfish enough to never want him to look at her with the brand of disgust everyone else had when she pulled a stunt. The longer she waited, the worse the unspoken threat Louella would snitch had become until it turned into her nightmare come true.

Louella had waited until their engagement party for a reason.

Impact. It was the final coup—the big win against Dixie, and it was exactly how Dixie would have played it had the roles been reversed.

Total public annihilation. She'd have let Louella think she'd won only to rip the rug right out from under her at the last possible second, too. That was when the grasshopper had become the sensei.

Dixie yanked herself back to the present when she realized no sound came from her earpiece. Damn it all. She'd let herself get too carried away, and way too intense. "Walker? Are you still there?" she asked, hoping he hadn't hung up because she didn't know when to shut up. The thought that she'd driven him away sent her into panic mode.

"I am, Mistress Taboo. I am."

His tone concerned her, making her heart stick to her ribs. "TMI?" she squeaked, with a wince.

Walker cleared his throat, his next words gruff, as if she'd hit a sore spot for him. "On the contrary. It helped a great deal."

"With your situation?"

She heard what sounded like Walker swallowing and then, "Could be. I have to go now, Mistress Taboo. It was a real pleasure."

Before she had the chance to protest or apologize, Walker was gone. Just like that. The dial tone in her ear signaled his obvious disgust.

Clicking her earpiece off, she rolled her head on her neck and stretched her sore arms. She'd blown it with a client.

A client whose voice she'd grown attached to hearing nestled against her ear in her dark, cozy office. One who asked inquisitive, if not personal, questions which were smart and well-articulated.

And made you say things you were better off not saying, Dixie. It only reopens the wounds and exposes what should remain private to a virtual stranger.

Despite all that, she still hoped Walker would call back.

* * *

"Emmaline?" On her 1:00 a.m. break, Dixie plunked down beside Em whose legs were dangling in the pool outside of Call Girls. The warm water felt particularly good on the soles of her feet, shredded from her barefoot run across the square last night.

"Mmm-hmm?" Em asked on a wobbly sway, leaning into Dixie.

"What are you doing out here so late? Everything okay? The boys all right? Where are they anyway?" she asked, spying droplets of spattered pink wine on the deck of the pool.

"Mama and Idalee have been lookin' out for them while I mediate you and Mr. Smexy. Gareth said to say hello."

Dixie smiled. She'd spent a little time with Em's boys recently, and she was falling madly in love with them. Even sullen Clifton Junior. "So, are you okay?"

"Everything's good, good, good," she chirped, too high and too forced.

"You sure? How would the good Reverend feel about you out here by the pool, drunk on wine, young lady?"

"Jesus drank wine." She leaned back and hiccupped, her chest rising and falling with a heave.

Dixie swallowed a snort. "Why, yes, he did, lightweight. But did *He* drink two and a half bottles of strawberry Boone's Farm? Nay. I think not. I think he drank the yucky kind made from his blood. The kind they have in church that makes you gag and gives you a heinous headache?"

Em giggled then took a hearty swig of the culprit, dribbling some on her pretty blue top. Her hair was mussed, her cheeks were flushed, and she looked more adorable and relaxed than she had since Dixie had been back. "It's not really Jesus's blood, Dixie. It's just cheap wine at church."

"Glad we cleared that up. So why are you out here drinking like you're still in college?"

Em snorted, spitting at a strand of hair caught in her mouth. "I took my college classes online, silly Dixie. There was no partying. Just me and a computer."

"In that case," she held up one empty bottle, "this means you're well on your way to righting an egregious wrong."

Em ran the tip of her finger over the bridge of Dixie's nose. "You're silly, Dixie. Silly and so pretty and too prideful to tell the man you love more than anyone ever how sorry you are. That's just plain dumb. Maybe you should be the one drinking?"

Maybe Em was right, but... "I'm not ready."

"To drink? Since when? As I recall, you were never afraid of a six-pack."

Dixie rolled her eyes at her. "No. To have—" she threw her fingers up to air quote "—the talk."

Em drove a finger into Dixie's arm and wrinkled her nose. "You know what you're not ready to do, Dixie-Doodle? You're not ready to get this sleeping with Louella thing all out in the open. That's what you're not ready to do. Know why? Because it hurts. Louella claims to have cuckolded you. Take charge of that. Face your demons is what you told me, right? So why not just ask Caine why or even *if* he did somethin' so vile and get it over with? The Dixie I knew would never let this fester."

"The Dixie you knew would have done something awful to Louella by now as a way to ease her pain.

Trouble is, I don't fully know the Dixie sittin' here before you yet, my friend. A Dixie who'd rather hide than break out the heavy artillery? Who is that? I'm either knocking people down like some sort of deranged linebacker or looking for my turtle shell to burrow into. I just can't seem to find my middle ground."

Or any ground. Everything felt soft beneath her feet. As if this tenuous grasp she had on her bad behavior would cave in if she didn't tread carefully.

Em's finger waggled under her nose. "Communication is the key. Just ask me about how wrong everything can go when you don't communicate."

"Speaking of communication, have I ever thanked you properly for helping me talk to Landon that one last time?" Em had called her the second the hospice nurse informed her it wouldn't be long until he was gone. She'd been driving all night, praying her crappy car would make it the last bit of the trip, praying the little money she had would be enough for gas.

Em shrugged. "There's nothin' to thank me for. It was one of his last wishes. We only spent a month together, but to be invited into his beam of sunshine is like bein' invited into a warm hug wrapped in a Snuggie. He had the best heart I've ever known."

Dixie forced back tears. Landon hadn't been able to say much, but she'd filled that void with a promise to make him proud. "That he did. Anyway, thank you, Em. I wanted to be there more than I wanted to take another breath."

"He knew that, Dixie. I need you to know, he *knew*. Now, no more thank-yous. Let's focus on you before I get to cryin'."

Her sadness made Dixie wrap an arm around her and

give her a squeeze. "Let's not talk about me anymore, please. I'll just say this, I'm not ready. Okay?"

Em nodded with a sigh.

"So what brought the drink on? 'Cause this sure isn't like my girl Em."

Em sat up straight with a jerk. "Am I your girl, Dixie?" she asked, pouring wine into her discarded glass and handing it to Dixie.

Dixie held up her glass to clink the bottle. "How about we're each other's girls?"

"You mean each other's person—like on *Grey's Anatomy?* Like Mer and Cristina?"

Dixie cocked a half smile, swishing her feet in tiny circles to ease the cramps in her calves. "Minus the surgeon part. Though, if we stuck in a McDreamy, I wouldn't be broken up."

Her glassy eyes focused on Dixie with fire in them. "You're the devil, Dixie. Is anyone the devil's person?"

"I dunno. Wanna find out?"

Em touched her bottle to Dixie's glass, her aim slightly off. "I'll drink to that."

Dixie winked. "Then to each other's person. Hear-hear!"

Em's head tipped before the wine bottle was actually on her lips, sending the pink liquid gushing straight down her chin and onto her chest. "Hey, person?"

Dixie grinned as best she could with her eye half hanging out of its socket. "Yes, other person?"

"Cleanup in aisle ten," Em slurred, with a lopsided smirk.

Dixie giggled, digging around in her purse for a tissue. She dabbed at the splotch of wine in a hopeless attempt to wipe it away. "So, person, I have a question for you."

"I don't know if the 'person handbook' requires that I answer said question, but I'm all ears. And wine."

"What's the real reason you're out here drinking, Em? You wanna talk about it or do you want me to hush and leave it alone?"

"I met a man today."

She dropped the statement between them as if she was dropping a hand grenade. It was a very un-Em-like admission. One Dixie was almost positive she didn't mean to make and certainly held unnecessary guilt. "So soon?"

Em's lips thinned. "Are you judging me again, S.S?"

"Me judge? Nope. I was just making an observation. Wasn't it you just the other day who told Marybell men were akin to locust and the black plague?"

Em scrunched her nose and waved an unsteady hand at her. "I was just spoutin' off because I was angry with Clifton, is all."

"So, person, you feel inclined to tell S.S. all about this man?"

Em sighed and smiled. "I didn't really meet him-meet him, I guess. He met Louella, actually. I was sort of eavesdropping on their conversation. Despicable, I know, but there was just somethin' about him…."

"Has Louella gone and had his name tattooed on her arm yet? Just so he's properly branded?" Dixie teased.

Em rolled her eyes, reaching out to clutch Dixie's arm to steady herself. "Well, you know Louella. Any new man in this podunk town is fresh meat. So can't say as I blame her for makin' a move as fast as she can."

"Forget Louella. Who's this man?"

"I only heard his first name. He was here lookin' at real estate, of all things. Lawd knows there isn't much of that to be had in the PO. He's some kind of software developer or something smart. Like I said, I was just fringing the conversation like some kind of stalker right there in front of Brugsby's. But we did make eye contact...."

As Em's words trailed off, her smile became a little like Dixie's once had over a particular Backstreet Boy. "So I'm guessing you thought he was handsome?"

She shook her head in absolute, alcoholically infused disagreement. "Oh, no."

Dixie kept her response relaxed as she looked up at the twinkling clusters of stars and watched the palm fronds from the surrounding trees sway with the warm air. "Explain?"

"He wasn't handsome. To say as much would be to deny his very essence. He was hot, Dixie. So very, very hot," she whispered, licking her index finger and making a sizzling sound. "Handsome is meant for a more distinguished man, in my humble opinion. This man— ohhhh, this man made me think all sorts of dirty things. The kinds of things the girls talk about on the phone with their clients."

Dixie gave her shoulder a playful nudge, thrilled Em was beginning to feel comfortable enough to admire someone of the opposite sex. It meant she was considering moving forward. "Wow, huh?"

"Wow-wow, for sure."

"So he's why you're out here drinking?" Dixie clucked her tongue. "Because if it was me, and I saw a man who was wow-wow hot, I'd be out there givin' Louella Palmer a run for her money."

"That's because you're a shameless flirt. Not a well-mannered lady like me," Em said on another inebriated giggle.

"Reformed shameless flirt, thank you." She tipped an imaginary hat at Em and smiled.

Em let her head drop. "I have no place thinkin' about other men when I couldn't manage to keep the one I had."

The mention of Clifton reminded Dixie of something she needed to clear up. "Speaking of the one you had, why did I hear Nanette telling Essie Guthrie that you were the one responsible for the breakup of your marriage the other day?"

Em made a face. "Because I've done nothing to right that wrong, and why're you listenin' in on someone else's conversation, oh thee of the reformation?"

Dixie gazed at her with astonishment. "Oh, no, person, I was not listening in. I couldn't help but hear her. I was in Madge's, picking up some of those yummy lattes for you and the girls before my shift. She doesn't hide the fact that she loves to gossip, and I reminded her of that on my way out the door."

Em sighed. "Better that go 'round town instead of the truth then."

"Hold on there. Why are you taking the blame for Clifton's misdeeds? While I admire you taking one for the team, I absolutely do not agree with him shifting the blame. Where's that spine of yours you're always shoving in my face?"

"What else was I supposed to do, Dixie?" she hissed, pressing a finger to Dixie's lips. "Tell my children and his parents that Clifton moved off to Atlanta because he wants to wear makeup and high heels and live with the most understandin' female this side of the galaxy? He's a descendant of one of Plum Orchard's founding fathers, for heaven's sake. You know how much pride Clifton's parents, Harlow and Idalee, take in that. How could I let them be humiliated that way? And Harlow's health isn't good. I won't have his heart attack on my hands."

No, damn it. This wasn't okay. How dare Clifton leave Em to clean his mess? "Will it be any better if Harlow ever learns the truth, Emmaline?"

"For now, this is the way it's gonna be, Dixie. It's better everyone think I was a terrible homemaker and wife than know the truth. Now, I won't hear any more of it."

"Fine," Dixie said between clenched teeth. "But for the record, Clifton's no kind of man if he'd let you take responsibility for his dirty pool. It's wrong to make you keep his secret and take the blame, too. I don't like it, Emmaline Amos."

Em's face relaxed again, the fiery anger in her eyes subsiding. "Well, I appreciate your concern. It's over and almost done now, and all that matters is everyone stay out of the line of fire. Which means I shouldn't be thinkin' about other men or Nanette and the senior Mags will surely have something to gossip about then."

Dixie leaned back on the palms of her hands, swirling the water with her feet. "Wanna know what I think?"

"About Nanette's gossip?"

"No, about how you're feeling when you think about this man and starting new relationships."

"Because relationships are your specialty—yours with Caine bein' so successful and everything." She stuck her tongue out at Dixie playfully.

"Here's what I think. Maybe you weren't meant to keep the man you had, Em. The one you had just wasn't good enough for you, in my opinion. So maybe there's someone else you're supposed to be keepin'?"

Em's gaze was faraway, full of guilt mixed with excitement. "His name is Jax. The hot-hot man, that is. I heard him say it to Louella while she was makin' those big round moon-eyes at him. How ridiculously soap opera, melt-your-knees sexy, is that?"

A lot like ridiculously soap opera, melt-your-knees sexy as Walker was. "Look at my knees—all melty," Dixie teased.

Em took another long swig of the now almost empty wine bottle and laughed. "Hah! Your knees don't count. They're just scarred from sittin' on 'em so much while you begged the man upstairs for forgiveness."

"Touché. So is this Jax why you're drinking?"

"No," she said on a sniff. "Though maybe he's just a small part of it. He just made me really think. I'm at a crossroads, one foot in my old world and the other somewhere undefined. I'm still stuck in the confines of marriage to Clifton—on paper anyway. Still sad I couldn't keep the promises I made the day I married him, but I'm itchin' to move on, too, you know? I feel so dirty bein' cheated on. I know it's absolutely ridiculous, but I feel like once we have a piece of paper that says it's over, I'll be clean again. Like I'll have a fresh start, and his sins won't be the boys' or mine anymore."

Dixie grabbed her shoulders and gave her a light shake. "Listen up. As your person, it's my responsibility to tell you, you didn't break those promises, Em. *You did not.* Clifton did. This was about Clifton's insecurities, not yours. It was easier to find another woman who already knew all his secrets than be man enough to tell you about them."

"He never even gave me a chance to decide how I'd feel about him wearing women's clothes, Dixie. But the truth is," she whispered, low and ragged, "I just don't know how I feel. The only thing I'm sure of is I don't know what I know anymore."

Dixie squeezed her arm then patted her shoulder, lifting it up and pointing to it. Em laid her head there. "I know, honey. But you know what else I know? I know that you're loyal, and generous, and probably the kindest human being I've ever met. I also know you won't always feel like this—so lost, so sad. It sounds meaningless right now, but this, too, shall pass."

"Like it did for you?" she asked in a whisper.

Dixie nodded in agreement because it soothed Em, not because she really believed anything would ever pass for her. "You bet," she whispered back against her hair. "Just like me."

Seventeen

Dixie sat on a bench under a big maple whose leaves were just beginning to turn while Caine watched her from behind a real-estate magazine like some kind of town-square voyeur.

She chatted with some of the senior men of Plum Orchard as they played chess and she ate her dinner out of a take-out box from Madge's. The sunlight danced on her hair, casting golden highlights on her long, loose curls and leaving her cheeks dusted a pretty pink. Her words were filling the air, and her laughter filled his head.

The days were finally cooling off a bit, allowing her to wear jeans and a light pink button-up sweater that made his mouth water for the way it hugged her curves and his fingers burn to pop the small pearl buttons right off it.

His mother had ordered him to locate and escort Dixie back to her house for a date they'd set to indulge in some pecan pie, coffee and girl talk. Because he couldn't resist, knowing she'd be here in the park with the seniors like she was most evenings lately, he'd arrived twenty minutes early to get his fix of her.

Since the night she'd decked Louella, she'd been purposely avoiding him again. This time, he knew why. Their relationship, the complexities and reasons they were at each other's throats all the time, had changed.

He'd apologized to Dixie for his crappy treatment of her, and now neither of them knew what to say if they weren't searching for an available artery or a bed while they said it. It was crystal clear neither of them knew what the hell to do with this fragile declaration of peace.

So neither of them said anything.

Add to that, Dixie's new vulnerability. She'd been vulnerable in that shower with him—*to him*—and it scared the shit out of her.

It scared the shit out of him more. She was no longer just the flirty, sexy woman he'd fallen in love with. She was ten times more. She had depth—scars he didn't understand—regrets she actually felt. He wanted to know them, hear them, soothe them.

"Candy Caine?" A phone with a text message was shoved beneath his nose followed by the sweet scent of fresh pear and Dixie's husky voice in his ears. "I've been ordered by your mother to find you and come directly to her house for pecan pie."

He rolled the magazine up and tucked it into his back pocket, glancing up at her with a smile. "I curse the damn day I taught her how to text. There's no hiding from her, ever."

Dixie's giggle, light and easy, drifted to his ears on the soft breeze as the shadows of the trees in the square played across her face. She hiked the strap of her purse over her shoulder and tucked it under her arm. "Well, it is homemade pecan pie. Seriously, what's more text-worthy?"

He rose, tearing his eyes from the swell of the tops of her breasts, just barely skimming her sweater's opening. "You ready? Or do you have more men left to charm the pants off?"

She tossed her empty dinner carton in a trash can as they began to walk. "Don't be ridiculous, do you really believe I left a crowd of men uncharmed *and* with pants on? Impossible," she said on a flirty giggle.

The bruises Louella had left on her eye were finally beginning to fade, but it still made him wince to see it. "How's the eye?"

"Still in my head."

"Phew. Good thing. One-eyed Southern belles are a hard sell these days, I hear." She let him slip his hand under her arm as they crossed the street, the temptation to place it at her waist stronger than ever.

She cocked her head in his direction and raised an eyebrow. "Then it's a good thing I'm not for sale. Sadly, my reputation precedes me."

Caine heard the teasing lilt to her voice, but that underlying hint of seriousness, the one that continually self-deprecated and punished, remained, and it was becoming like a kidney punch every time she used it. "Reputations can change. Or should I say perceptions can?" Why he couldn't just tell her his perception of her changing was a testament to his own damn insecurities. He didn't want to fall into another trap.

She gave him a strange look before saying, "Uh-huh. Just like a leopard's spots and a Kardashian's love of publicity. But let's not talk about me. We do that a lot. It's overrated. How about we talk about you?"

"Okay, floor's yours."

"How's the real-estate business in Miami? Yours in particular."

Mostly flailing due to his lack of on-site management for over a month now. "It's been good to me, despite the economy."

Dixie shook her finger along with her head. "I don't mean overall. I mean now, as in right now. Because I heard you just the other day talking to someone named Geraldo about escrow and all sorts of big words simple girls like me don't understand. And when I say talking, I mean you were sort of yelling. Which leads me to believe Miami's finest golden boy turned real-estate agent should be back home, managing the empire he built from scratch. You sounded pretty stressed."

She was right. Things were slipping back in Miami while he was in Plum Orchard, trying to figure out where the hell to go from here.

The realization that he wasn't ready to leave yet was unsettling. That he wasn't ready to leave because Dixie was here left his brain all kinds of shit-wrecked. But he had a feeling there was still much more to discover about her, and he wanted to do that.

"The big words are just a front for the real problem, which is that I'm not there to micromanage everything. They'll get over it. I pay them a lot of money to figure it out."

Dixie slowed a bit, the rhythm of her heels clicking against the sidewalk changing. She stopped at the cross section where his mother's street met the old dirt road they used to race bikes on.

This was the road where he'd threatened to take out Dixie's first boyfriend, Wayne Hicks, for getting her drunk and trying to take advantage of her. Little had he known Dixie was anything but drunk, and no one, least of all poor Wayne Hicks, took advantage of her.

The memory, vivid and in living color, made him smile.

It was also the road where they'd first made love in the back of his father's old pickup truck. And where he'd proposed to her.

Dixie tapped him on the shoulder. "Hey, where'd you go?"

Obviously to a place she didn't remember quite the way he did. He spun around on his heel and began walking back toward the intersection. "Sorry. What was the question?"

"Do you like living in Miami, Caine?"

He stopped again. Did he? He liked the money. He liked the challenge of selling high-end real estate in a less than desirable market. "Do you like Chicago?"

She smiled up at him, her dimples deepening in that enticing way she had of using their innocence only to later nail you with her sexy. "I asked first."

Caine shrugged, unsure of what she was getting at. "At first, I was in culture shock. It's very unlike Plum Orchard, but it grew on me." He'd forced himself to adjust because no way in hell was he going back to a place where Dixie lived in every nook and cranny.

Dixie wiggled a finger into his belt loop and tugged at it before letting go, a familiar gesture from their past when she'd wanted his attention. "But do you like it? *Really* like it? Do you think of it as home? Lately I'm discovering it's important to like the place you're going to set up shop with your life."

When he'd moved to Miami to follow up on a job

offer from a college friend's father, it had been the answer to getting the hell out of Plum Orchard and away from the memory of Dixie, but did Florida feel like home?

Did he look forward to going back to his ultra swanky town house after a long day? Did it make him feel comfortable and welcomed like his mother's kitchen with its hardwood floors, antiqued white cabinets and woodburning stove did?

No. It was just a place to hang his hat—a place to grab some sleep, have the occasional beer, and watch a game on a flat-screen TV he almost never had the time to turn on. "I have a nice town house," he replied, almost defensively.

"I bet you do. You deserve a nice town house. Town homes are what make life worth living," she teased.

Caine squared his shoulders. "So, Chicago?"

Dixie rubbed her arms. "Cold. Brrr."

Caine's eyes zeroed in on hers, trying to read where this was leading. "Did you like it?" Had she missed home as much as he was discovering he did?

Her eyes darkened momentarily then clouded over to hide whatever it was she was hiding. "It served a purpose. Did I love it? Sometimes, if I'm honest. The shopping was great, the nightlife even better. But mostly, not so much as I got older."

And? There was something beyond her getting older and her financial struggles that made Chicago not so likeable, and he wanted to know what. Yet, the way her eyes avoided his told him she wasn't ready to tell him what it was.

In fact, her eyes said she especially didn't want to

tell him. He kept his next question as casual as possible. "So, you thinking about staying here in the PO?"

"Well, of course I am. Who's going to run Call Girls when I beat you senseless and win this whole thing?" she asked on a laugh, sticking her hands in the pockets of her jeans as her feet began to move again.

"Tsk-tsk," he chided with amusement. "That has yet to be determined, Mistress Taboo. We still have a couple of weeks left. Don't pack your stilettos just yet."

She slowed as they neared the white rose-covered front gate to his mother's. "Can I ask you something?"

"You can always ask."

"If you win will you stay here, Caine? Move back?"

Would he? It was damn good to be home, to see his mother more often than holidays. It was good to walk down the center of town and be greeted with smiles that were familiar. It was good to share a beer or two and chicken wings with some of his old high school buddies at Cooters while they watched the game.

He'd missed the hell out of Landon the second he'd left this earth. Yet he'd thought it would be painful to return home and remember his friend as vividly as he did Dixie. Instead, he found it comforting to be surrounded by the things both he and Landon had once loved.

Was he ready to admit that? Not yet. So he avoided the answer to her question much the way he was internally avoiding it, too. "I don't need to be here to run things, Dixie."

"Like you're running them in Miami from here?"

Her skepticism was apparent. Ouch. "Hey, give a guy a break. Landon's will and his little game were a surprise. I wasn't ready for it, so I didn't make the proper arrangements. But remember, Cat's here. She can run things until I get everything sorted out and make decisions."

Dixie pushed her way through the gate topped with roses, stopping at the hammock his father liked to nap on. "But what about the girls?"

"What about them?"

The sun had become a setting ball of fiery orange behind her head, matching the flash of her eyes. "Please don't be such a man right now just to avoid any hint of female drama. You don't really think Plum Orchard's going to just let this go, do you? All this sin they claim has been cast upon them by having Call Girls right under their noses? Landon wasn't one to take pressure from people lightly, Caine. He responded in the way he always did, by doing what he damned well pleased because he had the money to do it. Which is a great attitude to have if you're dead and don't have to live with the consequences. He left that for us to do."

"Why does that require me to physically be here?"

Her eyes went wide. "Did you miss the knock-down drag-out Louella and I had because she was taunting LaDawn? I think we all know their idea of progress is allowing Rayvonne Purnell to open up a coffee shop that has, and I mean no disrespect, 'That fancy coffee with serving sizes in Eye-talian and full up with whipped cream and purty sprinkles,'" she mimicked the mindset of nearly everyone at the last town council meeting.

Caine noted his mother's house was strangely dark, which meant the doors were locked. He dropped down into the hammock, pulling Dixie with him as he considered her very valid point. "Well, to be fair, they did vote in Reyvonne's favor."

Dixie turned to face him, slipping her leg underneath her. She shook her head. "That's a far cry from a phone-sex line, Caine. The Mags want to preserve the integrity of small-town America. That doesn't include women like LaDawn who list companionating as a skill on their résumés. The girls need someone here to fight off ornery Nanette and the Mags. They'll eat LaDawn and the others alive if someone isn't here to take up for them."

Her fierce response left him full of admiration for her and just a little offended. "You know I'd never let anyone hurt those girls, Dixie. I like them, too."

The hard line of her lips softened then curved into a smile before she looked down at her lap, spinning her thumb ring. "I do know that. I do. I'm just being ridiculously overprotective, I guess. But just so we're clear, if you win this I want you to promise me you'll make regular appearances to check on them, Caine. Make sure Louella isn't baking them pies with the paring knife she uses to stab them in the backs."

Caine grinned and playfully nudged her to avoid addressing how incredibly sexy and passionate she looked when protecting the women of Call Girls. "Look at you coming to terms with me winning. That's good. Get used to it, pretty lady."

She clasped her hands together and reached skyward to stretch, revealing the silky smooth skin of her lightly tanned belly. Her lips curved upward. "Not on your life. I'm just saying it to distract you and stroke your ego before I swoop in like the mean-girl ninja I am and snatch that golden headset of yours right out from under you," she taunted good-naturedly, leaning back on her elbows and exposing the tops of her breasts to his hungry eyes.

Would she go back to Chicago if she lost? What would she go back to? "So does that mean you'll leave Plum Orchard if you lose?"

"Would you give me a job if I stayed?" she asked, but it wasn't with a challenge in her tone. There was a hint of fear in it—one that cut him off at the knees. Made him want to drag her into his arms and tell her he'd take care of it all.

"I need a full-time job, Caine. I have…debts."

Damn it, he wasn't willing to feel that way again— not yet.

Yet, friend? Landon taunted.

Her take-no-prisoners attitude about her financial mess surprised him. She didn't *have* to pay off the people who'd invested in her restaurant. They were mostly family friends and connections that wouldn't miss the money.

Somehow, Dixie had managed to find some principles. His curiosity about what had led to that was eating him alive.

Dixie poked at his rib cage, her eyes hopeful when she gazed at him from behind the curtain of her hair. "So would you? Hire me?"

"Sure, Dixie. I'll give you a job if I win. You can be Mistress Taboo for as long as you want."

She whistled. "Wow. I like this being friends thing. It's made you all warm and squishy."

"Do you, Dixie? Do you like us being friends?" The intensity of his question shook him up. He no longer wanted to crush her—at least not in phone sex.

Jesus.

"It beats wearing my boxing gloves all the time. They're hell on a manicure."

Pushing off with his foot, Caine set the hammock to rocking with a chuckle. The motion moved Dixie so close to him he had to fight with his arm to keep from wrapping it around her before she righted herself. "We used to spend a lot of time out here, didn't we?"

The pretty tint to her cheeks, the way she avoided eye contact told him she remembered exactly what he was remembering. "We did," she murmured, then gave him a look he pegged for surprise. "You still think about… about that?"

"More than I care to admit." Or more than was healthy.

Dixie shuddered a breath, a breath he read as touchy territory. "Me, too."

But he didn't want to walk on eggshells tonight. He needed to know those memories, that bittersweet chunk of time they'd spent together during their courtship, meant the same things to her they did to him. "Do you remember the time my mom came home, and we were out here, right on this hammock, buck naked like we were the only two people in the world?"

Dixie's head fell back on her shoulders, exposing her throat when she laughed out loud. "I remember it vividly. Me hiding in that big bush of rhododendrons while you stumbled through that lame story about how you thought you heard Digger Radcliff's dog rooting around in the garbage cans." She laughed again, care-free and soft.

"It would have worked, too, except for your damn pink bra, glowing under the moonlight, screaming,

'Hey, Jo-Lynne! Dixie and Caine just racked up some hammock miles!'"

Dixie began to laugh so hard she had to put a hand to her stomach. "Well, there's that—and the fact that it was still stuck around your ankle."

Caine began to laugh, too, making the hammock shake until somehow, they were only inches away from each other. Seeing her so untroubled, so like she used to be before her life had taken this abrupt turn, changed everything about what was supposed to be a piece of pecan pie and coffee with his mother. "Do you remember that bra, Dixie?" He couldn't stop himself from asking.

Her breathing hitched when he leaned over her, brushing her hair from her eyes. She nodded, and Caine thought he caught her swallowing nervously. "I think you said it was your favorite."

"Yeah," he muttered, transfixed by the swell of her peach-colored lips parted just enough to reveal her tongue. "Yeah. It was."

Dixie's chest rose and fell in choppy breaths, pushing against his. Her full breasts swelled with each breath she took. He used his knuckles to caress the underside of them, loving the fullness of them, aching to tear the tiny pearl buttons of her sweater off with his teeth before burying himself between them.

Her fingers automatically went to his hair, gripping a fistful of it as his tongue wisped over her bottom lip, nibbling it before pulling at it, relishing the plump flesh.

"Caine…" she whispered as the tip of her tongue caught his.

"Dixie?" he asked, before dragging his index finger between her breasts.

"We have to…" She moaned at the pop of the buttons on her sweater. "Talk. I need to…" She gasped when he pressed his open mouth to the column of her neck. "Ask you—and…tell you something."

He chuckled, cupping her breast, still encased in a lacy confection of interfering bra. *"After."*

Gripping his hair tighter, she dragged his head upward, forcing him to look at her. What he saw was desire, hot and sweet, but there was something else—something gritty. *"Please,"* she almost begged.

Her tone was so urgent, so primal and hoarse Caine paused, looking directly into her eyes, alarmed. "Anything."

Dixie's eyes shone bright under the full moon. "Did you sleep with Louella the night our engagement ended? Look at me when you answer me, Caine. *Look at me.*"

Where the hell had that come from? Was she serious? Yet, the almost desperate question, the way she demanded he look at her when he answered, said she meant it.

Caine looked down at this woman he was fighting tooth and nail not to fall in love with all over again, waiting with dread for his answer.

He pinned her with his gaze, his hand encircled her wrist, squeezing it. "No, Dixie. *Never.*"

Everything stopped when he spoke those words.

There was nothing but Dixie, staring up at him as if she was seeing him for the first time, his blood pumping in his veins, and the crushing thump of his pulse.

But she didn't leave him any time to think about it before she wrapped her arms around his neck and pressed her mouth to his.

She drove her tongue into his mouth, her lips covering his in a hungry kiss, lifting her legs and wrapping them around his waist.

Caine reacted, grinding his cock into the V of her soft thighs, pulling away and clenching his teeth when she tore her mouth from his to put her hands on his chest and roll him from her body.

She straddled him right there on the hammock, while crickets chirped and the breeze blew through her tousled hair. His breath caught in his chest, seeing her like this, sitting on top of him, her bare shoulder exposed from his anxious hands tugging at her sweater.

The rise and fall of her chest. Her waist, narrowed and flaring out to accentuate the swell of her full hips. Her lips, now red and swollen from their kiss.

"Wait," he said huskily, unwilling to lose this moment—this small window of opportunity when their inexorable need for each other wasn't clouded by angry words or revenge. He grabbed hold of her wrists, imprisoning them. "Let me look—*touch*."

Dixie clenched her fingers into fists, resting them on his abdomen, her breathing heavy, her eyes colliding with his.

Caine walked his fingers up over her shoulder and along her neck until he reached her mouth. He pressed his index finger to her lips. "I want you, Dixie. Need you. *Now*."

She shivered at his insistent words. "I need you, too, Caine," she breathed before reaching for his belt buckle. Dixie's eyes captured his for only a moment before she pulled the belt open and unzipped his jeans.

He throbbed against the tight cotton of his boxer-briefs for agonizing seconds, and then her hands were around him, stroking him as she slid downward. Her hands tugged at the material at his waist, yanking his jeans down until they were around his ankles.

The cool air washed over his skin. Caine's boots dug into the soft earth to keep them anchored and to prevent himself from losing his mind when Dixie's hot breath made contact with his bare cock.

His hiss of pleasure wheezed from his lungs at her lips, wrapping around him and taking him into her mouth with a slow swipe of her tongue. His hips bucked upward as she swirled it around the heated length of him, dragging along the sensitive skin with raspy precision.

His hands went to her head, palming the back of it, following the movement of her up-and-down motion. "Christ, Dixie. More. I need more." He ground out the demand just seconds before her passes intensified.

White-hot need raged in his veins, his cock swelled in the wet cavern of her mouth, and his balls drew up tight against his body in preparation. Caine's hand found hers gripped firmly around him. He covered it, increasing the pressure, clenching his teeth as their fingers entwined. The tips of his fingers drifted into the wet heat of her mouth, and Dixie nipped at them, pushing them aside.

He drove upward, heedless to anything but the wet heat of her tongue, and the soft noises she made as she devoured the length of him.

He reared upward one last time when she used her tongue to tease the sensitive spot just beneath the head of his cock before he pulled back, and her hands took the place of her mouth.

Caine lost control when she whispered, "Come, Caine. Come for me." He exploded in a brilliant flash of color, and Dixie's soft hair splayed out over his abdomen. His lungs screamed out a rush of air, and his cock pulsed in her hand with hot release.

He reached for her shoulders, pulling her upward until her forehead rested on his chin, fighting for breath. Her arms slipped under his shoulders the familiar way they always had after she made love to him and his cradled her, fusing them together.

The easy sway of the hammock rocked them, while Caine struggled to find the words that would express what was happening to him.

Both of them jumped when the floodlight attached to his mother's porch bathed them in the glare of light.

Jo-Lynne's voice seeped from behind the screened windows. "Attention Caine Donovan and Dixie Davis! If I find one wayward bra in my backyard, someone's in for a lickin'! Now both of you make yourselves fit to sit at my kitchen table and join me inside for some pecan pie. Fully clothed, please!"

Dixie muffled a giggle against his shirt, her shoulders crumbling in the effort.

"Caught," he said on a laugh.

She nodded with a snort. "Like a fly on sticky paper."

Before they succumbed to the decadence of his mother's pecan pie, he needed to know—to understand—what had brought about the question of Louella. Or more importantly, *who* had planted that notion in her pretty head.

Her urgency left him restless to settle whatever had her so troubled. He cupped the back of her head, kissing the top of it. "So hey, that talk? After pecan pie and coffee? Jo-Lynne's not exactly known for her patience."

She sat up, the warmth of her body replaced with the

cool air of nothing but space between them. The carefree look of moments ago was replaced with a troubled pair of eyes, but then Dixie smiled, leaning in to press a quick kiss to his lips. "After pecan pie. And there are tissues in my purse."

Dixie squirmed off the hammock, toeing the jeans around his ankles with a grin full of mischief. She began to back up into a light trot toward the house and yelled, "Race ya to the kitchen, Donovan. Last one in gets no pie!"

Caine pushed off the hammock with his knees and dived for the shadow of the big maple in his mother's backyard, grunting when he tripped on the tangle of his jeans and hit the ground hard. Reaching for Dixie's purse, he made good use of the tissues and pulled his jeans back up.

Rolling to a sitting position, he glanced up at the warm glow in the kitchen, shining through the screen porch windows. Dixie was pouring coffee with one hand while the fingers on her other folded napkins, and his mother sliced her famous pecan pie. They were smiling and chatting, their mouths moving in time with their bobbing heads, making him smile along with them.

Caine's gut tightened. It was exactly like the visual he'd created in his mind a long time ago when he'd thought about their future together.

Exactly.

Eighteen

Em and Dixie strolled arm in arm across the square toward the brightly lit gazebo where the annual Founder's Day parade was wrapping up and the slide show of Plum Orchard's founding fathers would begin.

The early-evening air was sweet with the scent of cotton candy and hot buttered popcorn. Children played in the grassy area in front of the gazebo, small American flags in hand. Replicas of pilgrim hats and Puritan bonnets tossed on blankets as far as the eye could see made Dixie smile. This was what her childhood had been filled with: town events concocted specifically to inspire gatherings full of family, food and Plum Orchard residential pride.

Plum Orchard celebrated their Founder's Day in the tradition of Thanksgiving—only without the turkey and dressing. Her father had always told her it was exactly like when the pilgrims hopped off the *Mayflower* at Plymouth. Except no one accused the original settlers of Plum Orchard of stealin' anything, he would joke with a chuckle.

Em plucked at the sweater covering Dixie's arm as

they strolled past a local dressed as a pilgrim, making balloon animals for the children. "So, I hear there was some funny business in the backyard of one Miss Jo-Lynne Donovan yesterday. I thought I was your person. You're supposed to tell your person about all funny business."

Dixie stopped in her tracks, rocking back on her heels. "Is there nothing sacred in this town?"

"Oh, now stop bein' offended. Digger was in Madge's, and he casually remarked he'd seen you and Caine swingin' on the hammock in Jo-Lynne's back-yard when he let Dewie out for his nightly run. I just assumed funny business occurred because it always does whenever you two are anywhere near each other."

Dixie breathed a sigh of relief. The last thing she needed was everyone in town abuzz with her private matters. She was still trying to process Caine's denial. Process the fact that she'd been beating herself up, ago-nizing over her lack of self-esteem and willpower, only to discover nothing had happened between Caine and Louella. Her gut told her Caine wasn't lying.

"So did you talk to him?" Em pressed, stopping in front of a table brimming with punch and delectable desserts made by the locals.

"Sort of. I think I cleared one thing up. Hey, as my person, can I tell you something? You don't have to get involved if you don't want to. Just say the word, and I'll hush."

Em's face was relaxed and open. "Tell away."

"Caine said he didn't sleep with Louella."

Em's red-glossed lips thinned. She tucked a strand of her hair back into the neat bun at the back of her head and clucked her tongue. "Told you I didn't believe it.

Not for a daggone second. The impression I got was that Louella was just salvaging what was left of her pride. As if to say the smoke from Caine's love haze for you had finally cleared, and he realized she was the better woman. But I never totally believed it because I saw that man's face after you hightailed it outta there, Dixie. Once the dust settled, he was hurtin'. We could all see it even though he tried to hide it while he handled the aftermath."

Caine's pain, voiced out loud, was like a knife in her back. Em's words left her breathless.

"So you asked him about it?"

Dixie gulped in some air. "I did, and he said never." *No, Dixie. Never.*

Those words had haunted her throughout last night while she'd waited for Caine to come back to the big house so they could talk. Finally, around dawn, she'd given up and fallen asleep, but before she had, she'd had an epiphany.

The agony she'd suffered just thinking something had gone on between Louella and Caine had been true, was nothing less than she deserved. She'd deserved to have it chip away at her heart bit by ugly bit.

"Hah! I knew it," Em chirped, slapping her hand against her thigh. "That Louella's a lyin' snake! I think we all knew it. We were all just too afraid to call her a phony to her face. But not anymore. No, ma'am. I'm gonna march right up to her and—"

Dixie grabbed at her arm. "No, Emmaline!"

Em's gasp of shock rang out. "No? *No?* What is this word *no?* Maybe I'll even beat it out of her with a microphone."

Dixie took a deep breath and closed her eyes. When

she reopened them, she shot Em a pleading look. "I'm going to ask you to let it go. It's enough that Louella knows she lied. When she goes to bed at night, she's not right with herself. That's plenty of guilt. Trust me."

Em gave her a sour look. "You know, Miss Dixie, there's a time for letting things go, and there's a time for loadin' up your gun for bear. Louella made you miserable for over a month now, and you want to just forget it ever happened?"

"It's nothing I didn't do to her, Em," she whispered harshly, letting her eyes skim the crowd that had begun to gather for the Founder's Day speech. "So I spent a month fretting over something that didn't happen? That's nothing compared to what I did to her in high school."

Em's sigh of exasperation sliced through the air, raspy and crisp. She put her hands in the wide pockets of her ruffled skirt and rocked back on her heels. "You were in high school, for heaven's sake! Not well over the age of consent, still carrying a childhood grudge. You made a stupid bet with Louella. Yes, it was childish and for no other reason than to show her you could best her, but it was most certainly not like claiming you'd made the hokey-pokey with her man. You've done nothin' but good since you stepped back on Plum Orchard soil, and still, you beat yourself up. The Mother Teresa act ends now, Dixie. You stink at pulling it off anyway. Mother Teresa would never have red hair with gaudy nails to match. And if you won't let me take that viper Louella to task, at the very least, promise me you'll stop this ridiculous need to accept whatever's handed to you as a bizarre form of just deserts!"

Dixie broke the intense moment by pinching Em's

cheeks with a grin. "Does this mean you like me now, Em? Like really, really like me? Because I like you," she teased.

Em burst into a fit of giggles. "It means I like you better 'n I did a month and a half ago, but no more than that. Hear me?"

Dixie rolled her eyes. "If I can't have you, I don't want nobody, baby," she sang, doing her version of John Travolta's infamous *Stayin' Alive* move by jabbing her finger up and down.

But Em wasn't impressed. She folded her arms over her chest and gave her an eyeful of admonishment. "Oh, Dixie Davis, how the tides have turned."

"Yup." She nodded, dancing around her in a circle. "You wanna use it against me at a later date? Dixie Davis Begs Emmaline Amos to Be Her BFF. It'd make a good *Plum Orchard Gazette* headline."

Em bumped butts with her and wiggled, letting out another giggle. "Gloating is a deadly sin." She grabbed Dixie's hand and twirled her.

"That's gluttony," Dixie said, ducking under her arm and giggling with her.

Em's laughter mingled with Dixie's, but the sudden sharp screech of the microphone in the center of the gazebo made them both turn their heads. "C'mon. It looks like Mayor Hale's gettin' ready to give his ump-teenth, long-winded Founder's Day speech. I don't want the boys to miss seeing their daddy's picture up on that big projection screen."

Em's soon-to-be ex-husband's family would be hon-ored tonight in the slide show they did every year as a memorial to those who'd made Plum Orchard what it was today. Dixie hoped it would make Em's boys smile again, proud their father—even if he wasn't physically here—had left his mark.

After spending a great deal of time with Em's sons in the guesthouse pool and on several very messy dining excursions, Dixie privately worried about Clifton Junior and his angry take on his parents' divorce. He was so sullen and withdrawn, it hurt her to the very core to see him so torn and broken.

They made their way across the grass, stepping over spilled cups and popcorn kernels. Dixie's eyes loosely scanned the crowd for Caine while she kept an eye out for Em's mother and the boys.

A chubby older hand rose from a quilted blanket in the corner of the square, waving at them. Em's face lit up at the sight of her mother and two sons. Their smiles, so much like Em's, were covered in gooey pink and blue cotton candy.

Gareth jumped up from the ground, propelling his stout five-year-old body at Dixie's legs. His arms wrapped around her, and he smiled up at her. "Miss Dixie!"

She bent and scooped him up, swinging him in the air before settling him on her hip. "Well, who's this fine-lookin' gentleman?" She lifted his pilgrim hat and tweaked his nose.

"It's me, Miss Dixie. Garef," he replied with serious, indignant eyes.

The pronunciation of his name melted her on the spot. "Oh, my gravy, it is!" She batted her eyelashes at him. "Why, I hardly recognized you without your swimmies, Gareth. When did you get to be such a man?" Dixie walked her fingers up his stomach and planted a kiss on his sticky cheek.

"I'm not no man. I'm five." He held up five sticky fingers to prove it.

She gave him a squeeze before setting him back on the blanket in order to dig through her purse to find some wet wipes. Clifton Junior sat quietly, as stoic as she'd ever seen any eight-year-old, on the edge of the quilt, his eyes, the same blue as Em's, taking everything in and sharing none of it.

Her heart shuddered in her chest for Clifton. He was angry and hurt over his father's departure, according to Em. He had little to say these days—not even to the pediatric divorce therapist Em had insisted he make weekly visits to.

Dixie wiped Gareth up, said her hellos to Em's mother then plunked down beside him, fanning her dress out over her knees and following his eyes to a delicious man with a child around Clifton's age.

The man, with hair so dark it gleamed like the feathers on a raven, and features so chiseled you could strike a match on them, threw a baseball to a young girl with fiery red hair. He was gorgeous and graceful, and between throws, he was eyeing up Em as if she was the last woman on earth.

Clifton Junior's hungry eyes watched the ball, but he said nothing. He didn't have to. His eyes did all the talking.

Damn Clifton Senior for abandoning his sons. Dixie looked off into the distance with him, taking on the same air of indifference he exuded. "Do you like baseball?"

His small shoulders shrugged under his Sponge-Bob sweatshirt with a hearty dose of that indifference. "Sort of."

"Really? Not me. I think it's kind of stupid."

"Everything's stupid."

Dixie nodded. "Yep. Pretty much everything."

He almost looked at her, but instead lifted his chin, giving it a defiant edge. "You don't think everything's stupid. You're an adult."

"I do so. And adults think stuff's stupid, too. Kids aren't the only ones allowed to hate stupid stuff."

Clifton's lips thinned at her response, clearly irritated his efforts to spoil a lovely evening weren't working out. "Being here is stupid. Who cares about Founder's Day anyway? My dad's not even here to see it."

Dixie let a bored sigh escape her lips while gazing up at the fading sun. "Yeah. Who wants to sit around and eat cotton candy and popcorn? I mean, seriously. And sparklers? For sissies."

"And girls."

"Not this girl. No way would I even consider holding a sparkler."

"Really?"

"Truly."

"You're not like most girls."

"Nope. I'm a bona fide not-like-most-girls kind of girl. Ask anyone."

"You don't make any sense."

"Which is probably pretty stupid."

He laughed. It was faint, and it wasn't willingly, but it was. "You're weird."

Em gasped her disapproval, latching onto Clifton's chin and forcing him to look at her. "Clifton Junior! You apologize this instant to Miss Dixie! I'm sorry, Dixie! I don't know what's come over him as of late."

Dixie held up a lazy hand, one that indicated she

was neither upset nor offended. "No, no. Clifton and I were just talking about things that are stupid. And being weird is definitely not stupid. Right, Clifton?" She gave him a sidelong glance and winked as if they had a special secret.

He smiled back at her. A real smile. One filled with the kind of mischief eight-year-olds should have glued to their sweet faces at all times. "Right, Miss Dixie, and I didn't mean that you were weird in a rude way. I meant it in a good way," he said, before jumping up and running toward the direction of the good-looking man and his daughter. He didn't approach them. Rather he stood on the outskirts of their game of catch, watching.

Em leaned into her and patted Dixie's leg with affection. "He smiled. I haven't seen him smile in near three months now. Leave it to you and your charm to turn even the crankiest, most sullen of boys into a puddle of goo."

"It just takes time, I guess. He's missin' Clifton Senior. He'll adjust. I know he will. He's of your loins. That means he's a fighter just like you."

"My loins…" Em snorted, settling in next to her between a basket of fried chicken and the potato salad.

"Speaking of your loins, I was wondering…did they have anything to do with him?" She hitched her jaw in the direction of tall, dark and lickable. "Because I don't think wow covers all—" Dixie made a circular motion with her hand "—that."

Em peered into the twilight of the coming evening, halting all movement. Dixie saw her throat work up and down in a nervous gesture, and her hand, always a sure sign she was flustered, go directly to her throat. "My."

"Uh-huh. He's worthy of an ohhhh," she cooed. "So is he that Jax you were talking about?"

"So what if he is?" Her response was defensive, as if it were unseemly to be caught looking at any other man but Clifton.

"Because if it is, it's my duty to tell you, he's been gobbling you up with his eyes since you plunked your cute behind on the ground."

"Oh, he has not."

"Has so, has so, has so. Watch. In three—two—one."

And right on cue, the gorgeous Jax looked up in Em's direction. Their eyes met and held, locking gazes for a brief moment.

Even Dixie held her breath at the sizzle between the two of them before he broke the spell by nodding to Em in acknowledgment, then returned to his game of catch.

Dixie cleared her throat. "So don't you ever tell me you're not attractive, Emmaline Amos. Because you managed to attract the likes of Mr. Sinfully Sexy on a Stick. Go, you."

"I did not," Em blustered, hiding her eyes with the curtain of her hair by unleashing her tight bun and giving her locks a shake. "He was probably looking at you. It's neither here nor there. I'm not on the market. Speaking of markets, where's Caine?"

"He texted me to tell me he had some emergency with work in Miami, and he'd be back soon." She was a bagful of vulnerability. She didn't understand where last night left them, if it left them anywhere at all.

She was afraid this new Dixie and Caine was nothing more than a long goodbye. Caine hadn't made any commitments to her last night other than he was willing to hear her out, and he hadn't even shown up for that.

Caine's words had contradicted themselves. He'd said if he won Call Girls, he could run it from Miami. Yet, when he'd looked up at her, lying beneath her on that hammock, and whispered, *I need you,* with such intensity, she'd been certain they meant something more than just physically.

Or had they? Win or lose Call Girls, he could go right back to his life in Miami and run the company from some beach house while women in colorful bikinis strolled past his lounge chair in the sand under a blazing Florida sky.

He still might not trust her the way she needed him to. Worrying that Caine was just holding his breath until she made another horrible mistake was no longer an option. He had to trust her enough to believe she'd begun to make the right choices.

How could anyone live like that when you knew you'd surely make more mistakes?

Her chest tightened when she realized, she couldn't go on with Caine this way anymore.

Wouldn't.

Em was dead on. Dixie was all about punishing herself, and being with Caine, making love to him, spending time with him while almost certain she'd lose him all over again, was the biggest form of self-inflicted harm going.

To postpone the inevitable, to drag out the end, hurt almost as much as letting go. The very idea of letting Caine go—actually saying the words out loud—was almost more than she could wrap her mind around. Her throat went dry, and her limbs went buttery soft simply thinking about it.

Somewhere, in the crazy recesses of her mind, she'd

always thought she and Caine would find each other again. Now that she'd grown up and experienced one of the hardest journeys of her life before returning to Plum Orchard, she knew that was all just make-believe.

But it had been the old Dixie's way of thinking.

The reformed Dixie saw Caine needed more substance in a woman. He needed trust—deep trust. He needed someone who would match his brand of integrity one selfless act at a time.

As the world continued around her, as children waved sparklers, as people laughed and chatted, and the high school marching band pounded out a patriotic beat, everything screamed to a screeching halt for her.

She would do the right thing and stop torturing herself by ending whatever this was with Caine. She'd apologize to him once and for all, and then she'd walk away—for good.

Even if everything inside her rebelled against the very idea.

Her fingers twisted the quilt beneath her to quell the bone-deep ache.

Leaning forward, Dixie scrunched her eyes shut and fought for breath when her phone buzzed. Her hand blindly reached for it, stupidly hoping it might be Caine—afraid it might be Caine.

Do you know how much I love you, Dixie-Cup? More than I love my own spleen. That's a whole lotta love. Love yourself that much, too, would you, please?

She read the text from Landon again, hearing him in her head as if he was sitting right next to her, eating

Em's mother's potato salad. She pinched the bridge of her nose.

Love yourself, Dixie. Love yourself enough to know when to let go.

Upon Landon's words, Dixie knew exactly what she had to do.

"Hey! Where'd you go there?" Em asked, smiling down at her, holding her hand out to offer her help up. "The slide show's about to start. Gareth wants to be front and center to see his grandparents and Clifton Senior up on that big screen. You comin'?"

Dixie took a ragged breath and accepted Em's hand with a squeeze. "I wouldn't miss it." She held out her hand to Gareth who smiled his chubby grin from behind Em's knees. "Let's go see Daddy, little man."

Mayor Hale had begun to read off the prestigious list of the founders of Plum Orchard with their accompanying pictures while Em, Dixie and Gareth plunged into the crowd, pushing their way toward the front to get closer to the gazebo.

Sandwiched between a scowling Nanette and Reverend Watson, Dixie swung Gareth up in her arms so he could see the screen.

Em tugged on his T-shirt from behind. "Daddy's next!"

"Next up," Mayor Hale's voice rumbled into the microphone, "we have the Amos family, five generations strong and still going. One of our original founding fathers…"

She forced herself to focus on the pictures projected

and Mayor Hale's deep drone rather than dwell on what she planned to tell Caine.

"And next up, Clifton Amos Senior!" The crowd politely clapped and Dixie squeezed Gareth to show her excitement for him, bouncing him up and down. "Son of Harlow and Idalee, one-time all-state football champ, six-time 4-H blue ribbon holder, father of two fine young men, Clifton Junior, now a strapping eight years old, and little Gareth, five, and last—but certainly not least—husband to the lovely Emmaline Amos. Join me in a round of applause for such an esteemed member of our little burg, Clifton Amos, everybody!"

The projection screen flashed to the next picture, but the hands that had so heartily joined together moments ago, stopped—dead.

She heard Em's shrill scream just before the silence. From the corner of her eye, Dixie caught her covering her mouth in order to muffle it.

There were gasps from the crowd—piercing and out-raged.

There were faint whispers—hissed and uncomfort-able.

Then there was silence, and nothing but Gareth's words when he placed his chubby hands on each of her cheeks and stared down at her with stoic confusion. "Miss Dixie, that ain't my daddy up there. That's a lady."

A lady?

Oh, sweet fancy Moses, no.

Nineteen

The silence that met Dixie's ears was deafening. No one moved for what felt like an eternity while she put two and two together.

No.

Dixie tore her eyes from Gareth's face and looked up at the screen behind Mayor Hale's receding hairline.

No.

She closed her eyes tight. *Please. Please, whoever's in charge, you can have whatever you want from me, if when I open my eyes, this all turns out to be a horrible dream.*

Her eyes popped open again followed by her mouth.

Clifton swam before her line of vision, larger than life. But he wasn't the Clifton of the plaid flannel hunting jacket and John Deere ball cap.

He was, according to the small bio beneath his picture, Trixy LeMieux and second runner-up in the Atlanta Miss Cross Dresser 2014 pageant.

Dixie's eyes widened as she absorbed Clifton dressed as a woman. He wore a sapphire dress, dazzling in sequins from his toes to the curve-hugging bodice where breasts spilled from the sleeveless frock.

Enviable silver stilettos with black, glossy heels, pointed outward in a pose reminiscent of Miss America, from beneath the tapered hemline. He wore heavy makeup, thickly applied to his jaw to cover his stubble line, flirty false eyelashes, silver and pink glitter eye shadow, and bloodred lipstick. The crown on his head sat atop long, thick locks in a gleaming ebony where they fell, tumbling into an enormous bouquet of red roses.

Clifton eyed the camera with a half smile as kittenish as any Dixie'd ever been able to produce. Yet there was something in his eyes, something that stuck with her. He looked happy. Happy and alive.

As the yelling around her reeling head began to penetrate her slow-motion brain, Dixie clung to Gareth, instinctively spinning around so he wouldn't see any more, making a frantic search for Em.

Em stormed toward her, her fists tight at her sides, her feet crashing against the ground. *"Give me my child,"* she seethed between her clenched teeth, her red lips twisted into a sneer.

"Em! Oh, God, how can I help?" Who would have done something like this? How had someone found out?

Em handed Gareth to her mother who had Clifton Junior by the hand. "Take them where they can't hear me, Mama," she ordered in a tone that held one part ferocious, two parts livid. The three scurried off into the dark, their backs becoming tiny dots until the night swallowed them up.

Dixie gripped Em's arm in an urgent gesture. All she needed to do was get her away from the gaping, judgmental eyes of all of Plum Orchard. They'd figure out the rest when they found somewhere more private than the square. "Hold on to me. I'll get you out of here."

"The—hell—you—will!" she roared. She yanked her arm from Dixie's grasp and shook her off with a hard shove.

The crowd of people around them parted, making a half circle of more astonished eyes. Nanette and Essie hovered on the fringes of the circle, arms hooked together, eyes narrowed in Dixie's direction.

Dixie frowned, not understanding. "Em! C'mon. Let's get out of here!"

Instead of accepting Dixie's hand, Em circled her, her chest heaving beneath the scooped neckline of her red dress. Her sweet face, always so open and warm, was a closed mask of barely contained anger. Her mouth twisted into a sneer. "I'd rather be flayed alive under the noonday sun and have vinegar poured in my open wounds than ever go anywhere with you again, Dixie Davis!"

Startled, Dixie still didn't understand the words coming from her person's mouth. "What?"

Em moved in on her, shoving her face at Dixie, her finger pointed and suddenly digging into the spot beneath Dixie's collarbone as if she was hammering a nail. *"What?"* She mimicked Dixie's surprise in a sticky-sweet impression, giving her a poke so full of rage, it knocked Dixie backward. "Poor, poor persecuted Dixie. Everyone's always picking on sorry little ol' you. Don't you pull that—that—" she jammed her face farther into Dixie's "—*bullshit* with me! Don't you dare 'what' me like you're all innocence and light! You were only one of two souls alive who knew about Clifton. You don't expect me to believe it was Marybell, do you? *Do you?*" she screamed.

Dixie's heart throbbed in her ears while ice ran in her veins. "Em! *No!* I swear to you on everything I have, I didn't tell anyone. I made a promise to you—"

Em's snort ripped through the strange quiet of the square, cutting her off. "Just like you made a promise to Caine, Dixie? You're a filthy liar and a disgraceful human being. I told you, Dixie. I warned you, if you hurt my boys, you'd pay!"

Dixie was too stunned to speak. Her instinct to run, to hide from such a horrible accusation was thwarted only by the fleeting thought that this was what vengeance, the karma she so deserved, was all about.

But Em couldn't possibly believe she'd told anyone her secret. "Em, *please.*" She reached for Em's arm only to have it snatched from her vicinity as if she was riddled with plague.

Dixie held up her hands and backed away, forcing herself to remain calm. There was an explanation. There had to be an explanation. "Please listen to me. I would never, ever hurt those boys. I would never hurt you. I know I've said things like this before, but I swear to you, I never told a soul. Not a solitary soul. No one talks to me, Em. Everyone treats me like the town pariah. Think about that. Who'd listen to me if I told them anyway?" Dixie's eyes sought Em's, pleading, blinking back tears.

"Ohhh, you're good, Dixie. So, so good," she said with dripping sarcasm. "Those big, wide eyes, those crocodile tears. I'm sure you'd love me to believe that, wouldn't you? Stupid Emmaline, always chasin' after the trail of pathetic breadcrumbs you leave in your wake like some lovesick puppy. I'm sure you'd love for me to believe you had nothing to do with this so I could go on bein' your loyal minion. Well, *no—more!*" she bellowed.

Dixie held her ground. She ignored the spiteful eyes of the Mags, and the disgusted eyes of the Senior Mags. She turned her cheek to the onlookers, gawking at her public demise with knowing nods of their heads.

One more time, she forced herself to stay calm even as her stomach rebelled. "Em, I'm begging you. Please listen to me. Let's go somewhere where we can sit down and talk about this rationally, and you'll see I'm telling you the truth. I did not tell anyone. *No one.*"

"Well, you musta told someone, Dixie! You might not have done that," she pointed at the projection screen, still displaying the damning image of Clifton/Trixie. "But it got out somehow!"

Dixie shook her head, fighting her hysteria in order to make Em believe her. "Em, I'm telling you the truth—"

"The truth? You wouldn't know the truth if it slapped you in your two faces! Maybe you just wanted back in with those disgusting Mags, and this was your way to get it. A big juicy bit of gossip for you to spread like the vermin you all are." Em whipped around, turning her rant to the crowd, her eyes wild and shining with fury even as tears streamed from her eyes. "And yes!" she yelled, her scream coming out harshly hoarse, her finger stabbing out her targets. "I called the lot of you vermin, always takin' pleasure in someone else's pain. You hear me, Louella Palmer, Annabelle Pruitt, and Lesta-Sue Arnold? I meant *all* of you with your vicious mouths and backstabbin' ways! Be warned, Dixie, you will pay for hurting my children! I hope you all, and es-

pecially you, Dixie Davis, rot in hell!" she spat before
spinning around and running toward the curb.

Dixie watched as Em careened right into the man
who'd watched her while he played catch with his little
girl. He righted her with large hands, his eyes under the
streetlamp full of concern, before Em let out a sharp
cry and tore herself from his reach.

Dixie closed her eyes and swallowed so hard, she
was sure it echoed around the square. The eyes of Plum
Orchard burned holes into her back as sure as if they
were holding lit matches to her skin.

And still, she couldn't move. Not as their horror over
Em's accusations sank in, and the twitter of chatter ig-
nited. Not even as some residents made wide circles
around her as if her mere existence would bring them
harm.

She didn't move an inch, not a muscle. For all the
hurt that had resulted from the cruel pranks she'd once
perpetrated, she would not run from everyone's chance
to finally hold her accountable.

She lifted her chin and let them all look, refusing
to look away. Let them nod their heads as if to say, *No
big surprise here.*

As she stared straight ahead, she almost wished
Caine were here. Funny, even though she'd resolved
to end things between them she still looked for him,
needed his chest to bury her face in.

In her head, she heard Landon's voice, *Sugarpie,
someday, for all the mean things you've done, you're
gonna have to pay the piper, and I'm bettin' it won't
be pretty.*

Someday had arrived.

* * *

She didn't know how long she stood there. The only thing she could see was Em's face, angry and riddled with hurt, and it had immobilized her.

The only thing she could hear was Em's stifled cry of shock, Gareth's innocent question, Clifton Junior's tears as he sobbed, and Em's damning words. *You're a filthy liar. A disgraceful excuse for a human being!* over and over again as though someone had pressed replay.

If it had only been minutes, it certainly felt like an eternity judging from her stiff legs and ice-cold hands. Whether she breathed during that time also escaped her, though when she finally exhaled, she almost gagged.

The litter in the deserted square came into focus, just as the goose bumps on her arms made her shiver. Her clenched fingers, achy and tight, released. She shook them, looking down to find they were red and splotchy from the cold.

Dixie wrapped her arms around her waist and sank to her haunches, taking slow, deep breaths, aching for Em and the boys. How could she make this right so Em would allow her to help her through this?

"If it isn't Plum Orchard's favorite snitch."

Her head snapped up to see Louella, smiling down at her, ankles crossed, arms folded at her chest and eyes full of smug delight.

Dixie buried her face in her arms. "Go away, Louella," she mumbled into her folded arms, not caring that she was obviously here to gloat.

Louella toed the grass at Dixie's feet with her royal blue pump. "Somebody had a rough night."

Misery prevented Dixie from rising. Everything in her hurt. "Somebody asked you to go away."

"What comes around goes around, they say."

"Then *they* enjoyed a little full circle tonight, didn't *they*?"

Louella's laughter slipped from her lips. "I'll say. You really did it this time, Dixie. This was almost as good as your engagement party."

Her pride nudged her from the inside. *Just because you're paying for all those sins, doesn't mean you have to be Louella's whipping boy. Stand up, Dixie. Look her in the eye, take it like a man, but don't take it sitting down.*

Dixie pushed off her knees with her hands and rose. "Okay, you've had your due, right? See mean Dixie taken down a notch while everyone points and laughs. But in the process someone was hurt, Louella. Someone who's always kind to everyone. Worse, there were children involved. I can't think of anything more despicable than involving innocent children."

Louella's eyes shifted from smug to dark for a fleeting moment before settling on haughty. "Maybe you should have thought about that before you told everyone her secret. Who knew the king of the rednecks liked sparkly pretties? Surprise!"

Her anger spiked hard and fast, and it was all Dixie could do not to snake her hand out and flatten her palm against Louella's taut cheek. "Don't speak those words to me, Louella. I won't defend myself to the likes of you, but I won't have you speak about Em or Clifton that way either. Em's the most decent human being I know. How dare you poke at her when she's hurting so badly."

"You mean just like you used to do?"

"Is that enough? Or do you want blood?" Dixie held out her wrists as an offering.

Louella made a face and rolled her eyes. "No. I just want you gone. You're bad news, Dixie. Everybody knows it. So why don't you go on back to Chicago, and take your bevy of trashy women with you."

Suddenly, she was bone-weary. Exhausted from either having her guard up all the time, or trying to live down her bad reputation. "Look, Louella, let's just call a truce, okay? I'm asking you this because, though there were plenty of bad times, we had some good ones, too."

Louella put a finger to her chin as if in thought. "You mean like the time you knew I was crazy about Caine and you went out with him anyway? That was super good."

Dixie's sigh was ragged. "Okay, it's time for some reality here. You've let this eat you up for too long, and you've lost perspective. First, I wasn't in that bet alone. Second, you couldn't have known you loved Caine any more than I did. You'd been on *one* date with him. The rest was just hero-worship from afar, a high school crush. How do you know you would have fallen in love with him? Maybe you would have hated each other."

"Or maybe we wouldn't have," she said angrily. "You didn't exactly give him the chance to find out before you were all over him like some kind of fungus. You knew how I felt about him, and you chased after him anyway. So we'll never know, will we?"

Someone needed to give Louella the cold splash of reality she so deserved. She was so eaten up by her petty jealousy and anger she was headed straight for where Dixie was right now. "Obviously, he didn't want to find out, Louella. He didn't ask for another date. I'm not saying that to be cruel. I'm just saying it because it's the truth. But you won anyway, didn't you? You won big. Remember the microphone suspiciously placed by your phone at our engagement party? Remember the chaos?" The fire that broke out when Dixie had chased after Caine and knocked down all those beautiful candles. The pounding thunder and rain that had come out of nowhere like some foreboding sign.

God, she'd never forget the words she'd said. *I win, you lose, Louella Palmer! That'll teach you to bet Dixie Davis when it comes to a marriage proposal. Wish Caine and I lots of little Donovans.*

"You righted all the wrongs. We broke up. I can't figure why you're still so angry about it almost ten years later. You won in the end."

"I did that to right a potential wrong, Dixie. Marrying you was wrong. No man should marry a woman who was just in it to do a victory lap. You didn't deserve Caine then, and you don't deserve him now."

More truth. But she still had an ounce left of reason in her, and she was going to spend it on Louella because she had nothing to lose. "But I don't have him now. So if you still want him so badly, why don't you go get him? You got him mere minutes after I left our engagement party, right? Isn't that what you told Em and the rest of the Mags?"

Louella's mouth opened to construct a plausible denial, but Dixie held up a hand to stop her. "Let's lay all our cards on the table. You wanted me to believe you'd slept with Caine. Please don't insult me by denying it. You wouldn't have told the Mags, and Em specifically, if you didn't. It's a weapon to hurt me, but I'm here to tell you, whether you did or not, I'm over it. Caine was a free man, and you were free, too. Isn't the knowledge that it would hurt me enough payback for what I did? And if it isn't, what is? What will ever be enough?"

Dixie got the impression Louella didn't know the answer to that question any more than she did. "You're a sad excuse for a human being, Dixie. You turn my stomach."

She didn't have the energy left to fight with Louella when the very thought of what Em was going through was on the table. "Yes, yes, yes, Louella. I *was* a horrible person. Said it a hundred times since I've been back. The point is I'm trying to be better, but you're taking up where I left off. Do you want to end up like me? Like this? Didn't you just bear witness to what happens when you're an absolute bitch? It bites you in the ass."

Louella's face had disbelief written all over it. "When did this change come about? I'd love to know. We'd all love to know, in fact. Care to share what made cold-hearted snake Dixie turn into Dixie-Do-Gooder?"

No. There'd be no sharing something that was none of her business. It was personal and a deep pain she'd live with always. Ignoring the question, Dixie appealed to Louella from a different angle. "Here's the score. The girls and I aren't hurting anyone. We're just trying to make a living. Why does that make you see red? Is it because I'm involved in it? Are you just out to make me miserable simply because I exist? Because I have some news for you, I plan to exist for a long time."

Louella's silence gave Dixie hope she was at least reaching her.

She stuck her hand out to Louella, an olive branch of fingers attached to a wrist. "So can we just let this grudge go, please? People who had nothing to do with what happened between us are getting hurt. LaDawn and Marybell have never uttered an unkind word to you, so why involve them? To hurt me? There's nothing you have left in your bag of tricks that can hurt me, Louella. I'm all hurt out. Everyone knows everythin' there is to know about my jaded past. All the sharp thorns left in my backside have scarred over."

More silence as Dixie watched the wheels turn inside Louella's head. She hoped that meant Louella was considering her proposition.

"So if you stop, I'll stop," Dixie continued. "Swear it. And I'll never steal another man from you for as long as I live. My hand to God," she joked, hoping to lighten their conversation. "Deal?"

Louella looked at Dixie's hand as if it was smeared in cow dung, turning her nose up at it. She leaned in close so Dixie wouldn't miss a venomous word. "I won't stop until you're gone from this town, Dixie. You and your bunch of ex-hooker friends are a blight on Plum Orchard's good name. No one wanted you to come back to begin with. After what you did to poor Em tonight, I'd bet they want you here even less."

Louella spun on her heel, picking her way across the square, leaving behind a haunting tune of pending doom playing in Dixie's head.

Sanjeev's quiet presence made her turn around to acknowledge him before returning to packing her bags.

Mona and Lisa stretched their bulky bodies, whimpering their joy at his presence.

"So you're running away?"

"You heard?"

"Who hasn't, Dixie? The Maldives heard. They

called, by the way. Something about an offer for a place to hide?"

Dixie snorted. "Don't you start on me, Sanjeev. I'm not running away or hiding because I did something wrong. I would never, ever betray Em's trust. Are you kidding me? What little trust I had was like earning a seat on the space shuttle to Mars. But I can't seem to convince anyone of that." She'd texted Em five times since she'd walked back from the square to nothing but profound silence.

And it hurt. But it had proven something to her. No matter what the situation, no one would ever say, "Not a snowball's chance in hell would Dixie Davis ever do that." She'd always be the scapegoat. While that was more than fair, it was no way to live.

Sanjeev placed a comforting hand on her shoulder. "You've convinced me, Dixie. Landon always said you'd come around. He was right. I believe."

She scooped up a pile of her underwear and dumped them into the suitcase. "I'm a real beacon of hope for mean girls everywhere."

"Does this mean you'll forfeit the contest, too, Dixie?"

Yes. It meant she was forfeiting everything that had to do with Plum Orchard. Caine, Em, the Mags, and Call Girls. For a little while, she'd convinced herself you really could come home again. She'd basked in the familiar, fallen in love all over again with her small town, despite the small minds and gossip. She'd found a way to ignore the comments and whispers—until tonight.

"Yes. I'm forfeiting. I'm only causing trouble for the girls anyway, Sanjeev. Louella and every last one of the Mags want them gone. Me in the mix makes her want them doubly gone. If I'm out, maybe she'll ease up a little and let them live their lives in peace."

"And if she doesn't?"

"Poison some of that fabulous curry you make and take it to her house for dinner, for me, would you?"

Sanjeev laughed, tightening his hand on her shoulder and forcing her to turn around. "Dixie?"

"Sanjeev?"

His somber eyes, full of peace and understanding, gazed into hers. "It's always darkest before the dawn."

Her clipped laughter dripped sarcasm. "It doesn't mean my days aren't always going to be dark just because the sun comes up. I think I've proven that. You can have buckets full of sunshine and still have a really crappy day."

He tilted his dark head, his deep brown eyes searching hers. "I think what it really means is things have to be intolerable before they're tolerable."

She cupped his cheek and stroked the smooth, enviably perfect skin with her thumb. "Look at you, all learning the ways of the American. And after all this time. I'm so proud."

But Sanjeev frowned and shook his head. "Who'll see to Em and the boys? Who'll protect her from that wretch Louella and her evil Magnolia posse if not you?"

Dixie turned away and threw a batch of socks on top of her underwear. "I can't protect someone who would rather see my entrails wrapped around a tree and tied in a bow, Sanjeev."

"It isn't like you haven't stood up to things like this before. It never stopped you in the past."

"In the past I had no shame. Nowadays, I have so

much I could open a shame bank and share my endless supply with the shameless of the world."

"I wish you'd reconsider, Dixie. *You're meant to be here.*"

Dropping one of her scarves into the pile, she twisted her fingers into it to keep from screaming her frustration. "I wish you weren't the only one that believed me. But you're an island, my friend."

"You do know that your past will always make you have to prove yourself in the present, don't you?"

"Is that your way of telling me whenever something horrible happens, I'm always going to be the most likely suspect?"

"I suppose it is."

"Well, thanks for clearing that up. If I wasn't aware of that before tonight, I'm pretty clear now."

"You're being saucy."

"And just a little mouthy," she admitted. "I could do it as long as the gossip and sly comments were just about me. I can handle it because I invented it. But now it involves Em and her children. I can't allow that. I won't."

"Did you speak to Emmaline?"

"She's not talking to me. I want to help, Sanjeev. Can you even imagine how horrible this will be for her and the boys? She was so afraid everyone would find out. She knew exactly how everyone would react, and she was right."

"That you're more concerned for Emmaline and the boys than your own persecution surely proves you would never share such a sensitive issue, doesn't it?"

"Not when you've done the things I've done, Sanjeev. Wasn't it you just a minute ago who said I'd always be suspect? Though, I wish someone would look at the evidence a little closer. What could I possibly gain from exposing something like that? Or from gossiping about it? When I did some of the things I did, I did them to gain something. Like a boyfriend who had a car. Or a seat on the Miss Cherokee Rose float."

"Who do you think would do something so distasteful? Are you certain no one else knew?" Sanjeev prodded.

Dixie bobbed her head. "The only other person who knew was Marybell. She was there when Em told us, and I can promise you, she'd never betray Em."

Sanjeev's face grew skeptical. "Of that you're sure?"

Yes. She knew Marybell would never hurt anyone, let alone Em. "I'm positive, Sanjeev. I wouldn't even insult her by asking her a question like that. So how did someone all the way here in Plum Orchard find out about what Clifton's been doing in Atlanta? Besides, Marybell wouldn't think twice about someone cross-dressing. She's a phone-sex operator, for gravy's sake. It's no big deal to her. She loves Em. Everyone at Call Girls does."

She loved Em, damn it.

Sanjeev clapped his hands together as if they'd made some revelation. "Then we've narrowed our suspects, yes? It was clearly someone who is mean of spirit. I can name at least one woman. Cough—Louella Palmer—cough," he joked, running his words together.

Defeat crushed her just thinking about trying to prove it. If Louella had done this, she wouldn't leave a trail of evidence that led back to her. She wasn't that stupid. "Listen, Matlock, we're not narrowing anything. I almost don't want to know who'd do something so cruel because it would be all I could do not to bring the old

Dixie back for some good old-fashioned stoning. And what would Louella gain by doing something so evil?"

Sanjeev, usually so serene and unruffled, sighed in aggravation. He gripped her arm, making her stop what she was doing. "She'd hurt you, Dixie, of course! It's clear she'll use any avenue to get to you. You don't really think she opposes Call Girls, do you? She opposes you being here because of Call Girls, which is why she attacked LaDawn and Marybell. She saw your friendship with Emmaline blossoming. If she makes you miserable enough to give her exactly what she wants, which is your swift departure back to Chicago, she'll use whoever and whatever it takes to do so. How can you not see that?"

Dixie shook her head in disbelief. "But this involved Em's children, Sanjeev. That's unbelievably cruel, even for Louella."

"Bah," he groused, throwing an impatient hand up. "She eats nails for breakfast and kicks walkers out from under unsuspecting senior citizens. Louella's blinded by her jealousy of you. As you well know, that ugly emotion can produce uncharacteristic behavior."

That emotion she was painfully aware of. "Nobody knows the green-eyed monster like I do. In fact, I think I slept with him once."

Sanjeev wasn't biting at her joke. He was, however, becoming exasperated with her. The tic in his jaw pulsed, a rare occurrence for him to become ruffled. "Then the answer is clear. You have to stay in order to slay the monster."

"I can't slay something if my heroine is uncooperative. Em's never going to forgive me. And if what you say about Louella turns out to be true, then I'm going back to Chicago where no one knows me enough to hate my guts quite like that—or hurt anyone else who's even remotely involved with me."

"Ah, to lick your wounds," he baited with a sly smile.

She clenched her teeth together. "Yes."

"And to poverty."

"That, too." And to work at McDonald's until she paid off her debts.

"And Caine?"

Right. And Caine. Dixie's heart sank like a rock, landing in her stomach and settling there. "What about Caine?" she asked nonchalantly.

"You'll leave without saying goodbye to him? He'll be distressed to see he didn't have the chance to crow his phone-sex victory."

"I haven't seen him since last night. When the smoke clears, I'm sure he'll resurface. Give him my best." Her offhand attitude helped hide the searing pain in her heart.

"How unlike him to disappear when there's a damsel in distress."

"Well, you're forgetting who the damsel is. I'd disappear if I could, if I were him, too."

"Still, very curious…"

Dixie breathed deeply, forcing her next words out of her mouth. "It's better we don't see each other anyway."

"Really then? I wouldn't have thought that was how you felt by the way the two of you have *seen* so much of each other recently."

Her stomach twisted into a tight knot. She closed her eyes to wash away Caine's face—to keep the memory of their last moments together at bay. "That's all part of our dysfunction. We can't stay away from each other.

But it's time to end the cycle. I won't ever be the kind of woman Caine needs, and I definitely can't live up to his high expectations. There's no breathing room for me to screw up—or be accused of screwing up. If I'm always going to be suspect, I'll spend every waking moment proving to him and everyone else I'm innocent if something goes wrong. That's no way to have a relationship, and you know it, Sanjeev. It's done, and that's that."

"Then there's nothing left to say but goodbye, is there?"

Dixie dropped her makeup bag and turned around when she heard how hoarse Sanjeev's voice had become.

He held out his arms, and she went to him, squeezing her eyes shut to keep from shedding more tears. "I'll miss you so much, Sanjeev. Thank you—for everything. The wonderful meals, the company, but most of all, for your friendship."

"If I can't talk you into staying, will you at least remember this one thing?"

"More twisted clichés and metaphors to suit my pathetic existence?"

"Mona likes the cheesy beef kibble, but particular Lisa will only eat the chicken."

Dixie laughed into his shoulder and nodded, squeezing him extra hard so she had his soothing warmth to carry her back to Chicago.

Sanjeev pulled away first, tilting her chin upward with one finger, his eyes glossy. "Until next we meet, Dixie Davis."

"Until next time," she whispered, biting the inside of her cheek to fight the tremble of her lips.

And then he was gone, and Dixie was left alone with nothing but the tick of the clock on her dresser.

Right back where she'd begun.

Twenty

Caine dropped into the ugly red chair in his Miami condo living room and made a face at the chair the over-priced interior designer Landon had sent to redecorate when he'd bought the place had chosen. "It's still damn ugly, and it's still uncomfortable, and I don't give a shit if it's facing the ocean," he complained to his phone after reading another of Landon's texts.

Are you lonesome tonight? Is your heart filled with pain? Will you come back again? Tell me, Caine, are you lonesome tonight?

It was as if the bastard knew what he was doing—how he felt at any given moment. And yes, he was lonesome. Lonesome for home, lonesome for family, lonesome for Dixie and he'd only been gone a day.

There. All out in the open now.

Now, what to do about it. How to go about it. How to fix this for good. How to trust again. How to explain everything to Dixie.

He closed his eyes and took a deep breath—when he

opened them again, he saw nothing that made him feel as if any of this was even his. Everything in his condo had been picked out by someone else, carefully placed by a stranger's hand, and he hated most of it.

And he never realized how much he hated it until just this moment. How much he'd dreaded getting on that plane to come back to it.

He wanted to go home and stay home—for good.

With Dixie. If she'd have him after what he'd done.

Maybe she'd be angry. Maybe she'd be really angry.

He'd been hard on her. Too hard. Too unforgiving. An asshole. He'd tested, he'd pushed, he'd taunted—and still, she'd damn well soldiered on.

He wanted this Dixie. Maybe more than he'd ever wanted her.

But maybe she won't want you?

Maybe not, but he wasn't going out without a fight.

His phone chirped, leaving him leery. One more taunting text message from the grave…his eyes fell to the phone, concern instantly replacing his irritability. "Sanjeev? Is everything okay?"

"No, Caine Donovan, nothing is okay."

As he listened to Sanjeev tell him what happened at the Founder's Day picnic, his blood boiled over. "Son of a bitch," he growled into the phone.

"Something *must* be done, Caine."

"I'll handle it. Thanks, buddy."

Sanjeev's sigh of relief only added to his anxiety. Sanjeev rarely stuck his nose into anything. When he did, Landon always said that was when you should sit up and take notice.

Caine sat up, his fingers skipping through a quick Google search. Tapping the number that came up, he added it to his phone and dialed it while his teeth clenched tight.

"Louella? Caine Donovan. We need to talk."

"I'm sorry to drag you in here on your last night in Plum Orchard, Dixie, but Marybell's down with the flu, and you know how busy Saturday nights are around here," Cat apologized. "You were the only option. Sheree's out of town, and LaDawn can only handle so many calls. I'll divert the calls for the girls to you. Just do your best."

Dixie's plan had been to leave as fast as she could throw her bag and Mona and Lisa into her car, and drive until she was too tired to drive anymore, until Cat called and asked if she'd take Marybell's shift. "I'm happy to help," she offered dully, adjusting the box for her personal belongings.

"No you're not. You want to get in your car and drive the hell out of here as fast as your beat-up old car can go."

"Like I'm on fire," she tried to joke, but it sounded bleak and depressing.

Cat pulled her into a hug, rubbing her back. "I wish you'd reconsider. You were beating Caine by at least twenty-five percent. You could've had it all if that kept up."

Dixie breathed deeply, her stomach a jumble of butterflies, all fighting to find their way out of her intestines. "If all means Em hating my guts and the rest of Plum Orchard giving me the stink eye, I'd rather not have it all. I'll settle for just some."

"Not a single one of us believe you were responsible, Dixie. Not one of us. Em'll come around."

Dixie forced herself to smile. She would not be pathetic. If she was going, she was going with her head held high. "Not even LaDawn? Look at me, winning friends and influencing people."

Cat held her away from her. "LaDawn was your biggest supporter. She offered to find out who did this to Em and drop them off at her old place of business in Atlanta."

"Aw, LaDawn and me sittin' in a tree. Surely her offer to have someone beaten to death for me is a sign of her undying devotion," she teased, gripping Cat's hand. Despite her preconceived notions about what the women of Call Girls would be like, she'd fallen in love with them. Had come to respect their grit and determination to survive. "I'm really going to miss you guys."

"You don't gotta miss us if you don't go nowhere, Dixie. Closed mouths don't get fed, as my mama, rest her soul, used to say! Cain't win a contest if you ain't playin'!" LaDawn shouted from her office.

Dixie couldn't help but laugh before Cat sobered and said, "You're only givin' that awful Louella what she wants, Dixie. You know that, right?"

"Maybe so, but if she's responsible for what happened to Em, what's the right thing to do, Cat? Stay here so she can cause more damage just so I can say I didn't let Louella Palmer beat me?"

Cat's expression was grim. "I see your point, but—"

Dixie shook her head, moving toward the hallway leading to her office. "No buts. Em's children's suffering is absolutely not an option. Now, no more of this sad talk. Send some of those LaDawn calls my way, so I can leave y'all proud." She padded down the hallway. As she passed LaDawn's office, she taunted good-naturedly, "Look out, LaDawn! Mistress Taboo's in the house, and she's gonna turn your floggers inside out!"

LaDawn's cackle filled her ears, making Dixie's heart clench. "You go on, Vanilla. Do me proud now—show 'em you da man!"

Headset in place, Dixie gathered her personal belongings from her desk, taking a last glimpse of the picture of her and Landon. She traced his beaming smile with her fingertip, and wondered what he'd have to say about this mess. "Well, now look, would you? A fine mess you've made, pal. I hope you're happy up there, you big pain in my ass," she said fondly.

The realization that Landon had done this—the challenge between her and Caine for his company, the text messages—all of it—had been about bringing her home.

Sanjeev's words, *You were meant to be here* said with such conviction had been the final clue. He knew what Landon's motives were. He had all along.

Even in death, Landon had been trying to save her. He knew coming home, confronting her past, tying up all of the ugly loose ends she'd left dangling was what she'd need to finally move forward.

She might not have known she was ready to come home, though. So he'd invented a reason that would keep her here longer than just attending his funeral.

He'd known familiar places and treasured faces would comfort her at a time when her entire world was upside down. Someday, she'd like to know how he'd known what was really going on with her life in Chicago.

He just hadn't counted on the unforeseeable.

Her earpiece rang again, making her sit up straighter.

Taking over for LaDawn meant she'd better be on her toes. It took her mind off leaving, off the possibility that she'd never see Caine again. "This is Mistress Taboo. Are you worthy?"

"Mistress Taboo, it's real fine to hear your voice."

Walker. His deep, rumbly voice made her heart begin that excited thrum. Then it took a nosedive.

In all her mad preparation to leave, she hadn't given thought to what she'd say to the list of clients she'd managed to accrue—or if she'd say anything at all. But Walker probably wouldn't be too disappointed by her hanging up her phone-sex hat. He didn't really call for advice.

Why did Walker call? "Walker—it's nice to hear your voice, too."

"You don't sound like yourself tonight, Mistress Taboo. Why's that?"

How uncanny he should sense that when she was so focused on sounding normal. "I think I'm catching a cold." It was as good of an excuse as any.

"My mama always used to say, some milk boiled with onions and pepper in it'll cure all your ills."

Where had she heard that before? "Ugh. I think I'll stick to over-the-counter stuff."

"So how've you been, Mistress Taboo? What's new in your world since we last talked?"

"Well, I do have a little bit of news, and you're the first client I'm sharing it with."

"I'm all sorts of honored."

"I'm leaving Call Girls." Her heart squeezed at the admission.

Walker's pause was long before he cleared his throat and asked, "Better prospects somewhere else?"

Sure. Some might call the fast food industry a better prospect. "I don't know if you'd call it better, but it's better all round, better for me." Better for Em and her boys. She would miss Em so much.

"For you? You've got me frettin' now, Mistress Taboo. Does it have to do with what we talked about the last time?"

There was no twirling her hair or flushed cheeks over his supposed concern this time, just a dead weight in the pit of her stomach. "How is it we're always talking about me?"

"Because I'd bet my last dime you're prettier. Prettier wins the spotlight. Plus, if you're leaving Call Girls, who's it hurtin'? We won't talk to each other after tonight." His soothing voice somehow managed to lull her anxiety.

He was right. What difference would it make if she told him the truth? She relented, her reluctance to share ebbing away. "My past has come back to haunt me in ways I not only deserve, but it's also come back to haunt others, too. It's affected someone who's…" She stumbled. "She's very important to me. If I go back to Chicago, I'm hoping it'll all die down, and she'll be able to have some peace."

"So this isn't about the former fiancé you talked about? I'm confused."

It would always be about Caine, wouldn't it? "It's about him, and my friend, one who was reluctant to befriend me after the pranks I played on her in high school. It's about everyone, I guess," she said with stark honesty. "I guess the point here is I come from a place where everybody knows everybody, a small town that can be very judgmental and set in its ways. The things

I did here, the people I hurt, well…they don't forget. And I don't blame them. But a recent incident reminded me of something. I'll always be the usual suspect for everything that goes wrong. No matter how I go about redeeming myself, the first bad thing that happens, everyone's going to look to me."

"Do you want to share this latest incident?" he asked tentatively with what sounded like genuine concern.

Dixie shook her head at Walker's "no pressure here" inquiry even as she cringed with the memory of last night. "Not on your life. I will tell you, it made the Rapture look like a church social. Suffice it to say, it was ugly, and it devastated someone I really love in front of a bunch of people. It hurt members of her family, too. That's the worst part of this."

What would it be like for Clifton Junior and Gareth at school come Monday? Children could be so incredibly cruel. She couldn't bear the idea that everyone would be laughing and teasing them. Especially as fine a line as Clifton Junior was walking.

"Any idea who might have done this?"

Dixie tried to pinpoint something, anything from her conversation with Louella that was even a small hint she'd been involved, but she couldn't think of anything other than the boys and Em. "There's only one person I can think of. And if it was her, this person, she would have done it to hurt me. I can't live with that. I won't allow it."

"Still don't see what that has to do with your ex-fiancé."

"Basically, it's just another nail in my coffin. When he hears about what happened, I'll be the first person he suspects talked out of turn and spilled my friend's secret, because I'm the only other person alive who knew about it." The more she said that out loud, the harder the time she was having processing who could've found out about Clifton. Certainly no one from Plum Orchard frequented a place where they held a cross-dressing pageant.

Or did they?

"So he's pretty judgmental."

She leaned back in the chair, a visual of Caine's handsome face, smiling up at her, floating before her eyes. "No," she whispered into the phone, the true ache of longing strong and harsh. "He's not judgmental. I used to think he was, but now I realize, he just lives his life to a pretty high standard. He's an amazing person. The kind of person who expects everyone else to be as honest and decent as he is. And he should expect that, but it's damn hard to live up to when you know you're bound to make more mistakes. Perfect and I are about as far apart as they get."

"Do you really think he expects perfection from you? That's rather unrealistic."

"No. Maybe I'm not saying this right. I just mean that he deserves a woman who's as amazing as he is. I think if something like this happens again, he'll always suspect me first—even if he doesn't say it out loud. Who wouldn't? My past, our past, will always get in the way of him trusting me fully. Is that any way for two people to live? Him always waiting for the hammer to drop? Me always unsure if he completely trusts me. He deserves better, so much better. But I deserve better, too." As she said the words, Dixie nodded her head with conviction. She did deserve that. She'd earned it.

"So clean-slate mentality?"

Wouldn't that be a relief? She shrugged her shoulders, pushing the mouse on her desk back and forth. "I guess I'd like a clean slate. I'd like to start over with people who know me as I am now, who aren't tainted by the things I've done to hurt them."

"So answer me this, why did you do all those things to people?"

She dropped her head to her hand. "I've learned a lot about myself since I've been back, and one of those things was sort of coming to terms with my relationship with my mother. She wasn't an easy woman to please. She's…all about appearances and how much money she has in her bank account. So I stopped trying to please her and went out of my way to do everything in my power to displease her. I guess I rebelled. Big. It's certainly no excuse, but I think I manipulated and lied and forced people to give me what I needed because she didn't."

"That's pretty honest. So what brought about this huge change in your life?"

Dixie closed her eyes and swallowed. She'd never confessed this to anyone. Not even Landon—because it was a pain that might have dulled, but it would never really leave. It would always taint her soul. It would always ache when she least expected it.

"What do you have to lose by sharing, Mistress Taboo? If this is our last phone call, let's go out with a bang, huh?" he coaxed.

"Someone did to me what I'd done to countless others." There. She'd said it. She hated it, but she'd done it.

"Like?"

"Used me and discarded me."

The raspy breath Walker took almost hurt her ear.

"How?" he said, his question tight and clipped, striking Dixie as an odd reaction to someone he hardly knew.

"It's so cliché," she half joked. But wasn't that always the way life paid you back—in the way of a cliché you should've seen coming from a mile off?

"Tell me anyway. Pretend I'm someone else if it makes you feel comfortable."

Now that the floodgates were open, there was no stopping her. No stopping the guilt and anguish that ate her up from the moment she woke, until the moment she put her head on her pillow. She hid it with jokes, but it was always there.

It was the truth she'd wanted to share with Caine. So he understood she'd not just changed—she'd had a complete soul makeover. From the deepest part of her, her core had experienced a shift. There'd been plenty of dark during that shift, but then there'd been light. And it was that light she looked for whenever she began to falter.

"When I left home and went back to Chicago after my engagement ended, I was angry and bitter, sort of in an 'I'll show you' head-on disaster way. It's stupid, I know, but I acted out as if the person I was hoping to hurt with my behavior would actually see it or hear about it. I wanted him to think I'd gone right on living like he was just a bump in the road."

"The ex-fiancé again."

"Yes. He was my target. Anyway, I behaved badly. God. So badly." She closed her eyes to stave off the memories of how badly. "I stayed out all night. Drank too much, ignored my duties at my restaurant. You know the drill."

"I'm familiar with it."

"I became involved with a man, a rich man. It started out as me using him much in the way I did everyone who had something I wanted. He had a nice car, a nice credit card. All the stuff mean girls like me live for. So we became involved…."

"Did you love him?" His question sounded as if he'd asked it with a locked jaw.

Had she loved Mason? When she compared what she felt for Caine to how she'd felt about Mason, no. "No, it wasn't like that. After a while, I even liked his companionship more than I liked his credit card. But I wouldn't call what we shared love exactly. Though, arrogant ass that I was, I was sure he loved me. I was wrong, but at the time, I thought I held all the cards the way I always had."

"So what happened?"

Her fingers trembled, clutching the edge of her desk until her knuckles were white. *Just say it, Dixie. Say it. Own it.*

The silence between them crackled with an expectant hum.

"Mistress Taboo?"

"I got pregnant."

This time, the pause Walker made was painfully long. "You have a child?" he rasped into the phone.

Dixie closed her eyes, her throat threatening to close up. "No." The word shot from her lips like a ball from a cannon. "No. I lost the baby. I miscarried three months into my pregnancy." God, she didn't know if she could do this. It was a mistake to share something so personal. The hurt returned like a hammer, pounding nails into her heart.

"Damn. I'm sorry. So damn sorry."

His remorse sounded so genuine that she found herself reassuring him. "Don't be. It was almost two and a half years ago now." But sometimes, like now, it still felt like yesterday.

"If you say you deserved it because of your past, that it's some kind of karma for all your wrongdoin', I just might have to hunt you down and give you a good what-for. Don't say that, Mistress Taboo. Just don't."

Walker's insistent tone, his demand she not blame herself might have been cause for alarm had he been any other caller. Yet, Dixie only felt at ease. "I wouldn't go that far. I did deserve what happened in the aftermath."

"What could you have possibly done to deserve fallout after a miscarriage?"

"Well, for starters, the person I was involved with was married."

She thought she heard him hiss until he asked, "Did you know?"

"Not until I was two months pregnant and I finally told him." Thinking about Mason and that conversation now made her shudder. His suspicious disbelief. His cavalier dismissal of her tears. His final cruel words.

"So let me guess," Walker said, harsh sarcasm riddling his words. "He offered to help get rid of it."

Her disgust for Mason's solution to the problem came out in the way of a repulsed snort. "Among other things. Not that it wasn't a viable option, mind you. It was how he went about offering to dispose of his inconvenience. His callous disregard for how I felt about it. I'd planned to break it off with him anyway. I was foolish enough to believe I could raise the baby on my own, and in being honest with myself, I didn't love him. I didn't want to spend the rest of my life with him. But I did hope he'd want to be a father."

"But he couldn't because he was married." The disgust in his voice rang true to Dixie's ears.

"Right, and he made it clear he wanted to stay that way."

"So he was just using you as a fling?"

That no longer made her angry. Nowadays, it just made her sad that he'd go right on hurting his wife the way he had countless others before her. "He sure was. That I couldn't see the signs, that I never had a clue he was married, still blows me away. No one had ever done something like that to me. But Mason had me fooled for almost a year."

"And?"

"I got into a car accident," she said, almost choking the words. A horrible, metal-screeching, tire-gnashing collision that was totally her fault.

"And lost the baby," Walker responded quietly.

"But not a scratch on me…" she almost sobbed. Saying those words years later still held the same amount of crushing disbelief they'd held the first time she'd said it to a roomful of doctors and nurses. "It was almost as if it never happened. I lived, but the baby—*my* baby died."

When Walker spoke again, his voice was gruff. "I don't know what to say."

Now that she'd spoken the words that had haunted her to a total stranger, she couldn't seem to stop spilling her guts. "When I woke up in the hospital and realized how much I'd wanted the baby, I also realized something else—something more important. This was what it felt like to be humiliated—used."

"That son of a bitch."

"But I also realized I had not a single friend to turn to for help with my recuperation. There was no one to talk to about the gut-wrenching ache in my empty stomach with the baby gone, or the huge hole in my heart. There was just me, and an agonizing pain that stole my will to get out of bed each day."

"You really had no one?"

Dixie's bark of laughter into the quiet room was sarcastic. "After the things I'd done? Who do you call when the person who's always done the kickin' is suddenly the kicked? The only real friend I've ever had was overseas in the Baltic, or on safari, or something, and I couldn't call my mother. It would have infuriated her to find out I was pregnant with a married man's child. The shame alone would have made her turn her back on me. Though," she reflected derisively, "she probably wouldn't have been surprised."

Walker swallowed into the phone, his voice husky when he asked, "So what happened next?"

A smile rimmed her lips. Hope happened, hope and a hand to guide her to the path of self-forgiveness. "Mrs. Kowalski."

"And she was?"

She reached for her cell phone and clicked on her gallery of pictures, scrolling to Agnes's. The one of her holding up a bag of fresh peaches she'd scored at the farmer's market in order to make Dixie a peach pie so she'd have something from home to comfort her. Her smiling face, round and wrinkled, made Dixie grin.

"Who was Mrs. Kowalski?"

"My neighbor from downstairs in my apartment building. She'd seen the accident. It was raining. I was in a rush, and I pulled out in front of a big pickup truck.

Anyway, she came to the hospital every day. Brought me homemade cookies, muffins, all sorts of goodies to entice me to eat. When I came home, she'd knitted me a blanket and had a freezer full of casseroles and meals at the ready so I wouldn't have to cook. We became friends—good friends. Over many games of checkers and Parcheesi and lemon Bundt cake, she taught me what it was to give selflessly. She didn't have to nurse me back to health. She had a husband and two granddaughters. Her life was already pretty full. But she did it because she was kind, and loving, and she didn't judge me—not even after I told her everything about my horrid past."

"Acceptance," he murmured gently. "That's what healed you."

Dixie nodded, setting her phone down and promising herself she'd print out Agnes's pictures and frame them when she got back to Chicago. "That and something Mrs. Kowalski said to me one day that stuck like glue. When I let go of what I am, I become what I might be."

"Lao Tzu," Walker provided with a low rumble.

She smiled at his wisdom. "You know it?"

"I do."

That conversation with Agnes still warmed her. "I wanted to be a better person for a baby that was never going to exist. I know that sounds utterly ridiculous, but it's what helped me move forward after my miscarriage, stop blaming myself."

"I can't imagine losing a child, let alone thinking you were responsible for that loss." His quiet words washed over her like a warm balm. They rang deep with truth, honest and pure. "But you really weren't, Mistress Taboo. If it didn't happen that night, it might have happened on another. I believe there's a reason for everything, but I don't believe the reason is you were a horrible bitch."

Dixie closed her eyes and took a deep breath. "Thank you for that, Walker."

"So I'm guessing by this point your restaurant had failed?"

"It was mostly in ruins. I tried to save it at the eleventh hour, but it didn't work out. But Mrs. Kowalski's words reminded me, I didn't have to keep going in that direction. So I changed direction and decided no matter what, I'd pay off my debts to the people who took a foolish chance on a slacker like me. And that's why I'm at Call Girls."

"And Mrs. Kowalski? Is she still in your life?"

Dixie's breathing hitched again, her smile sad. "She died of a heart attack about a year after she saved me from myself. I'll never forget her, and I'll never be able to repay her."

"Maybe the idea is to pay it forward to someone who needs saving like you did?"

"Maybe it is," she murmured.

"So, I'm just gonna keep right on bein' nosy about this, Mistress Taboo. Why haven't you told your ex-fiancé about this? That these are the things that shaped you into who you are today? Wouldn't he understand?"

Shame. More shame than any one person had room for. "I wanted to. I was actually going to the other night, but he had to leave town, and now, after what's happened with my friend, there's no point. He'll come back to hear about this mess, and there'll be no goin' back."

"So what?"

Her eyes widened. "So what? Are you kidding me? Who wants to be persecuted over and over?"

Walker barked a rebuttal. "Who wants to have someone make decisions for them they have no right to make?"

Dixie's spine stiffened. "Huh?"

"You're deciding this man won't believe you at all before he has the chance to decide for himself. Maybe he'll look at you and say, 'Mistress Taboo, I believe. And no one could convince me otherwise.' It sounds like it's because you don't want to face the final piper. If you're so into movin' forward, then wouldn't it only be fair to tell him that? Is he such a jackass he wouldn't at least listen?"

"No. It's not that. He'd...listen. It's just that—"

"Then what can one more shot at it hurt? The worst that can happen is he says forget it, and you do what you originally intended. Go back to Chicago."

She sat in quiet contemplation.

"Do you want to run away again, Mistress Taboo?" he taunted. "Didn't you say you did that once when you went to Chicago?"

"Ye...yes."

"Then quit doing it again, Mistress Taboo."

A fire began to simmer in her belly. Maybe Walker was right. Maybe she should just confront Caine. Tell him about Mason and the baby, and how much she needed him to trust she was a different person.

Maybe she should search high and low until she found out who'd done this awful thing to Em?

Maybe...

"Mistress Taboo?"

"Yes?" she asked, out of breath and excited.

Walker chuckled. "I hear your wheels turnin'."

"Maybe you're right. Maybe I should do just that," she said with a definitive nod, her long-lost courage poking its head out.

Yeah. She didn't have to settle. She didn't have to be poor Dixie. If she was going to leave this town for good, by hell, she was going down in a blaze of truthful glory! The thought left her breathless and determined. "Thank you, Walker. *Thank you.*"

She heard him smile into the phone. "You're most welcome, Mistress Taboo. So I guess this is goodbye, huh?"

Dixie grinned. "I'm not sure now that you've pumped me up like I'm headed for a round with Mike Tyson. Maybe I'll stick around to fight another day, huh?"

"Boo-yah. Boo-yah."

Boo-yah, indeed. "So maybe I'll talk to you soon, Walker, but if I don't, thank you. You're…"

"The fire under your butt."

She laughed. "Sizzling hot."

"Goodbye, Mistress Taboo. It's always been a pleasure."

"Until another time, Walker, goodbye," she breathed into the phone, her throat clogged, her chest tight.

Clicking off the earpiece, she let her hand linger on her ear as though she could keep him close for just a little longer.

Whoever Walker was, wherever he came from, he'd been exactly what she needed tonight.

She sat back in her chair, entwining her fingers behind her head and closing her eyes. It was time to hatch mission "Make Everyone Listen."

"I'll be your Jewel of the Nile, baby," in Michael

Douglas's voice echoed through the wall to her office, catching her attention.

She jolted forward on her chair. Caine was back? Maybe he'd taken a red-eye?

Dixie popped out of her chair, the burning embers Walker had stoked under her backside cheering her on. By hook or by crook, it was time to set the record straight.

Dixie threw open the door to her office and rounded the corner to Caine's office door. She pressed her ear to it and heard. "C'mon, baby, take a voyage on the *Starship Enterprise*," in Jean-Luc's voice.

He was here. Her heart began to thrum, and a nervous smile flitted across her lips. It was now or never. She hesitated, her stomach a flutter of butterfly wings.

What if…

Maybe you should let him decide, Mistress Taboo. Walker's words came back in a rush.

Dixie used the side of her fist to bang on the door. "Caine! Open up—it's me. We need to talk!"

There it was again. "I love the way you look tonight," Frank Sinatra's voice sang.

Wow—this client sure liked variety. "Caine! Open up," she yelled, banging the wood again.

"Dixie! What are you doing?" Cat asked, her face worried. "Caine's not here. He's in Miami until tomorrow, honey."

Dixie grabbed Cat and pulled her close to the door. "Then he has a ghost or a twin in there. Listen."

"C'mon, baby. Take a voyage on the *Starship Enterprise*," Jean-Luc repeated.

Cat's mouth fell open just as Dixie reached for the doorknob. It was locked.

Cat dug around in her jeans and pulled out a shiny brass key with a conspiratorial smile, her hands steady as she drove it into the lock.

The door popped open, and they both peered inside.

To an empty office and a phone hooked up to a charger. The phone buzzed bright and blue each time it spoke—*recorded messages.*

"I'll be your hunk-a-hunk-a burnin' love," Elvis said.

Dixie's eyes narrowed.

Cat's did, too.

Caine had been cheating? Maybe even all along? Ohhh!

Oh, the dirty, low-down, let's-be-friends, son of a horse's ass! No disrespect to Miss Jo-Lynne, of course.

Dixie scooped up the phone and eyed it. All the tuning him out so she wouldn't have to suffer the indignity of hearing him talk dirty to a string of women, and he'd never been talking to anyone at all. They were the same phrases she heard over and over just before she put her headset on and listened to some loud Waylon Jennings until she had a call.

Oh. Oh, Caine Donovan. What have you done?

Dixie's eyes narrowed again, but her lungs worked right as rain when she yelped, "Caine Donovan, when I'm through with you, you're gonna wish for a slow, painful death!"

The ultimate challenge, the one where she plucked each luscious strand of hair from his head as she poked him with a cattle prod had begun.

May the odds be ever in your favor, Candy Caine!

Twenty-One

"Oh, Candy Caine... Wake up, sugahh plummm," Dixie cooed with a thick drawl in Caine's ear, moving her fingers along his sumptuously hard belly until she skimmed the top of his navy blue boxer-briefs. The reaction she received made her smile that much wider.

It was the evening after her discovery Caine had been cheating, and to Dixie's delight, he'd arrived home in the late afternoon, telling Sanjeev he needed a nap.

His arms, warm and strong, sculpted and hard, automatically reached for her, but his eyes remained closed. "Is that you, Mistress Taboo?" he asked, deep and sexy-sleepy.

"Uh-huh," she whispered, letting her tongue flit over the shell of his ear.

Caine moaned low and hot against her cheek, kneading her back with his hands. "To what do I owe this visit? Body snatchers, right? You're Dixie's doppelganger."

Dixie giggled in her best breathy Marilyn Monroe. "Now you're just talkin' silly." Her hand roamed over the width of his bicep as she nipped her way down his neck, purring as she went.

"Possession? A demon possessed you?"

"No possession."

"Too much plum wine?"

"Why I never," she said, pretending to be offended.

"Oh, you have so," he accused, though his voice was light.

"Okay, guilty. But I'm definitely not under the influence right now. Unless you count your intoxicating deliciousness."

Caine stilled his roving hands. "My *what?*"

Dixie lifted her head, letting her eyes meet his confused gaze. She fluttered her eyelashes. "You heard me." She returned her lips to the heat of his skin, taking pride in his hiss of pleasure.

"Question?" he squawked.

"Ask," she demanded, enjoying the tension in his muscles as her fingers skimmed the crisp hair on his belly just below the surface of the white band of his underwear.

"What's this about?"

Letting the length of her hair tease his stomach, something she knew drove him wild, Dixie rolled her head to see if he was looking at her. "You really wanna know what this is about, Candy Caine?"

"I do, Mistress Taboo."

Just the way she'd planned, she popped up, hopping off his bed.

"Here's what *this* is all about!" she bellowed like some demented warrior, dumping an entire pitcher's worth of ice-cold water on his head.

Caine reared up off the bed with a roar, water spraying everywhere. "What the hell?"

Dixie bolted for the door with a scream, Caine's Call Girls cell phone in her hand. She waved it above her head as she made a break for her bedroom. "Cheater, cheater, toe jam eater!" she singsonged, slipping into her room and turning to slam the door on his lying face.

When she'd hatched her payback, she hadn't counted on Caine still being as quick as he'd ever been. His dripping wet fingers grasped the edge of the heavy door and gave it a good shove, sending her backward to the frantic barks of Mona and Lisa.

She stumbled, but caught herself by stabilizing her feet and thanking her Zumba DVD for giving her the balance of a dancer.

Dixie held up the phone between them as if it was some sort of super shield. "You low-down, lying, underhanded, self-righteous *cheater!* Ohhhhh," she sneered up at him. "All that garbage about playing fair and bein' friends all while you were cheating!"

Caine, his tanned skin glistening from the water like some Adonis, went all humble and pleading, surprising her. "Okay, first, I'm not a cheater, and if you'll just let me explain, you'll know why I did it."

But Dixie threw her hand up, phone in place. "Don't you dare come any closer, cheater! I worked the phones legitimately while you were cheating! I'd bet you never answered a single call! All that Dixie bashing, all that takin' me to task over and over for being underhanded all those years ago, and you were doing the same thing. Racking all those fake numbers up for calls that never even existed. How did you do that, Candy Caine? One of your computer friends from Miami help you out, maybe? Like maybe the same person who designed your trashy website?" Cat had rechecked Caine's numbers, and they were solid. But if he hadn't been talking to anyone, how had he managed to finagle any numbers at all?

His chest, glorious and dripping wet, rose and fell. "Dixie, if you'll just hear me out."

"You should be ashamed of yourself!" She grabbed a picture of Landon from her nightstand. "Landon's ashamed of you, aren't you, Landon?" Dixie thrust the picture of Landon into Caine's face. "Tell him, Landon." She held the picture back up to her ear with a smirk. "What's that you say? Caine's just as smarmy as I am?"

"Dixie," he warned in that oh-so-reasonable tone of his, moving closer, the material of his boxer-briefs sticking to him in all the right places. "If you'll just hear what I have to say, I can clear—"

Dixie hopped up on her bed, making Mona and Lisa bark excitedly, cutting Caine off. "Don't you dare come near me, Donovan! Get out of my bedroom right now, or I'll start throwing things and have Sanjeev charge you for them," she threatened, reaching for a very expensive vase with her toe.

"Dixie," he said once more, inching closer, leaving behind a pool of water in his wake.

"Get—out!" she hollered, snatching the vase up and hurling it at his head with the speed of a torpedo.

Caine ducked just in time before the vase crashed against the wall, splintering into a million gold and green pieces.

Sanjeev flew around the corner as one of her perfume bottles sailed across the room. Dixie laughed out loud when it cracked and the room filled with the scent of pears. "Get out, Caine!"

"Dixie Davis!" Sanjeev bellowed, freezing all movement. Even Mona and Lisa stopped hopping around the bed. "The two of you will cease this instant!"

"But!" They both yelled together in protest.

Sanjeev threw a hand up, his normally calm eyes flashing all sorts of threats. "Enough! I will not have you desecrate the beauty of my housekeeping with your foolishness. Caine? You will leave this room now. You will go back to yours, and you will mop up every last drop of water on my meticulously maintained carpets!"

Caine frowned, but his expression was tame. "But she started it."

"Pay very close attention to me, Caine Donovan. I don't care who started this. You will do as I've told you, or you'll suffer the consequences!"

Caine's eyes grew petulant. He crossed his arms over his chest in a defiant gesture. "What're you gonna do? Take away my dessert?"

"Yes!" Sanjeev whisper-yelled.

"Damn," Caine muttered, backing toward the door.

Sanjeev's gaze swung to her, all hot and fiery. "And you, Mistress Taboo. You will clean up every last splinter of glass or never shall another of my curries pass your lips. Do we understand each other?"

Dixie pouted in response, straightening her sweater and smoothing it over her jeans.

"Oh, no, young lady. I'm not Landon. Your sullen act and sultry-pouty lips do not pull the wool over my eyes. Dustpan and broom, *nowwwww!*" He jabbed his finger toward her bathroom.

Dixie dropped on her butt to the bed, bouncing as she fell to the mattress. She tried one last sad face only to be greeted by Sanjeev's surprisingly stern eyes, before slinking off the edge with a huff.

Sanjeev turned his back to whistle to the dogs.

"Mona, Lisa, come! I won't allow you to dwell with heathens!"

While his back was turned, Dixie stuck her tongue out at a contrite Caine, jamming her fingers into her ears and wiggling them.

Caine's lips thinned.

Sanjeev whipped around as if he had eyes in the back of his head. "Dixie Davis! The bathroom. Now. March!" he ordered. "And not another word from either of you. Not. One."

Caine left first, stomping back to his bedroom and slamming the door like a ten-year-old.

The moment he left, Dixie collapsed, muffling a fit of giggles. She'd won—fair and square. No tricks, no loopholes, just her and a phone.

"This—" Sanjeev muttered, eyes ablaze "—is amusing how, Dixie?"

Dixie hopped off the bed and hugged him hard. "I'm sorry I made a mess of your floors, but it was for a good cause."

"Define a cause worthy enough to sully my housekeeping reputation?"

Dixie gave him another quick hug. "Soon. All shall be revealed soon."

Sanjeev gave her a quick squeeze of her shoulder before putting his stern face back in place. "But not before you clean this up!"

Dixie waved him off with a chuckle. "Like it never happened. Swear."

As Sanjeev took his leave, his face perplexed, Dixie smiled to herself, celebrating her victory on the inside.

It was official. She'd won Call Girls fair and square, and that meant she could pay back her investors. But before she decided if she'd run it from Plum Orchard or Chicago, there was one more thing left to do, and it would depend on Em.

Two things left to do if you counted Candy Caine.

"Why am I here again, Cat?" Dixie groused. She needed to set phase two of her plan in motion, and it didn't involve her operating the phones tonight.

"I told you, Dixie. Whatever Marybell had, LaDawn has, too, and now that Caine's out of the picture because he's a dirty, rotten, cheating scoundrel, we need your help. If Call Girls is gonna be yours, you gotta help in the bad times as well as the good."

"Okay," she conceded. "Let me get my headset and get settled." She moved toward the hall entryway leading to the offices.

Cat spun around in her chair. "Hey! Did I tell ya how glad I am you're stayin', Dixie?"

Dixie smiled at her, beaming when she remembered Cat's response to that information at Hank's office. They'd both gone and tattled on Caine together first thing this morning while Caine slept after a red-eye in from Miami, proving he'd been cheating.

Caine had found a way to rack up fake phone calls to his operator line, and fake money to the Call Girls kitty, but there was absolutely no way he'd been taking real calls like she had.

Oddly, he hadn't inflated his numbers, though he'd still cheated because, according to Hank, his clients weren't genuine Call Girls callers.

Oh, technicalities, how I love thee, she'd yelped in triumph.

All of Dixie's clients were real, and when Hank had ruled as such, Cat had jumped up and down over the fact that Dixie was considering staying in Plum Orchard.

Dixie sent Cat a warm smile. "I think you screamed your approval once or twice."

Cat rushed up behind her and gave her a hug. "Well, lemme say it again. I'm happy you're the new boss."

"Happier than if Caine was your boss?" she teased, tugging at Cat's hair.

"Now, don't go makin' me pick. I like Caine, too. I know there's an altruistic reason he did what he did. We just don't know it yet."

"Oh, fine. Keep the truth to yourself if it makes you feel better. I'm off to answer those calls." She gave Cat a quick hug and headed to her office.

Her office.

The words made her beam with pride. She'd done it, and she'd done it without taking advantage, twisting the rules—well, not a lot—and hard work.

She hoped somewhere up there, Agnes and Landon were proud.

When Dixie entered her workspace, there were pink and purple balloons attached to her chair and a banner on the wall behind her desk that read, You Are Worthy, Mistress Taboo!

Dixie grinned, but only briefly before her headset was buzzing. She grabbed it off her desk and placed it over her head, pushing balloons out of her way to sit down. "This is Mistress Taboo, are you worthy?"

"I hope I am."

"Walker!" she squealed in delight. "I'm so glad you called again."

"I'm assuming, because I was able to reach you, you're staying at Call Girls?"

She raised a fist upward. "You assume correctly. Boy, what a difference a day makes," she said, giddy and excited about the future for the first time in a long time. "You were so right."

"So you talked to your ex-fiancé, then?"

"Not quite, but I did revert back to my mean-girl ways—only momentarily. Promise." She was still patting herself on the back, rejuvenated by the sight of Caine, soaking wet in all his hard ab-ed, delicious half nakedness, dripping wet and in shock.

She almost heard Walker's smile turn to disappointment. "But I thought those days were over?"

"Well, so did I, until I caught him cheating."

"Cheating?" Walker rasped as though he were defending Caine. "He sure doesn't sound like the kind of guy who'd cheat. Not after the way you described him. Where'd Mr. Honorable go?"

"Well, I didn't think so either, but here we are."

"So he had another woman?"

"No! It's one of those long stories I'm infamous for, but here's the gist of it." Dixie briefly explained Landon, and the challenge to win Call Girls, and how they'd come to find out Caine hadn't ever taken any calls at all.

Walker whistled into the phone. "Wow. He's a crafty guy. Whaddaya suppose his motive for that was?"

Dixie paused for the thousandth time, wondering the same thing. "I don't know. It's really strange. He didn't inflate his call numbers—which is what I would have done back in the day if I'd had access to something like that. So it wasn't like he was trying to beat me that way. It makes no sense. He knew if he cheated he'd have to forfeit the company."

"Do you want to find out why he did it? I might be able to help."

Dixie stopped all motion. How could Walker help her find out what Caine had been up to? A rush of alarmed goose bumps skittered along her spine, but it didn't stop her from saying, "More than I want to keep a kidney."

"Can you meet me by the pool outside the guest-house?"

The pool? Outside? Now there weren't just alarms going off in her head, she was hearing DEFCON bells and whistles. "My pool? *In my town?*"

"Right here in Plum Orchard," he said low and sweet.

Dixie looked around at her office with suspicion, her breaths coming in choppy puffs. How did Walker know about Plum Orchard? Oh, God, what had she done by confiding in him? He'd tracked where her calls were coming from, and now he was stalking her. Damn technology. She forced herself to slow down. "Okay, what's going on? This isn't funny."

"Just come to the pool," he reassured in that lazy Southern accent. "And keep the phone to your ear while you walk over."

Dixie froze, her hands like ice. She shook her head. "No. If this is some kind of joke—not funny."

"Don't be afraid, Dixie."

Panic screamed in her veins. He knew her name. *Oh, Dixie Davis, of all the foolhardy, stupid, ill-informed things you've done, talking to a man who calls for sex on a phone has to be right up there with a too-stupid-to-live horror-movie heroine!*

"It's okay, Dixie. I promise," he coaxed, silky and smooth.

Dixie hesitated only a moment before she began making a break for the reception area where she'd left Cat, like, at any moment, Walker was going to pop out of the bedroom closet door, gleaming knife in hand.

She pushed out of her door and found all three women, Marybell, Cat, and LaDawn, waiting on her with expectant faces. Her mouth fell open then snapped shut as her mind raced forward. "I—I thought you had the flu, LaDawn? Hold on. What's going on here?"

"Don't you have a phone call right now, Mistress Taboo?" LaDawn reminded, smiling wide. "Remember what my mama said, closed mouth don't get no food. You need to eat. Keep talkin', honey."

Cat shooed her forward toward the door leading out to the pool as Marybell grabbed her hand with an excited giggle and virtually dragged her through the entryway door.

Dixie gripped the phone to her ear, even as her feet struggled to keep up with Marybell's. Her fear was replaced with bouts of panic. "Walker! I want you to tell me what's going on right now. This isn't funny, you hear? Not laughing!"

But Walker was laughing. Right in her ear. "Keep walking, Dixie. Trust, would you? There has to be trust in a relationship, right? Isn't that what you said?"

As they entered the pool area, Dixie stopped dead, refusing to move another inch.

She pulled her hand from Marybell's grip and turned on the women. "You three better tell me what's going on right now! I'm your boss now, you know, and if you thought for one fine second—"

"Dixie?" Walker interrupted her rant.

"What?" she hissed into her earpiece.

"Look up, honey," he insisted.

Oh, no she would not. In fact, she was going to close her eyes tighter. "I will not."

LaDawn gripped her chin and forced it upward. "Look up, *boss,* or I'm gonna pry your eyes open with my fingers like I'm pryin' open a can of sardines."

Her eyes propped open just as she was mentally putting on her boxing gloves to take on LaDawn.

And then her jaw dropped open to the sounds of the girls cheering, and Caine wiggling his fingers at her.

Always Caine.

Standing on the far side of the pool amidst the twinkling lights, as handsome as ever, a phone to his ear, he held out his hand to her. His eyes were tender, and his smile was wide. Dixie's heart responded with a clench.

LaDawn, Cat and Marybell squealed in delight, each giving her a quick hug before nudging her toward Caine who took her hand and pulled her close to his side.

Just to his left stood Em, holding Gareth in one arm and Clifton Junior's hand. Her face wreathed in a warm smile directed at Dixie.

Her confused expression was greeted with laughter and a cheerful vibe from everyone she didn't understand.

And there was cake just off to Caine's left, a beautiful confection of tier after tier of sparkling white iced cake with the words, *You Are Worthy.*

But forget the cake.

Caine was Walker?

She'd kill him.

Twenty-Two

Gareth leaned forward and placed both of his hands on either side of Dixie's cheeks. "My daddy's a lady just like you, Dixie," he informed her with a chubby smile. "But you're prettier," he exclaimed, making everyone laugh.

Despite her shock, Dixie couldn't resist reaching up and squeezing his wrists before he was swept away, and Em was reaching for her, her words tear-filled, her face full of anguish and worry. "I'm so sorry. As long as I live, Dixie Davis, I will never, ever doubt you again. Say you'll forgive me or I'll have to throw myself off the bridge all dramatic-like. That's always messy cleanup for Coon Ryder. You don't want poor old Coon overworked, do you? I need a person, Dixie," she pleaded. "Obviously, I really need a person to stuff a dirty sock in my big trap after my awful behavior the other night. Say you'll be my person again?"

Dixie didn't know what to say. No sooner had she grasped the idea that whatever was going on was about her, but Em was taking back what she'd said last night. "But I don't understand...."

"You will," Em whispered in her ear, grinning at her. "Right now, all you have to say is you'll be my person again."

Dixie squeezed her hand, trying not to choke on her words or her disbelief. "I'll always be your person, Em. For as long as you want me."

Caine pulled her back to him, fitting her to his lean side, holding up a microphone to his mouth. Seeing him with the phone in his hand made every fuzzy moment up till now clear.

Like a bolt of thunder, Dixie was struck and everything came together. "Wait! Warm milk boiled with an onion and pepper," she whispered up to him.

Caine laughed. "Mama always said it was the best cure for a cold. Can't believe I slipped up like that."

"You're Walker...." she murmured as all the confessing and cleansing came back to her in humiliating droves. "You?"

"I'm Walker, honey. Don't you remember? It's my grandfather's middle name, and the one my mother flatout refused to give me?"

Even though she nodded her head with a chuckle, she tweaked his arm, wrapped tightly around her hard, her senses returning in full force. "You do realize you have to die for toying with me this way, right? You'll pay, Donovan. Maybe not right now because I can't process this totally, but pay you will."

He turned Dixie toward him, pulling her close so their lower bodies fastened together. He dropped a kiss on her nose, brushing her hair from her eyes with tender fingers.

"Aw, c'mon now, Mistress Taboo. Don't be mad. I had to find a way to talk to you again without all the noise between us. There was just too much of it. We were always at each other's throats. Calling you as Walker was the perfect solution. In a sense, it gave both of us a clean slate. I wanted to get to know this new Dixie. The one who protected Em at Madge's and went a round with Louella. Once I started calling you, I couldn't stop. And even though I knew you'd kill me if you knew, it helped me to understand you in a way I never did before. I get it now, Dixie," he said, husky and low, his blue eyes honing in on her. "I get *you.*"

Dixie's lust for the lopping off of Caine's head ebbed, replaced with shock. Her words stuck to the roof of her mouth like thick peanut butter, refusing to cooperate.

"Forgive me, honey?" Caine asked, sweet as pie.

So many emotions assaulted her. This was Caine asking her for forgiveness. A Caine who now knew all her dirty secrets. A Caine who knew all her secrets and was still standing beside her. But wait...

On tiptoe, Dixie rose and pressed a kiss to his lips, savoring the firm silkiness before she let him have it. "Not just yet, Candy Caine. We have to talk *privately.* But first, explain the rigged phone calls. You were cheating! Can I tell you the flak I've taken for that sort of behavior?"

His smile was amused and smug—and perfect— so perfect. "I had a software developer I know hack the system and create calls that never really existed. It looked like calls were coming through, and my numbers reflected that. Then I had him hack Call Girls' bank accounts and dump some money into it so I wouldn't get caught."

Her eyes narrowed even if she had to admit it was genius. "Clever you."

"Right?" he teased.

She poked him in the ribs with a hard jab. "And exactly where were you while you were jeweling everyone's Nile?"

He barked a laugh. "You're gonna kill me."

"I can only do that once. So make sure you cover everything in your confession."

His granite face went sheepish, but his arms tightened around her. "Sleeping. Not at first. At first I did answer a call or two, but that was damn weird. After that, I recorded what you heard through the wall last night, hit play, locked the door, climbed out the window, and went back and watched TV, hot-tubbed, had some pie with Sanjeev. I just forgot to take the damn thing with me when I went to Miami."

Dixie gasped her outrage, but it wasn't real—her heart was too full for true outrage. "Sanjeev knew? My kill list grows."

"He knew. But it was all for the greater good, honey. Scout's honor."

"Explain your definition of the greater good."

"I did it so you'd win."

Her head fell back on her shoulders when she laughed out loud. "I knew it! I knew you couldn't be dishonest or cheat. I just didn't know what your motives were for rigging the calls." Dixie softened then, cupping Caine's hard jaw with trembling fingers. "But *why* would you do it? You could have just gone home, Caine and I would've won anyway."

He nodded his dark head, bringing her hand to his lips and brushing his mouth over it. "Yep. But then I couldn't have stayed to torture you—or win your favor."

Dixie's heart pumped hard against her ribs, her stomach a bundle of knots, but she managed to give him a coy batting of her eyelashes. She didn't bother to harp on the fact that Caine had handed her Call Girls. She didn't balk at the fact that it was a win by default— something she no longer took any pleasure in.

Instead, she smiled at the fact that Caine was in it to win *her*. "Why, Candy Caine, you want to win my favor? Little ol' me? I do declare. Mistress Taboo is listening. The real question is, are you worthy?" she asked in her best Scarlett O'Hara impression.

"You'll see, Miss Davis," he teased, dropping a gentle kiss to her lips, leaving her wanting more. So much more. "But first, I need to know something."

"Ask me anything."

"You wanna give this thing another go? A real one? No secrets. No agendas, just you, me and a phone-sex business?"

All the years of missing him, all the angry words that had passed between them, her guilt over that horrible night, every last doubt she'd had about whether Caine would ever be able to trust her the way she needed him to, exploded and disappeared in one word. "Yes," she whispered, throwing her arms around his neck and lifting her lips for the kiss she'd waited for since the night they'd parted ways.

The girls cheered as they surrounded them, but Dixie only heard about that later, when everyone retold the story about the night Caine Donovan threw a multimillion-dollar contest in Dixie Davis's favor just to win her heart.

She was too busy kissing the life out of him.

Dixie caught Caine's gaze from across the pool where he was parked beneath a palm tree, holding a longneck and listening to LaDawn and Marybell tell him how they'd met Landon.

She tilted her head toward the road leading away from Landon's and to his mother's house just off the square with a come-hither smile, waggling a finger at him in invitation.

Recognizing what she meant, Caine wiggled his eyebrows with a delicious grin and held up two fingers to signify he needed a couple of minutes.

The evening was cool, and she only had a T-shirt on. She rubbed her arms and smiled at the pool, abuzz with food and music and faces that actually smiled back at her.

Em came up behind her, throwing a sweater over her shoulders. She spun Dixie around to face her. "I'm despicable."

Dixie couldn't resist the temptation to tease. "The despicablest."

"That I ever in a million years thought you could do something so horrible to us." Em shook her head with disgust. "Well, I'll have to bring you lattes for a million years to make up for it."

"And some of that pizza with anchovies," Dixie said on a giggle.

"I'll bring you all of the Backstreet Boys, if you'll forget all the horrible things I said."

Dixie pursed her lips in mock thought. "Only if it's Nick Carter. I'll settle for nothing less."

"Done."

Dixie threw her arms around Em's neck and squeezed her tight. "It's okay, Em. Really. I get why you thought it was me. What I don't get is, who was it?"

Em swiped at a tear, escaping down her cheek.

"Know what? I'm gonna let the hero in all this tell you all about it. If looks could devour a person, from the way Caine looks at you from across that pool, we won't have time to talk anyway."

Caine came up behind Dixie, slipping his arms around her waist. "Let's blow this Popsicle stand, huh? We have business to attend to," he murmured in her ear, sending a shiver of anticipation along her spine.

She leaned back against him, sheltered, warm, accepted. "We'll talk tomorrow, Em?"

Em blew her nose into a tissue and flapped her hand at them. "You two go do unseemly things to each other. I'll be at the offices tomorrow." She blew them a kiss before making her way back through the shrubs and disappearing.

Dixie turned in Caine's arms, planting small kisses on his jawline. "I believe we have a date, Candy Caine. Lead the way."

"I know the perfect place." He grabbed her hand and began walking in the shadows.

Dixie ran behind him, forcing herself to focus on the road rather than his perfect butt in tight jeans.

When he finally came to a stop, Dixie had to muffle a giggle. "You remembered," she said with a breathy sigh.

He planted a quick kiss on her lips, rubbing his nose against hers. "I'll always remember. Now hurry it up, Dixie Davis. I need you naked, but I know you're gonna make me wait until you have all the answers to your questions just like a typical female," he teased.

Dixie cocked her head at him, planting her hands on her hips. "A typical female, huh? I'll have you know, I'm

anything but typical. Race ya to our spot!" she shouted
before she took off running toward the dirt road.

Caine was hot on her heels, his footsteps thundering
behind her until he caught up, looping an arm around
her waist and carrying her the rest of the way to their
favorite tree.

Dixie's laughter rang out when he plunked her down
on a warm plaid blanket where glasses and a bottle of
wine sat. "You had this all figured out, didn't you? Pre-
sumptuous much?"

Caine dropped down beside her, raising himself up
on one arm while slipping the button of her jeans open.
"I sure as hell am," he teased, rimming the outline of
her mouth with his tongue.

Her nipples beaded, tight and hungry, just as her fingers threaded through his hair. "But wait," she moaned.
"You promised me answers."

His sigh was ragged, but his fingers didn't stop moving. Pulling up her shirt, he dragged it over her head.
"Right, answers," he repeated, unhooking the clasp on
her bra with nimble fingers and cupping her breast.
"What am I answering?"

"What about Miami?" *Please don't go back.*

"Well, now, you don't think I'm going to go back
to Miami when there's this hot, rich, totally awesome
Southern belle right here in Plum Orchard? Why work
when I can lounge by the pool and watch you work?"

Dixie laughed, snuggling closer to his broad chest.
"I'm being serious."

"I'm giving up the real-estate business. If this trip
taught me one of many things, it was that I miss the
hell out of my mama's pecan pie. Oh, and you. And PO
and life here in general. That's why I was in Miami—

to close up shop. So is there anything else? Or can we get to the business of tearing each other's clothes off. If I'm not inside you soon, it's gonna get ugly."

Dixie almost forgot everything but the firm warmth of his hand, his thumb as it caressed her nipple. "Who took those pictures of Clifton? How did they get mixed in at the Founder's Day celebration?"

Caine's hands stilled for a moment, almost eliciting a whimper from her. "Louella Palmer hired an investigator from Atlanta to take them."

Dixie sat straight up, astonished. "But how did she know? How did you find out it was her?"

"Sanjeev called me in Miami to tell me you were leaving and why, and when I heard the whole story, I knew it was her."

"You really believed I had nothing to do with it?"

Caine cupped her jaw, bringing her in for a brief kiss. "Don't look so surprised, Dixie. Of course, I didn't believe you had anything to do with it. I saw how you defended Em at Madge's. I was there when you took out Louella, remember? I gotta confess, all those talks with Walker, all that honesty, stung, and it made me see what a judgmental prick I'd been. All this time you were beating yourself up, and I was still angry with you. Angry about what happened. Angry about wanting you even after what happened."

Dixie let her hands thread through his hair, loving the silky feel of it. "I get it."

"That has to stop, Dixie," he grated. "Stop thinking it's okay for anyone to treat you badly because of something that happened a decade ago. It's not your due, and if I damn well see it happen, whoever it is, is going to wish they'd stayed the hell in bed."

His overprotective stance left her breathless. Dixie gazed at him intently, loving him so completely. "I think Walker hashed that all out enough for one lifetime, don't you?"

Caine's face went from hard to soft in seconds. "The baby. Jesus, Dixie. If I'd known…"

She shook her head, the hot swell of tears pricking her eyelids. "Please, please don't," she whispered up at him, caressing his cheek. "It's done now. I just have to let it heal the rest of the way, okay?"

"But I need you to know I see what an ass I was being."

"Oh, I've seen," she teased, reaching for the buttons on his shirt. "Just tell me how you figured out it was Louella. How could she have possibly found something like that out when only three people here in Plum Orchard knew?"

Caine gave her a smile of satisfaction. "I did what every good golden boy does, I plied her with wine over a late lunch today, cornered her and got it out of her. She overheard you and Em talking about it one night outside of Call Girls when you were by the pool, according to her."

Dixie fell back on the warmth of the blanket, pulling Caine with her, but she couldn't hide her surprise. "You made Louella Palmer confess? I didn't think Jack Bauer could get her to confess."

"Oh, you'd be surprised at my interrogation tactics. I know things about Louella she wouldn't like getting out. I hated to resort to it, but I was willing to do whatever it took to prove you were innocent. To prove to Em you were innocent. Next, we work on damage control so Em and the boys don't suffer. I'll do the best I can to keep the gossip mill from percolating."

That wasn't enough for Dixie. No good would come from the entire town seeing that picture of Clifton. "But it's Plum Orchard. The gossip mill is set on percolate."

"You know what, sweetheart, you don't give everyone in Plum Orchard a fair shake because you've been on their bad side for too long. When someone's struggling, they don't just gossip about it, they rally together, bake a cake *and* gossip about it while the batter sets. Sure, plenty of them are small-minded, especially the Mags, senior and junior, but those are just the loudest hens in the henhouse."

"And they rule the roost. I'm worried, Caine." Dixie shook her head, incredibly sad for Louella. "She went too far. This involved children, Caine."

"If there's fallout, we'll help Em and the boys. *Together*. Now, can we get back to what's important here?"

"What's that?" she purred, pushing his shirt out of the way to allow her hands free rein over his pecs.

"You. Naked," he muttered, closing his mouth over hers.

She tore her lips from his. "Hold that thought for one second, Golden Boy."

"Woman, if you aren't naked in ten seconds and counting, I won't be held accountable for the lack of foreplay."

"Just one more thing. And it's really, really important," she said, bracketing his face with her hands.

"Nine…eight…"

"Thank you," she murmured, her eyes filling with tears for this new beginning. "Thank you for trusting me. You'll never know what that means."

"I don't know if I told you this, but that's what some-one does when they love you."

"I love you, too, Caine." So, so much it might have hurt if it wasn't so sweet with fulfillment.

"So quiet time now?" he asked with a smile before he didn't give her the chance to answer.

Caine planted his lips on hers, and Dixie responded by rearing up against him, stroking his tongue, revel-ing in his hot skin.

His lips slipped away, moving along the column of her throat until he was skimming her breasts, tonguing her nipples to sharp peaks, pushing at her jeans until they were off, and she was naked.

Caine's head lifted, his eyes hungry, devouring her as he slid his fingers between the folds of her flesh, thumbing her clit. "Christ, Dixie, you're so wet and hot." His voice, husky and low, sent a thrill of pleasure through her.

His words always stirred something in Dixie she couldn't quite define. Something wicked and untamed. Pulling at his shoulders, she dragged him upward, fum-bling with his jeans until he was free of clothing, and his cock was hard against her hip.

"I say we skip the foreplay," she managed to squeak out on a whimper. "I can't wait."

Caine's response was primal, his growl of pleasure from somewhere deep in his chest. He pushed her legs up high around his waist, and without another word, drove deep within her.

Dixie's head thrashed, pressing her hips hard against his until he was embedded in her slick heat. She fought a scream of pleasure at his first thrust, writhing, clutching his back, begging him with her body to make her come.

With each thrust, Caine's cock scraped her clit until she was swollen and so needy, tears seeped from the corners of her eyes.

Dixie opened her eyes briefly to watch Caine as he thrust into her, his muscled back under the moonlight, her fingers digging into his solid flesh, his body calling to hers to be one with his—forever.

At that very moment, she understood what it was to love someone so completely—so deeply—she felt it in her pores, her bones, her heart, her mind.

"Come, baby," he said, brushing his lips over hers, his words ragged and raw. "Come hard."

With those words, she tensed around him, moving faster beneath him until she exploded with a sharply sweet burn of release. Her head reeled with the pleasure roaring through her veins. Her pride swelled at his hot release.

And then there was the heave of chests, crashing together to pump air back into their lungs, and Caine was enveloping her in his arms, crushing her against him, pulling her closer, burying his face in her neck.

Her soul was full again, heavy with the piece of her she'd been missing all these years.

Full and finally complete.

Sanjeev awaited them at the wide front door of the big house, Mona and Lisa at his feet. "I see we've thoroughly debauched one another?"

Dixie's face turned red, and she buried it in Caine's shoulder, running her guilty fingers through her mussed hair.

"You missed a leaf," Caine remarked, winking at

Sanjeev before he picked it out of her hair and let it flutter to the ground.

"Well, now that you've taken care of that," Sanjeev said on a smirk, "we have at least an hour before you absolutely must continue your mad race to procreation. This leaves us time for the final bit of business to tend to. Follow me, sex-starved lovebirds."

Sanjeev began making his way down the marble-floored hallway to Landon's study.

Dixie had avoided this room almost the entire time she'd been here. Everything about it screamed Landon at the top of its lungs. From the large desk made of cher-rywood, to the wall with dozens of pictures of all of them together, smiling, laughing, loving each other, to the teak giraffe figurines and African masks.

She inhaled, savoring the smell of his cologne, clos-ing her eyes and remembering his warm hugs, his deep voice full of excitement about his next adventure.

Sanjeev motioned to the chocolate-colored leather couch. "Sit. I have a message from Landon."

Neither Caine nor Dixie spoke. She couldn't if she'd tried anyway. Being so near Landon's things brought back a sharp pain—one that reminded her he wasn't here to see who she'd become—how far she'd gone—and that she'd finally landed right back in Caine's arms. Where she belonged.

"What's going on, Sanjeev?" Caine asked, sitting next to Dixie on the sofa and drawing her close to him.

Sanjeev located the remote for Landon's flat screen, covering almost an entire wall in front of them, and pointed it at the Blu-ray player. "Watch."

The DVD flickered on, making Dixie gasp at the image of Landon in his hospital bed. His face was drawn and pale, his lips chapped, but the twinkle in his eyes was as bright as it had ever been—the purest of souls reflected in his kind handsome face.

Dixie stifled a sob, her eyes riveted to the TV. Transfixed by the tubes hanging from his arm, the bottles of medication to the right of his bed, the oxygen mask lying beside him.

God, I miss you so much, friend.

When Landon spoke, his voice was thready and weak, but Dixie's heart clutched it tight to her chest.

"So, by now you've either gotten those fool heads of yours on straight, or you've killed each other. I'm hopin' for the former, but I've prepared for the latter. By now, you also know, I set you both up, because how much pinin' can a BFF take from the two of you?" he said on a chuckle.

Clearing his throat after a blast of oxygen, he continued. "Ten years is long enough for you both to come to your senses, and if it isn't, then you shouldn't be allowed a second longer of precious time on Earth when it could be used by someone who wants to really live.

"Call Girls was an opportunity I knew both of you couldn't resist. I know you, my Dixie-Cup. I knew you were in dire financial straits with all those investors. I also knew you were determined not to ask for help. But I couldn't just leave money to ya, honeybee. First, you'da been mad, and your pride would have ruined everything. Second, you woulda just taken your mound of cash and gone right back where you don't belong. You belong in Plum Orchard, Dixie, not Chicago. I'm bettin' it didn't feel like it at first with all the anger and resentment some feel, but I'm also bettin' you showed everybody what you're really made of these days. It was time to heal up your wounds after you lost your little one."

A sob escaped Dixie's lips. That Landon had known, and never said a word....

Caine kissed the top of her head, pulling her hand into his to hold it tight.

"I know you're clutchin' your pearls in shock right now. I know all about your miscarriage, Dixie-Cup. I don't have all this money for nothin'. You hurt me bad when I found out about it. But I was off on some trip I can't remember now, unreachable, so I'm choosin' to believe you just couldn't find me instead of believin' it was a pain so deep you couldn't even tell me. But you did find Agnes, right? I left a whole bunch o' money to that Agnes's grandkids—a nice college fund for takin' such good care of you.

"Point is you needed to come home and be surrounded by the people who would eventually love the new Dixie. By the people you love despite bein' a bunch of gossipy old biddies. You just have to look hard. I put Em in charge because not only did I grow to love her in this last month or so, but also because she's pretty dang honest. And I knew she'd keep y'all on the straight and narrow.

"Most of all, Dixie, you needed Caine, and he needed you. In fact, I'm not sure who needed who more at this point. Caine was lost, too, you know. No social life to speak of, work, work, work. And still, he was always thinkin' about you. He'd never say it. For a while your name was strictly forbidden until I reminded him that my life was a part of yours, and if he couldn't hear about our friendship, he wasn't just a sissy, he was gonna be one less friend. Same way I did you.

"So what's a BFF to do but die a dramatic death, hatch up a devious plan while he's doin' it, and leave behind a will that forced you two to do what you do best—hand-to-hand combat. Then I set up texts to taunt you both—spur you both into some action, let you know I was thinkin' about you."

Dixie and Caine looked at each other with wonder. "You got them, too?" she asked.

Caine nodded with a grin and a shake of his head.

"I laughed and laughed when I thought about what your faces would look like when you found out I owned a phone-sex company. Then I laughed some more when I thought about what you'd look like when you both heard the rules of the game. I laughed harder when Sanjeev suggested we make the rule about you both stayin' in the big house together while you competed.

"But I didn't laugh when I considered what you'd get out of this if you'd just listen to your hearts. Dixie, honey. You. Are. Worthy. Of love and trust and all the good things that come with livin' a clean life.

"I wanted you to have each other forever. That part didn't make me laugh. I cried. I cried because I wouldn't be there to see it. I cried because I wouldn't finally have the two people I love most in the world together again with me—just like it used to be. I'm sure sorry I'm missin' that, y'all.

"But wherever I am, I want you two blind asshats to know this—I love you both more than I loved some of my very own family members.

"So I hope you jackasses found each other. I hope it was a hard road, too. You owe me for ten years of my life I lost listenin' to your whinin'. I don't know which of you I hope won, because if this went the way

I laid bets with Sanjeev, who won won't matter. You're now a couple, and you're gonna have that big weddin' you were supposed to have ten years ago to seal the deal, and Call Girls is rightfully both of yours—the big house, too.

"Hang on to what you have. Live. Really, really live. Be happy. Laugh. Smile. Argue. Make up. But do it. Don't let the past keep you from anything.

"And last, know that I love you more than my spleen, Dixie-Cup. I'd do anything for you. This time, I did the thing I knew was right for you. Caine. Caine *is* right for you, and you're right for him.

"Go make babies. Call one of 'em Landon, okay?

"As for me, well, I'll see ya when I see ya. I love you both, even from all the way up here."

The DVD clicked off, and Dixie buried her face in Caine's chest, tears streaming from her eyes, leaving the silence of Landon gone forever, weighing heavy in the room.

Caine cleared his throat, the muscles clenched and straining. "You've had this the whole time, Sanjeev?"

Sanjeev's eyes met Caine's, earnest and soft. "I have. I had two, actually. The other, the one where you two don't figure this whole thing out shall be burned promptly. On that note, I did as the man who rescued me so many years ago asked. One hundred lifetimes could never repay that debt—or do justice to the love and gratitude I felt for him."

Dixie let a breath escape her lips, shuddering on its way out. She wiped the tears from her eyes and rose, breaking her silence by pointing a finger at Sanjeev. "You are the master at keeping secrets, pal. I bow to you."

Sanjeev gave them a small smile. "I've also mastered the art of texting. I'm rather proud of that."

"It was you?" Caine asked.

"I was only the messenger. Landon was the author. He wrote them all out before he passed and left them for me to send to you both."

Dixie shook her head and grinned. "Was there anything he didn't think of? Bet he's feeling pretty pleased with himself right now."

Sanjeev nodded with another smile. "Oh, he was pleased long before now. I was laughing at you. Silly, lovesick fools. Oh, the moping and carrying on from the two of you is enough to make even the happiest of people seek a painful death."

They all laughed at that as Caine rose, too, sticking his hand out at Sanjeev to shake it and slap him on the back. "So, I guess this means you'll stay on here at the big house? Keep running things for us?"

"Surely you jest if you think I'd leave all of this and Mona and Lisa in the hands of the two of you?" he said on a chuckle. "The big house would fall to ashes, and Mona and Lisa would starve for all the attention you'd give them while you're sequestered in that bedroom up there. Now we're off, aren't we, precious beasts?" he said, looking down at Mona and Lisa who sat at perfect attention. "Come, furry friends, there's celebratory kibble to be had!"

Sanjeev left them, the dogs following his every step in a rustle of toenails against the marble floor.

Caine held his arms open, and Dixie went to them, slipping her hands under his biceps and curling into him. "I miss him so much. It aches, you know?"

Caine nodded against the top of her head. "I do know. I miss him every day."

At that very second, both of their phones chirped an incoming text.

They each fumbled in their pockets to pull their phones out, sharing a gasp of laughter.

"Sanjeev! Knock it off!" Caine yelled toward the kitchen.

"Last one, I promise!" Sanjeev yelled back, making them both laugh.

Caine held up his phone just as Dixie did so they could read each other's message.

Have you started making those babies yet? Your ovaries will dry up if you don't make with the haste, Dixie-Cup, and Caine, your sperm will turn to dust if you both don't get a move on. The big bed awaits you...

Love you both more than Bobby Flay.

Always, my friends,

Landon

Caine took Dixie in his arms, nuzzling her cheek with his lips, stirring that familiar ache deep inside her. "So how do you feel about making babies?"

She gave him a flirtatious smile. "Oh, I dunno. Do you think you're worthy?"

Caine shot her a smile before planting a hard kiss on her lips, one that made her moan in anticipation. Then he let her go and began to back away, pushing open the double doors to Landon's study and taking off up the stairs, "Argh, matey! Last one to the big bed be unworthy!" he said in Captain Jack Sparrow's voice.

Dixie chased after him, racing up the wide staircase, giggling like a schoolgirl. Whatever would happen, it would happen with Caine.

She stopped short of the bedroom's door and looked up at the ceiling, closing her eyes and summoning a picture of the last time she'd seen Landon—dapper, healthy, plowing through life and telling her all about it over her favorite wine. "I love you more than I love my own spleen, Landon Wells. Thank you, friend, thank you," she whispered, blowing a kiss into the palm of her hand and shooting it upward.

Placing her fingers on the partially opened door, Dixie walked right through, a smile on her face—and this time, she was going to keep walking—toward Caine.

Toward the love she'd waited a lifetime to find her way back to.

Toward whatever their kind of forever meant.

* * * * *

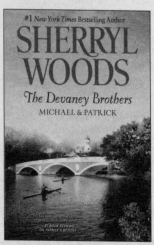

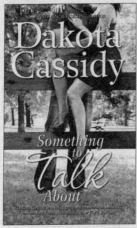

A NEW YORK TIMES BESTSELLING AUTHOR

Dakota Cassidy

Something to Talk About

$7.99 U.S./$8.99 CAN.

Limited time offer!

$1.⁰⁰ OFF

From
National Bestselling Author

Dakota Cassidy

Emmeline and Jax settled on no strings attached. That's when things got tangled…

Available May 27, 2014, wherever books are sold!

HARLEQUIN® MIRA®
www.Harlequin.com

$1.⁰⁰ OFF the purchase price of
SOMETHING TO TALK ABOUT
by Dakota Cassidy

Offer valid from May 19, 2014, to June 16, 2014.
Redeemable at participating retail outlets. Limit one coupon per purchase.
Valid in the U.S.A. and Canada only.

52611461

Canadian Retailers: Harlequin Enterprises Limited will pay the face value of this coupon plus 10.25¢ if submitted by customer for this product only. Any other use constitutes fraud. Coupon is nonassignable. Void if taxed, prohibited or restricted by law. Consumer must pay any government taxes. Void if copied. Millennium1 Promotional Services ("M1P") customers submit coupons and proof of sales to Harlequin Enterprises Limited, P.O. Box 3000, Saint John, NB E2L 4L3, Canada. Non-M1P retailer—for reimbursement submit coupons and proof of sales directly to Harlequin Enterprises Limited, Retail Marketing Department, 225 Duncan Mill Rd., Don Mills, Ontario M3B 3K9, Canada.

U.S. Retailers: Harlequin Enterprises Limited will pay the face value of this coupon plus 8¢ if submitted by customer for this product only. Any other use constitutes fraud. Coupon is nonassignable. Void if taxed, prohibited or copied. Consumer must pay any government taxes. Void if copied. For reimbursement submit coupons and proof of sales directly to Harlequin Enterprises Limited, P.O. Box 880478, El Paso, TX 88588-0478, U.S.A. Cash value 1/100 cents.

5 65373 00076 2   (8100)0 11920

® and TM are trademarks owned and used by the trademark owner and/or its licensee.
© 2014 Harlequin Enterprises Limited

MDC1627CPN

REQUEST YOUR
FREE BOOKS!

2 FREE NOVELS
FROM THE ROMANCE COLLECTION
PLUS 2 FREE GIFTS!

YES! Please send me 2 FREE novels from the Romance Collection and my 2 FREE gifts (gifts are worth about $10). After receiving them, if I don't wish to receive any more books, I can return the shipping statement marked "cancel." If I don't cancel, I will receive 4 brand-new novels every month and be billed just $6.24 per book in the U.S. or $6.74 per book in Canada. That's a savings of at least 22% off the cover price. It's quite a bargain! Shipping and handling is just 50¢ per book in the U.S. and 75¢ per book in Canada.* I understand that accepting the 2 free books and gifts places me under no obligation to buy anything. I can always return a shipment and cancel at any time. Even if I never buy another book, the two free books and gifts are mine to keep forever.

194/394 MDN F4XY

Name   (PLEASE PRINT)

Address   Apt. #

City   State/Prov.   Zip/Postal Code

Signature (if under 18, a parent or guardian must sign)

Mail to the Harlequin® Reader Service:
IN U.S.A.: P.O. Box 1867, Buffalo, NY 14240-1867
IN CANADA: P.O. Box 609, Fort Erie, Ontario L2A 5X3

Want to try two free books from another line?
Call 1-800-873-8635 or visit www.ReaderService.com.

* Terms and prices subject to change without notice. Prices do not include applicable taxes. Sales tax applicable in N.Y. Canadian residents will be charged applicable taxes. Offer not valid in Quebec. This offer is limited to one order per household. Not valid for current subscribers to the Romance Collection or the Romance/Suspense Collection. All orders subject to credit approval. Credit or debit balances in a customer's account(s) may be offset by any other outstanding balance owed by or to the customer. Please allow 4 to 6 weeks for delivery. Offer available while quantities last.

Your Privacy—The Harlequin® Reader Service is committed to protecting your privacy. Our Privacy Policy is available online at www.ReaderService.com or upon request from the Harlequin Reader Service.

We make a portion of our mailing list available to reputable third parties that offer products we believe may interest you. If you prefer that we not exchange your name with third parties, or if you wish to clarify or modify your communication preferences, please visit us at www.ReaderService.com/consumerschoice or write to us at Harlequin Reader Service Preference Service, P.O. Box 9062, Buffalo, NY 14269. Include your complete name and address.

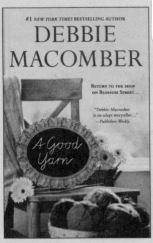